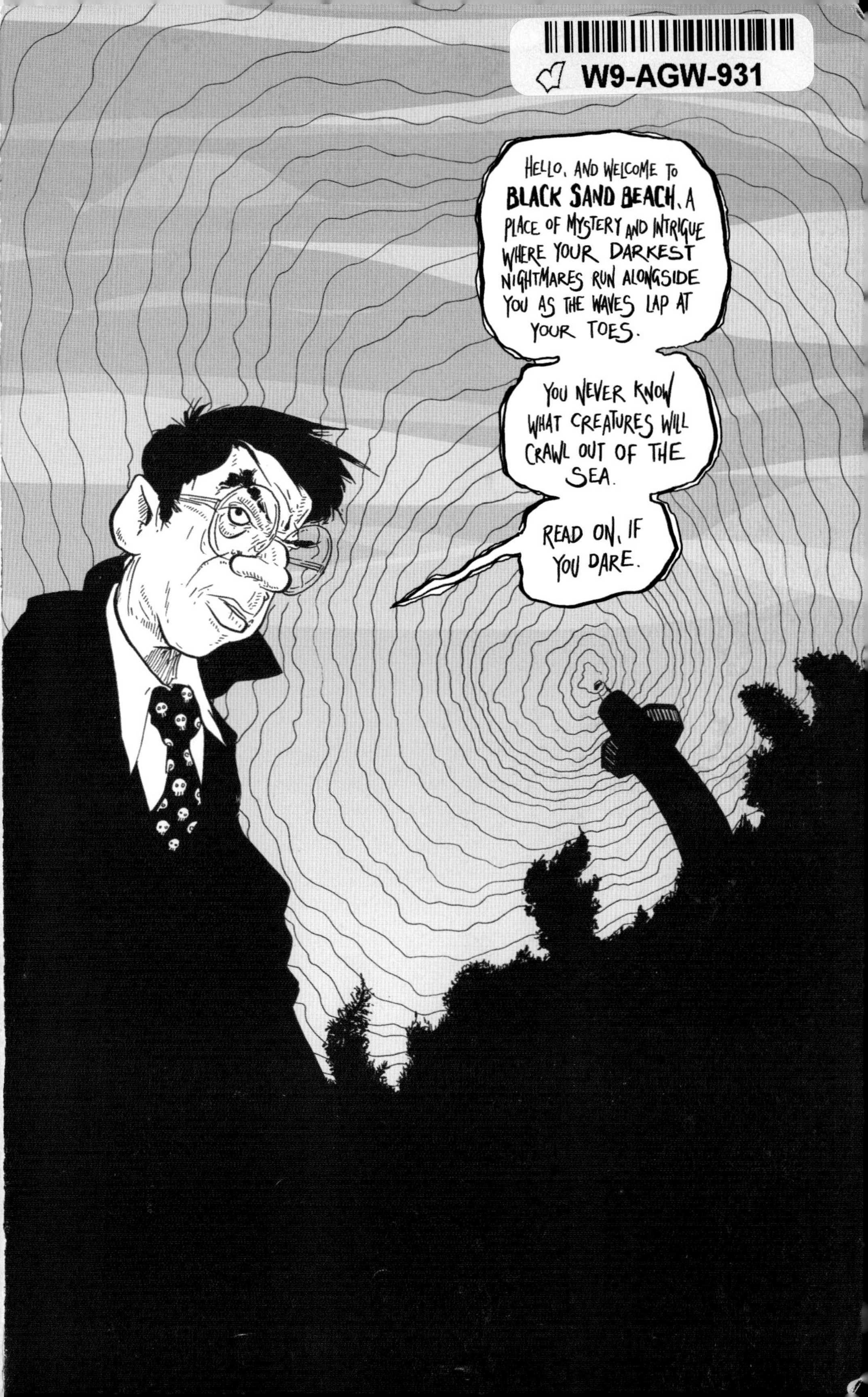
HELLO, AND WELCOME TO BLACK SAND BEACH, A PLACE OF MYSTERY AND INTRIGUE WHERE YOUR DARKEST NIGHTMARES RUN ALONGSIDE YOU AS THE WAVES LAP AT YOUR TOES.
YOU NEVER KNOW WHAT CREATURES WILL CRAWL OUT OF THE SEA.
READ ON, IF YOU DARE.

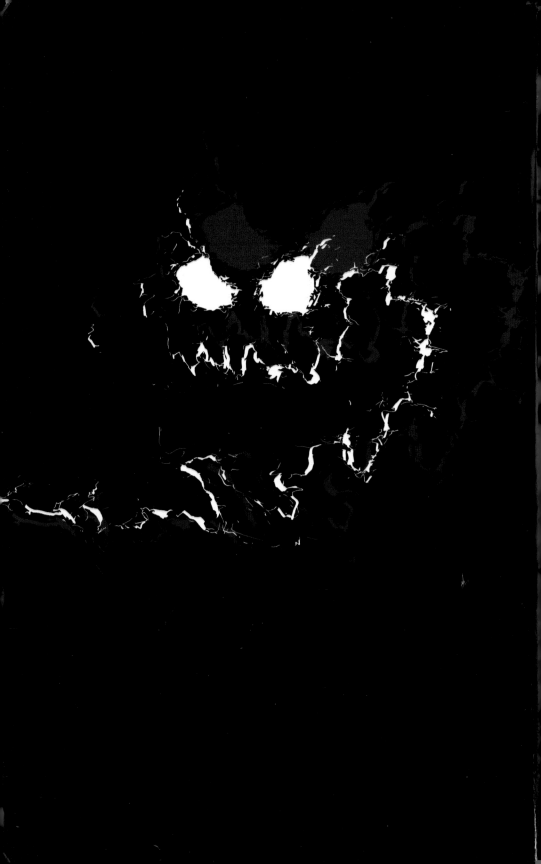

BLACK SAND BEACH.

ARE YOU AFRAID OF THE LIGHT?

BY RICHARD FAIRGRAY

PIXEL+INK

For Dasher

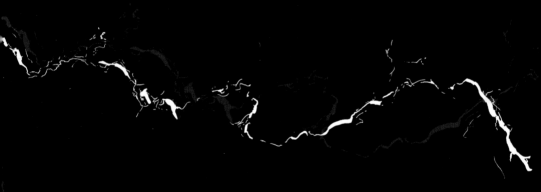

Pixel+Ink Books

Text and illustrations copyright © 2020 by Richard Fairgray
All Rights Reserved
Pixel+Ink is a division of Trustbridge Development Corp.
Printed and bound in 2020 at Tien Wah Press, Malaysia.
Book design by Richard Fairgray
www.pixelandinkbooks.com
First Edition
1 3 5 7 9 10 8 6 4 2

Library of Congress Cataloging-in-Publication Data is available upon request.

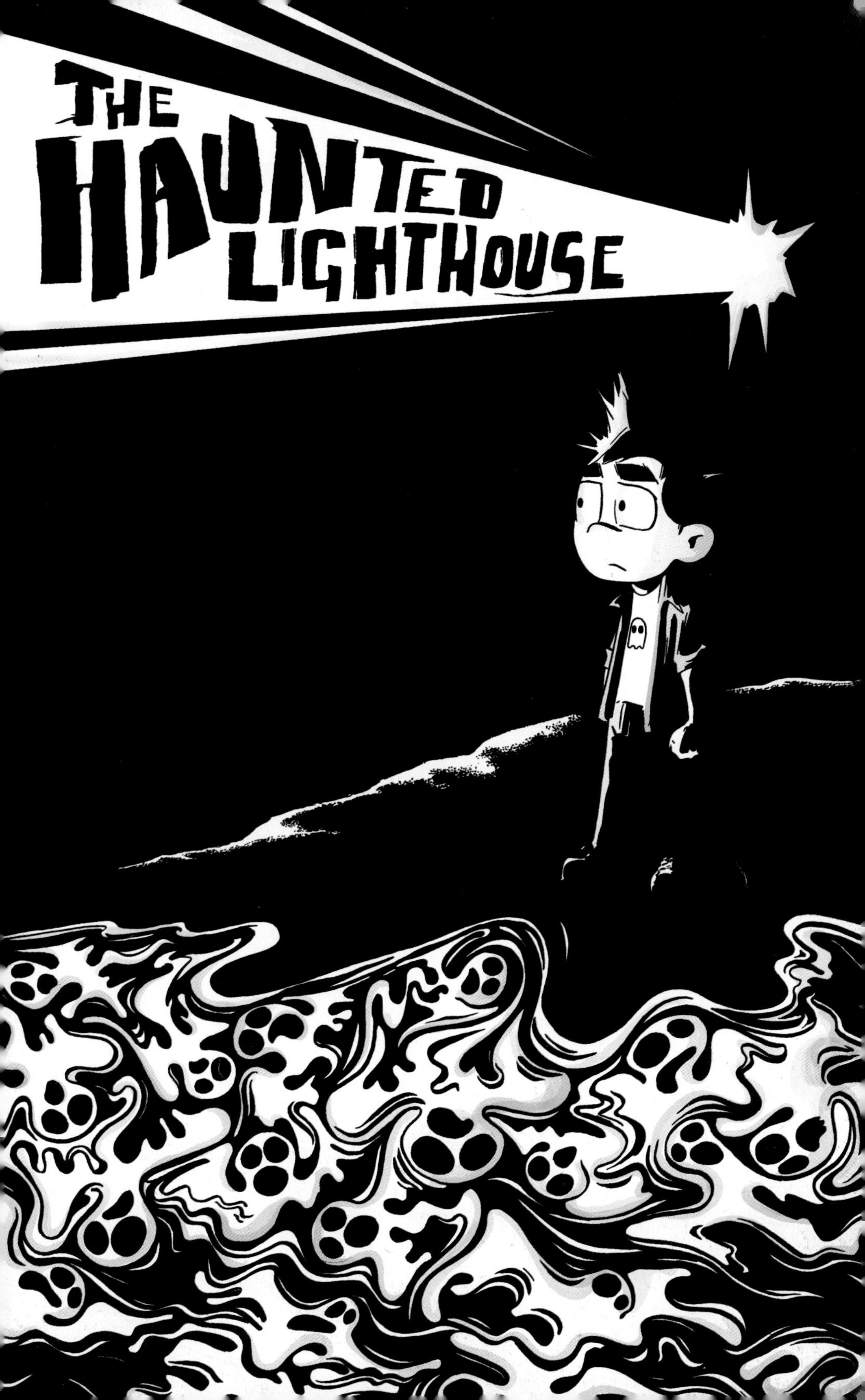
THE
HAUNTED
LIGHTHOUSE

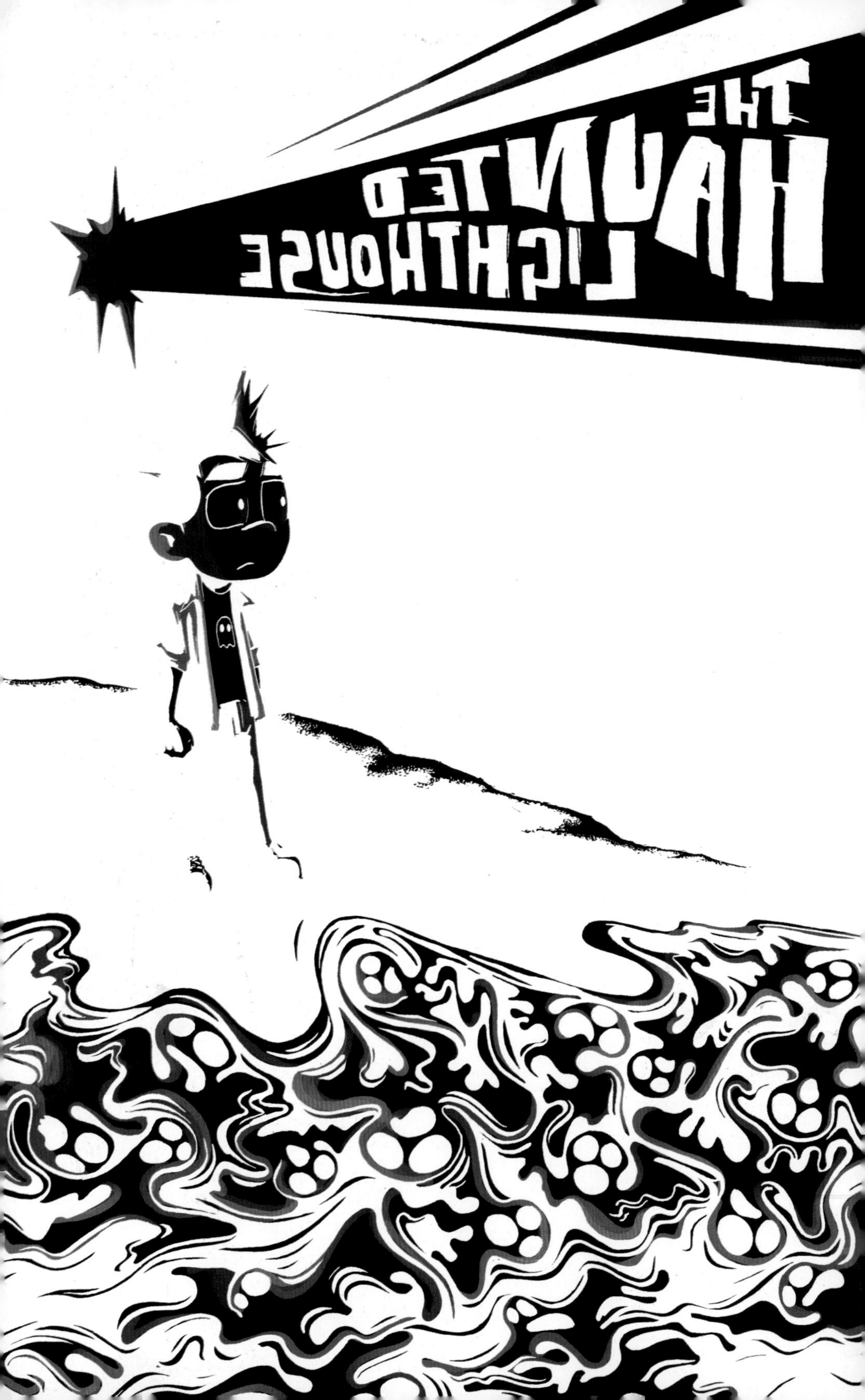
THE HAUNTED LIGHTHOUSE

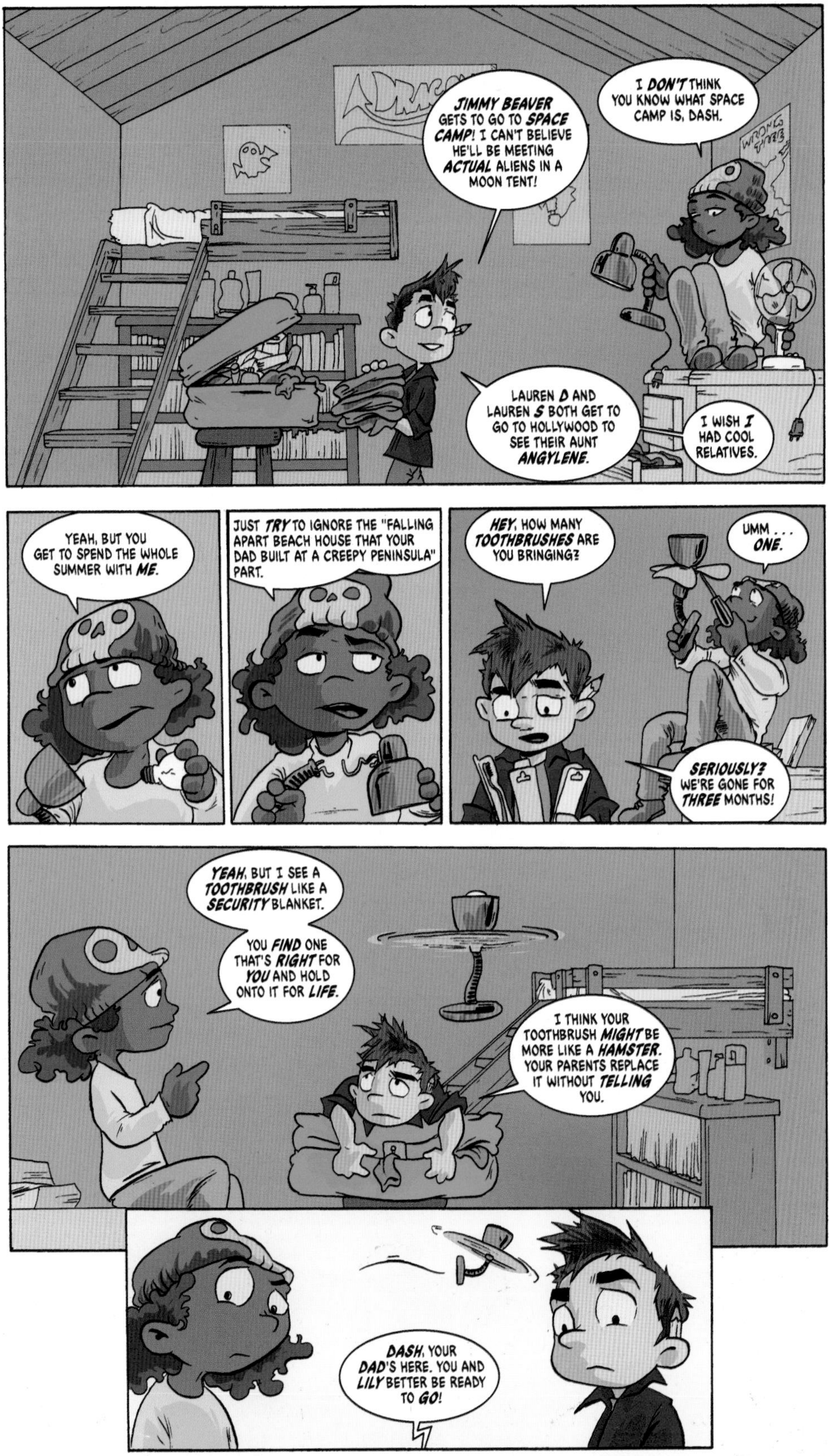
JIMMY BEAVER GETS TO GO TO SPACE CAMP! I CAN'T BELIEVE HE'LL BE MEETING ACTUAL ALIENS IN A MOON TENT!
I DON'T THINK YOU KNOW WHAT SPACE CAMP IS, DASH.
LAUREN D AND LAUREN S BOTH GET TO GO TO HOLLYWOOD TO SEE THEIR AUNT ANGYLENE.
I WISH I HAD COOL RELATIVES.
YEAH, BUT YOU GET TO SPEND THE WHOLE SUMMER WITH ME.
JUST TRY TO IGNORE THE "FALLING APART BEACH HOUSE THAT YOUR DAD BUILT AT A CREEPY PENINSULA" PART.
HEY, HOW MANY TOOTHBRUSHES ARE YOU BRINGING?
UMM . . . ONE.
SERIOUSLY? WE'RE GONE FOR THREE MONTHS!
YEAH, BUT I SEE A TOOTHBRUSH LIKE A SECURITY BLANKET.
YOU FIND ONE THAT'S RIGHT FOR YOU AND HOLD ONTO IT FOR LIFE.
I THINK YOUR TOOTHBRUSH MIGHT BE MORE LIKE A HAMSTER. YOUR PARENTS REPLACE IT WITHOUT TELLING YOU.
DASH, YOUR DAD'S HERE. YOU AND LILY BETTER BE READY TO GO!

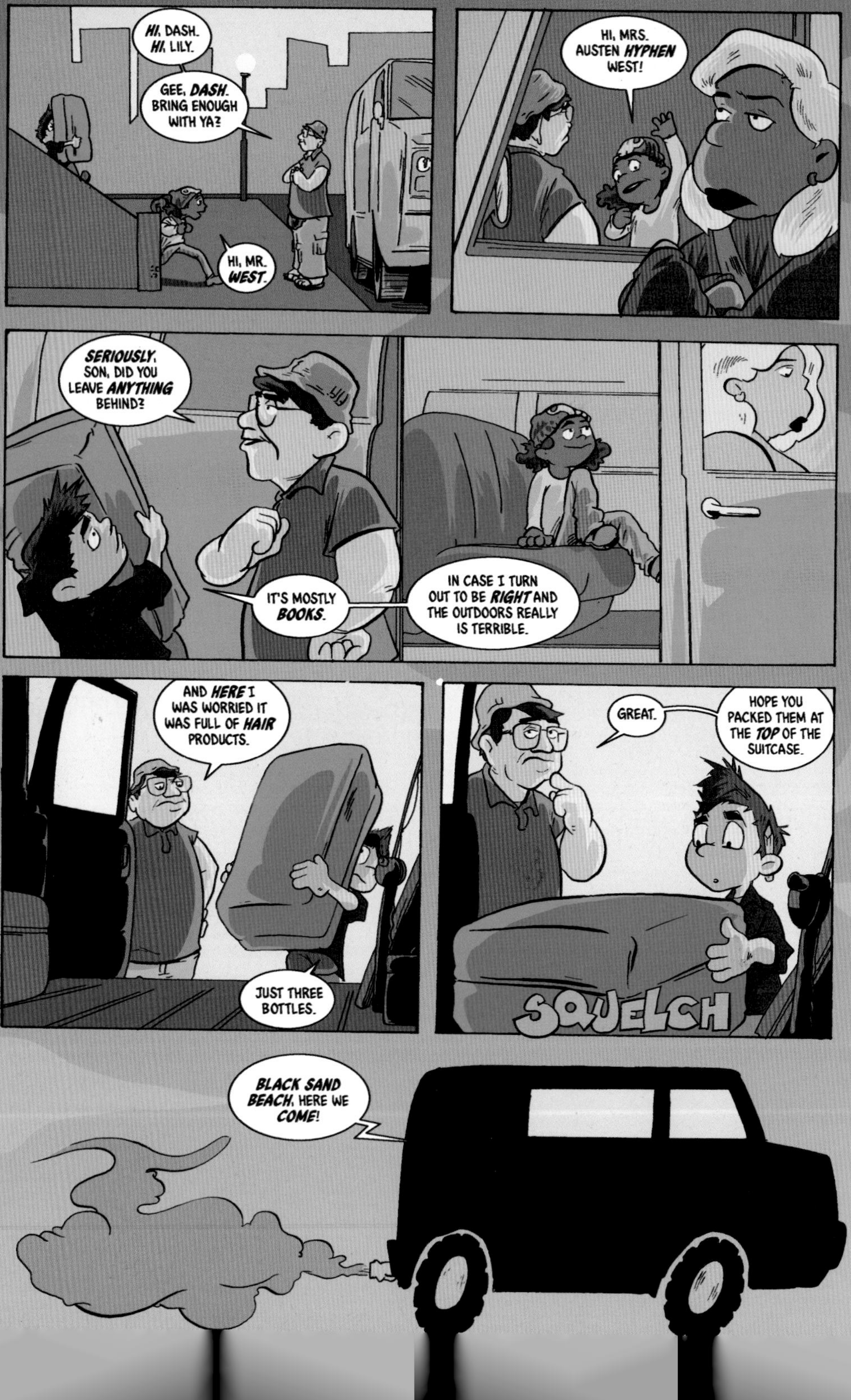
HI, DASH. HI, LILY.
GEE, DASH. BRING ENOUGH WITH YA?
HI, MR. WEST.
HI, MRS. AUSTEN HYPHEN WEST!
SERIOUSLY, SON, DID YOU LEAVE ANYTHING BEHIND?
IT'S MOSTLY BOOKS.
IN CASE I TURN OUT TO BE RIGHT AND THE OUTDOORS REALLY IS TERRIBLE.
AND HERE I WAS WORRIED IT WAS FULL OF HAIR PRODUCTS.
JUST THREE BOTTLES.
GREAT.
HOPE YOU PACKED THEM AT THE TOP OF THE SUITCASE.
SQUELCH
BLACK SAND BEACH, HERE WE COME!

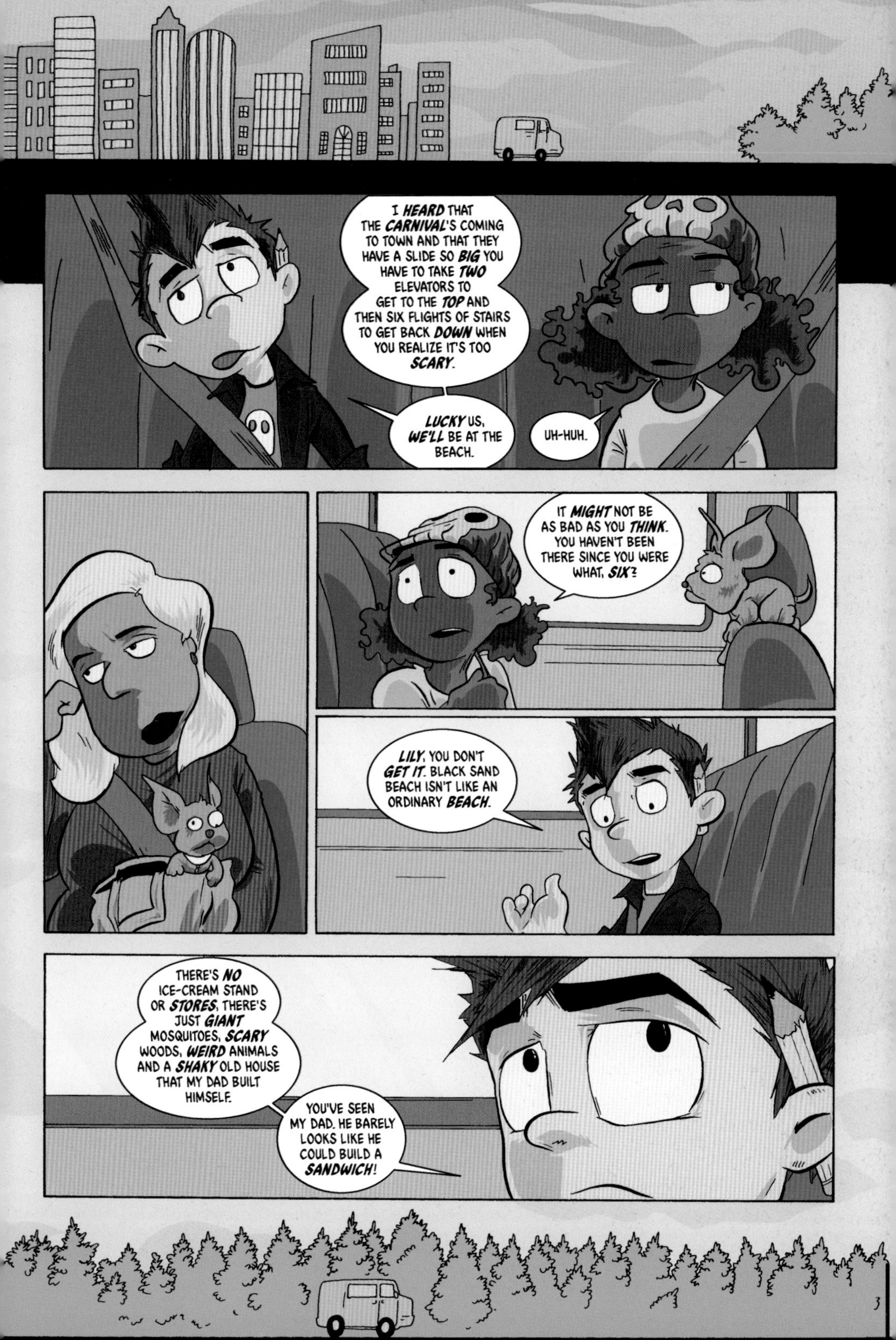
I HEARD THAT THE CARNIVAL'S COMING TO TOWN AND THAT THEY HAVE A SLIDE SO BIG YOU HAVE TO TAKE TWO ELEVATORS TO GET TO THE TOP AND THEN SIX FLIGHTS OF STAIRS TO GET BACK DOWN WHEN YOU REALIZE IT'S TOO SCARY.
LUCKY US, WE'LL BE AT THE BEACH.
UH-HUH.
IT MIGHT NOT BE AS BAD AS YOU THINK. YOU HAVEN'T BEEN THERE SINCE YOU WERE WHAT, SIX?
LILY, YOU DON'T GET IT. BLACK SAND BEACH ISN'T LIKE AN ORDINARY BEACH.
THERE'S NO ICE-CREAM STAND OR STORES, THERE'S JUST GIANT MOSQUITOES, SCARY WOODS, WEIRD ANIMALS AND A SHAKY OLD HOUSE THAT MY DAD BUILT HIMSELF.
YOU'VE SEEN MY DAD. HE BARELY LOOKS LIKE HE COULD BUILD A SANDWICH!

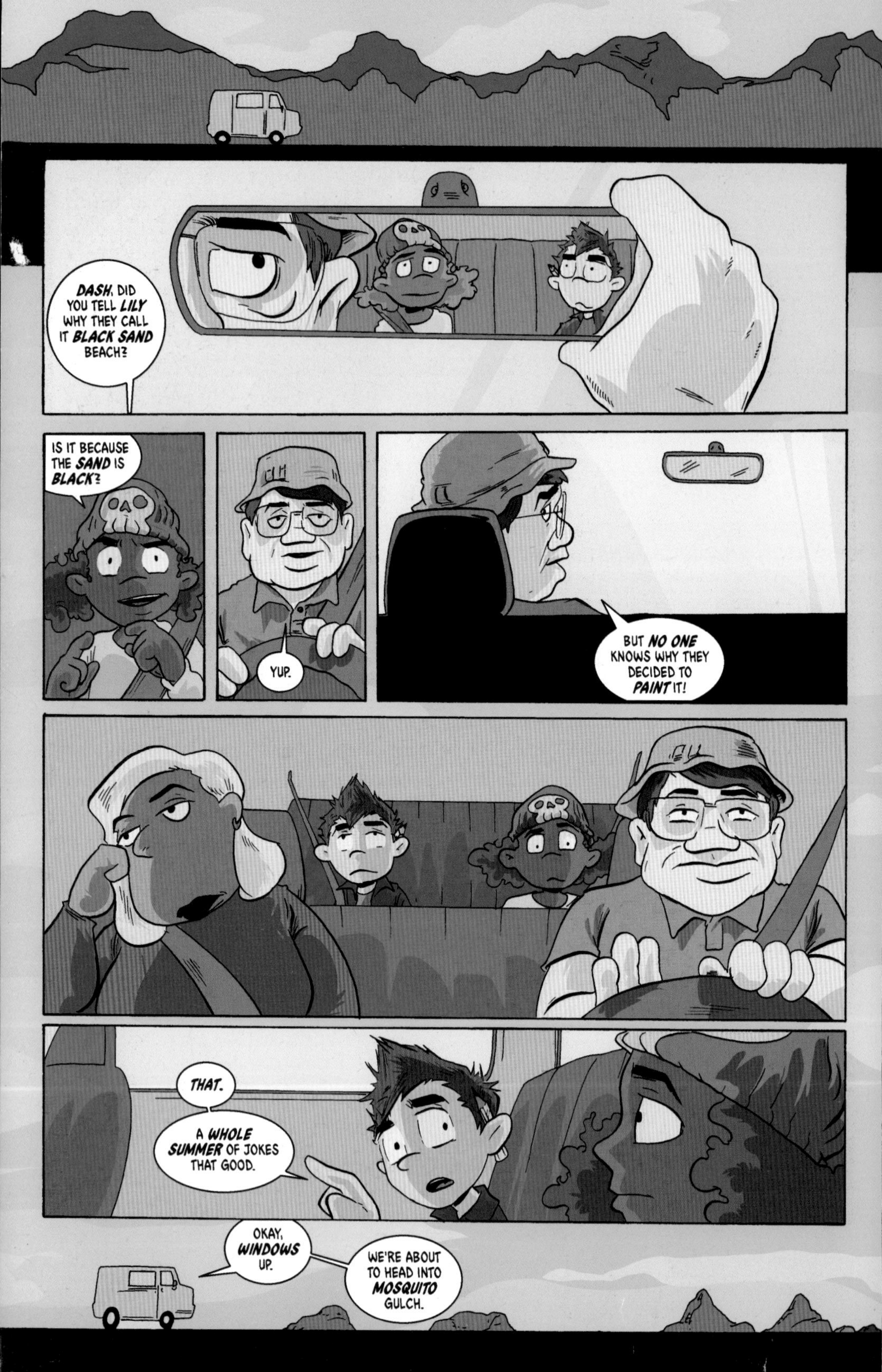
DASH, DID YOU TELL LILY WHY THEY CALL IT BLACK SAND BEACH?
IS IT BECAUSE THE SAND IS BLACK?
YUP.
BUT NO ONE KNOWS WHY THEY DECIDED TO PAINT IT!
THAT.
A WHOLE SUMMER OF JOKES THAT GOOD.
OKAY, WINDOWS UP.
WE'RE ABOUT TO HEAD INTO MOSQUITO GULCH.

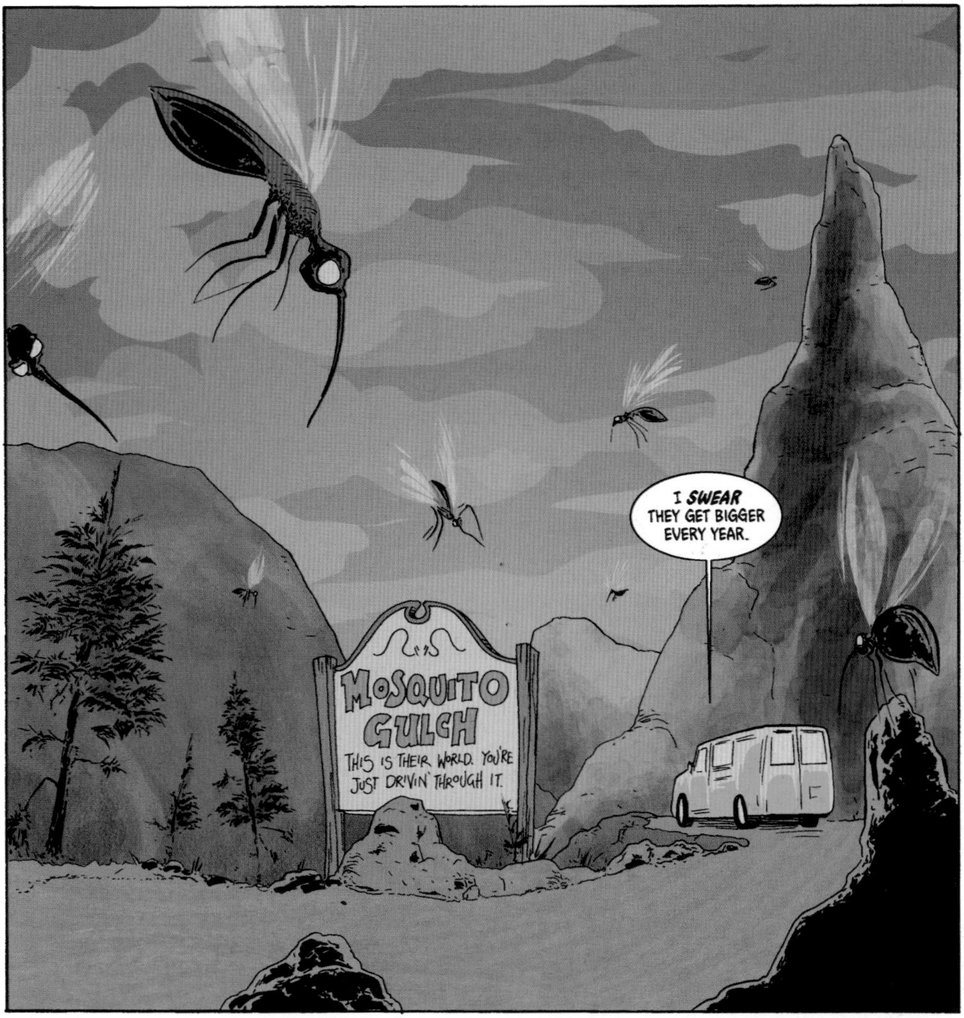
MOSQUITO GULCH
THIS IS THEIR WORLD. YOU'RE JUST DRIVIN' THROUGH IT.
I SWEAR THEY GET BIGGER EVERY YEAR.

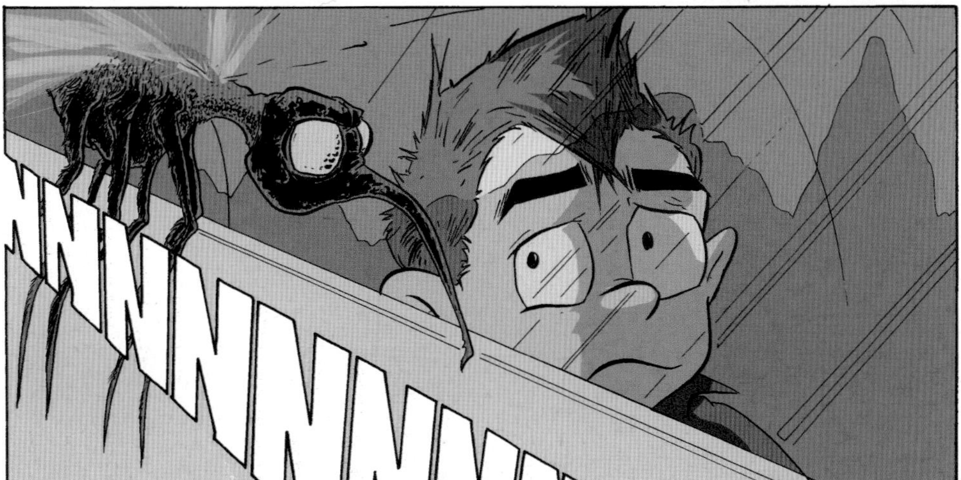
NNNNNNNNN

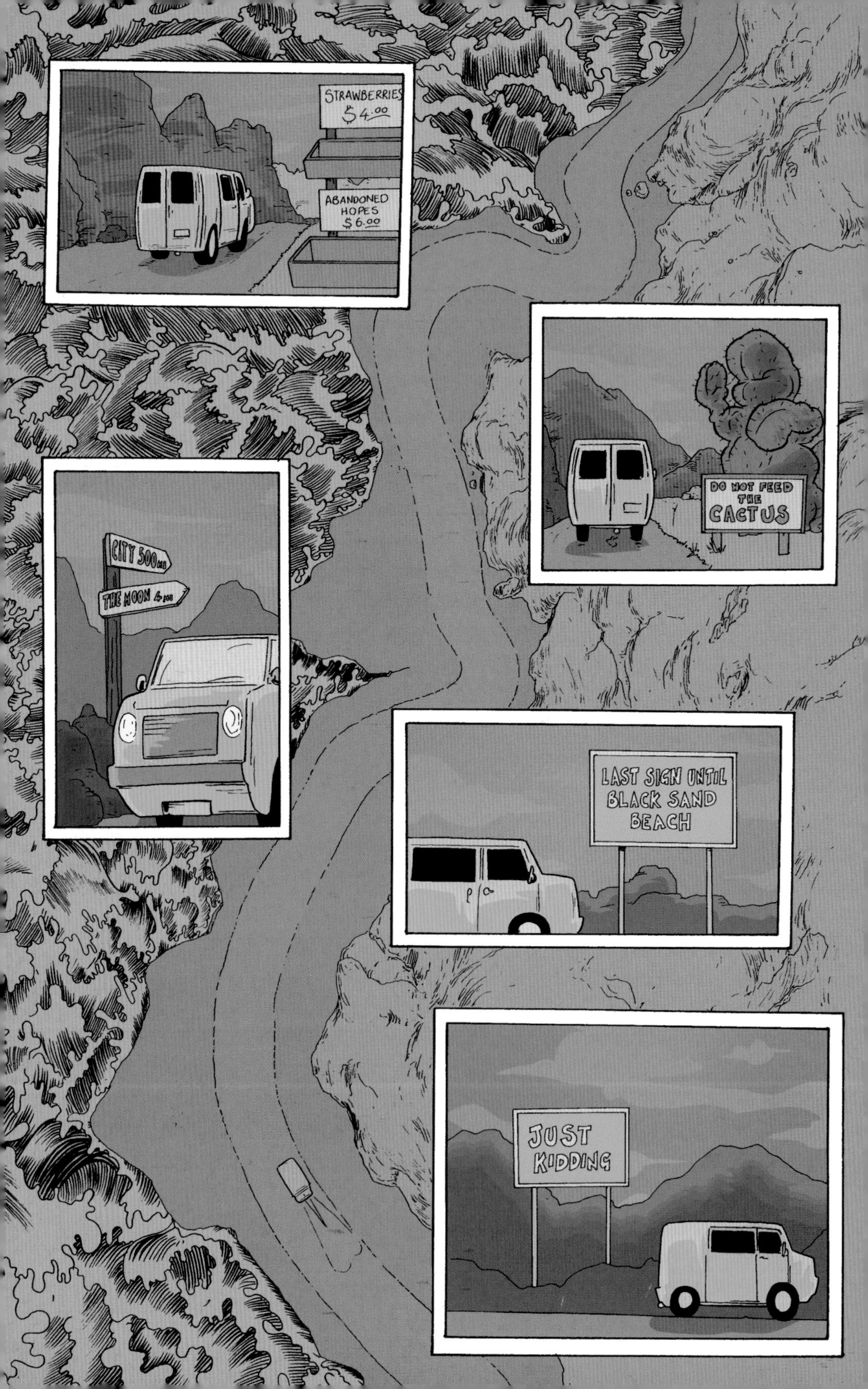
STRAWBERRIES $4.00
ABANDONED HOPES $6.00
DO NOT FEED THE CACTUS
CITY 500 MI
THE MOON 4 MI
LAST SIGN UNTIL BLACK SAND BEACH
JUST KIDDING

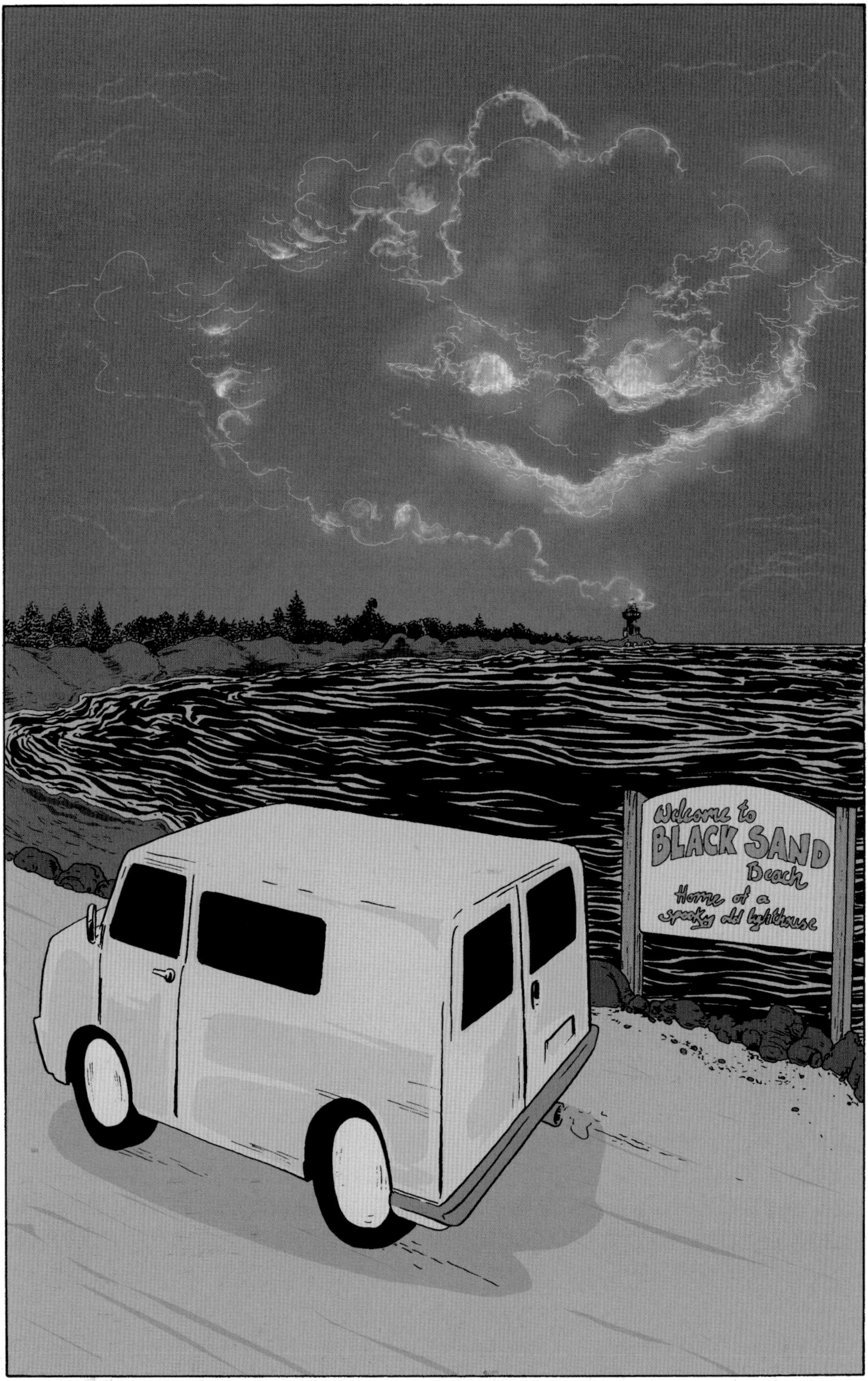
Welcome to
BLACK SAND
Beach
Home of a
spooky old lighthouse

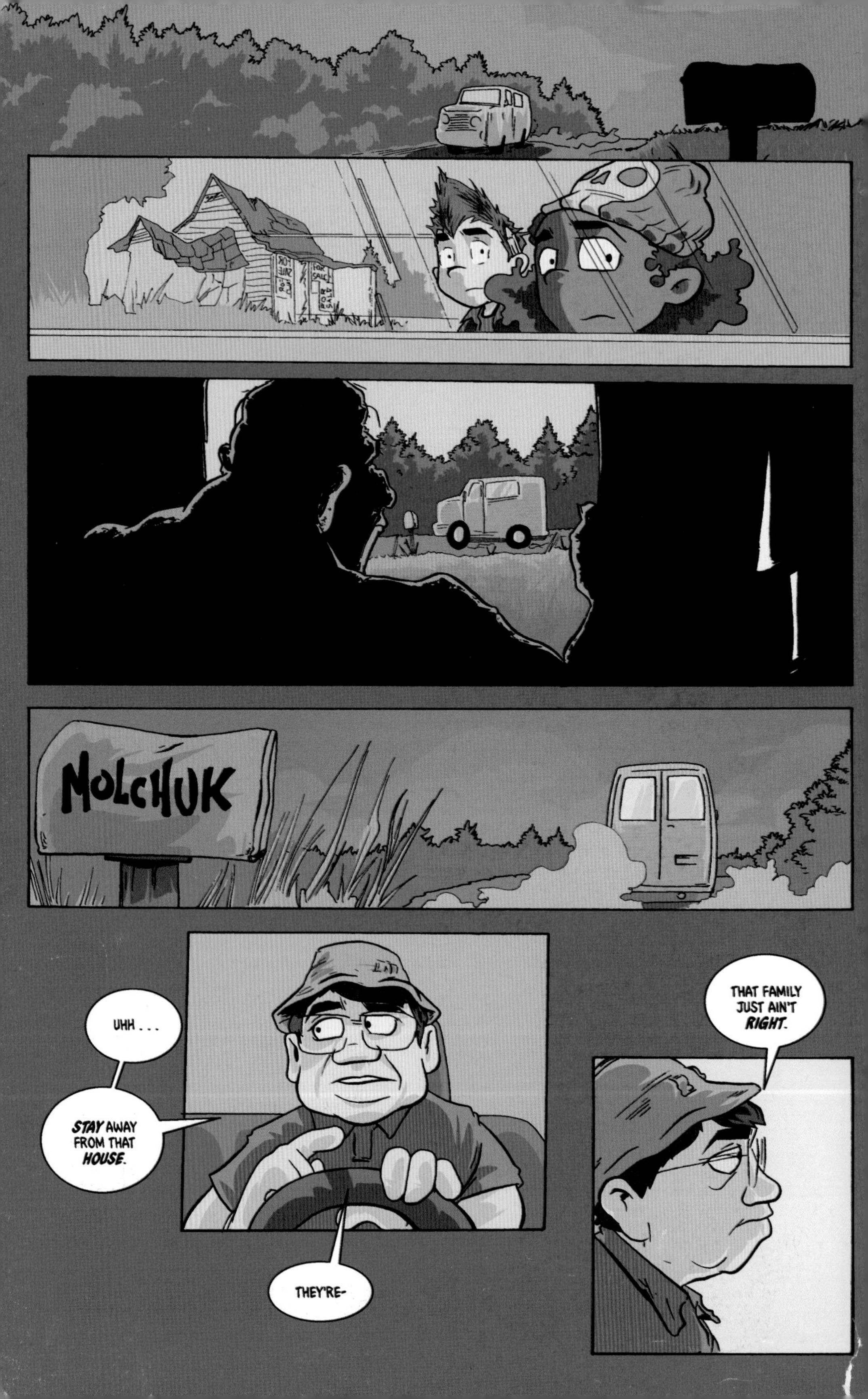
FOR SALE
FOR SALE
MOLCHUK
UHH . . .
STAY AWAY FROM THAT HOUSE.
THEY'RE-
THAT FAMILY JUST AIN'T RIGHT.

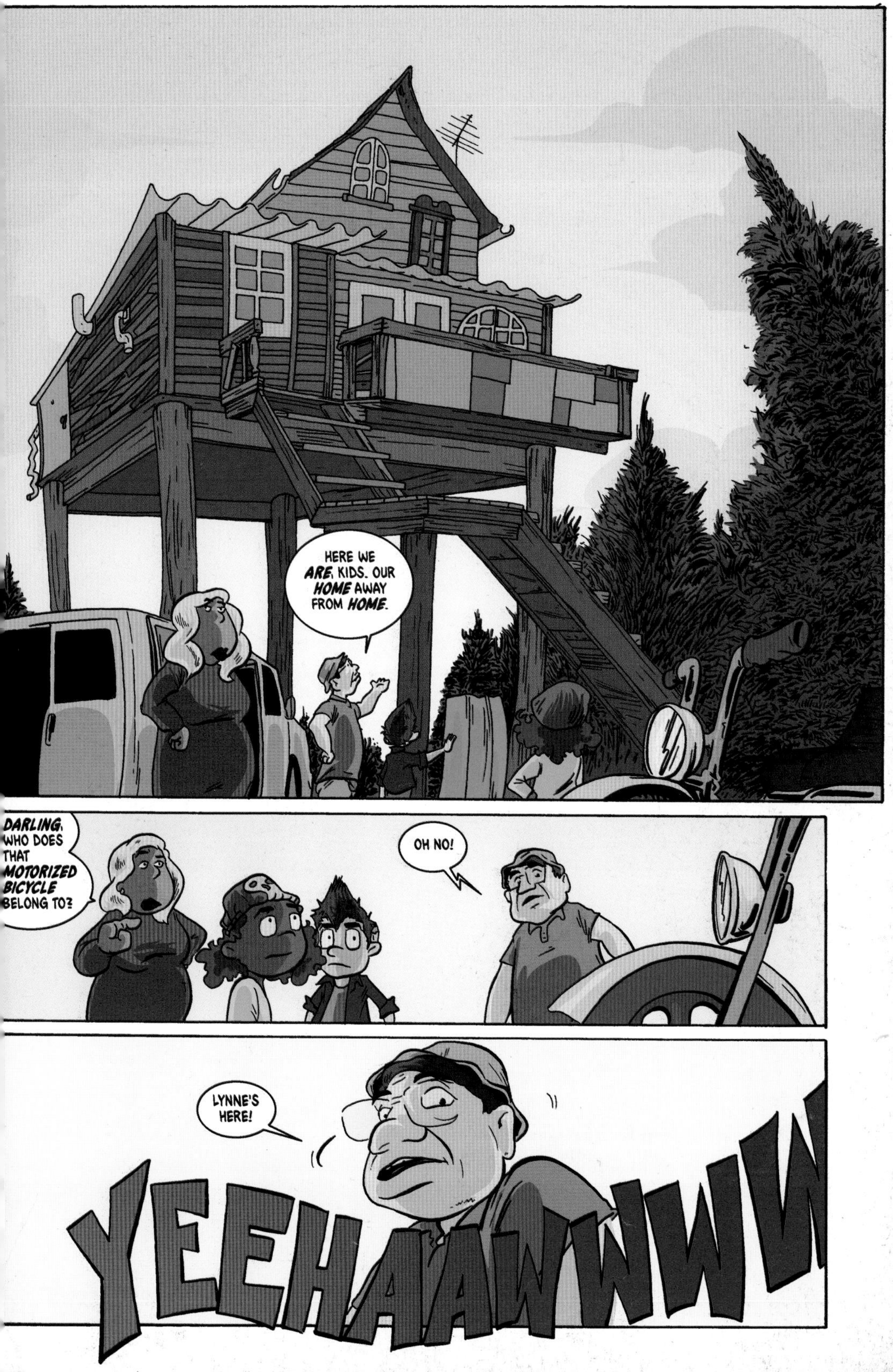
HERE WE ARE, KIDS. OUR HOME AWAY FROM HOME.
DARLING, WHO DOES THAT MOTORIZED BICYCLE BELONG TO?
OH NO!
LYNNE'S HERE!
YEEHAAWWWW

CLIPPITY CLOP · CLIPPITY CLOP · CLIPPITY

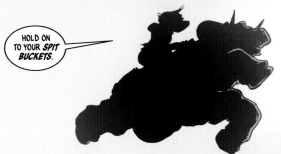

HOLD ON TO YOUR *SPIT BUCKETS*.

YA LOUSY *CITY DWELLERS*.

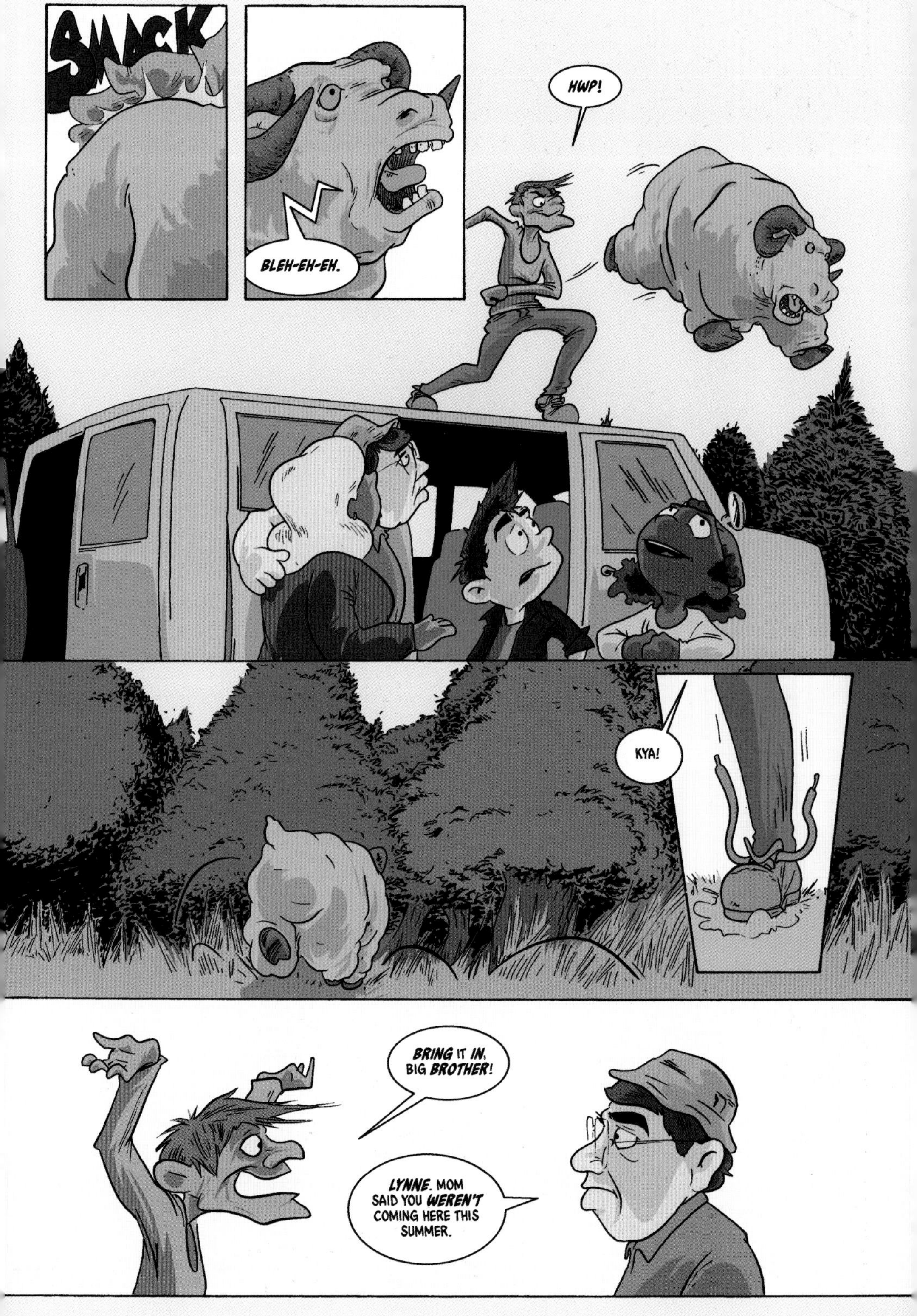
SMACK
BLEH-EH-EH.
HWP!
KYA!
BRING IT IN, BIG BROTHER!
LYNNE. MOM SAID YOU WEREN'T COMING HERE THIS SUMMER.

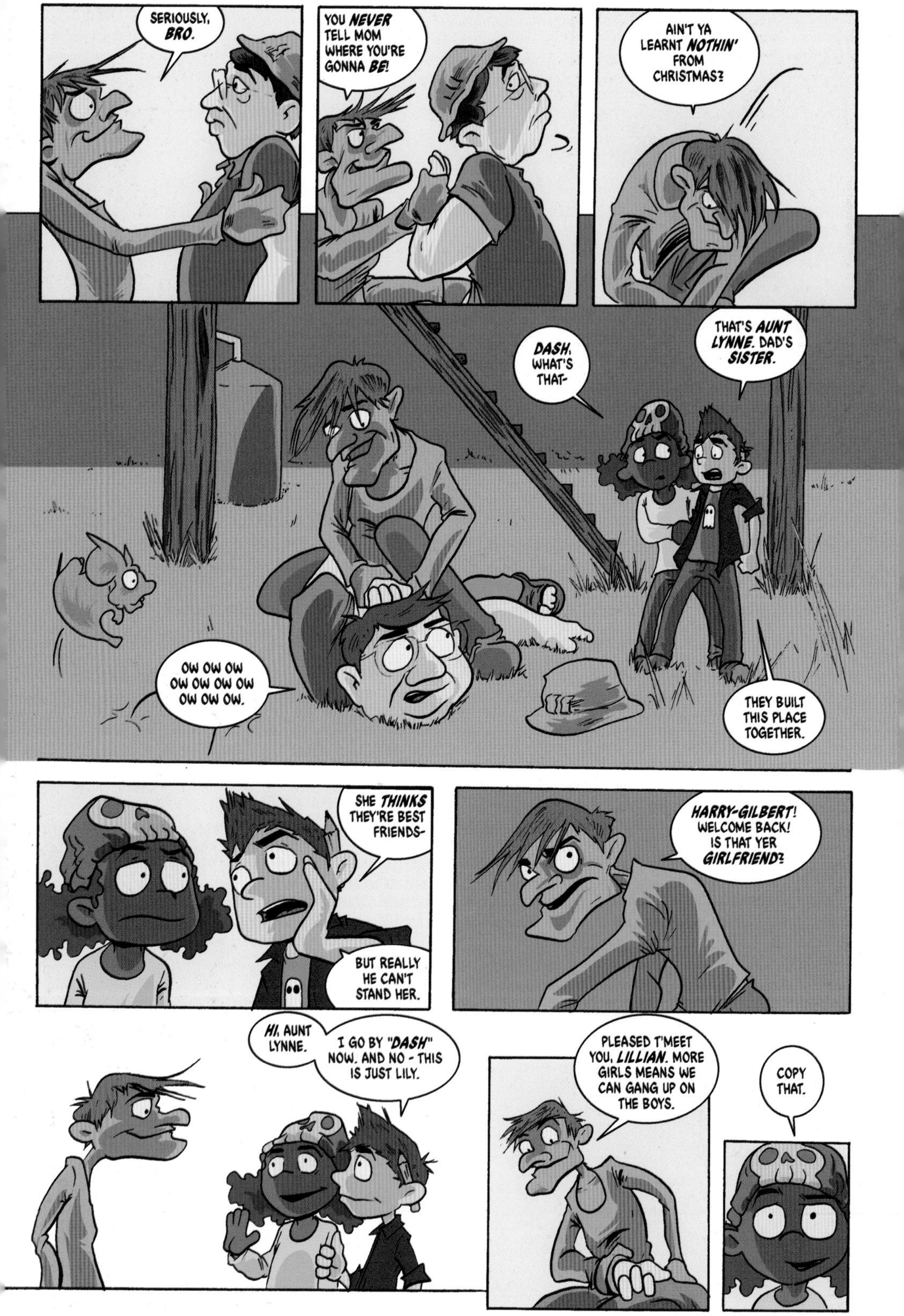
SERIOUSLY, BRO.
YOU NEVER TELL MOM WHERE YOU'RE GONNA BE!
AIN'T YA LEARNT NOTHIN' FROM CHRISTMAS?
DASH, WHAT'S THAT-
THAT'S AUNT LYNNE. DAD'S SISTER.
OW OW OW OW OW OW OW OW OW OW.
THEY BUILT THIS PLACE TOGETHER.
SHE THINKS THEY'RE BEST FRIENDS-
BUT REALLY HE CAN'T STAND HER.
HARRY-GILBERT! WELCOME BACK! IS THAT YER GIRLFRIEND?
HI, AUNT LYNNE.
I GO BY "DASH" NOW. AND NO - THIS IS JUST LILY.
PLEASED T'MEET YOU, LILLIAN. MORE GIRLS MEANS WE CAN GANG UP ON THE BOYS.
COPY THAT.

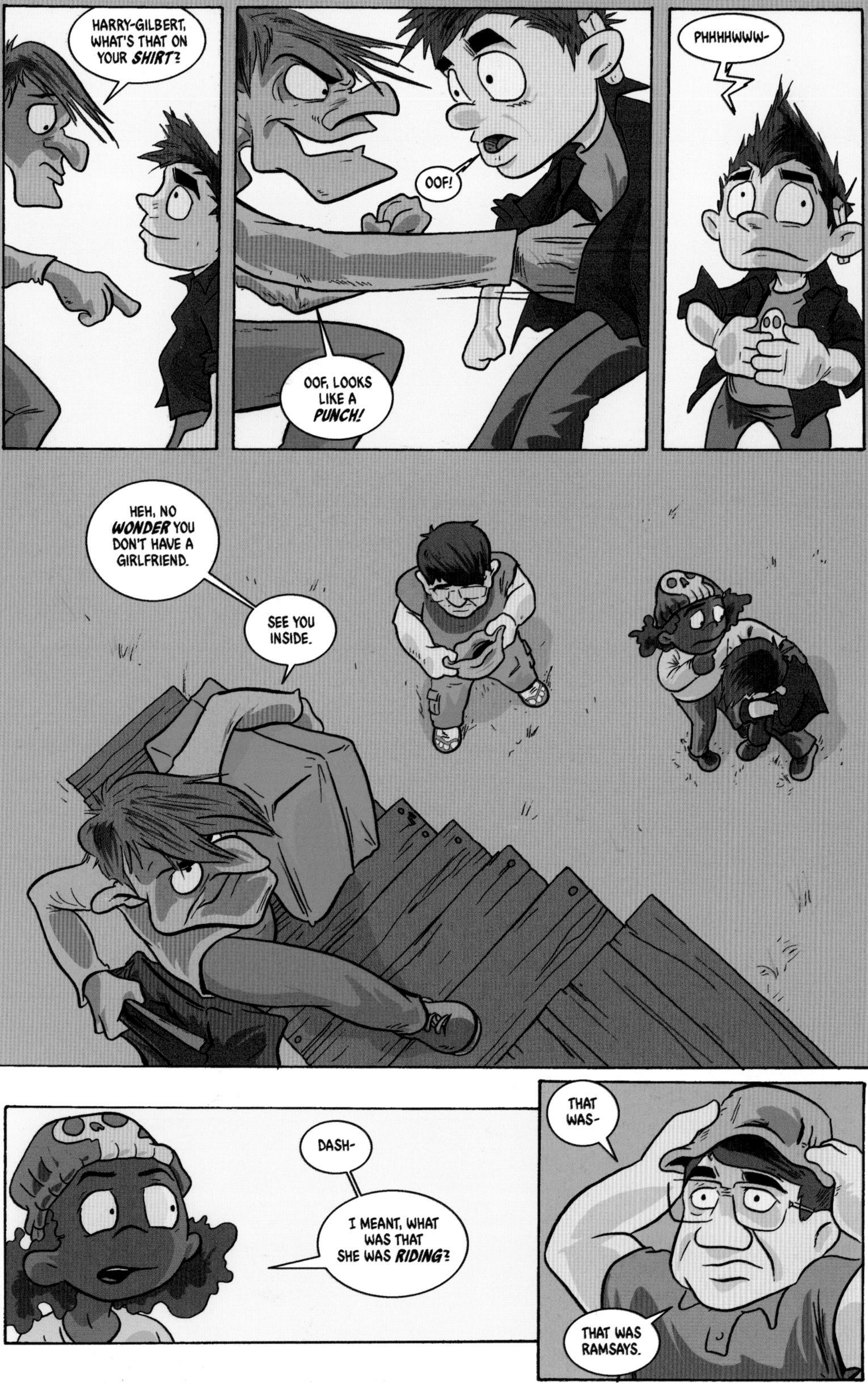
HARRY-GILBERT, WHAT'S THAT ON YOUR *SHIRT*?
OOF!
OOF, LOOKS LIKE A *PUNCH!*
PHHHHWWW-
HEH, NO *WONDER* YOU DON'T HAVE A GIRLFRIEND.
SEE YOU INSIDE.
DASH-
I MEANT, WHAT WAS THAT SHE WAS *RIDING*?
THAT WAS-
THAT WAS RAMSAYS.

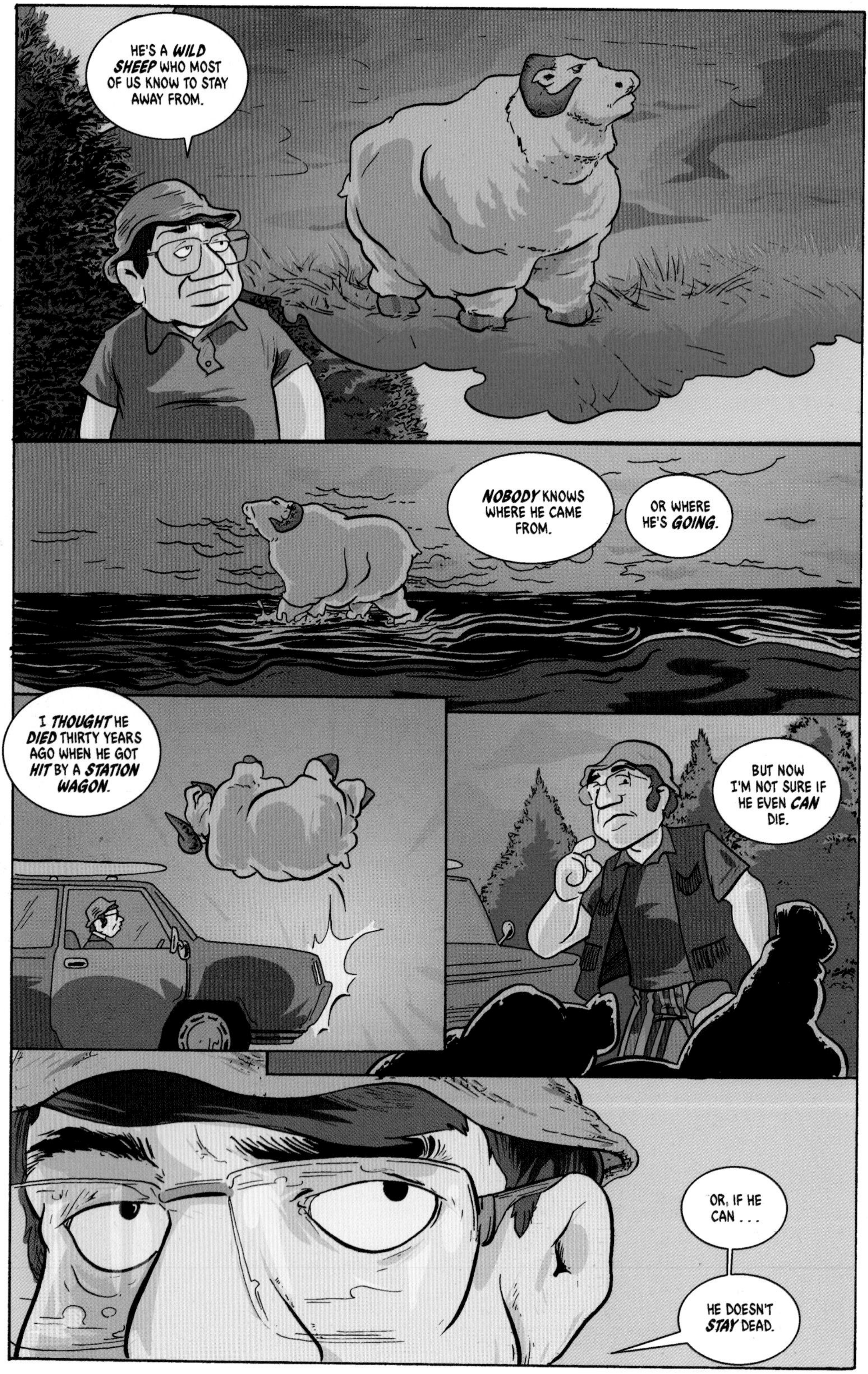
HE'S A WILD SHEEP WHO MOST OF US KNOW TO STAY AWAY FROM.
NOBODY KNOWS WHERE HE CAME FROM.
OR WHERE HE'S GOING.
I THOUGHT HE DIED THIRTY YEARS AGO WHEN HE GOT HIT BY A STATION WAGON.
BUT NOW I'M NOT SURE IF HE EVEN CAN DIE.
OR, IF HE CAN . . .
HE DOESN'T STAY DEAD.

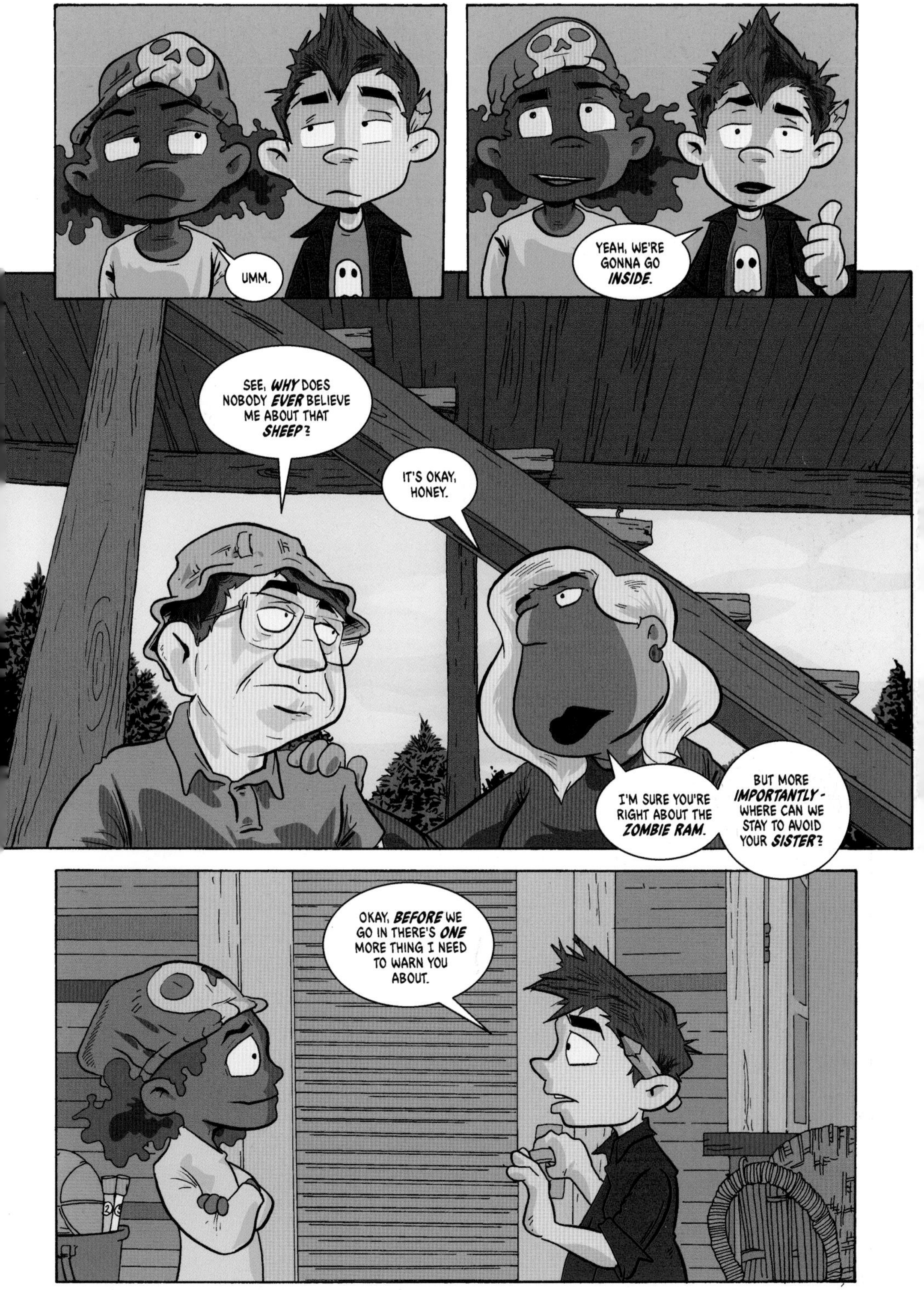
UMM.
YEAH, WE'RE GONNA GO *INSIDE*.
SEE, *WHY* DOES NOBODY *EVER* BELIEVE ME ABOUT THAT *SHEEP*?
IT'S OKAY, HONEY.
I'M SURE YOU'RE RIGHT ABOUT THE *ZOMBIE RAM*.
BUT MORE *IMPORTANTLY*- WHERE CAN WE STAY TO AVOID YOUR *SISTER*?
OKAY, *BEFORE* WE GO IN THERE'S *ONE* MORE THING I NEED TO WARN YOU ABOUT.

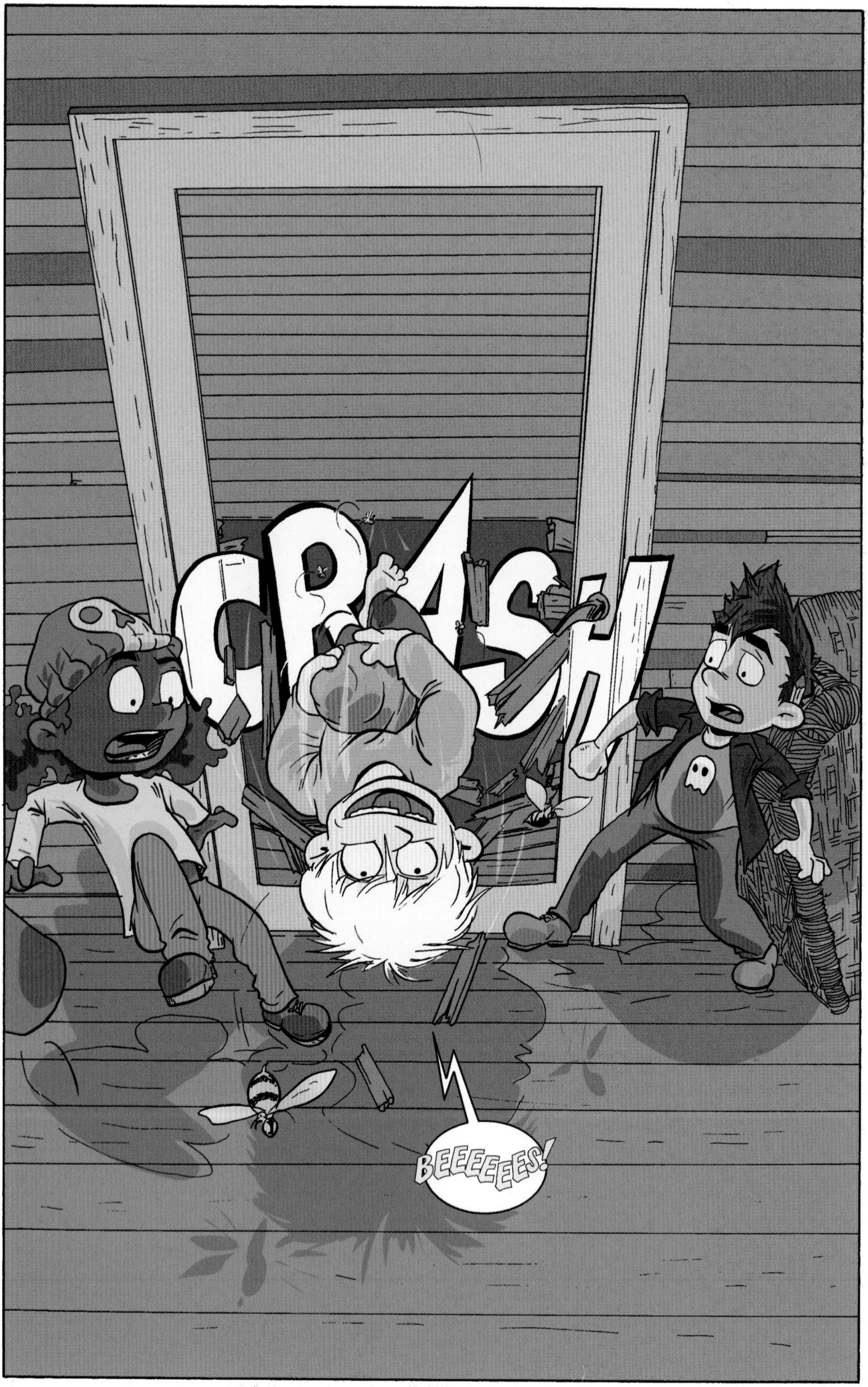
CRASH
BEEEEEEES!

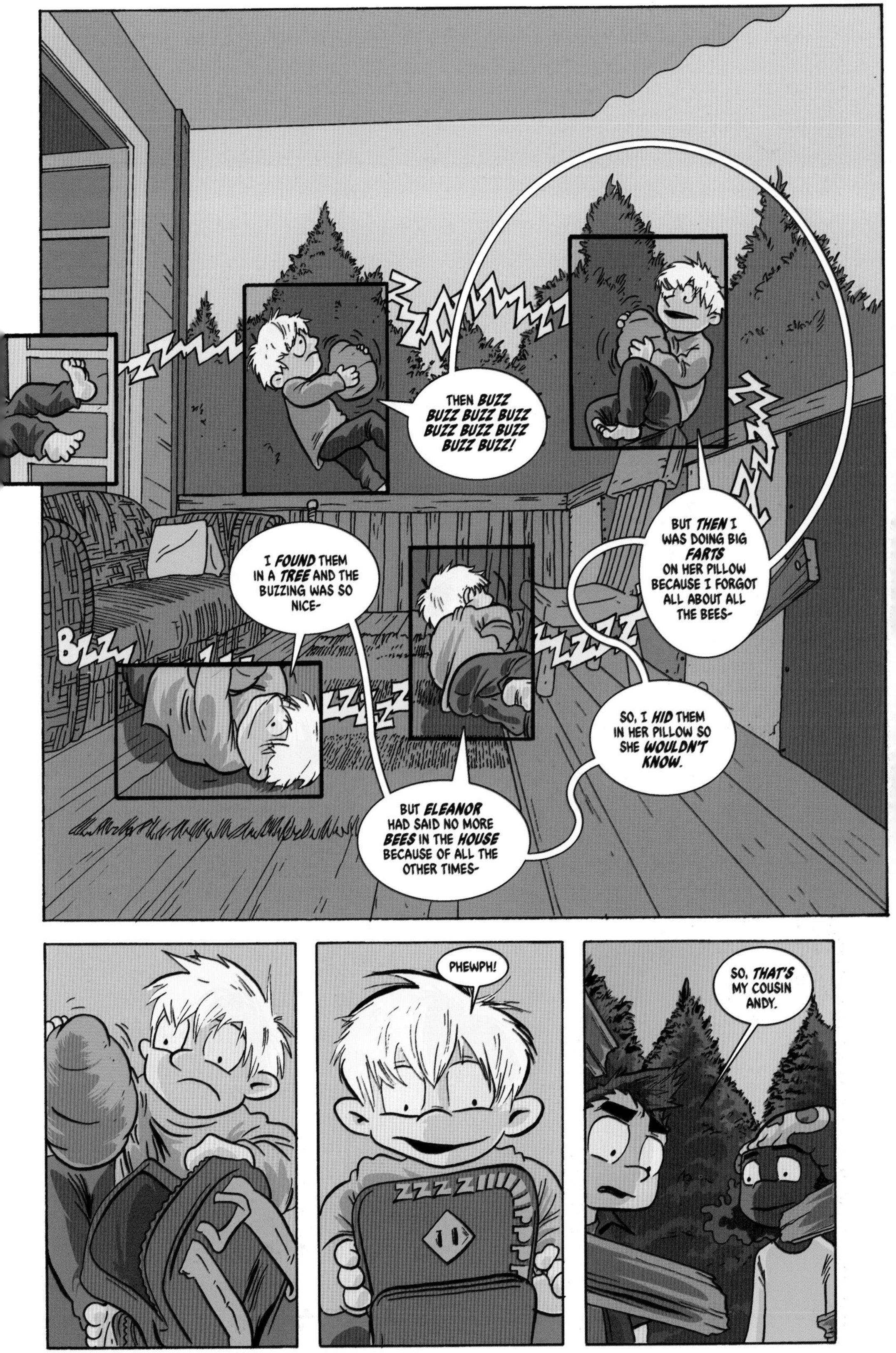
ZZZZZZZ
THEN BUZZ BUZZ BUZZ BUZZ BUZZ BUZZ BUZZ BUZZ BUZZ!
BZZ
I FOUND THEM IN A TREE AND THE BUZZING WAS SO NICE-
BUT ELEANOR HAD SAID NO MORE BEES IN THE HOUSE BECAUSE OF ALL THE OTHER TIMES-
SO, I HID THEM IN HER PILLOW SO SHE WOULDN'T KNOW.
BUT THEN I WAS DOING BIG FARTS ON HER PILLOW BECAUSE I FORGOT ALL ABOUT ALL THE BEES-
PHEWPH!
ZZZZ
SO, THAT'S MY COUSIN ANDY.

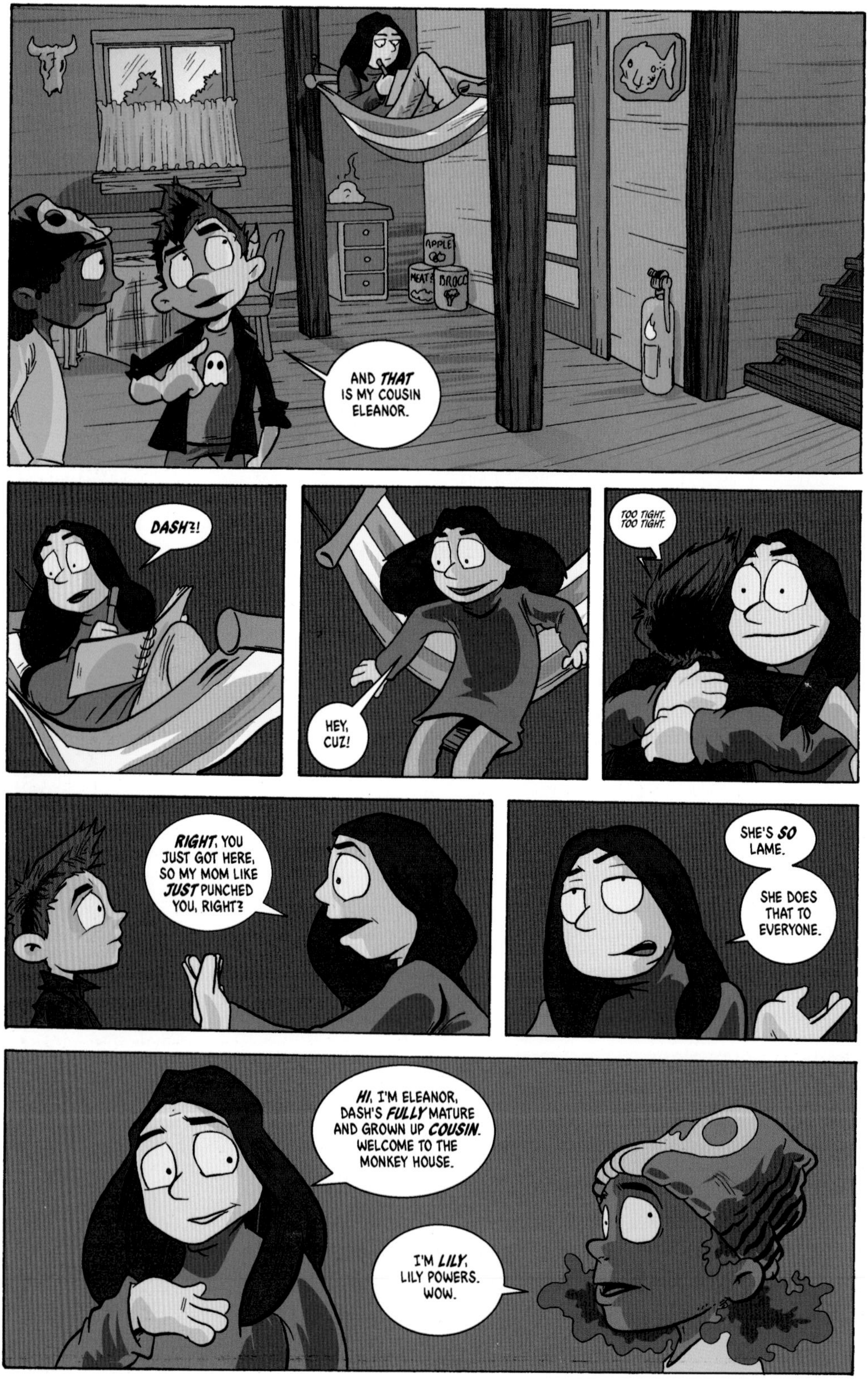
APPLE
MEATS
BROCC
AND THAT IS MY COUSIN ELEANOR.
DASH?!
HEY, CUZ!
TOO TIGHT. TOO TIGHT.
RIGHT. YOU JUST GOT HERE, SO MY MOM LIKE JUST PUNCHED YOU, RIGHT?
SHE'S SO LAME.
SHE DOES THAT TO EVERYONE.
HI. I'M ELEANOR, DASH'S FULLY MATURE AND GROWN UP COUSIN. WELCOME TO THE MONKEY HOUSE.
I'M LILY. LILY POWERS. WOW.

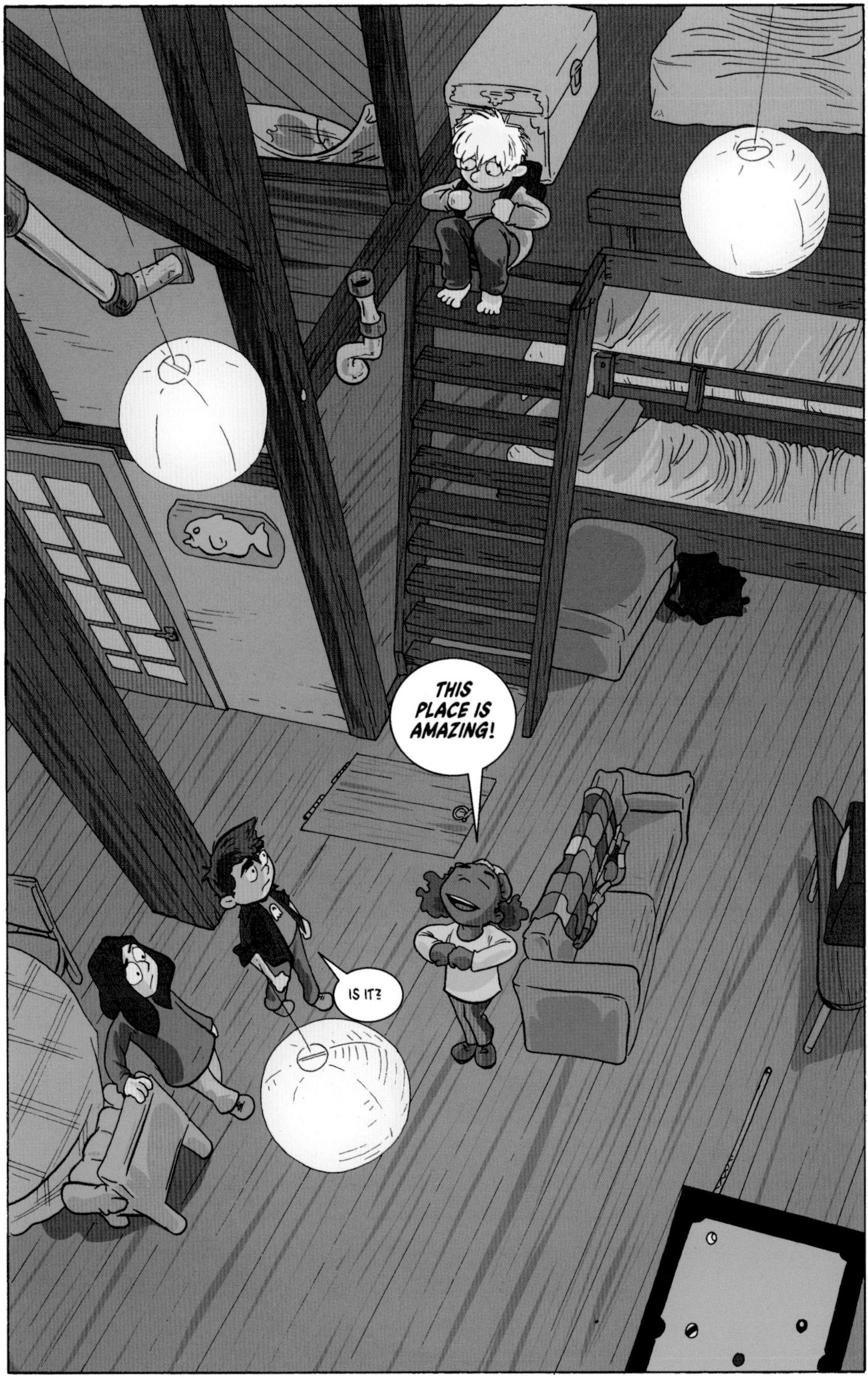
THIS PLACE IS AMAZING!
IS IT?

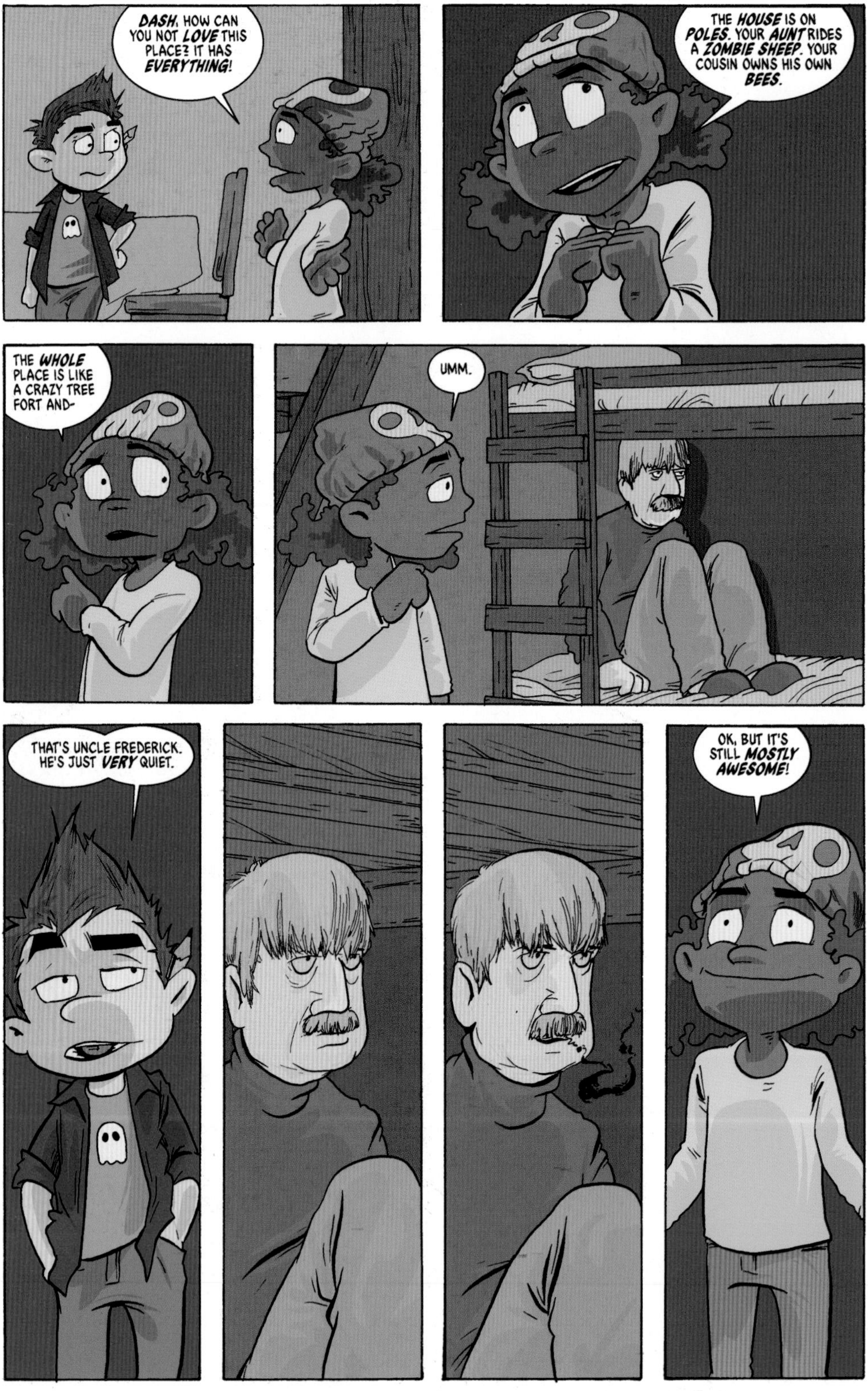
DASH, HOW CAN YOU NOT LOVE THIS PLACE? IT HAS EVERYTHING!
THE HOUSE IS ON POLES. YOUR AUNT RIDES A ZOMBIE SHEEP. YOUR COUSIN OWNS HIS OWN BEES.
THE WHOLE PLACE IS LIKE A CRAZY TREE FORT AND-
UMM.
THAT'S UNCLE FREDERICK. HE'S JUST VERY QUIET.
OK, BUT IT'S STILL MOSTLY AWESOME!

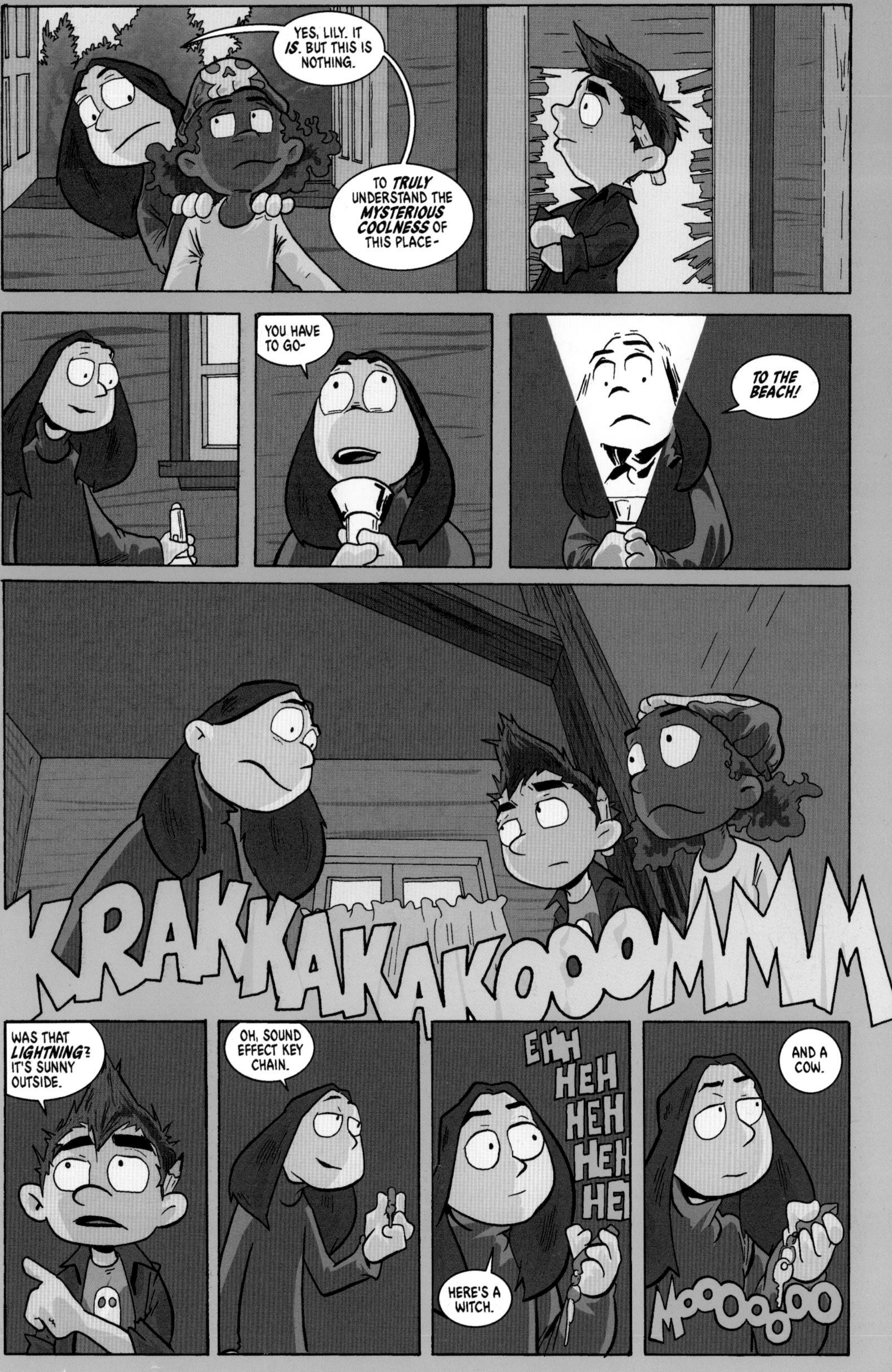

YES, LILY. IT *IS*. BUT THIS IS NOTHING.
TO *TRULY* UNDERSTAND THE *MYSTERIOUS COOLNESS* OF THIS PLACE-
YOU HAVE TO GO-
TO THE BEACH!
KRAKKAKAKOOOMMMM
WAS THAT *LIGHTNING*? IT'S SUNNY OUTSIDE.
OH, SOUND EFFECT KEY CHAIN.
EHH HEH HEH HEH HE
HERE'S A WITCH.
AND A COW.
MOOOOOOO

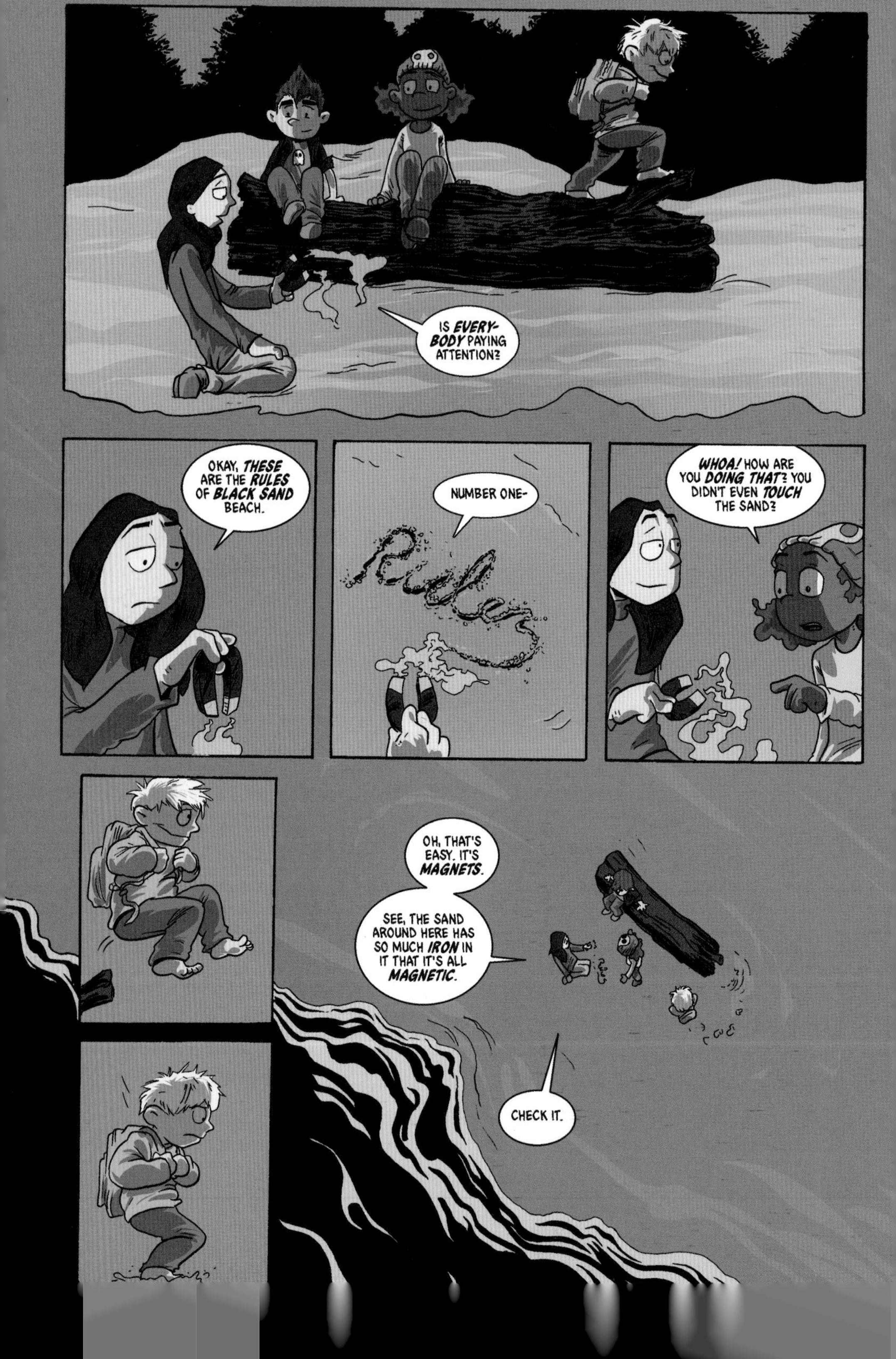
IS EVERY-BODY PAYING ATTENTION?
OKAY, THESE ARE THE RULES OF BLACK SAND BEACH.
NUMBER ONE-
Rules
WHOA! HOW ARE YOU DOING THAT? YOU DIDN'T EVEN TOUCH THE SAND?
OH, THAT'S EASY. IT'S MAGNETS.
SEE, THE SAND AROUND HERE HAS SO MUCH IRON IN IT THAT IT'S ALL MAGNETIC.
CHECK IT.

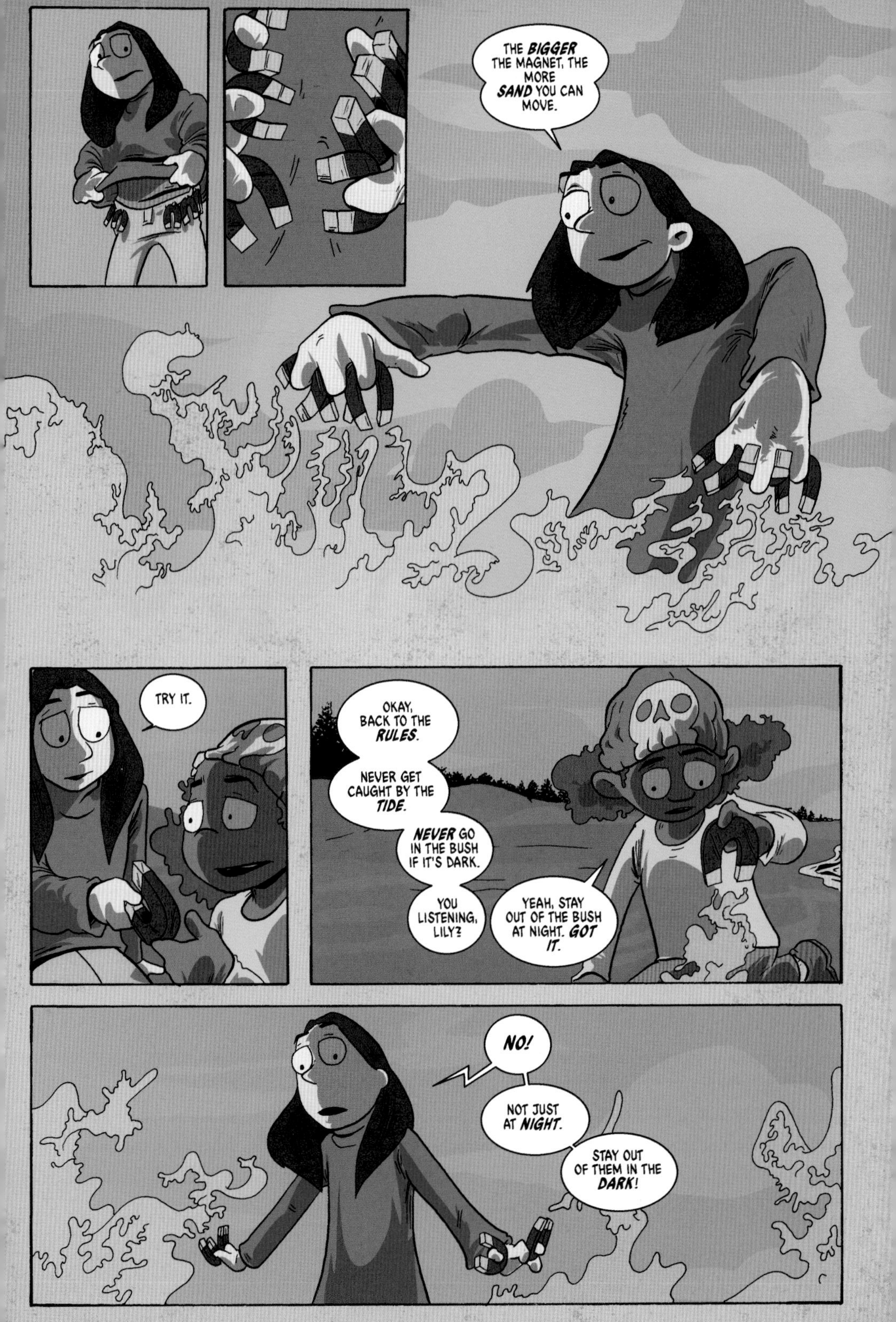
THE BIGGER THE MAGNET, THE MORE SAND YOU CAN MOVE.
TRY IT.
OKAY, BACK TO THE RULES.
NEVER GET CAUGHT BY THE TIDE.
NEVER GO IN THE BUSH IF IT'S DARK.
YOU LISTENING, LILY?
YEAH, STAY OUT OF THE BUSH AT NIGHT. GOT IT.
NO!
NOT JUST AT NIGHT.
STAY OUT OF THEM IN THE DARK!

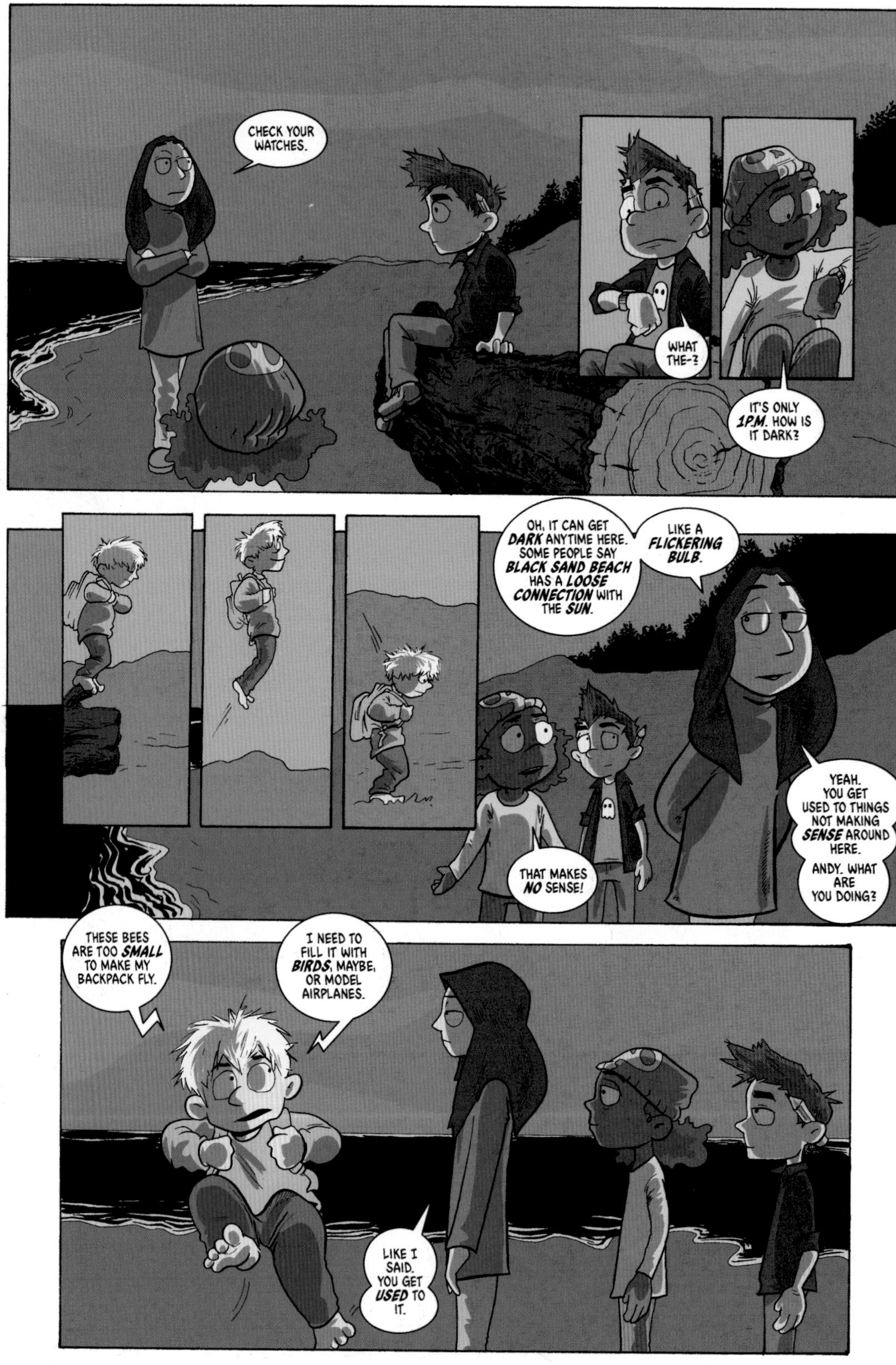
CHECK YOUR WATCHES.
WHAT THE-?
IT'S ONLY 1P.M. HOW IS IT DARK?
OH, IT CAN GET DARK ANYTIME HERE. SOME PEOPLE SAY BLACK SAND BEACH HAS A LOOSE CONNECTION WITH THE SUN.
LIKE A FLICKERING BULB.
THAT MAKES NO SENSE!
YEAH. YOU GET USED TO THINGS NOT MAKING SENSE AROUND HERE.
ANDY. WHAT ARE YOU DOING?
THESE BEES ARE TOO SMALL TO MAKE MY BACKPACK FLY.
I NEED TO FILL IT WITH BIRDS, MAYBE, OR MODEL AIRPLANES.
LIKE I SAID. YOU GET USED TO IT.

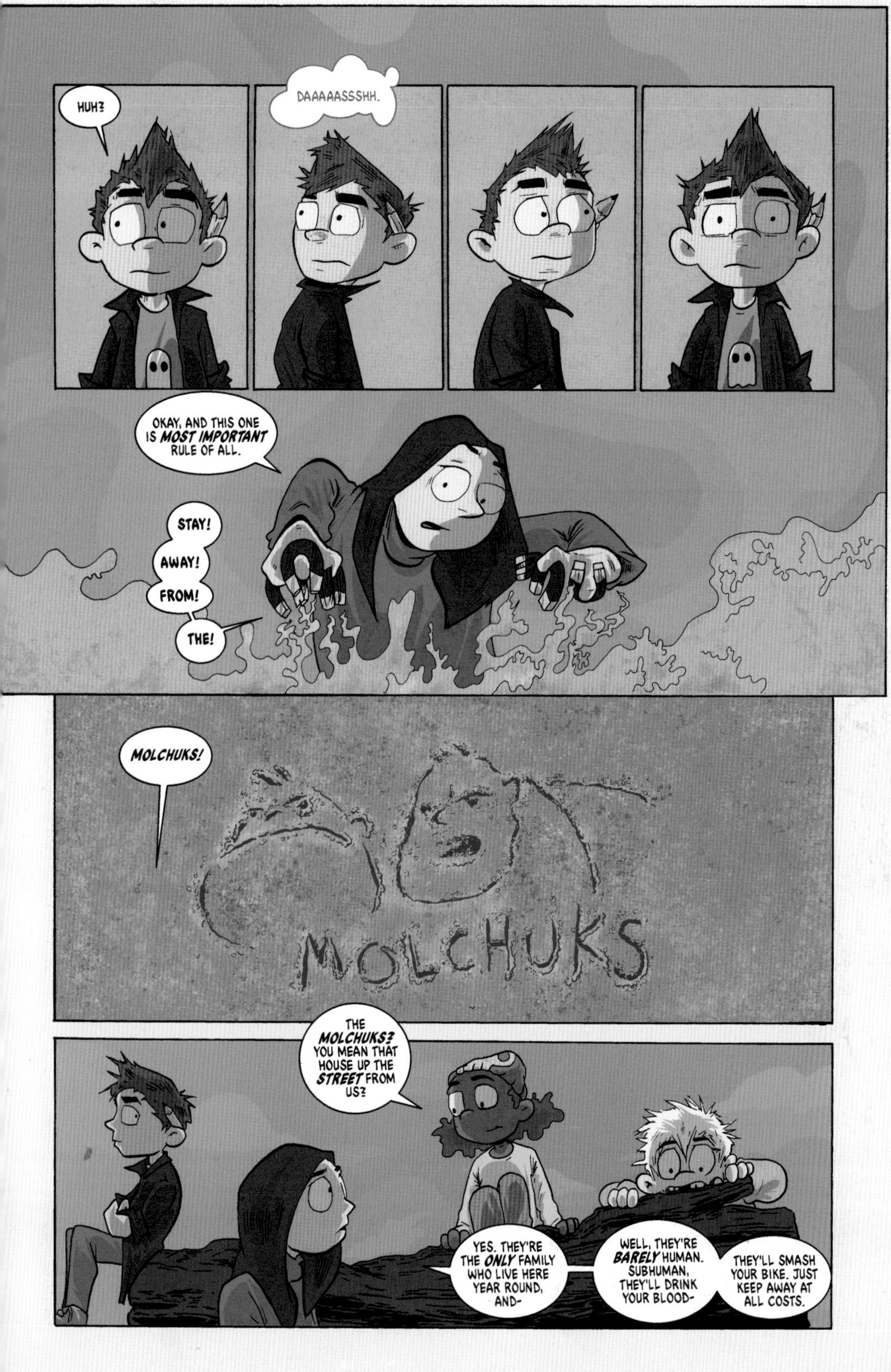
HUH?
DAAAAASSSHH.
OKAY, AND THIS ONE IS MOST IMPORTANT RULE OF ALL.
STAY!
AWAY!
FROM!
THE!
MOLCHUKS!
MOLCHUKS
THE MOLCHUKS? YOU MEAN THAT HOUSE UP THE STREET FROM US?
YES. THEY'RE THE ONLY FAMILY WHO LIVE HERE YEAR ROUND, AND-
WELL, THEY'RE BARELY HUMAN. SUBHUMAN. THEY'LL DRINK YOUR BLOOD-
THEY'LL SMASH YOUR BIKE. JUST KEEP AWAY AT ALL COSTS.

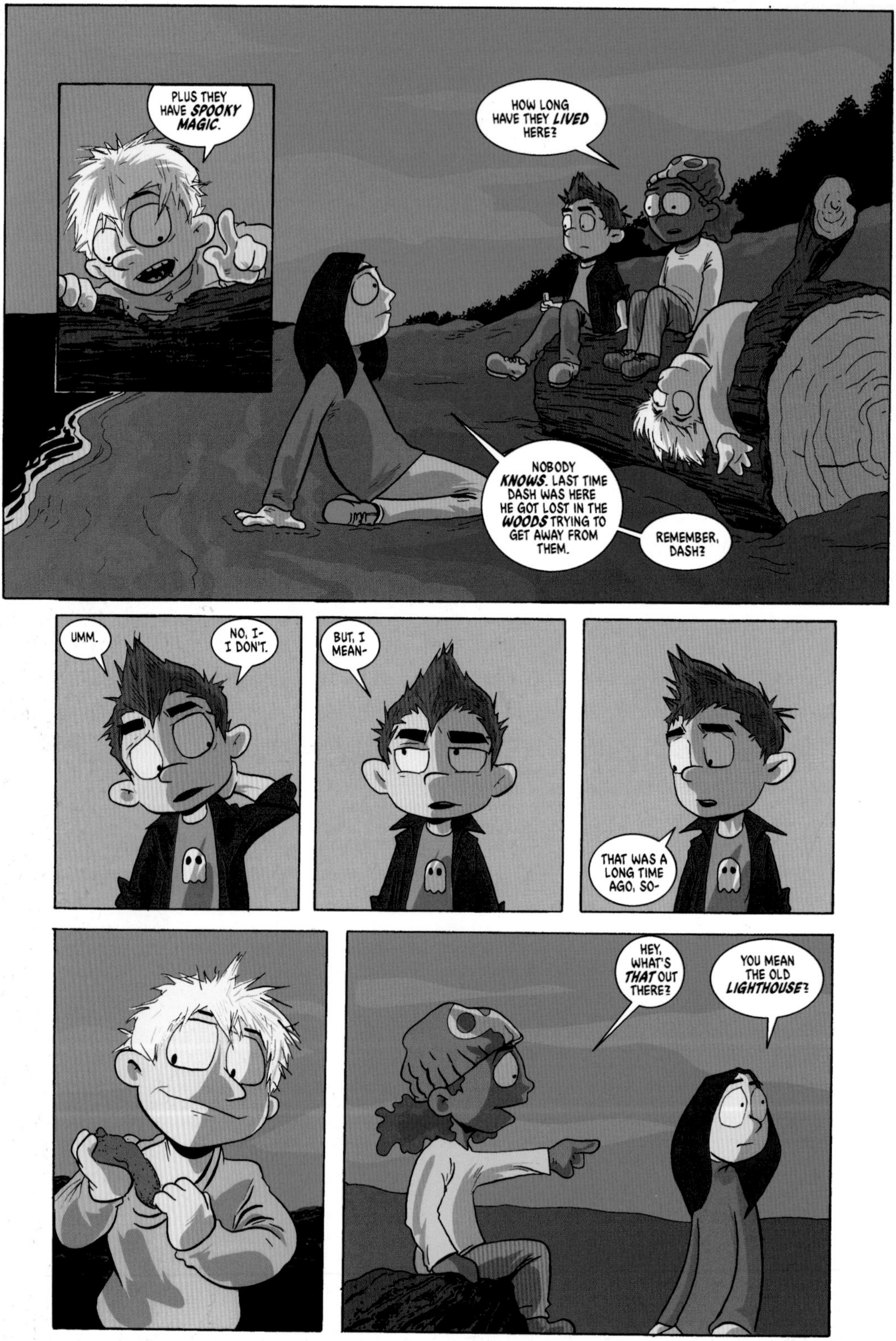
PLUS THEY HAVE **SPOOKY MAGIC**.
HOW LONG HAVE THEY **LIVED** HERE?
NOBODY **KNOWS**. LAST TIME DASH WAS HERE HE GOT LOST IN THE **WOODS** TRYING TO GET AWAY FROM THEM.
REMEMBER, DASH?
UMM.
NO, I- I DON'T.
BUT, I MEAN-
THAT WAS A LONG TIME AGO, SO-
HEY, WHAT'S **THAT** OUT THERE?
YOU MEAN THE OLD **LIGHTHOUSE**?

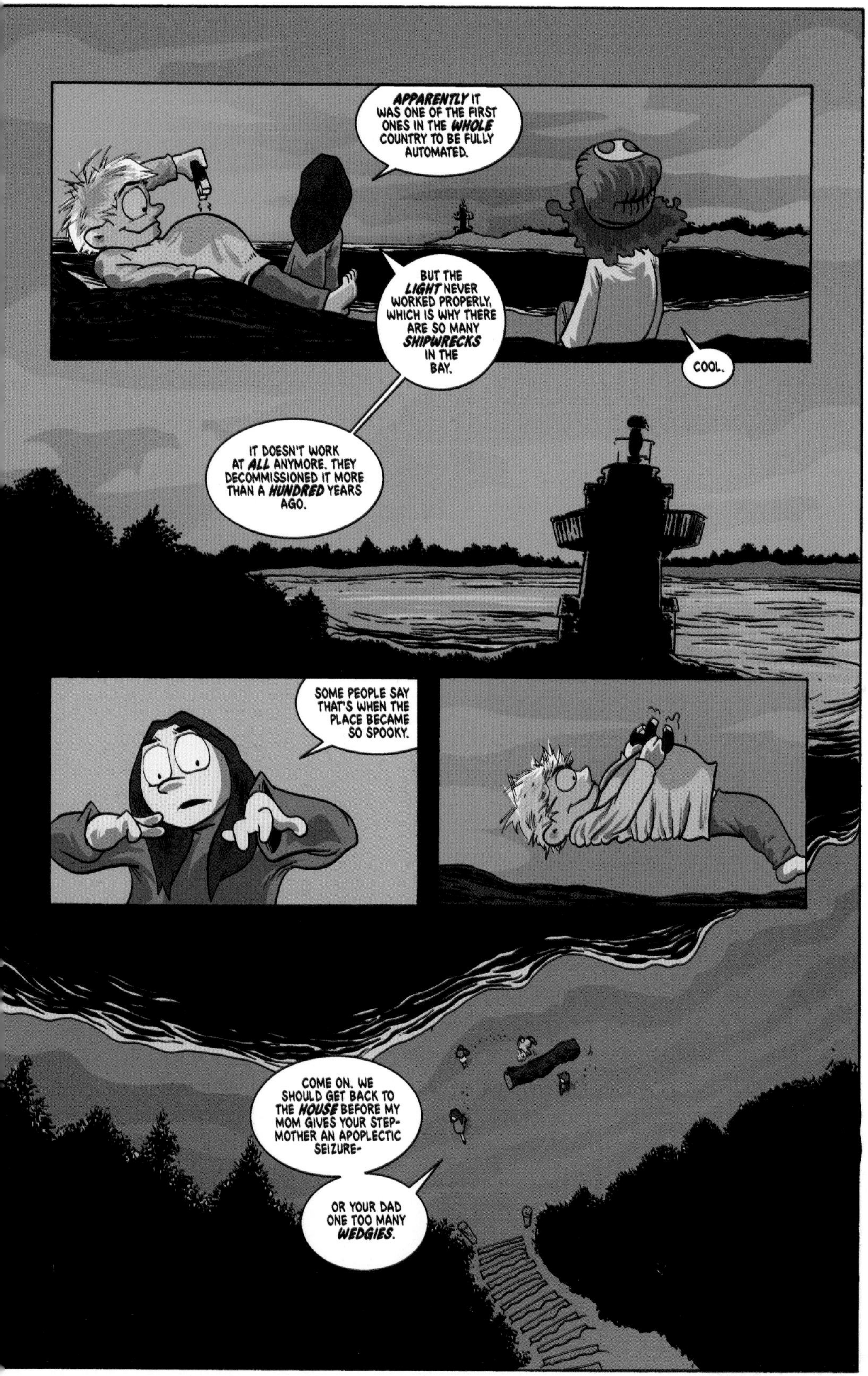

APPARENTLY IT WAS ONE OF THE FIRST ONES IN THE WHOLE COUNTRY TO BE FULLY AUTOMATED.
BUT THE LIGHT NEVER WORKED PROPERLY, WHICH IS WHY THERE ARE SO MANY SHIPWRECKS IN THE BAY.
COOL.
IT DOESN'T WORK AT ALL ANYMORE. THEY DECOMMISSIONED IT MORE THAN A HUNDRED YEARS AGO.
SOME PEOPLE SAY THAT'S WHEN THE PLACE BECAME SO SPOOKY.
COME ON. WE SHOULD GET BACK TO THE HOUSE BEFORE MY MOM GIVES YOUR STEP-MOTHER AN APOPLECTIC SEIZURE-
OR YOUR DAD ONE TOO MANY WEDGIES.

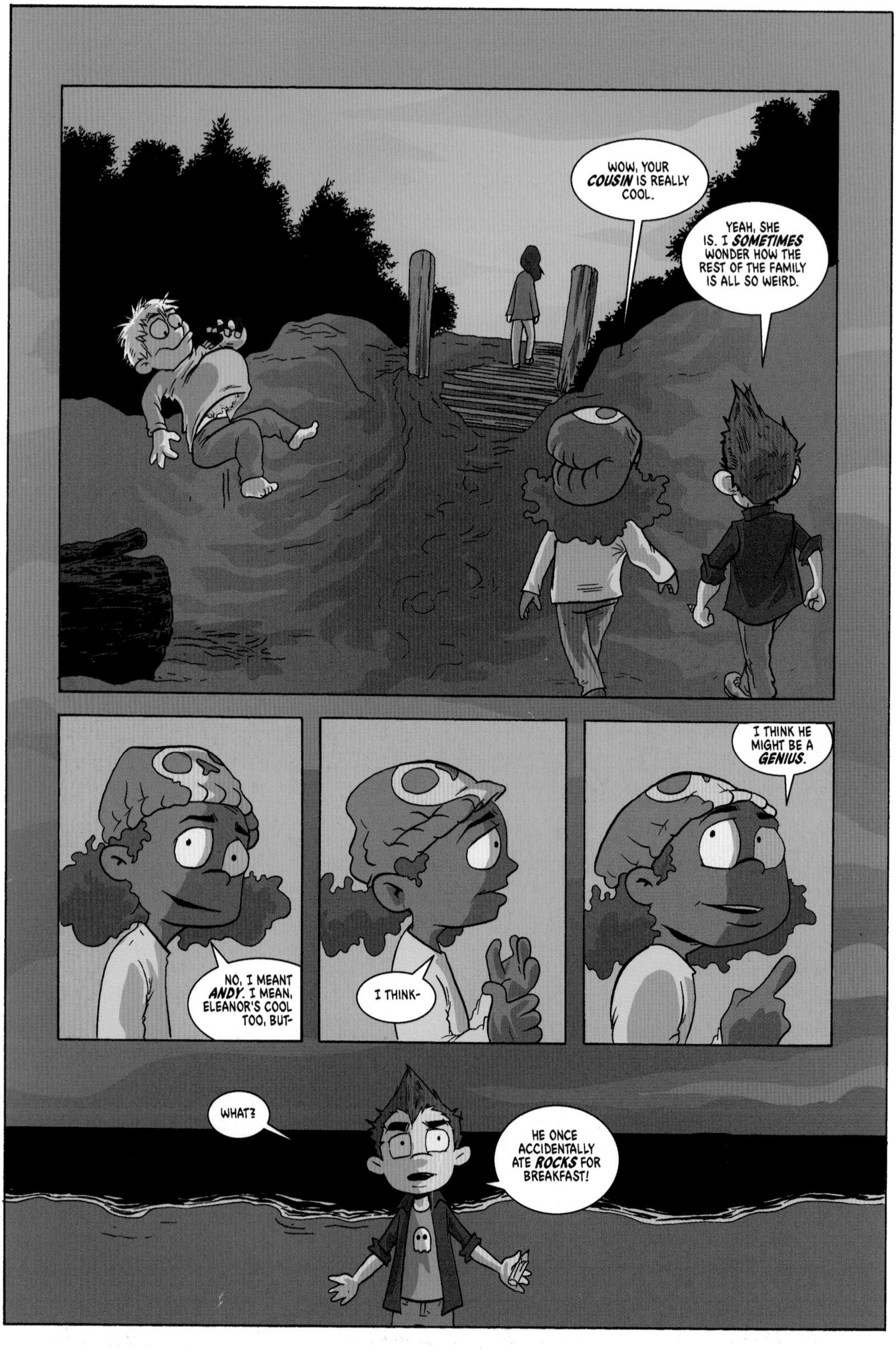
WOW, YOUR COUSIN IS REALLY COOL.
YEAH, SHE IS. I SOMETIMES WONDER HOW THE REST OF THE FAMILY IS ALL SO WEIRD.
NO, I MEANT ANDY. I MEAN, ELEANOR'S COOL TOO, BUT-
I THINK-
I THINK HE MIGHT BE A GENIUS.
WHAT?
HE ONCE ACCIDENTALLY ATE ROCKS FOR BREAKFAST!

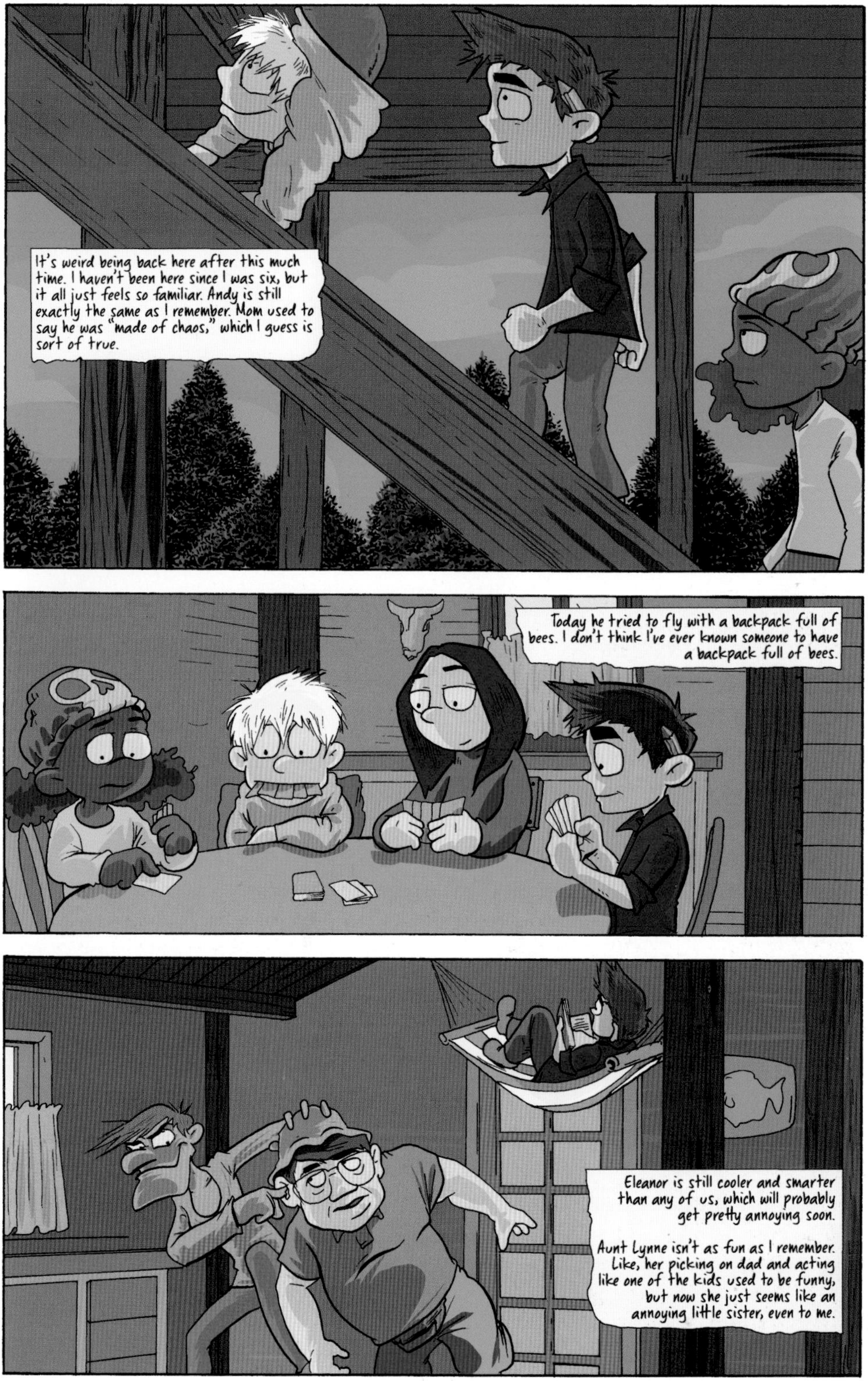
It's weird being back here after this much time. I haven't been here since I was six, but it all just feels so familiar. Andy is still exactly the same as I remember. Mom used to say he was "made of chaos," which I guess is sort of true.
Today he tried to fly with a backpack full of bees. I don't think I've ever known someone to have a backpack full of bees.
Eleanor is still cooler and smarter than any of us, which will probably get pretty annoying soon.
Aunt Lynne isn't as fun as I remember. Like, her picking on dad and acting like one of the kids used to be funny, but now she just seems like an annoying little sister, even to me.

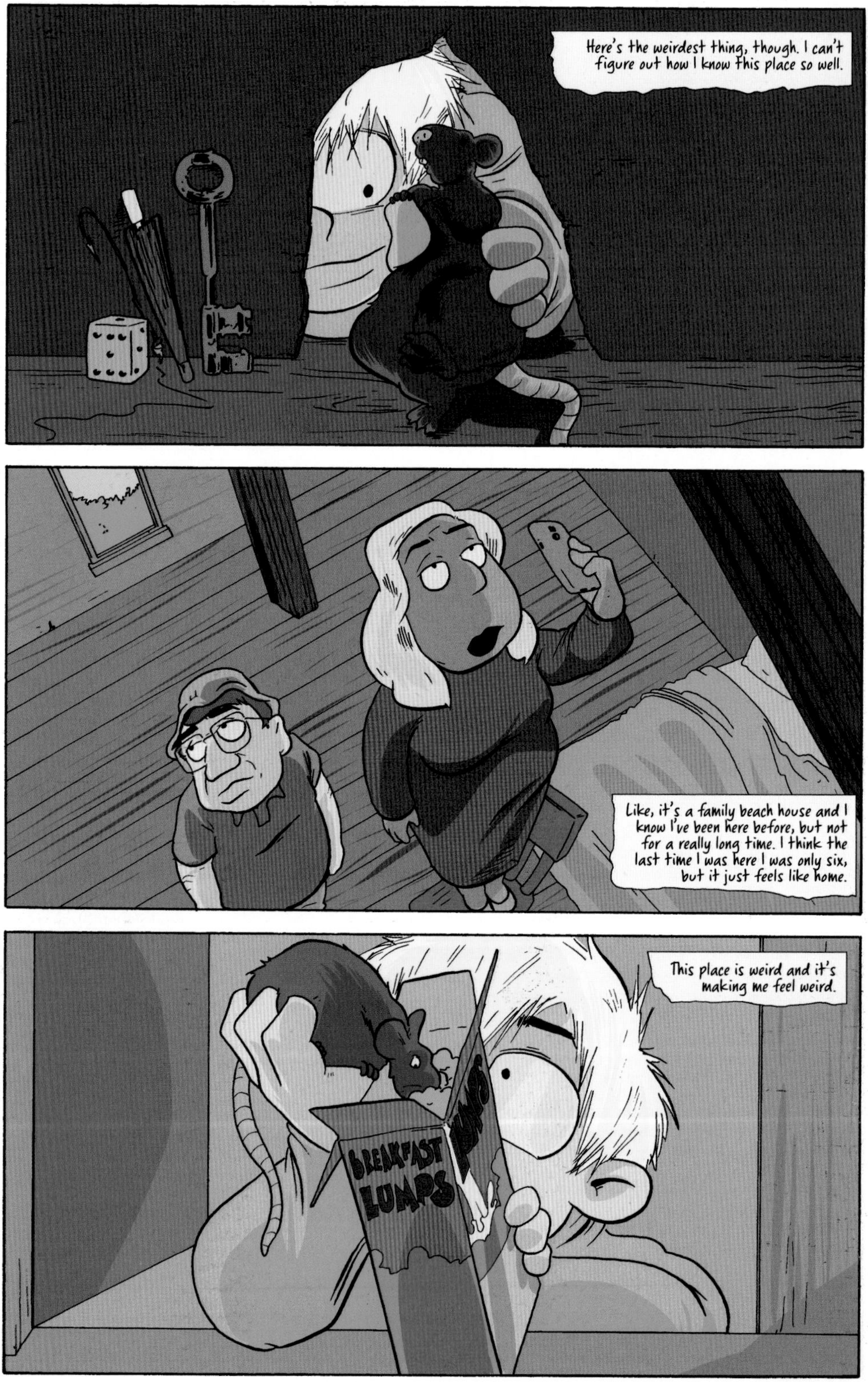
Here's the weirdest thing, though. I can't figure out how I know this place so well.
Like, it's a family beach house and I know I've been here before, but not for a really long time. I think the last time I was here I was only six, but it just feels like home.
This place is weird and it's making me feel weird.
BREAKFAST LUMPS
LUMPS

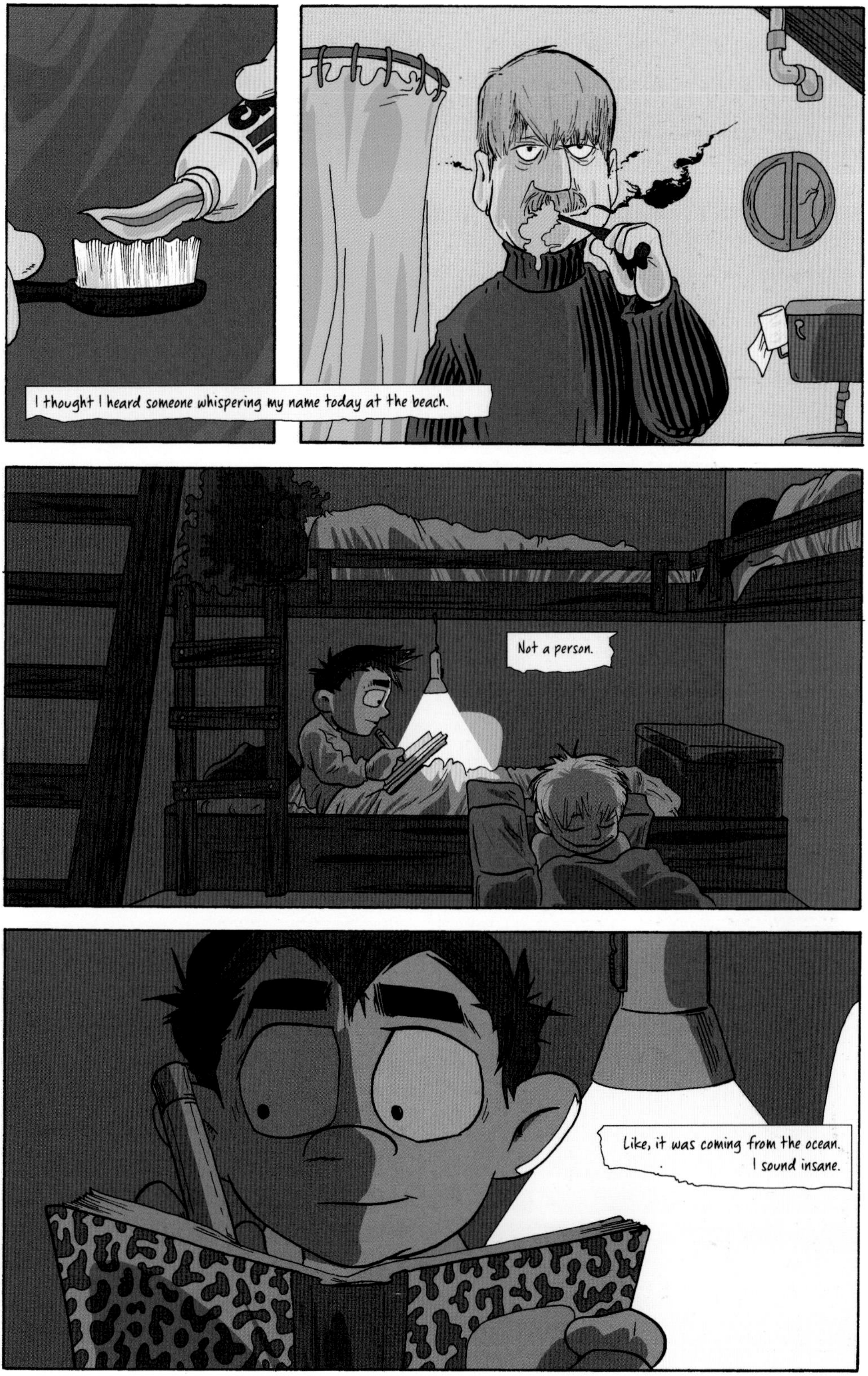
I thought I heard someone whispering my name today at the beach.
Not a person.
Like, it was coming from the ocean.
I sound insane.

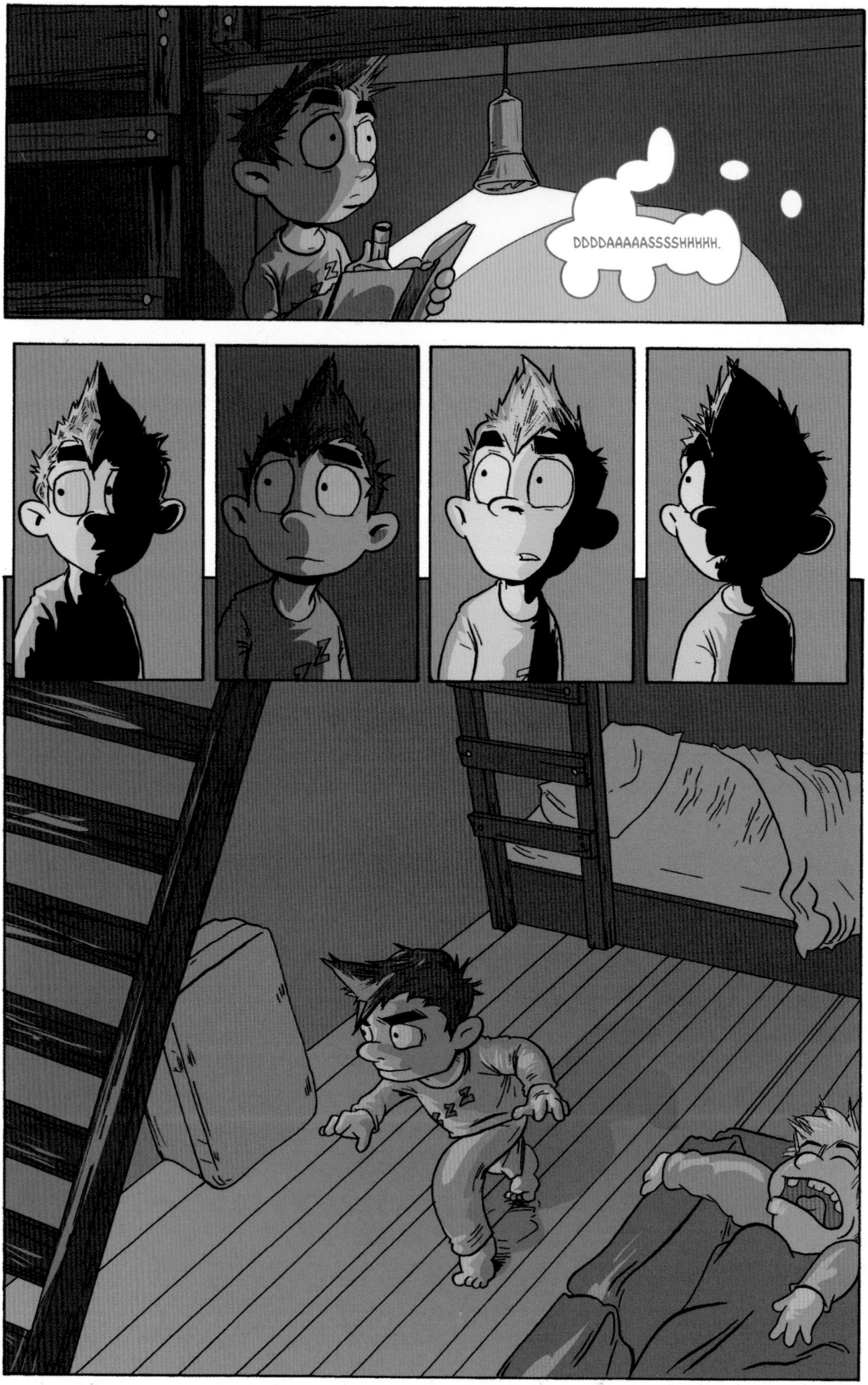
DDDDAAAAAASSSSHHHHH.

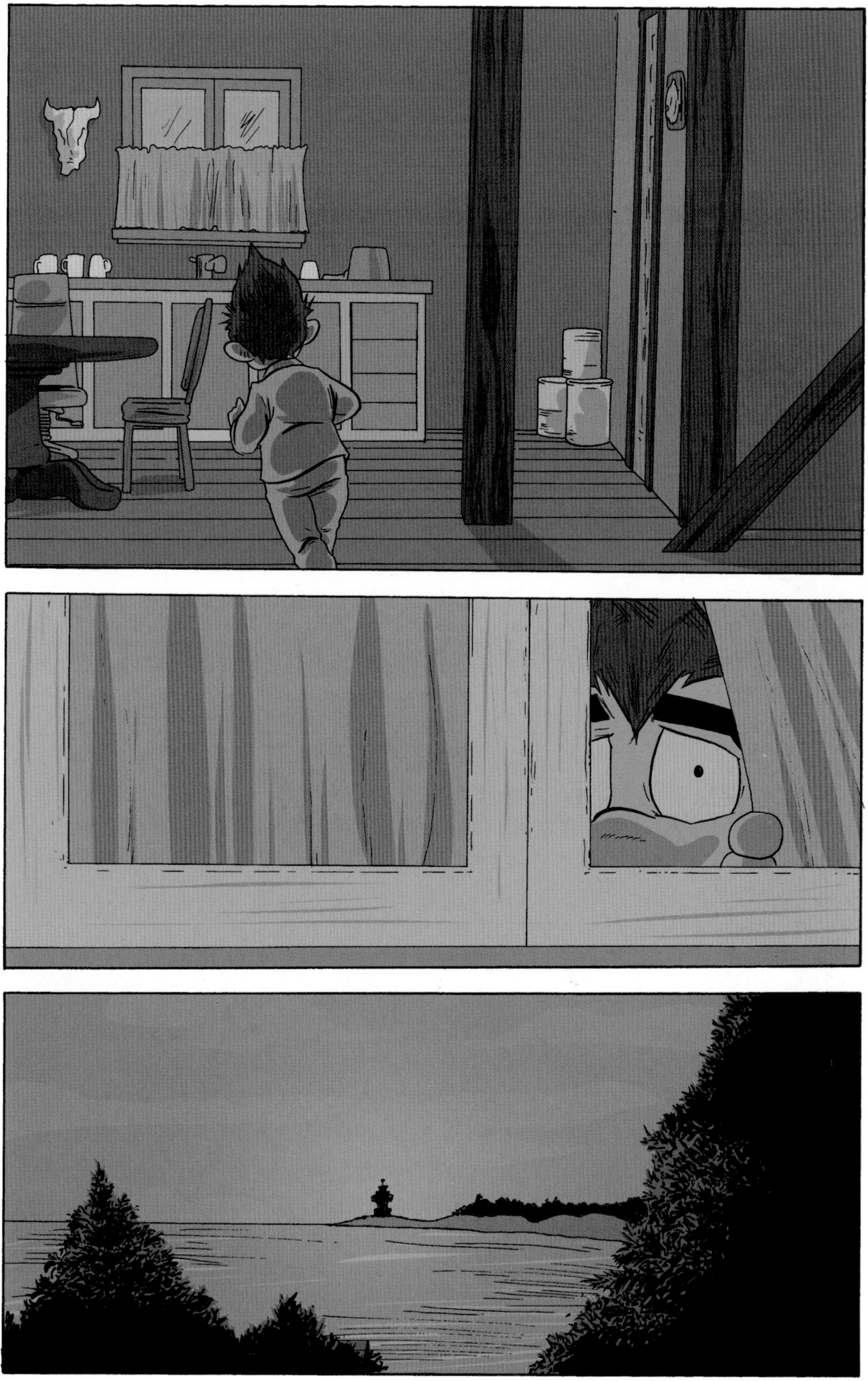

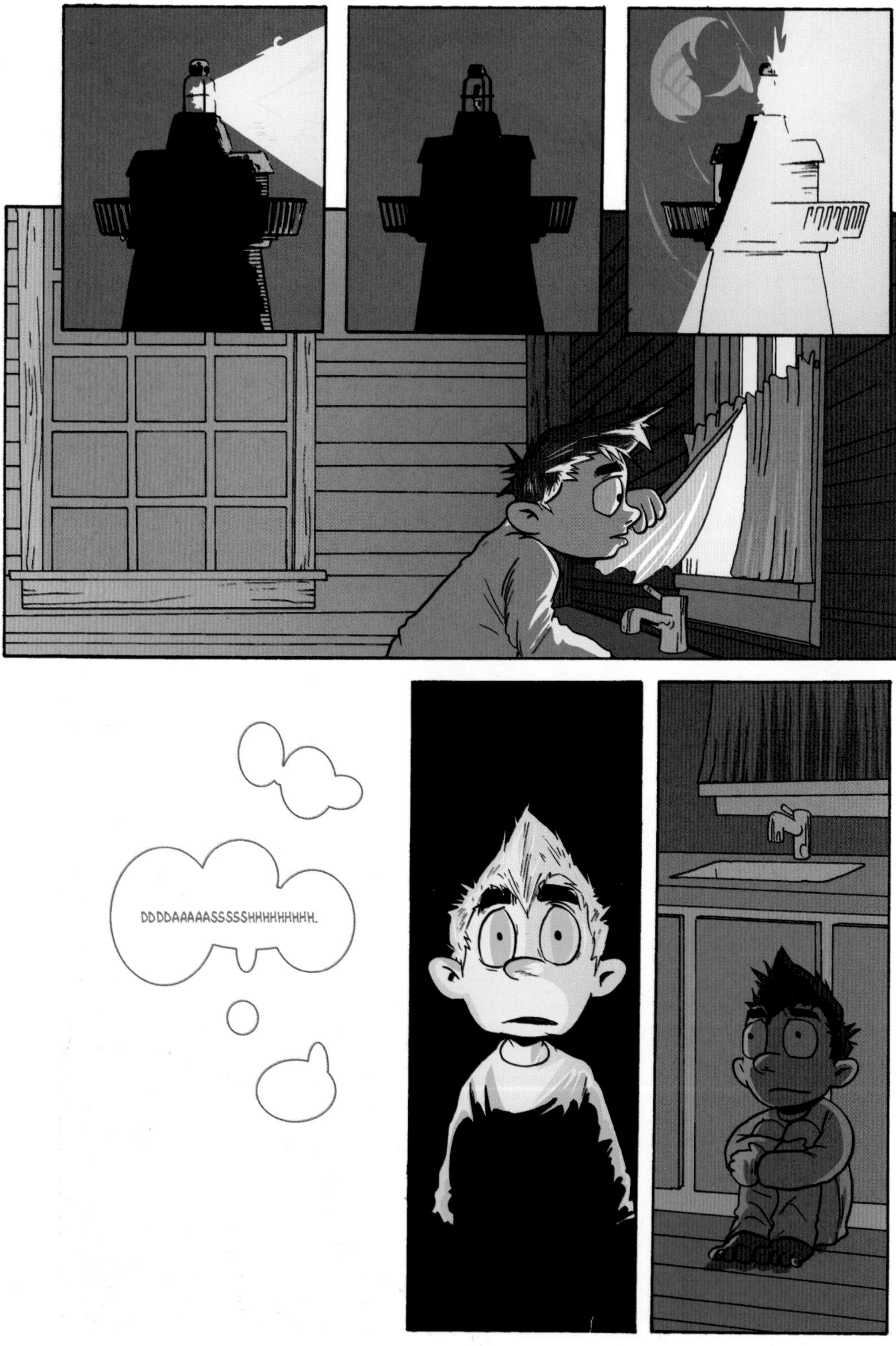
DDDDAAAAASSSSSHHHHHHHHH.

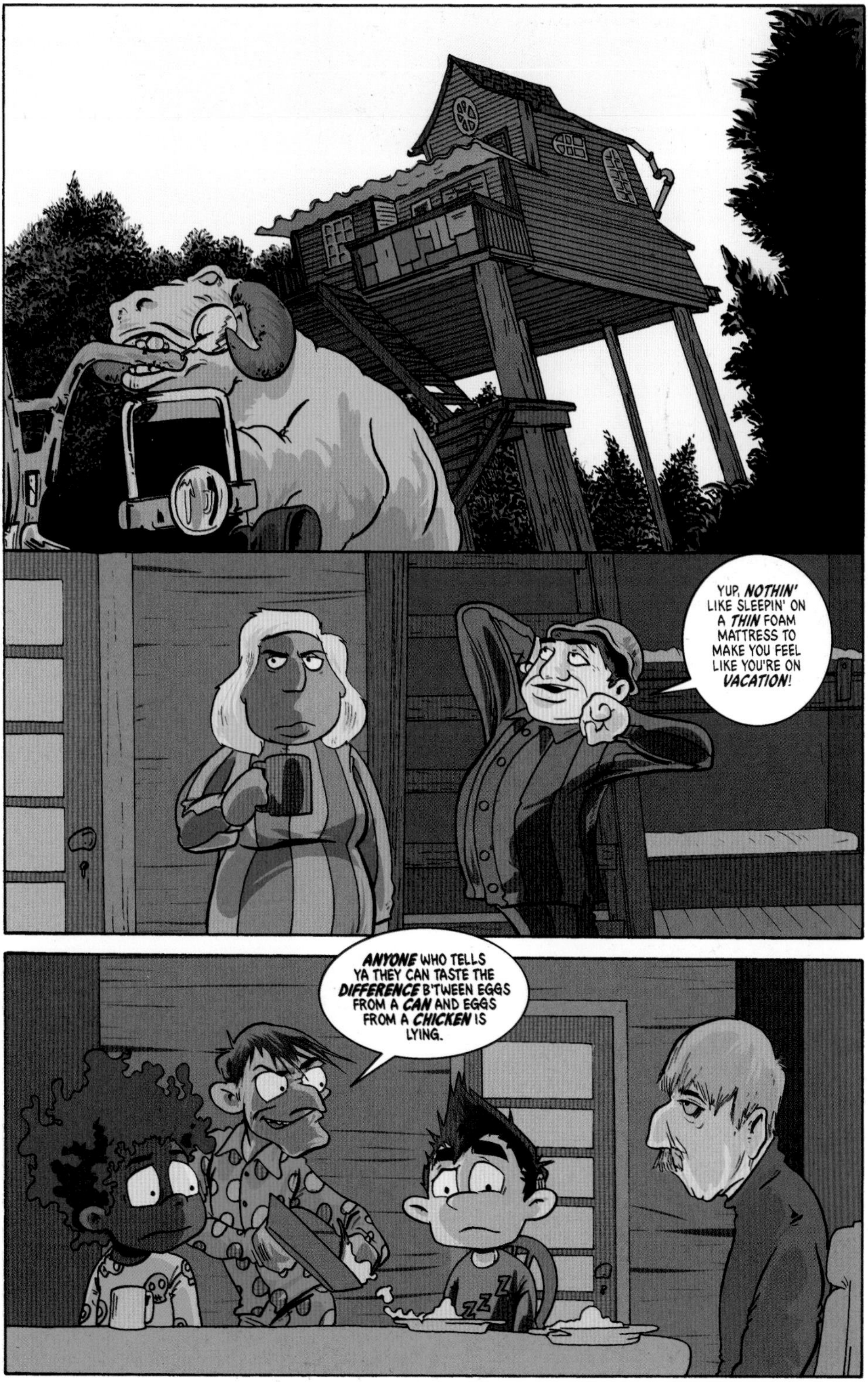
YUP, NOTHIN' LIKE SLEEPIN' ON A THIN FOAM MATTRESS TO MAKE YOU FEEL LIKE YOU'RE ON VACATION!
ANYONE WHO TELLS YA THEY CAN TASTE THE DIFFERENCE B'TWEEN EGGS FROM A CAN AND EGGS FROM A CHICKEN IS LYING.

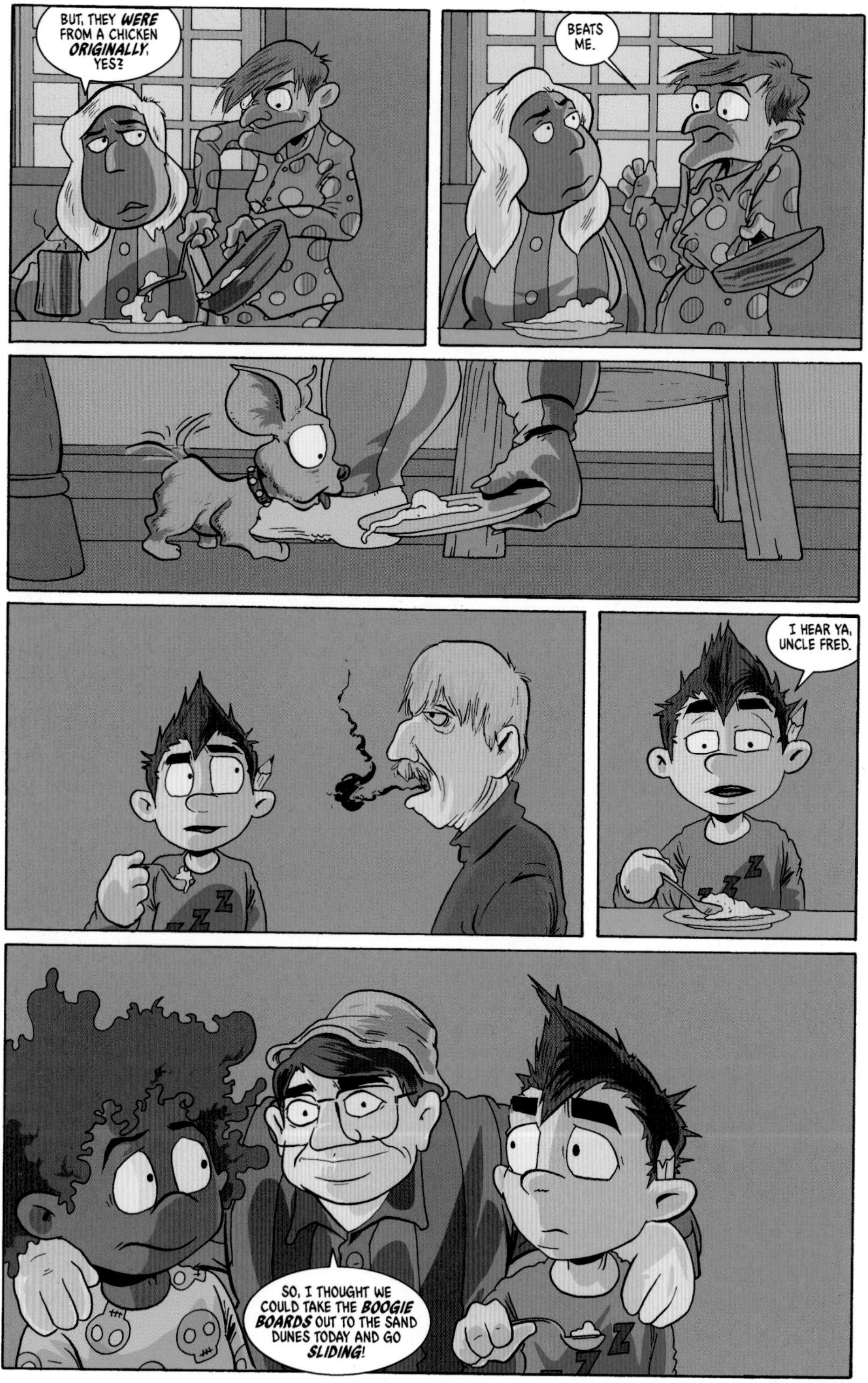
BUT, THEY WERE FROM A CHICKEN ORIGINALLY, YES?
BEATS ME.
I HEAR YA, UNCLE FRED.
SO, I THOUGHT WE COULD TAKE THE BOOGIE BOARDS OUT TO THE SAND DUNES TODAY AND GO SLIDING!

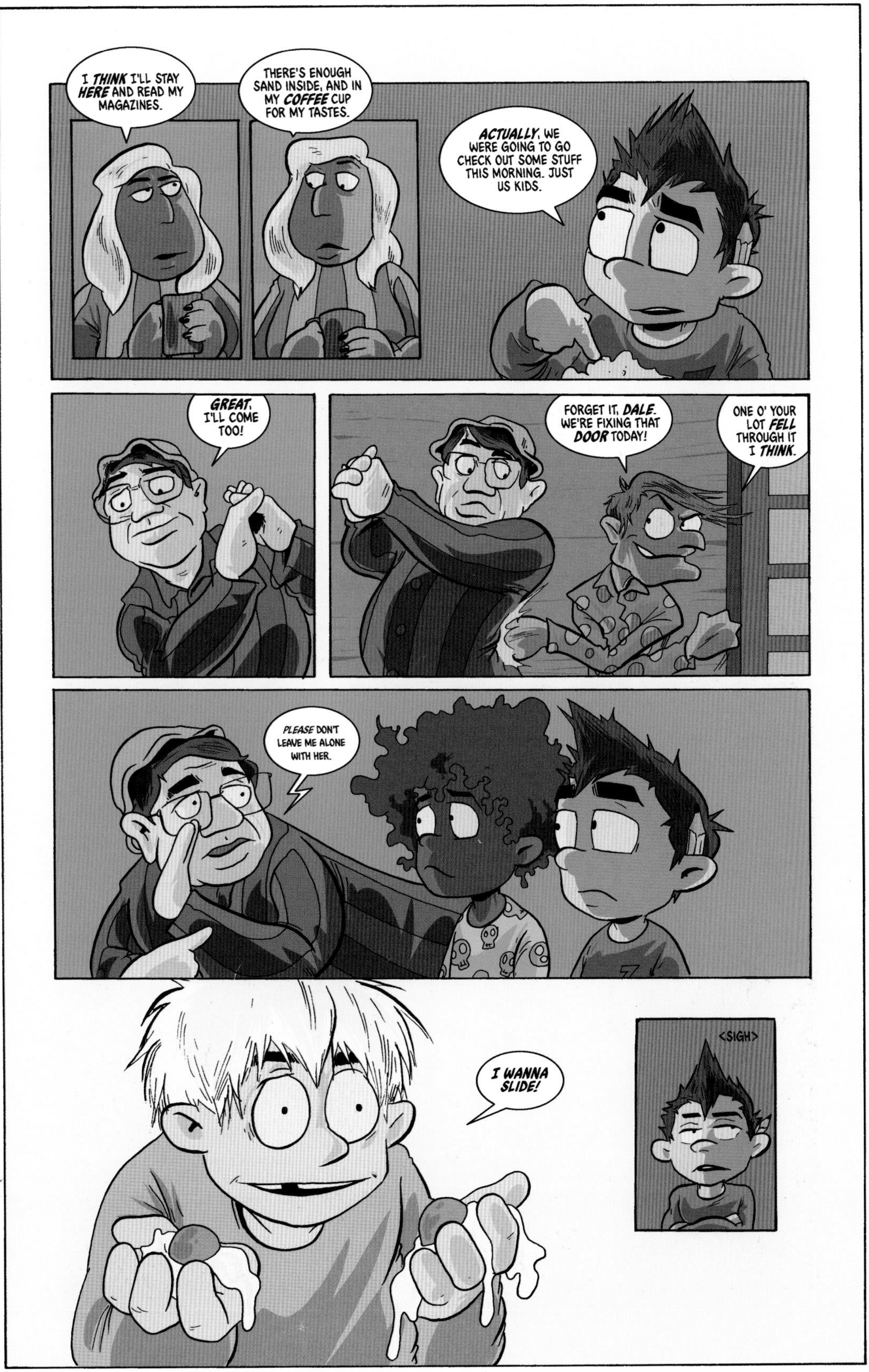

I THINK I'LL STAY HERE AND READ MY MAGAZINES.
THERE'S ENOUGH SAND INSIDE, AND IN MY COFFEE CUP FOR MY TASTES.
ACTUALLY, WE WERE GOING TO GO CHECK OUT SOME STUFF THIS MORNING. JUST US KIDS.
GREAT. I'LL COME TOO!
FORGET IT, DALE. WE'RE FIXING THAT DOOR TODAY!
ONE O' YOUR LOT FELL THROUGH IT I THINK.
PLEASE DON'T LEAVE ME ALONE WITH HER.
I WANNA SLIDE!
<SIGH>

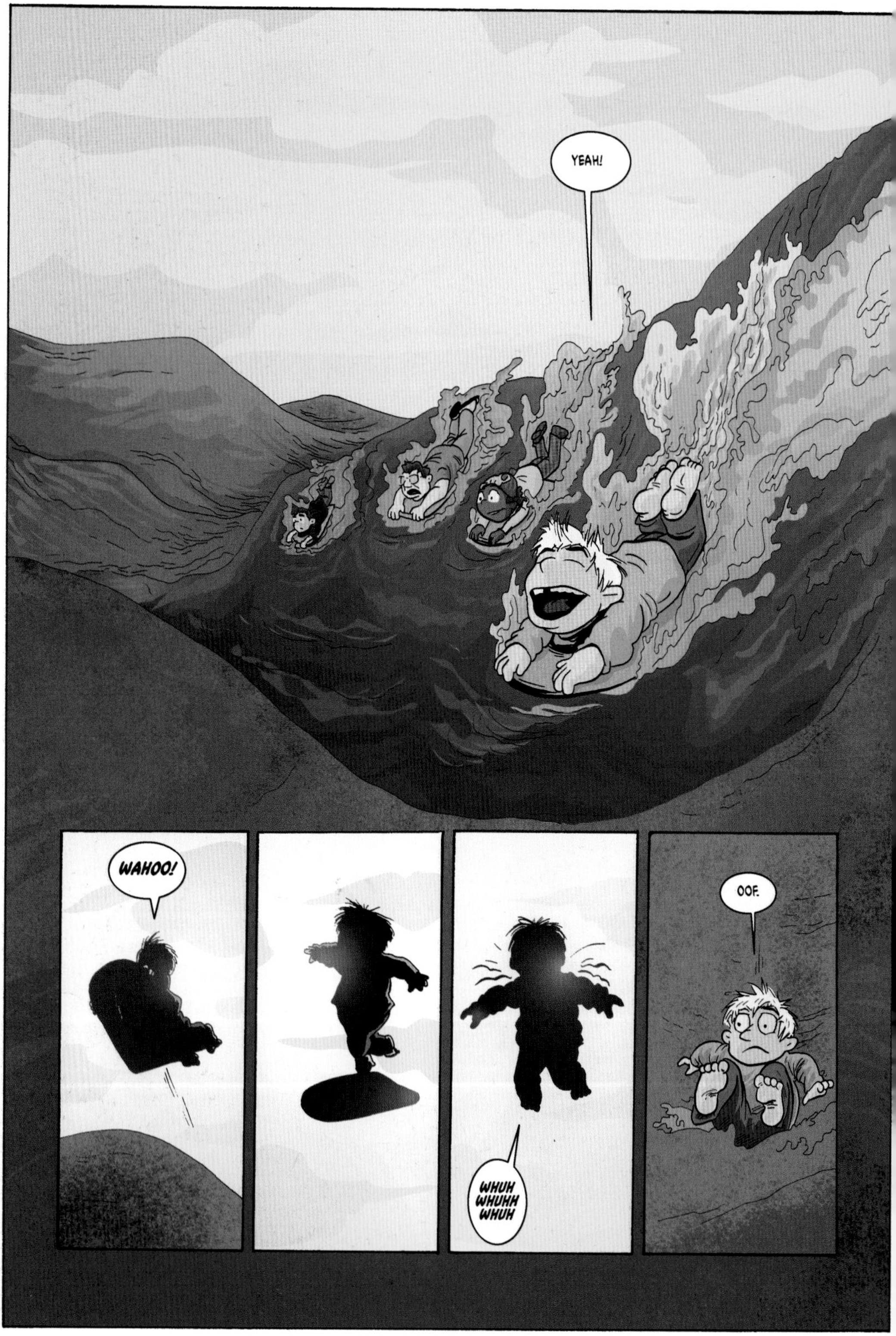
YEAH!
WAHOO!
WHUH
WHUHH
WHUH
OOF.

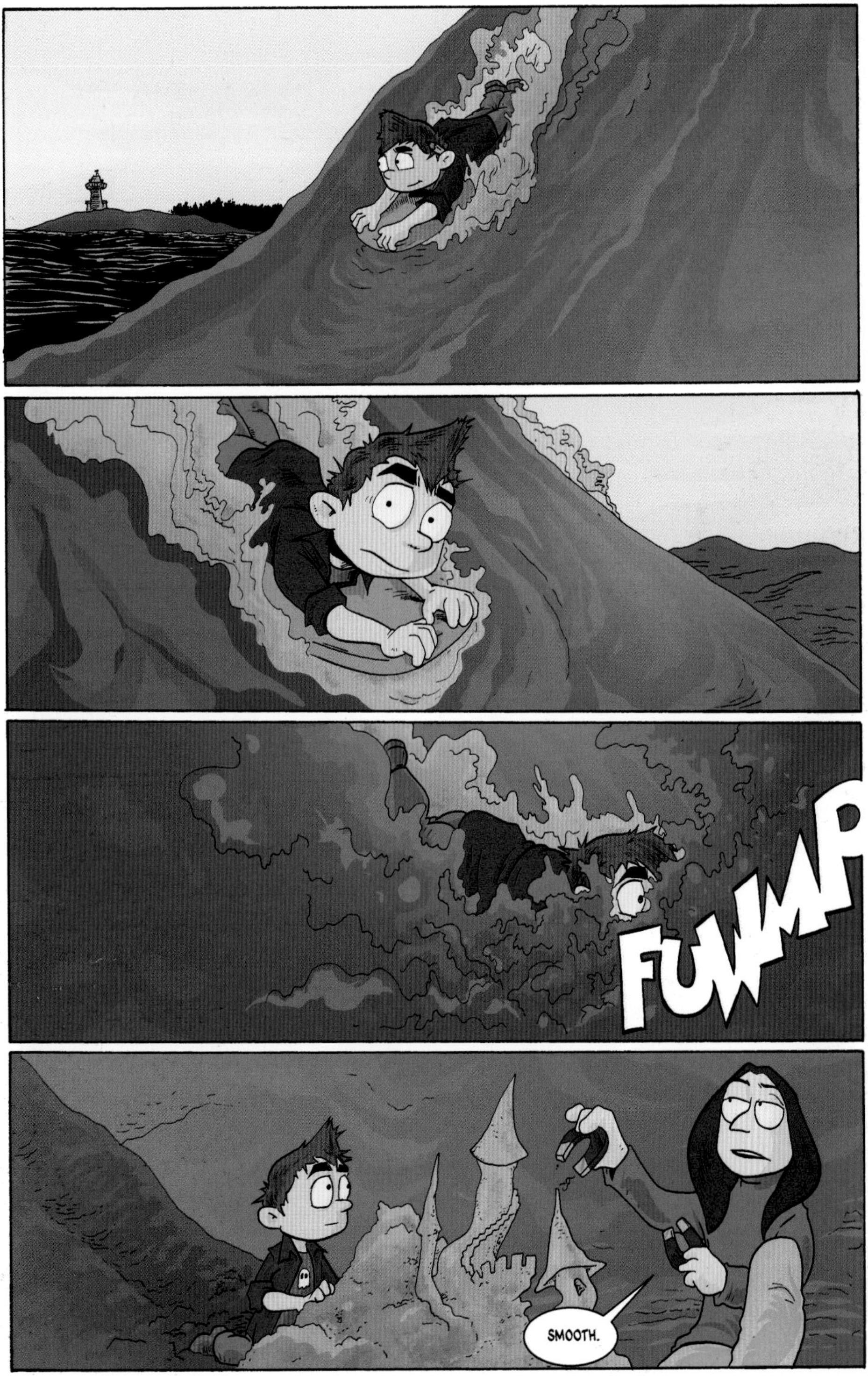
FUMP
SMOOTH.

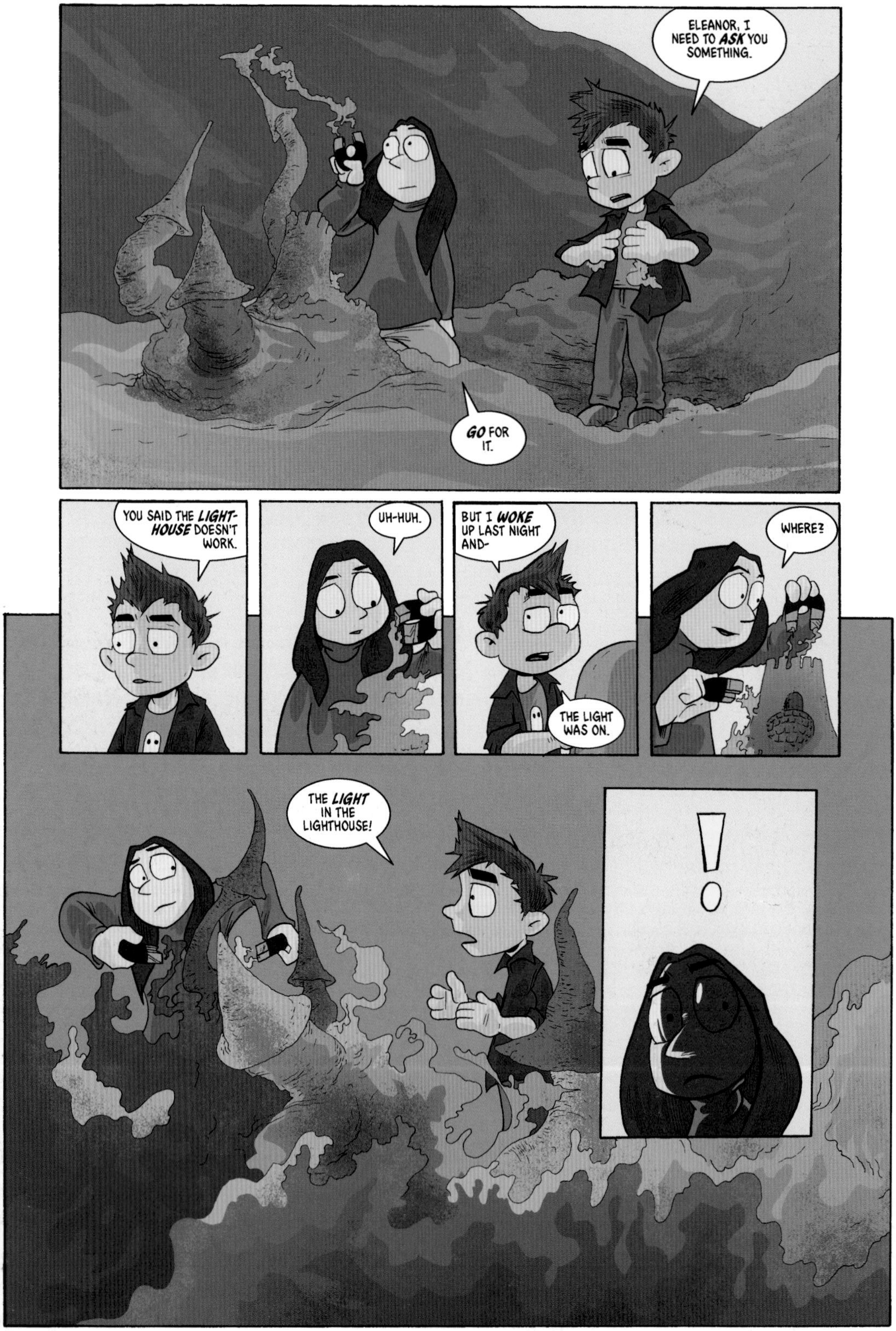
ELEANOR, I NEED TO ASK YOU SOMETHING.
GO FOR IT.
YOU SAID THE LIGHT-HOUSE DOESN'T WORK.
UH-HUH.
BUT I WOKE UP LAST NIGHT AND-
THE LIGHT WAS ON.
WHERE?
THE LIGHT IN THE LIGHTHOUSE!
!

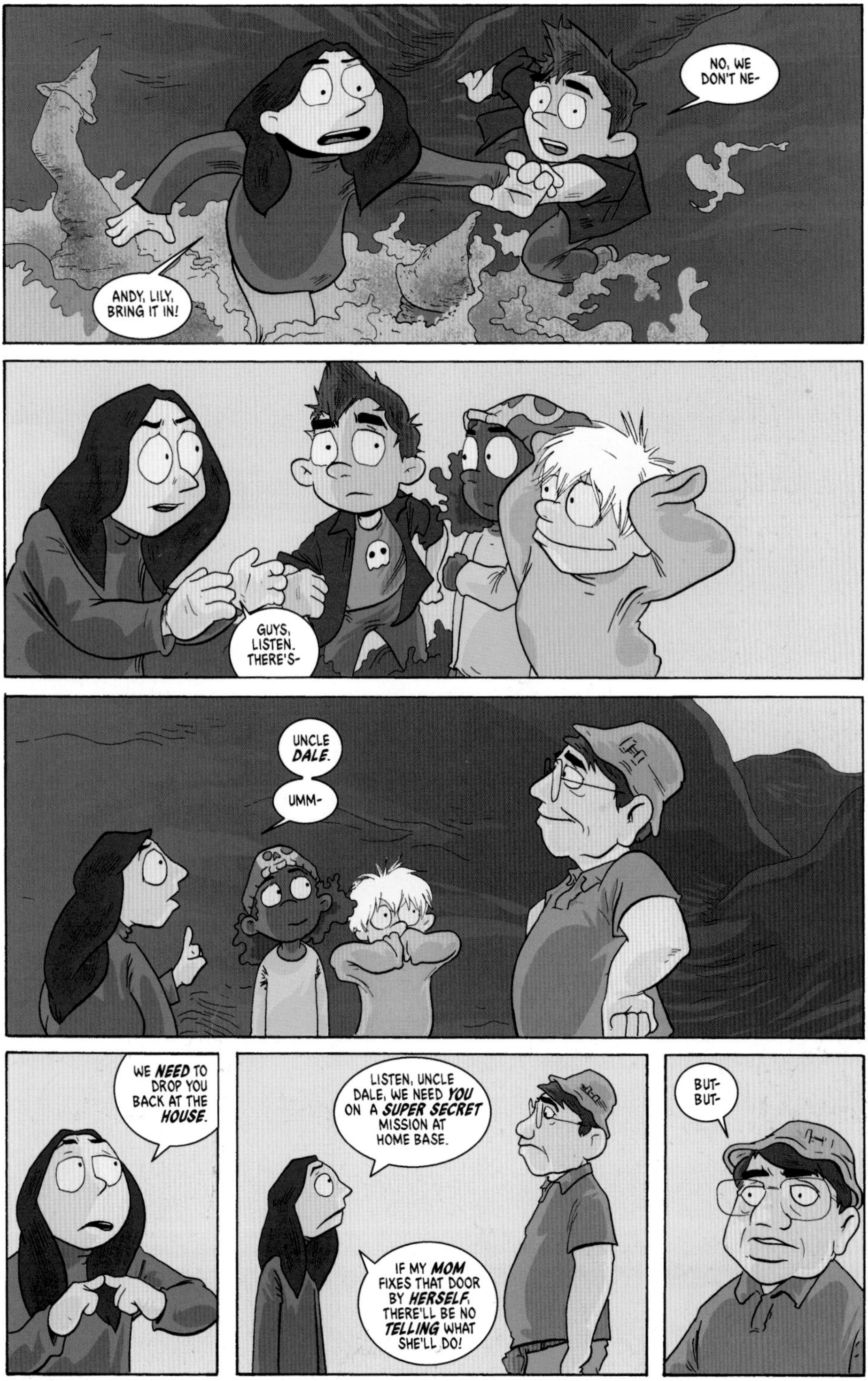
NO, WE DON'T NE-
ANDY, LILY, BRING IT IN!
GUYS, LISTEN. THERE'S-
UNCLE DALE.
UMM-
WE NEED TO DROP YOU BACK AT THE HOUSE.
LISTEN, UNCLE DALE, WE NEED YOU ON A SUPER SECRET MISSION AT HOME BASE.
IF MY MOM FIXES THAT DOOR BY HERSELF, THERE'LL BE NO TELLING WHAT SHE'LL DO!
BUT-
BUT-

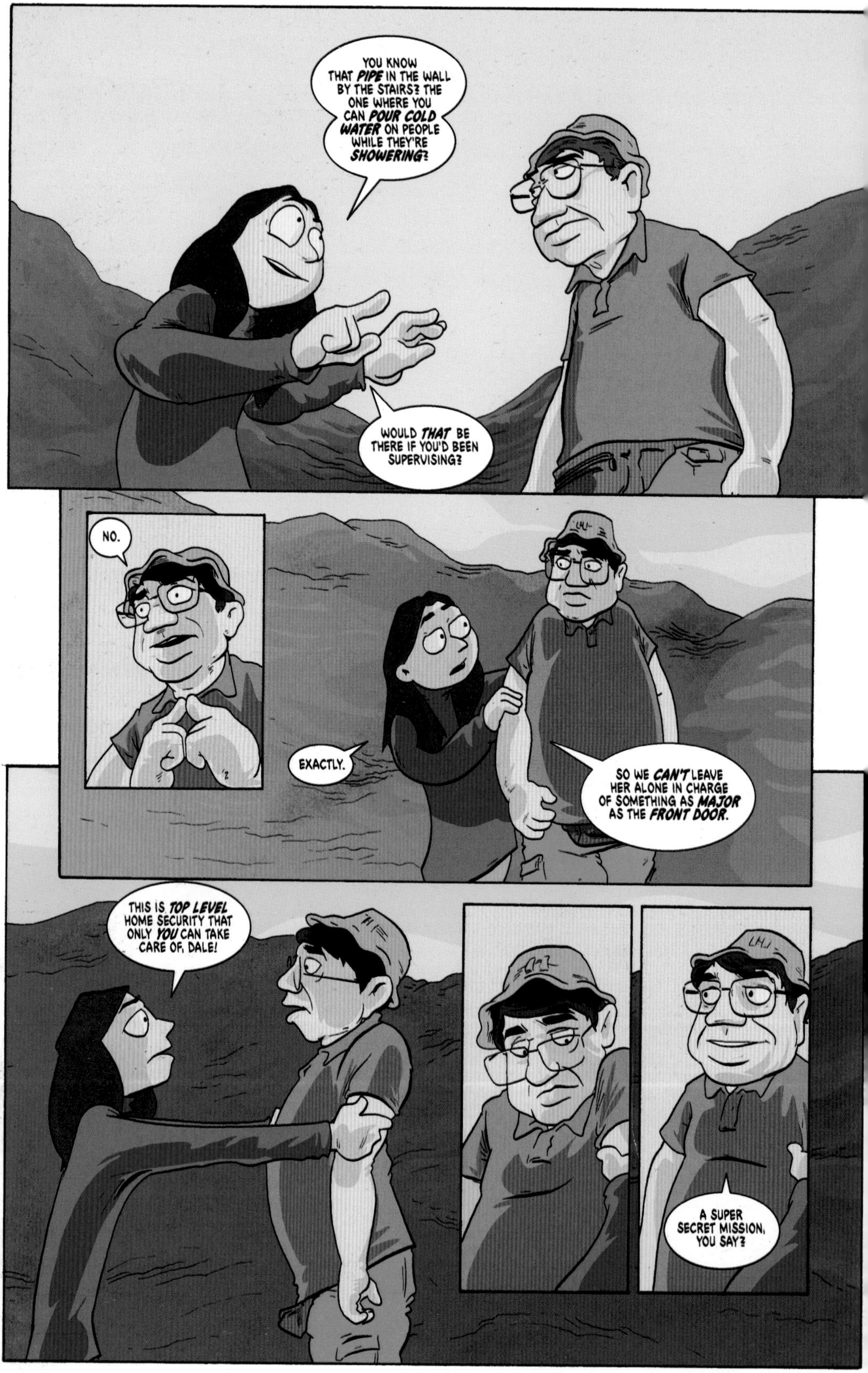
YOU KNOW THAT PIPE IN THE WALL BY THE STAIRS? THE ONE WHERE YOU CAN POUR COLD WATER ON PEOPLE WHILE THEY'RE SHOWERING?
WOULD THAT BE THERE IF YOU'D BEEN SUPERVISING?
NO.
EXACTLY.
SO WE CAN'T LEAVE HER ALONE IN CHARGE OF SOMETHING AS MAJOR AS THE FRONT DOOR.
THIS IS TOP LEVEL HOME SECURITY THAT ONLY YOU CAN TAKE CARE OF, DALE!
A SUPER SECRET MISSION, YOU SAY?

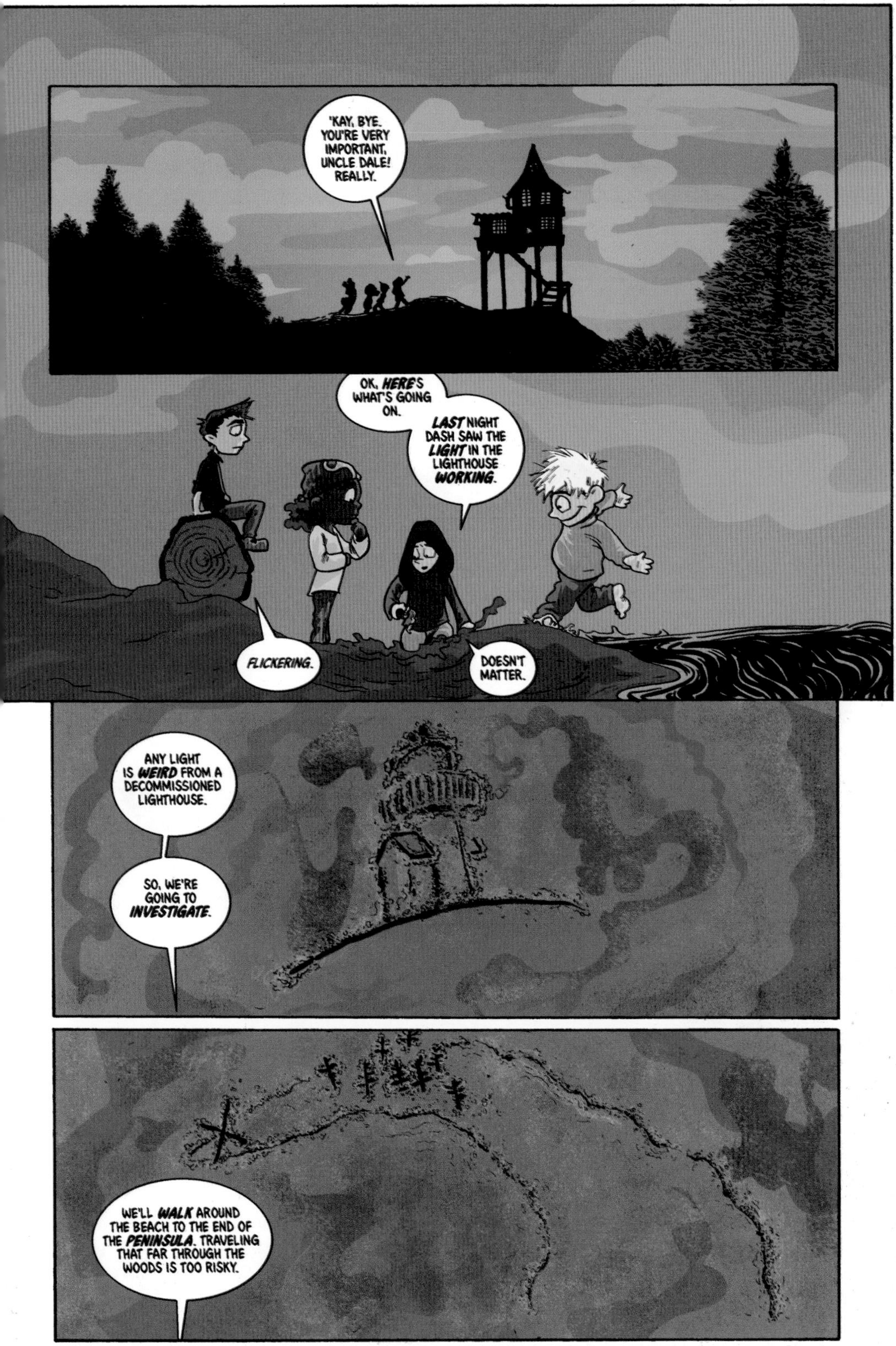

'KAY, BYE. YOU'RE VERY IMPORTANT, UNCLE DALE! REALLY.
OK, HERE'S WHAT'S GOING ON.
LAST NIGHT DASH SAW THE LIGHT IN THE LIGHTHOUSE WORKING.
FLICKERING.
DOESN'T MATTER.
ANY LIGHT IS WEIRD FROM A DECOMMISSIONED LIGHTHOUSE.
SO, WE'RE GOING TO INVESTIGATE.
WE'LL WALK AROUND THE BEACH TO THE END OF THE PENINSULA. TRAVELING THAT FAR THROUGH THE WOODS IS TOO RISKY.

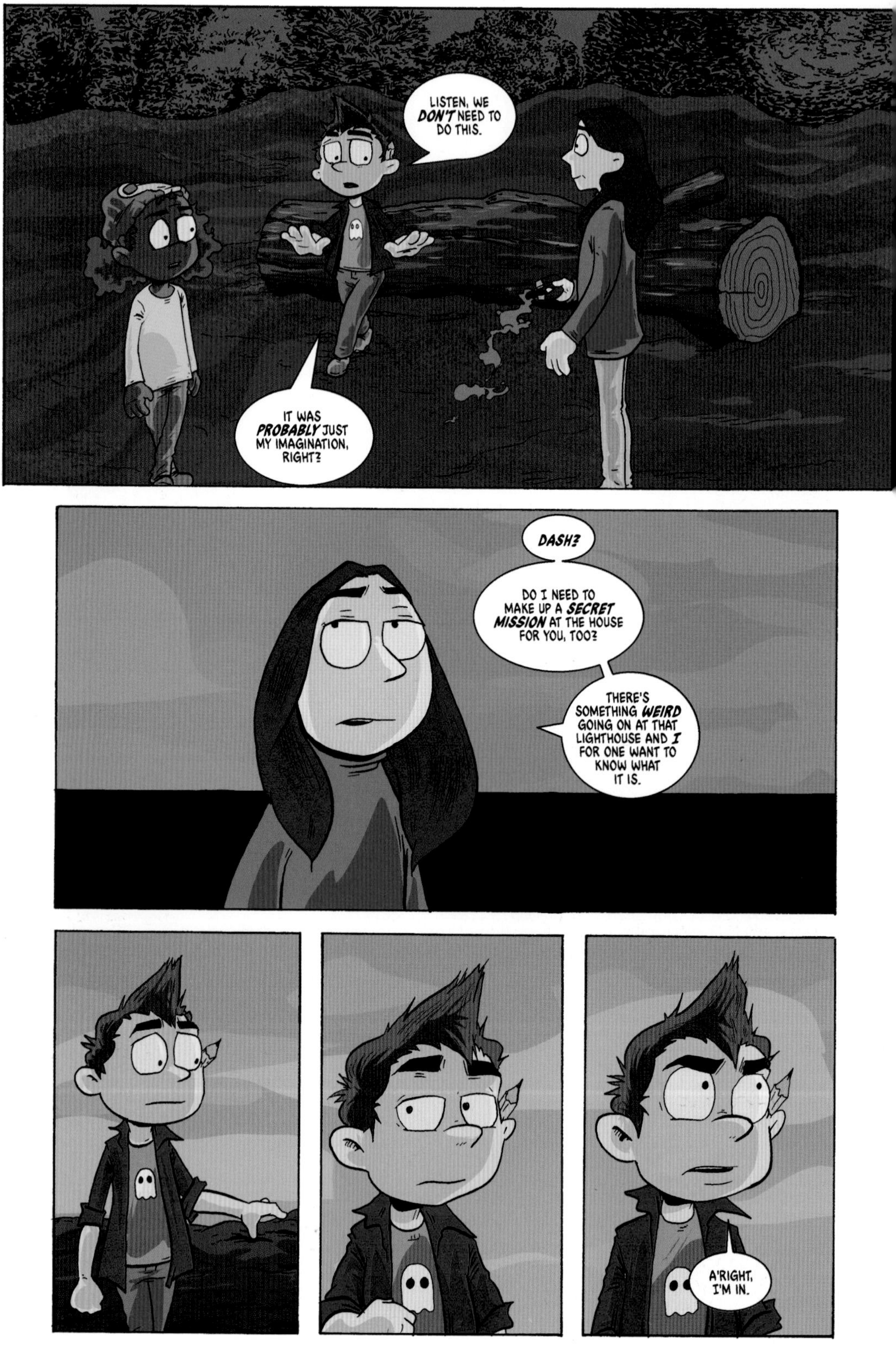
LISTEN, WE DON'T NEED TO DO THIS.
IT WAS PROBABLY JUST MY IMAGINATION, RIGHT?
DASH?
DO I NEED TO MAKE UP A SECRET MISSION AT THE HOUSE FOR YOU, TOO?
THERE'S SOMETHING WEIRD GOING ON AT THAT LIGHTHOUSE AND I FOR ONE WANT TO KNOW WHAT IT IS.
A'RIGHT, I'M IN.

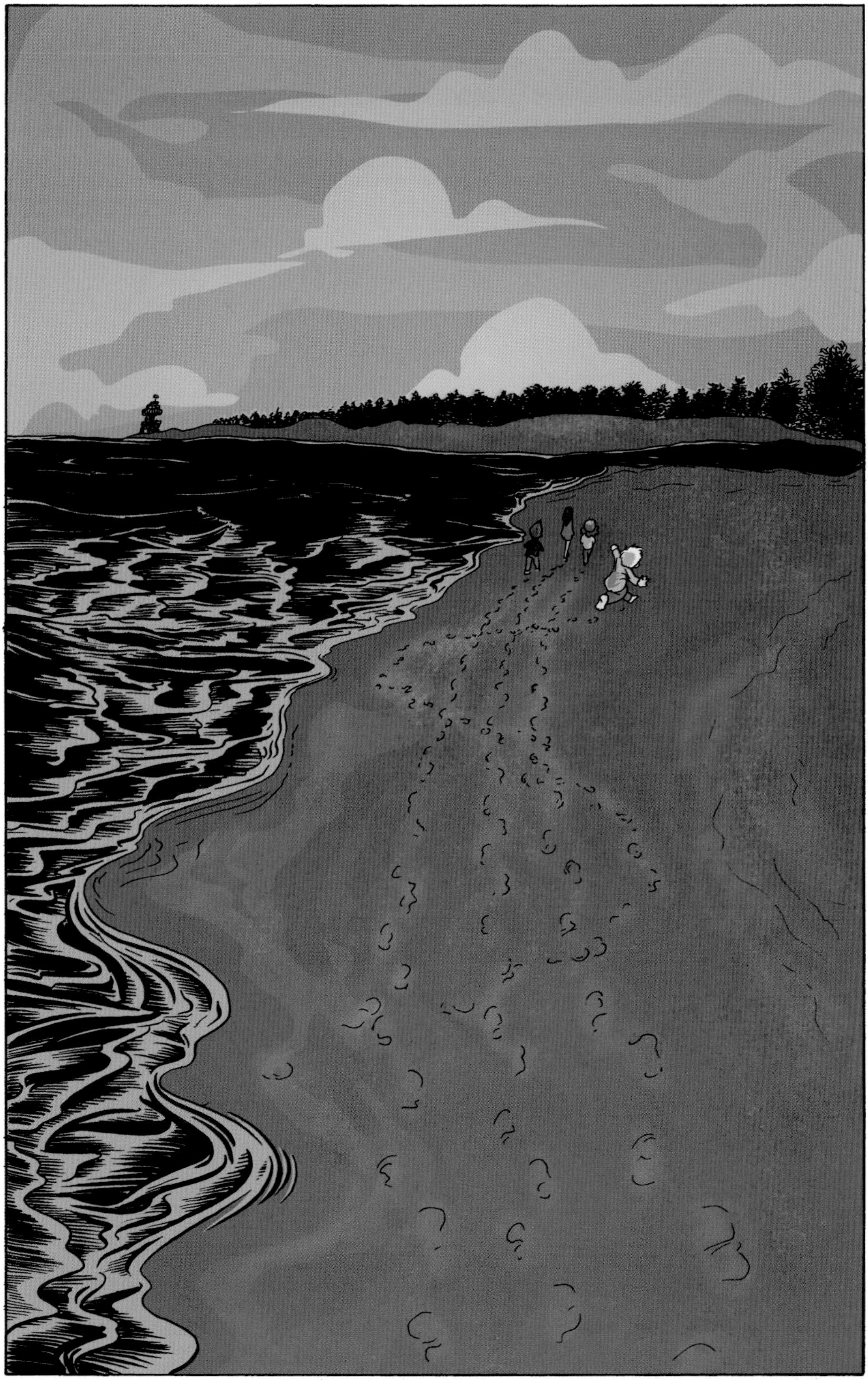

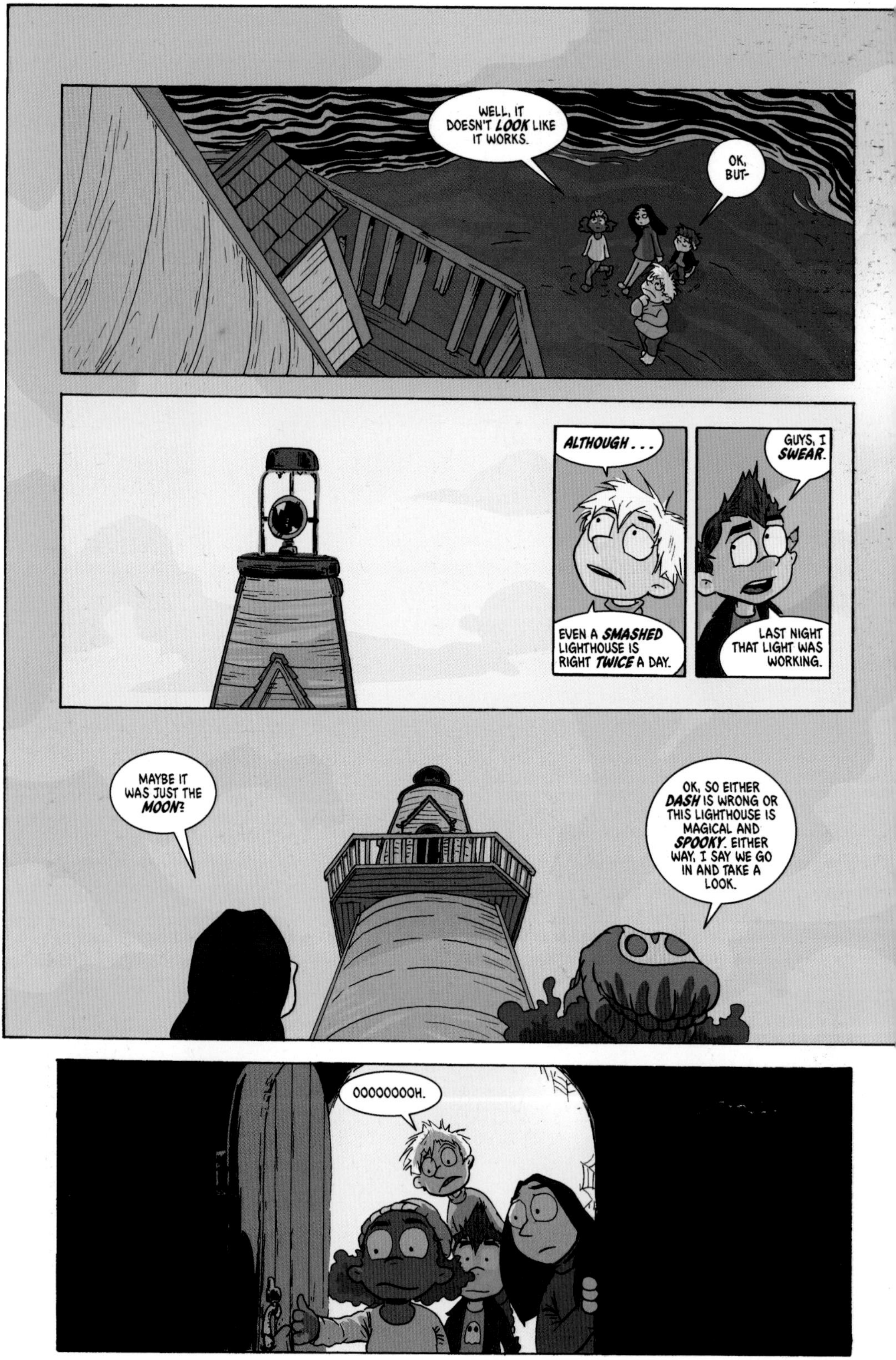
WELL, IT DOESN'T LOOK LIKE IT WORKS.
OK, BUT-
ALTHOUGH . . .
EVEN A SMASHED LIGHTHOUSE IS RIGHT TWICE A DAY.
GUYS, I SWEAR.
LAST NIGHT THAT LIGHT WAS WORKING.
MAYBE IT WAS JUST THE MOON?
OK, SO EITHER DASH IS WRONG OR THIS LIGHTHOUSE IS MAGICAL AND SPOOKY. EITHER WAY, I SAY WE GO IN AND TAKE A LOOK.
OOOOOOOOH.

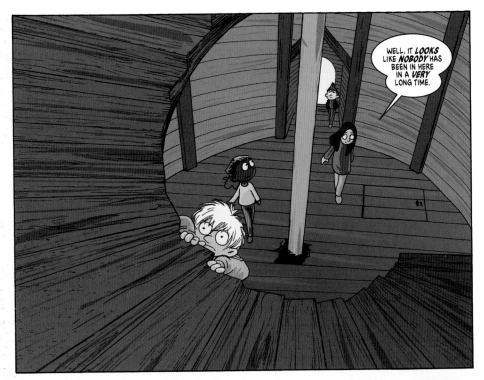

WELL, IT *LOOKS* LIKE *NOBODY* HAS BEEN IN HERE IN A *VERY* LONG TIME.

SO, IF WE'RE THINKING *SOMEONE* WAS TURNING THE LIGHT ON—

DIDN'T YOU SAY THIS LIGHTHOUSE WAS FULLY *AUTOMATED?*

YEAH, BUT I ALSO SAID IT NEVER *WORKED* PROPERLY.

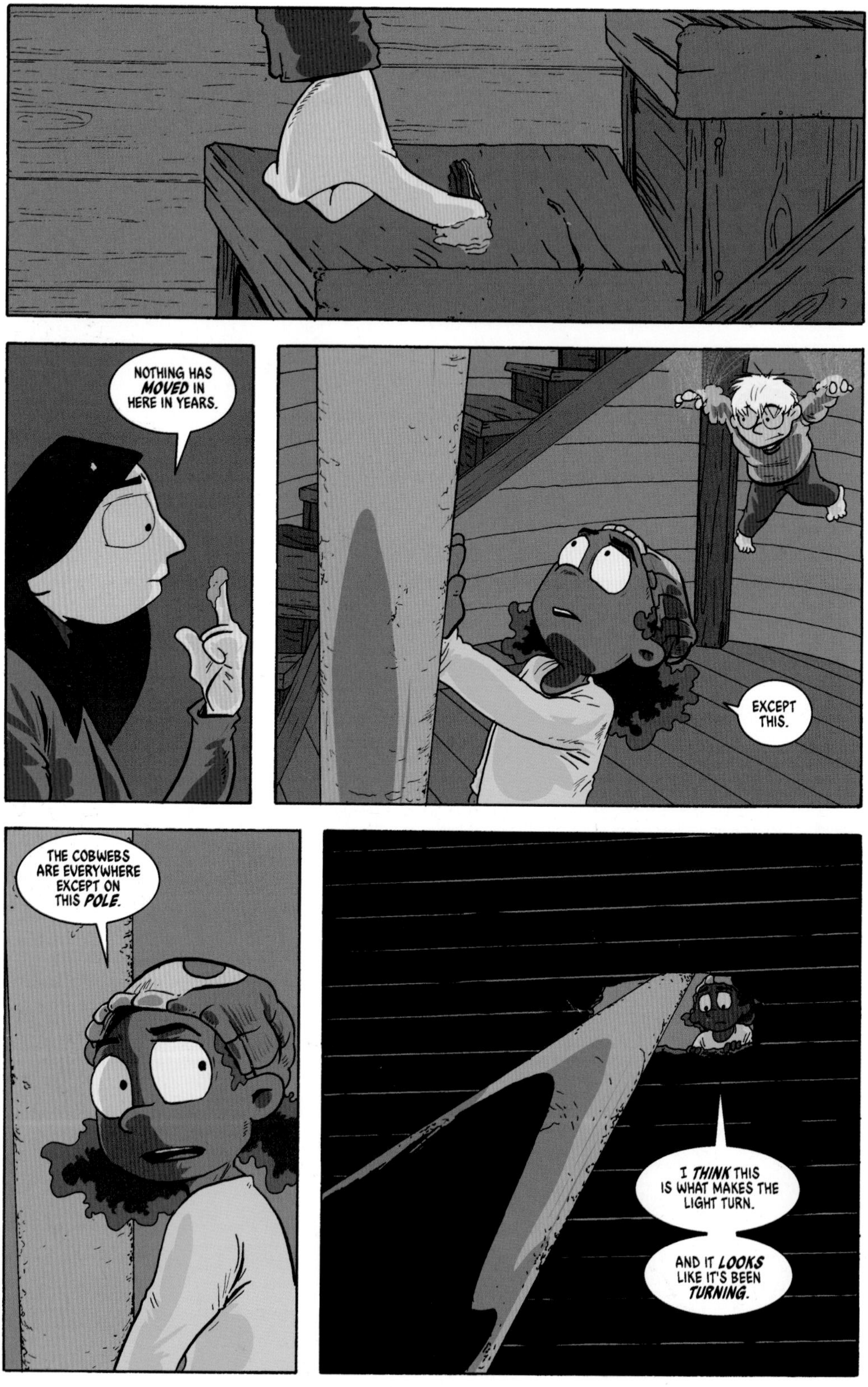
NOTHING HAS MOVED IN HERE IN YEARS.
EXCEPT THIS.
THE COBWEBS ARE EVERYWHERE EXCEPT ON THIS POLE.
I THINK THIS IS WHAT MAKES THE LIGHT TURN.
AND IT LOOKS LIKE IT'S BEEN TURNING.

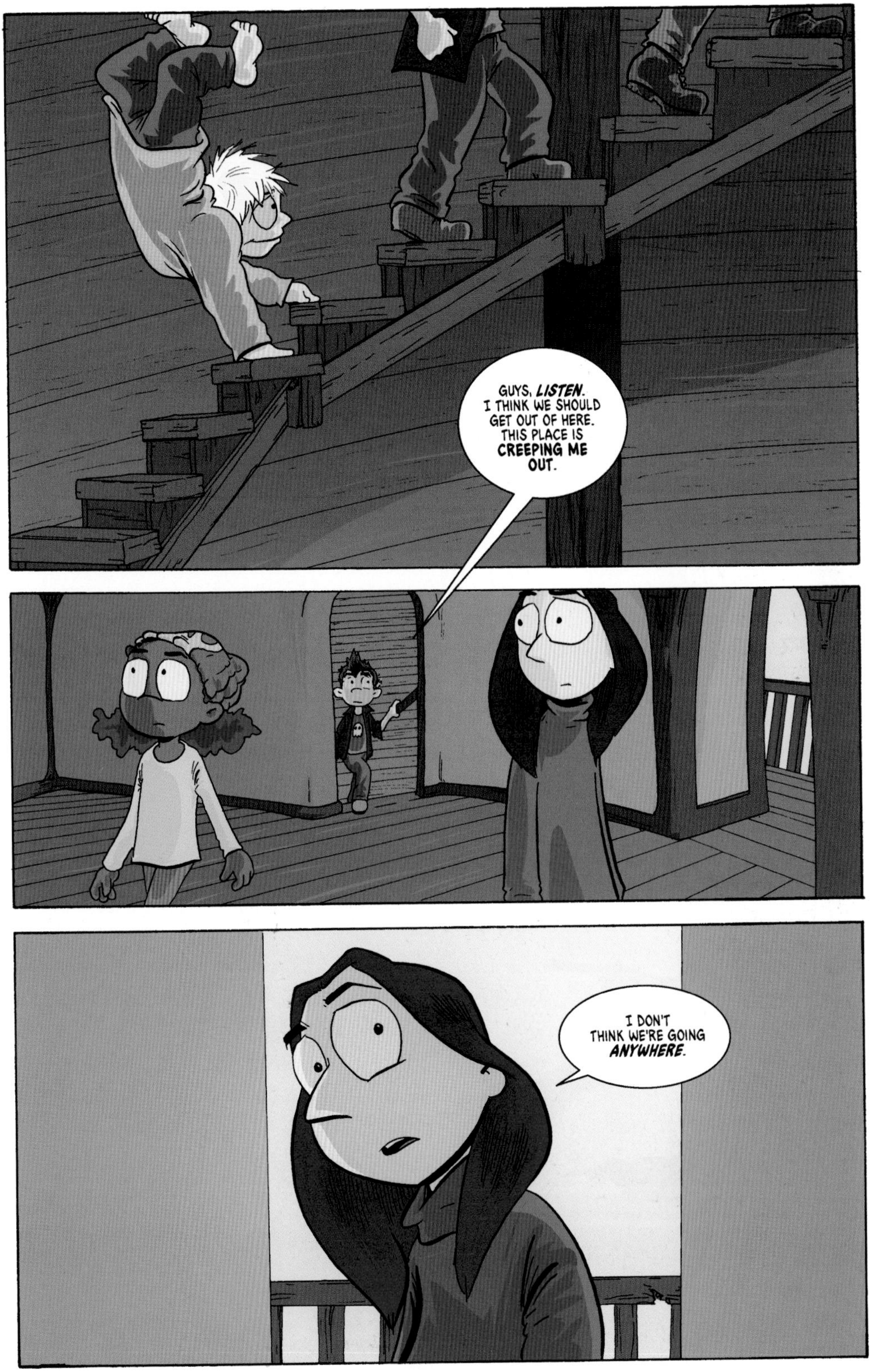
GUYS, *LISTEN*. I THINK WE SHOULD GET OUT OF HERE. THIS PLACE IS **CREEPING ME OUT**.
I DON'T THINK WE'RE GOING *ANYWHERE*.

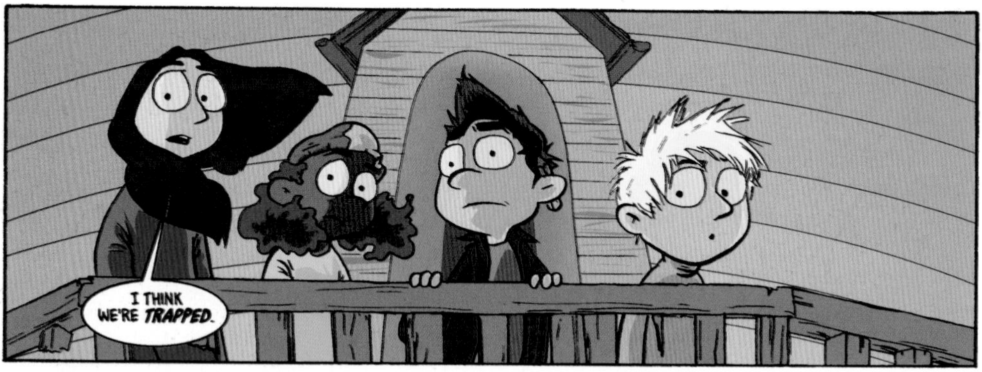
I THINK WE'RE TRAPPED.

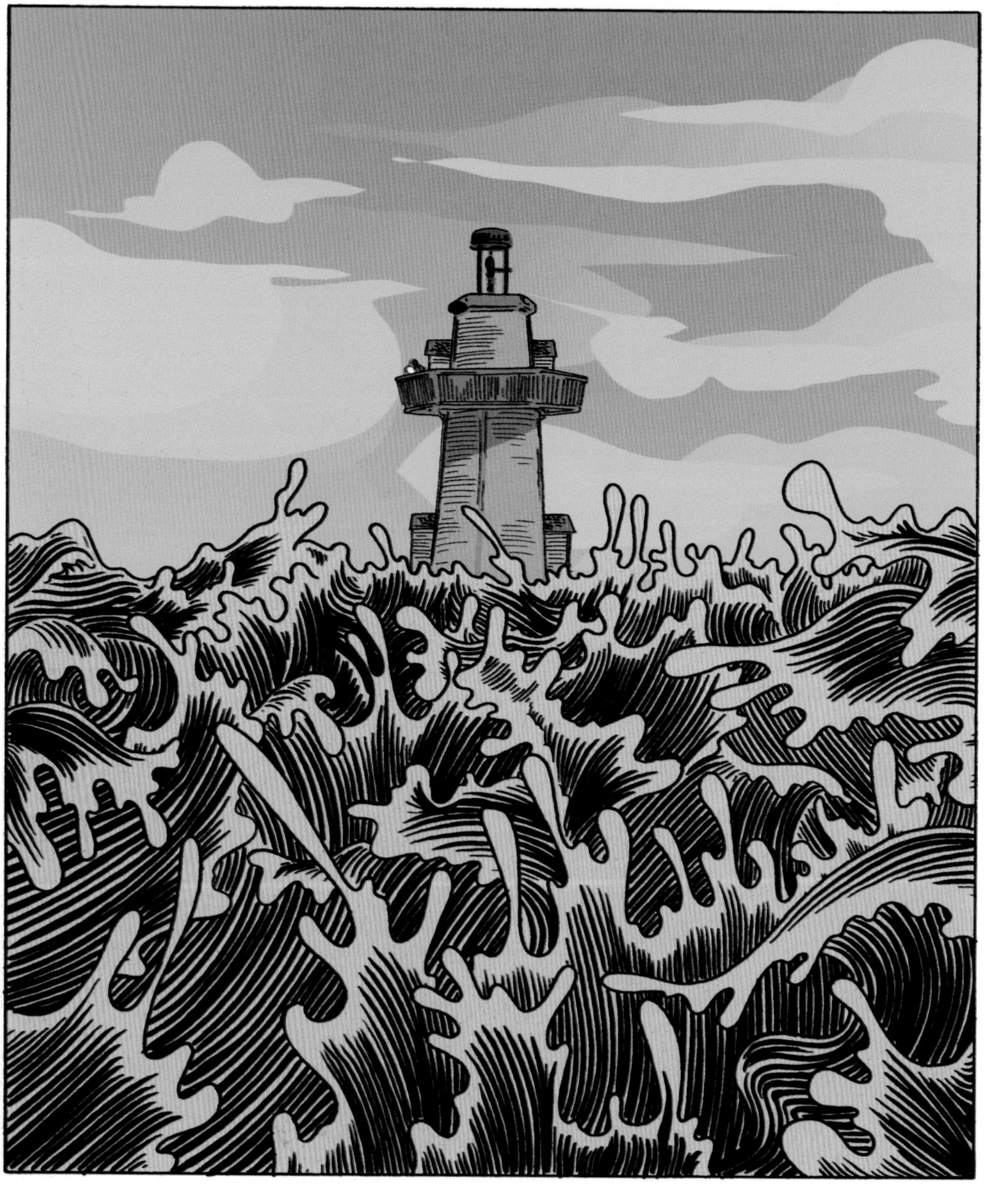

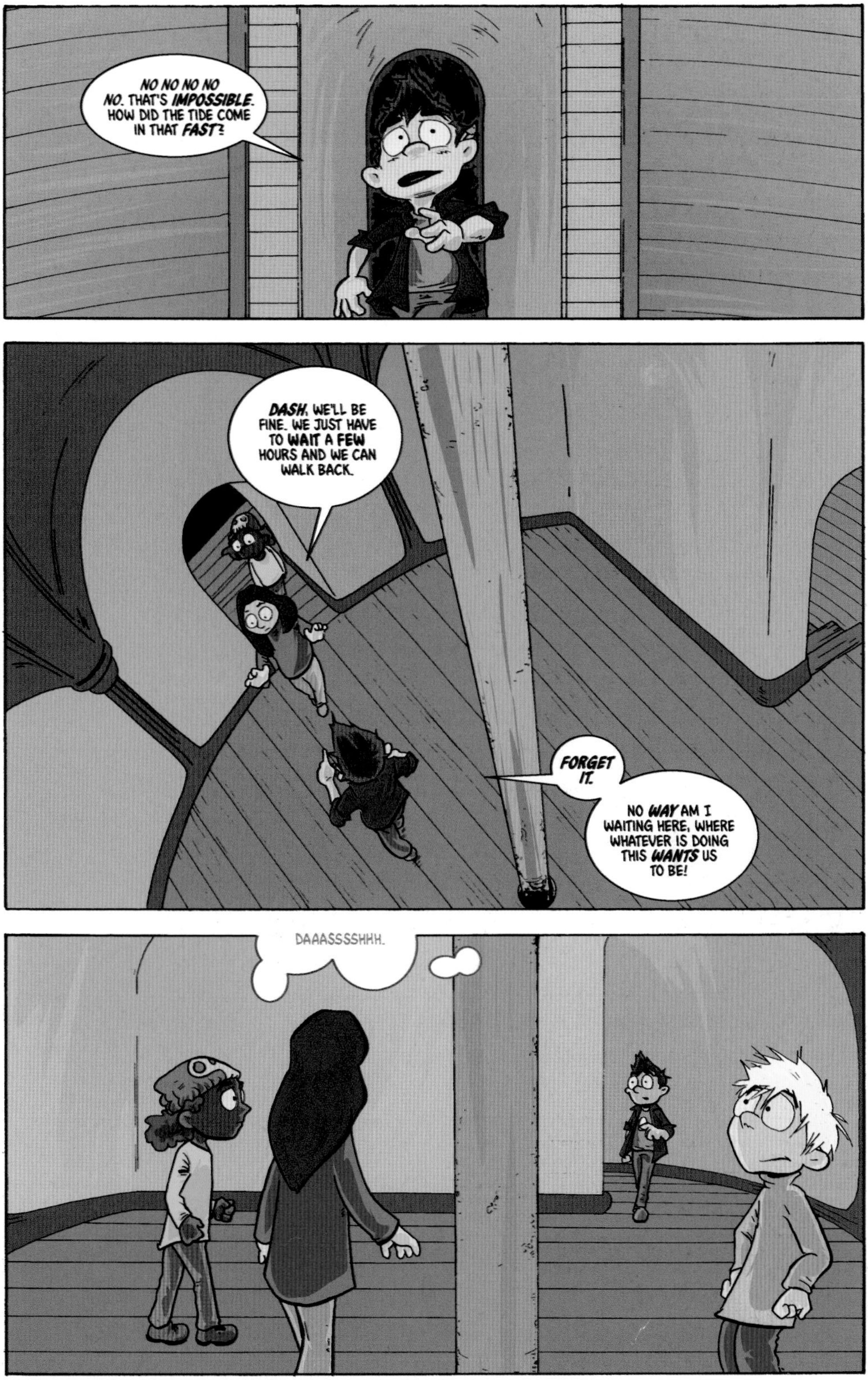
NO NO NO NO
NO. THAT'S IMPOSSIBLE. HOW DID THE TIDE COME IN THAT FAST?
DASH, WE'LL BE FINE. WE JUST HAVE TO WAIT A FEW HOURS AND WE CAN WALK BACK.
FORGET IT.
NO WAY AM I WAITING HERE, WHERE WHATEVER IS DOING THIS WANTS US TO BE!
DAAASSSSSHHH.

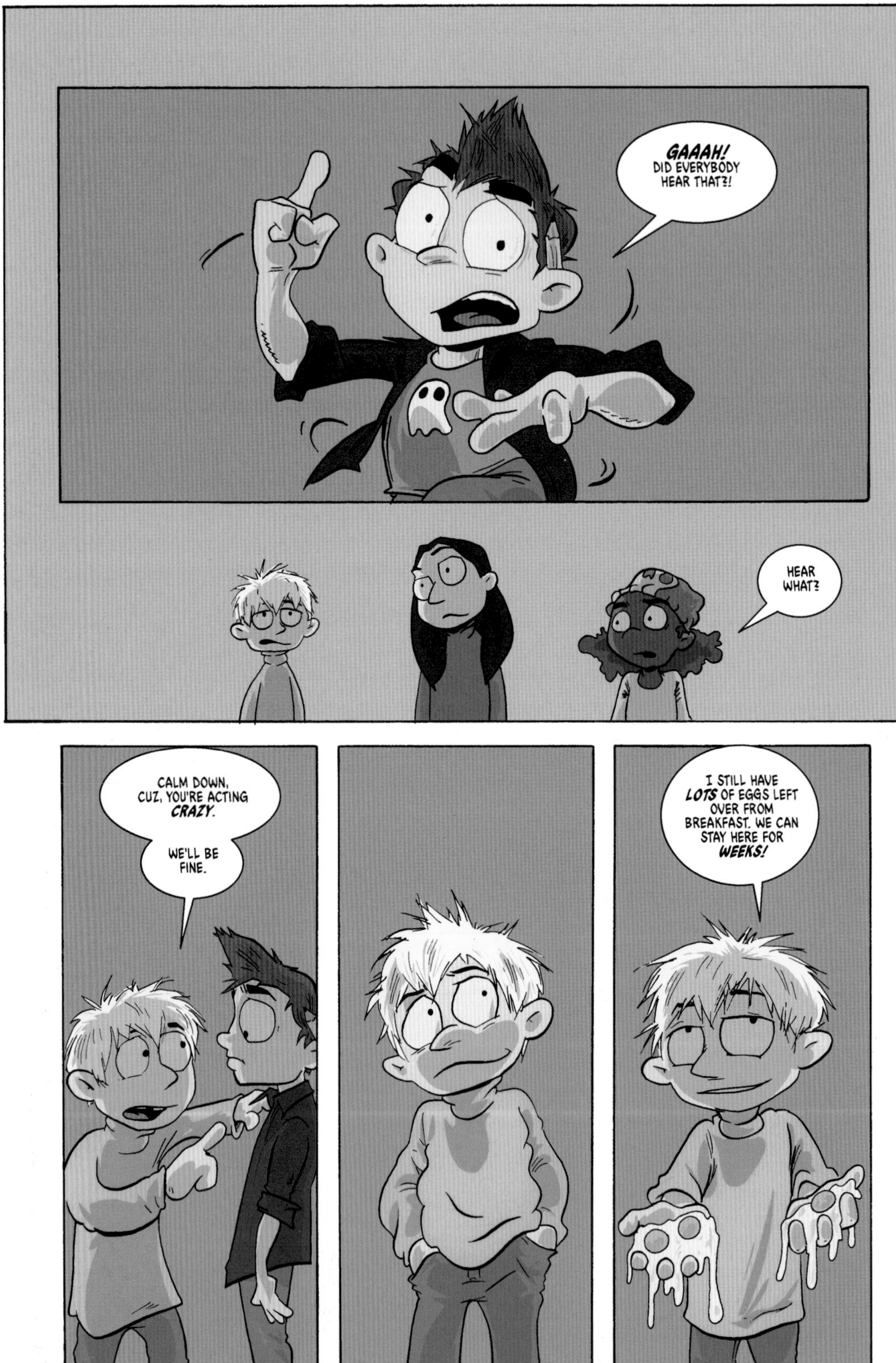
GAAAH!
DID EVERYBODY HEAR THAT?!
HEAR WHAT?
CALM DOWN, CUZ, YOU'RE ACTING CRAZY.
WE'LL BE FINE.
I STILL HAVE LOTS OF EGGS LEFT OVER FROM BREAKFAST. WE CAN STAY HERE FOR WEEKS!

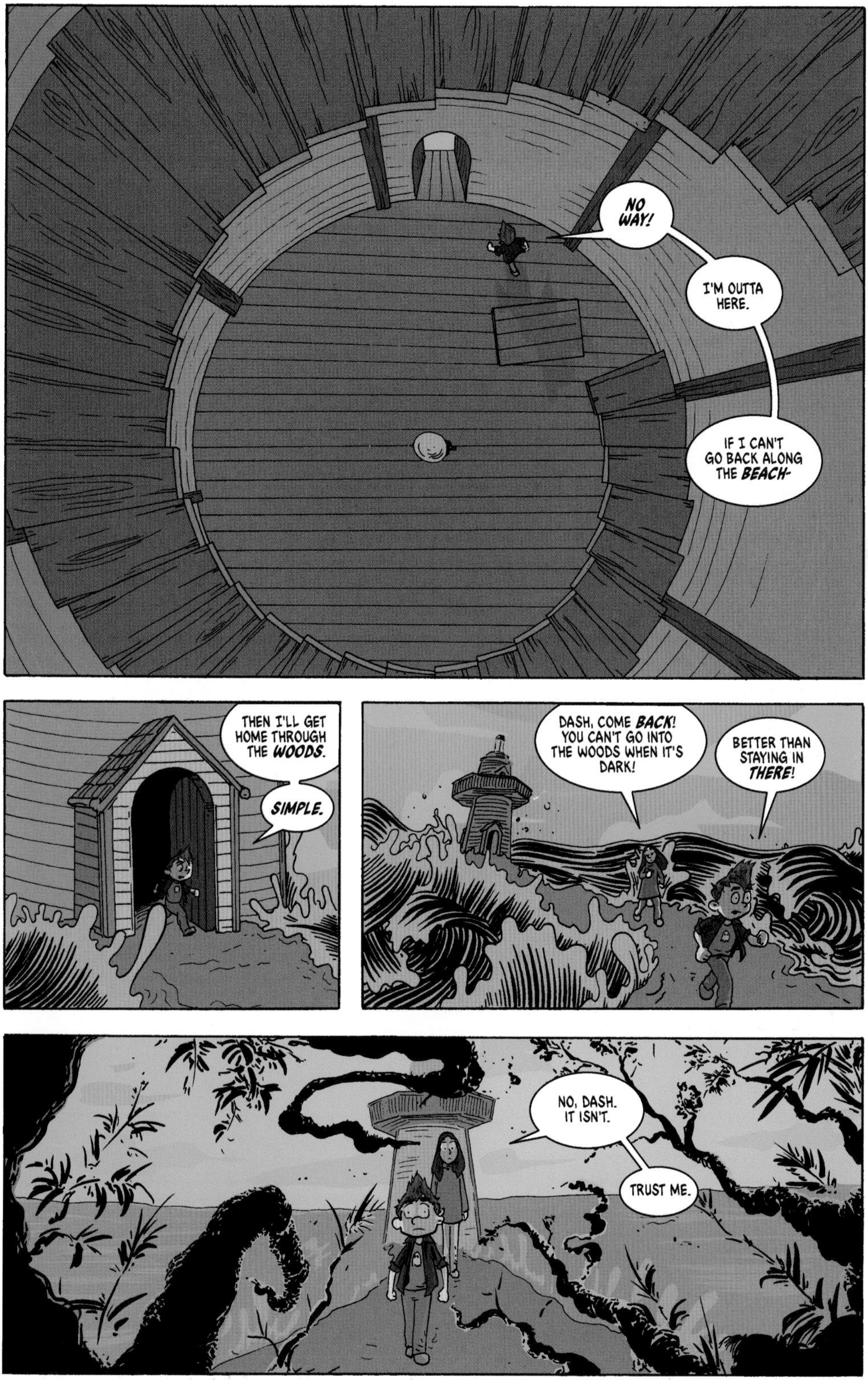
NO WAY!
I'M OUTTA HERE.
IF I CAN'T GO BACK ALONG THE BEACH-
THEN I'LL GET HOME THROUGH THE WOODS.
SIMPLE.
DASH, COME BACK! YOU CAN'T GO INTO THE WOODS WHEN IT'S DARK!
BETTER THAN STAYING IN THERE!
NO, DASH. IT ISN'T.
TRUST ME.

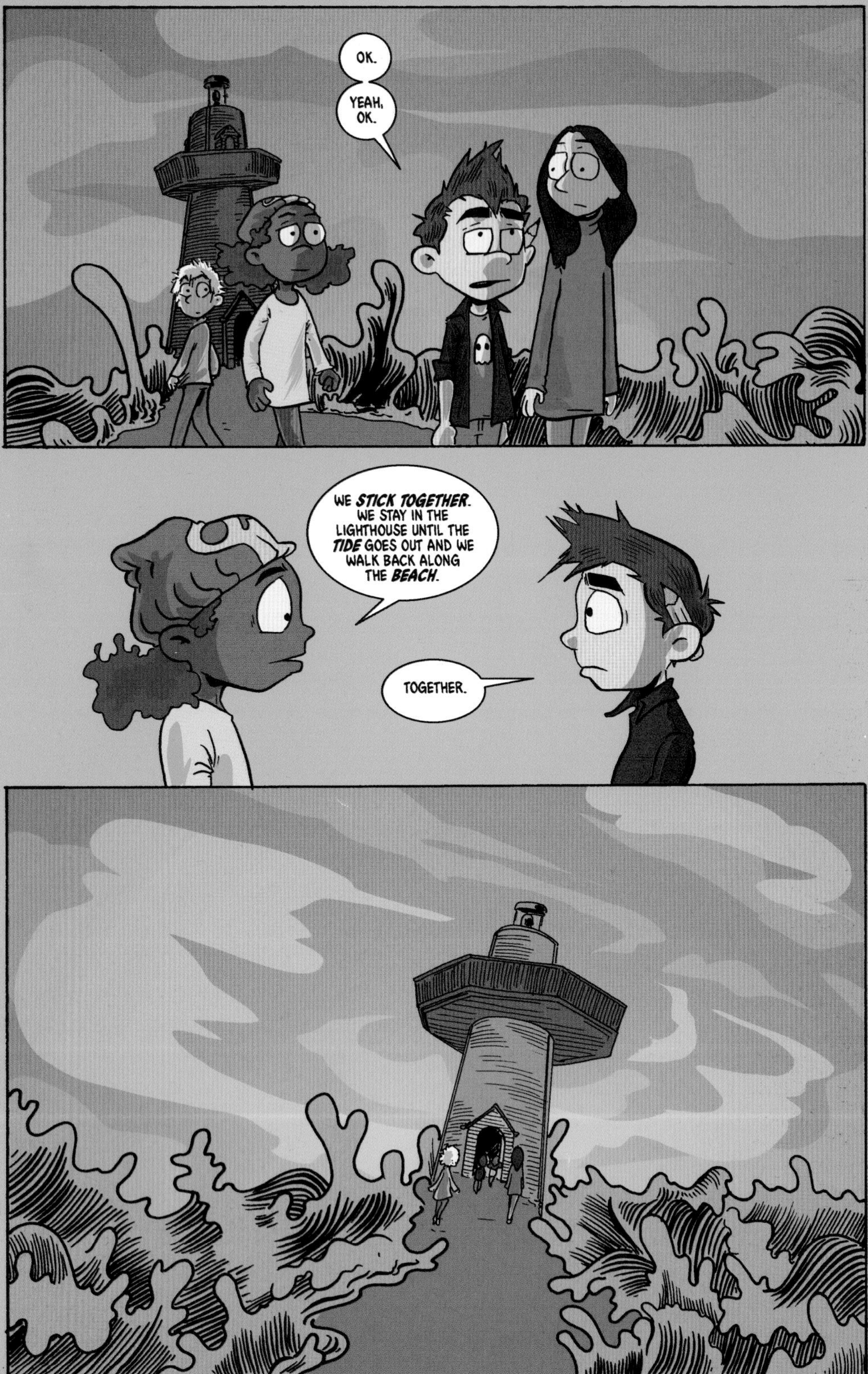
OK.
YEAH, OK.
WE STICK TOGETHER. WE STAY IN THE LIGHTHOUSE UNTIL THE TIDE GOES OUT AND WE WALK BACK ALONG THE BEACH.
TOGETHER.

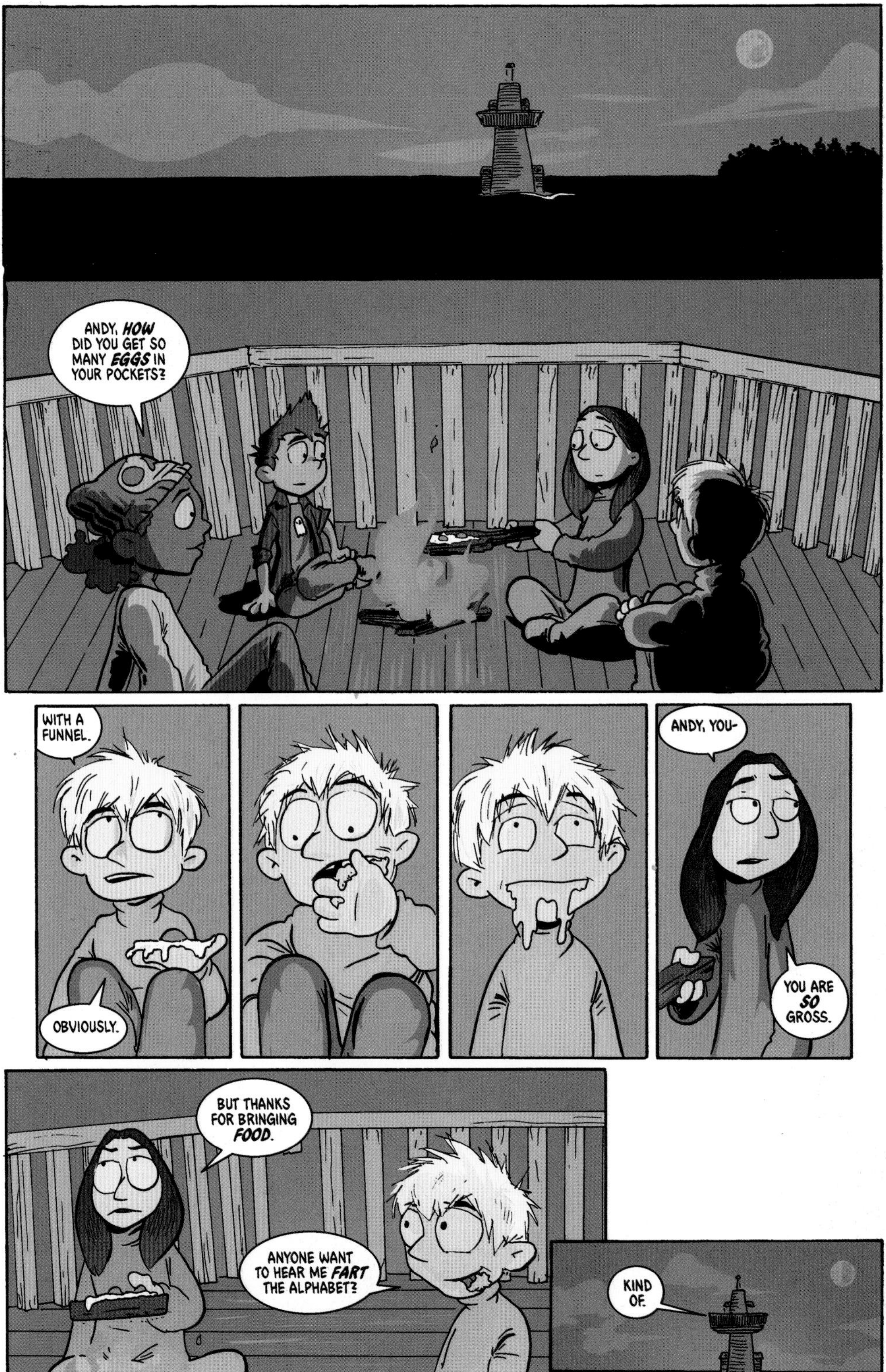
ANDY, HOW DID YOU GET SO MANY EGGS IN YOUR POCKETS?
WITH A FUNNEL.
OBVIOUSLY.
ANDY, YOU-
YOU ARE SO GROSS.
BUT THANKS FOR BRINGING FOOD.
ANYONE WANT TO HEAR ME FART THE ALPHABET?
KIND OF.

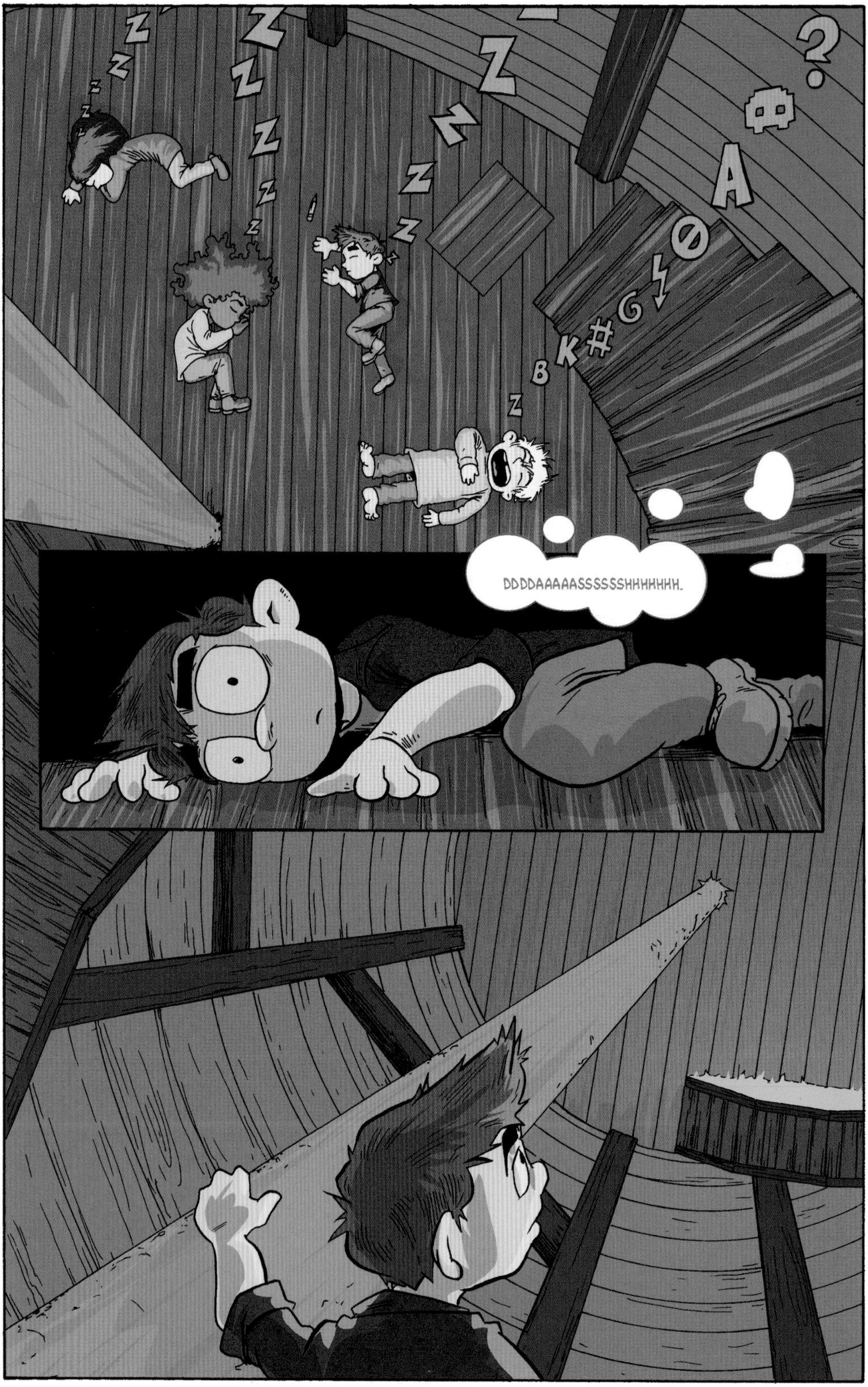
DDDDAAAAASSSSSSHHHHHHH.

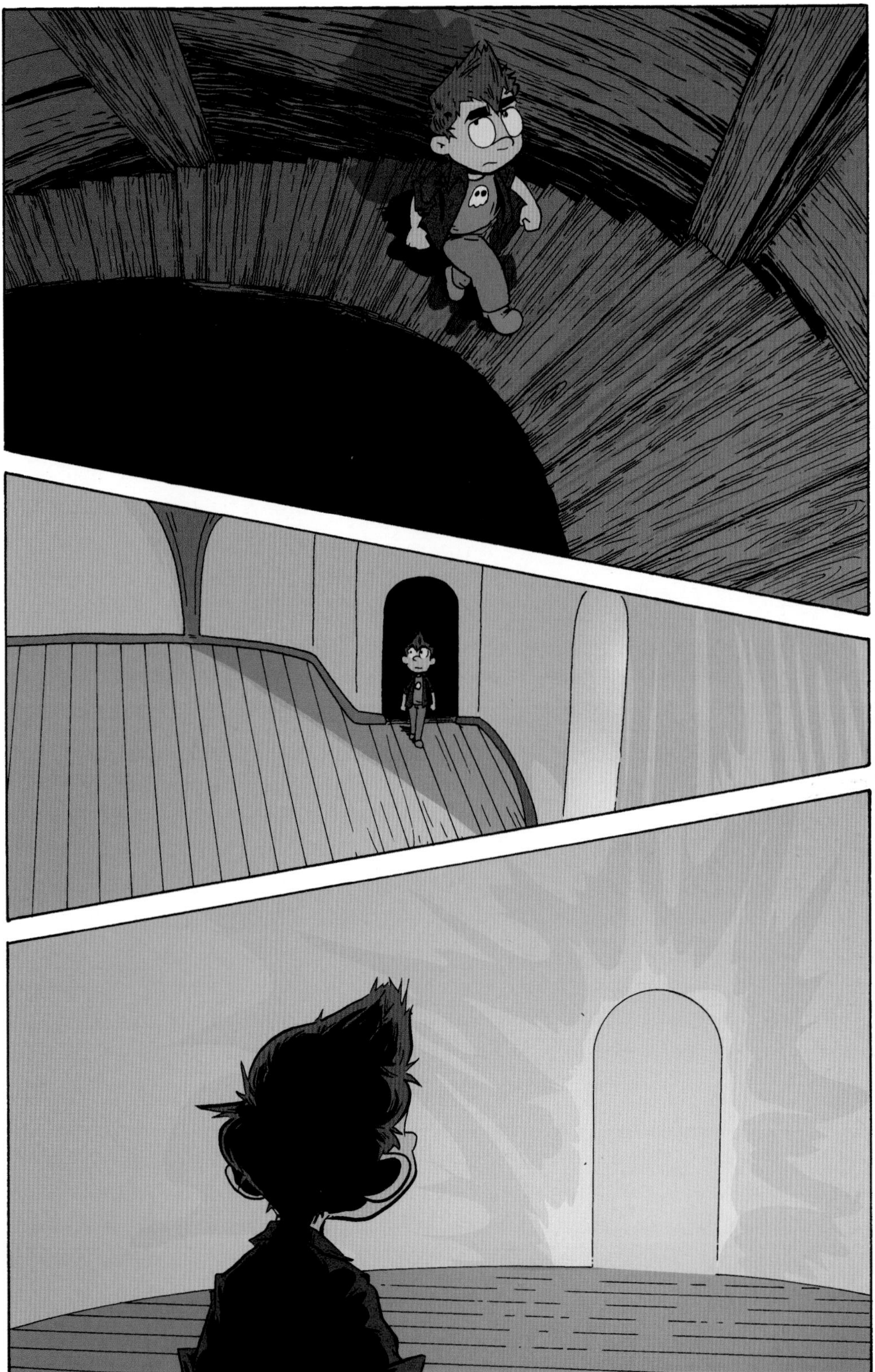

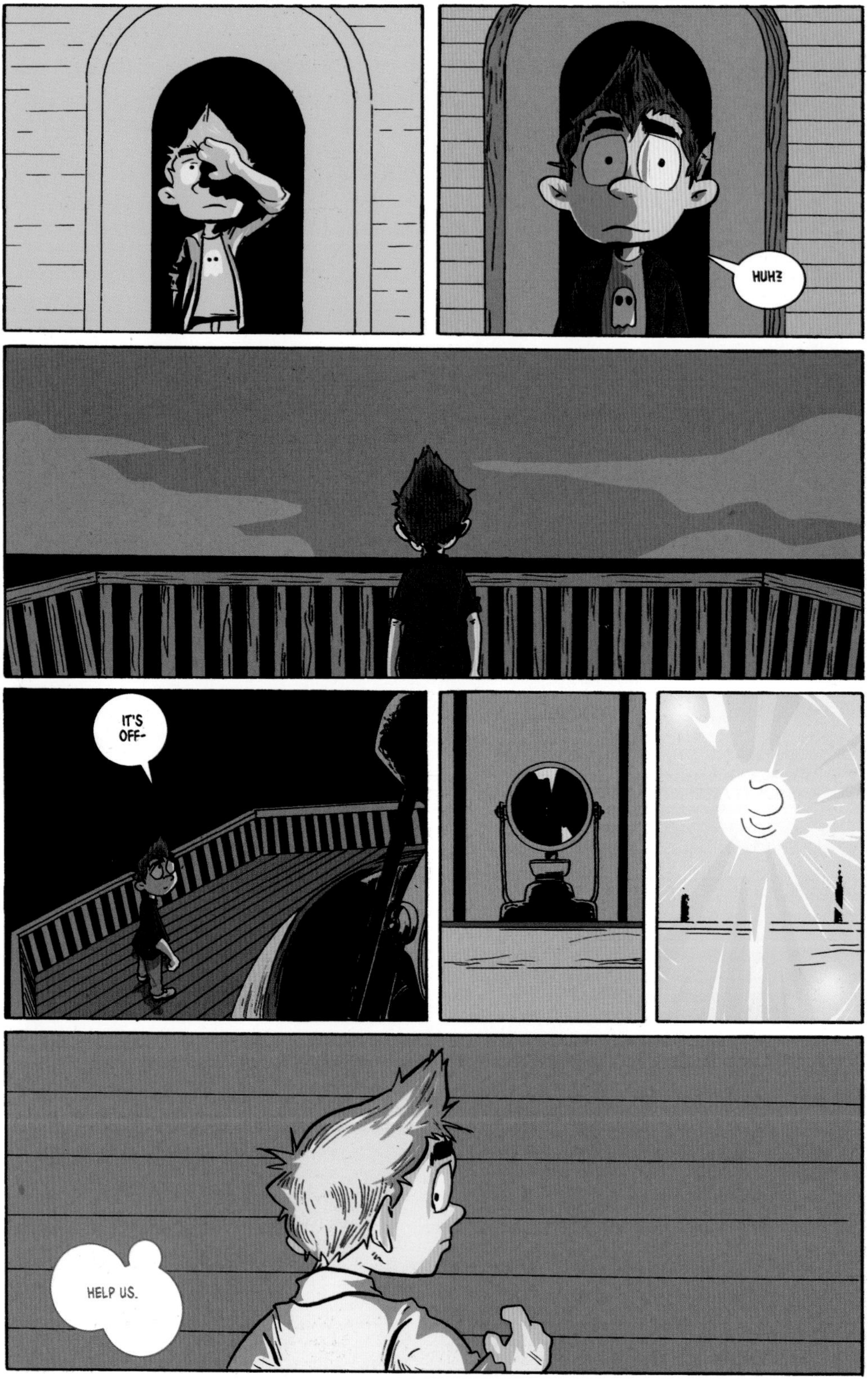
HUH?
IT'S OFF-
HELP US.

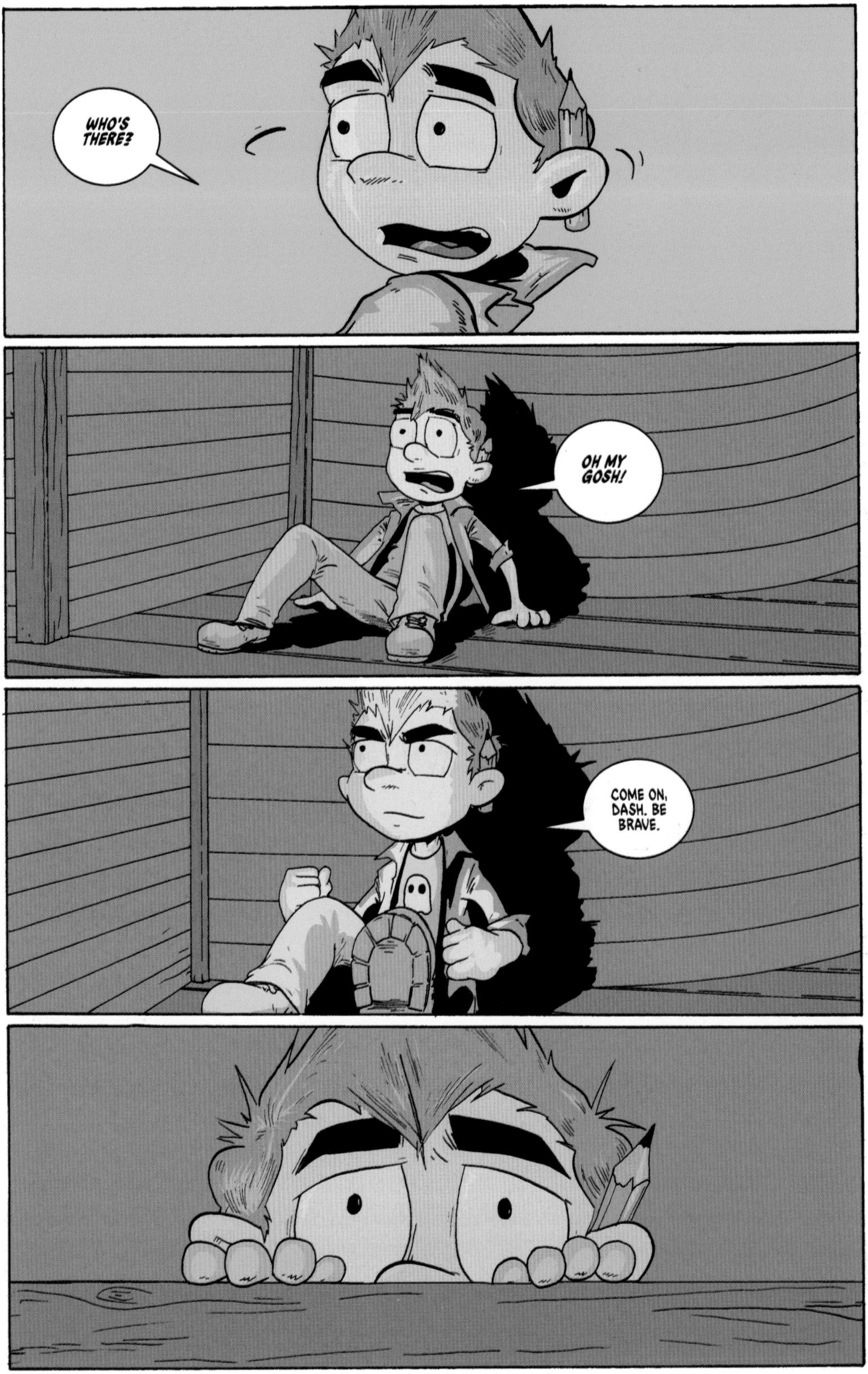
WHO'S THERE?
OH MY GOSH!
COME ON, DASH. BE BRAVE.

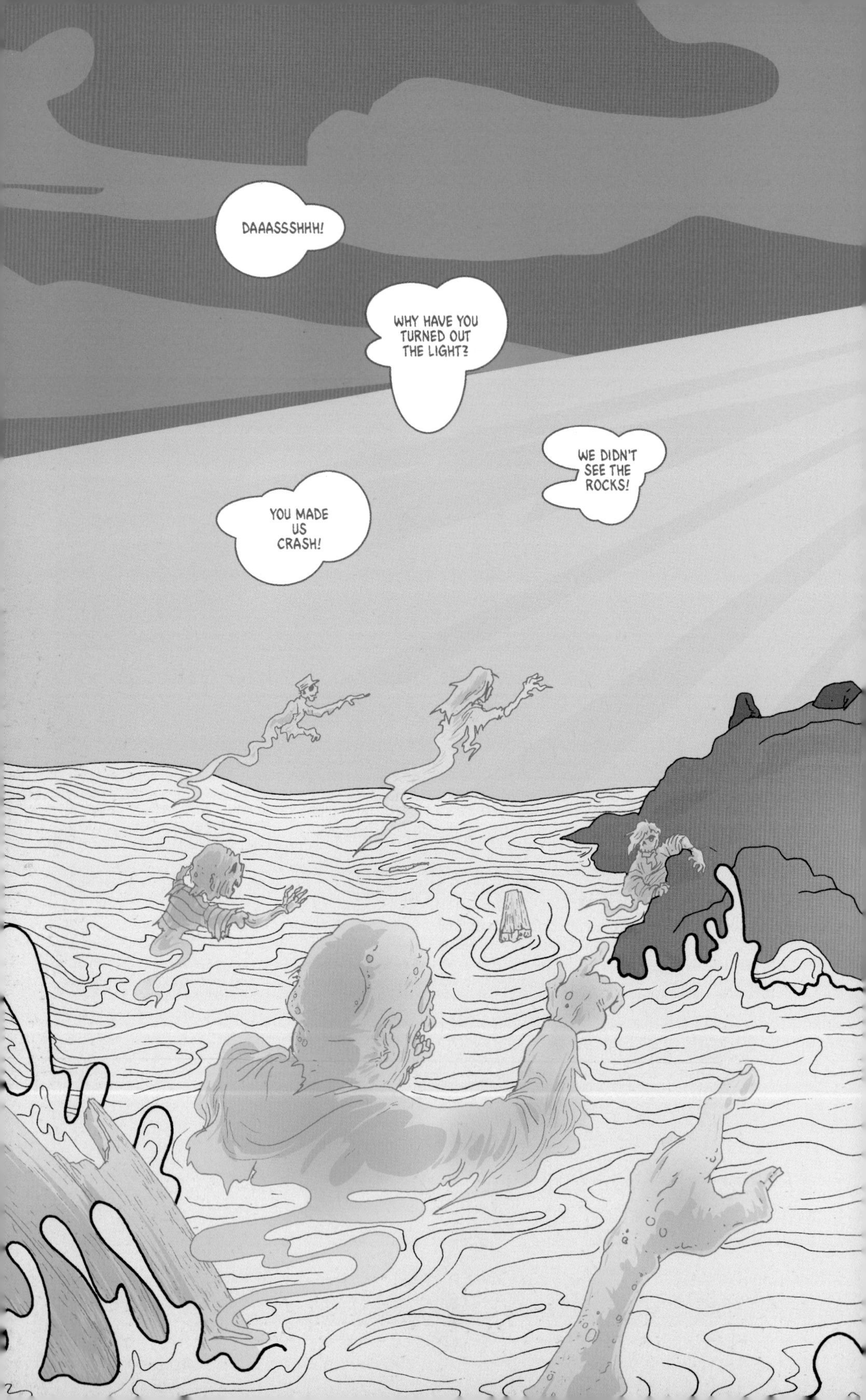
DAAASSSHHH!
WHY HAVE YOU TURNED OUT THE LIGHT?
WE DIDN'T SEE THE ROCKS!
YOU MADE US CRASH!

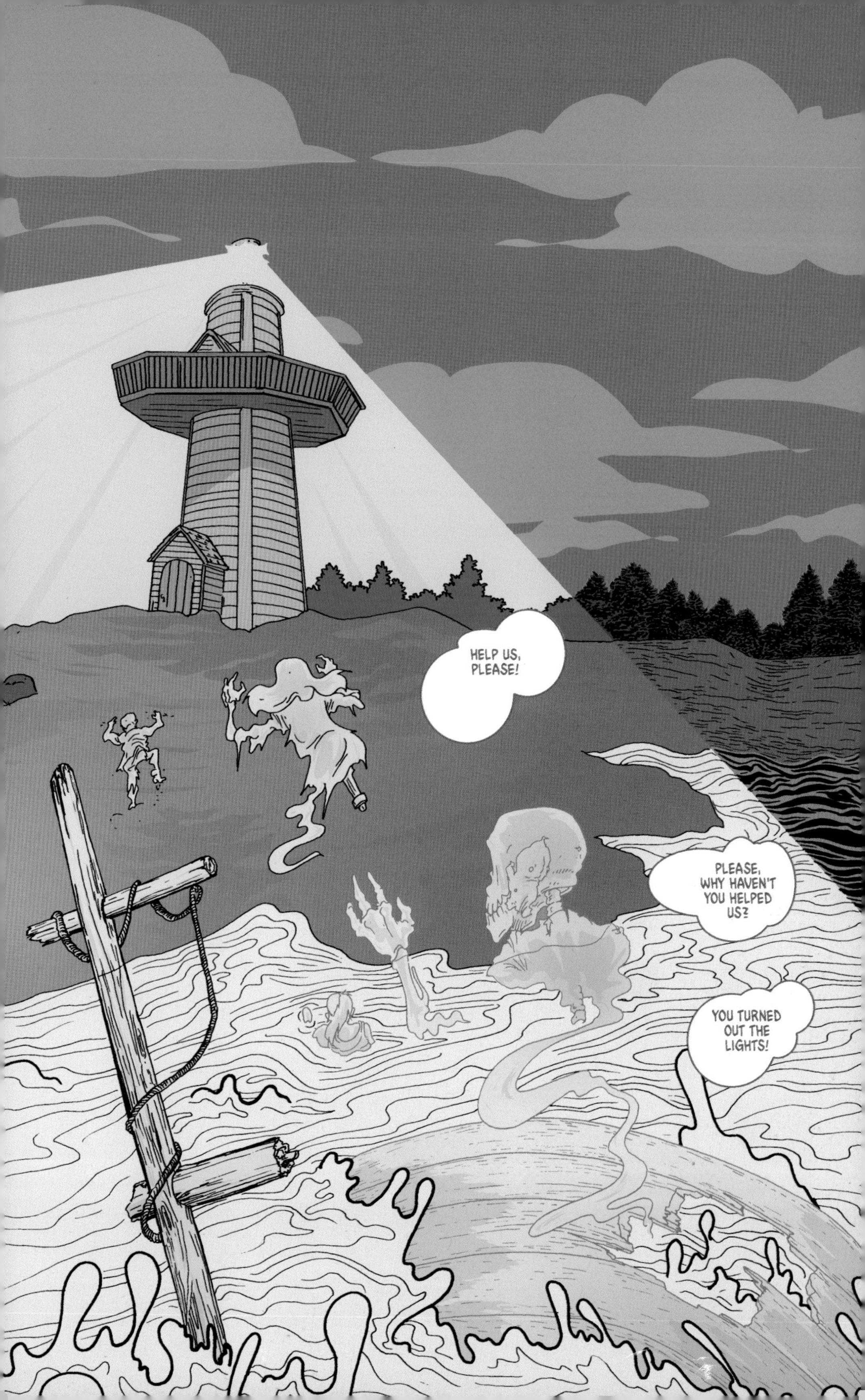
HELP US, PLEASE!
PLEASE, WHY HAVEN'T YOU HELPED US?
YOU TURNED OUT THE LIGHTS!

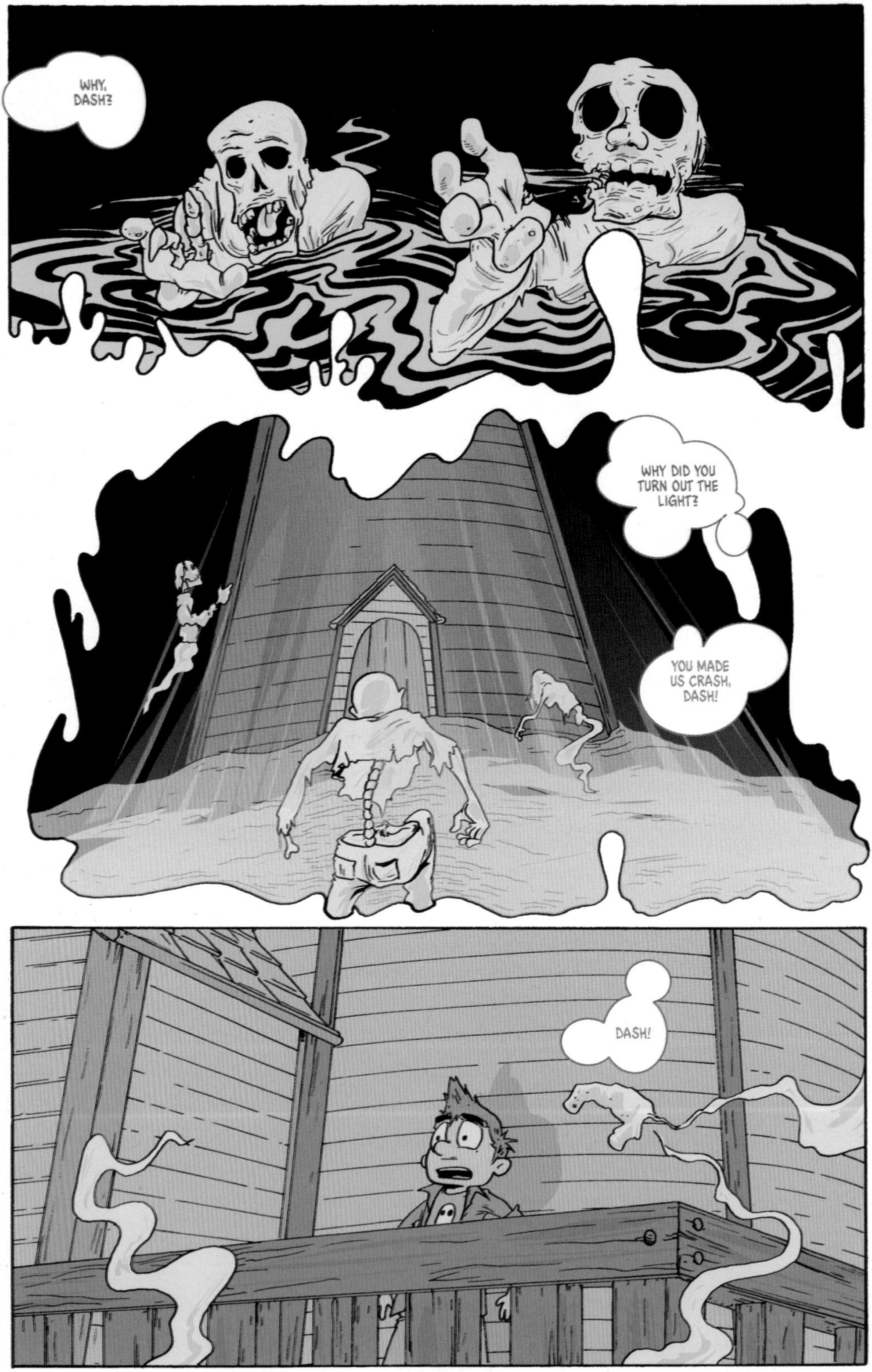
WHY, DASH?
WHY DID YOU TURN OUT THE LIGHT?
YOU MADE US CRASH, DASH!
DASH!

TO BE CONTINUED.

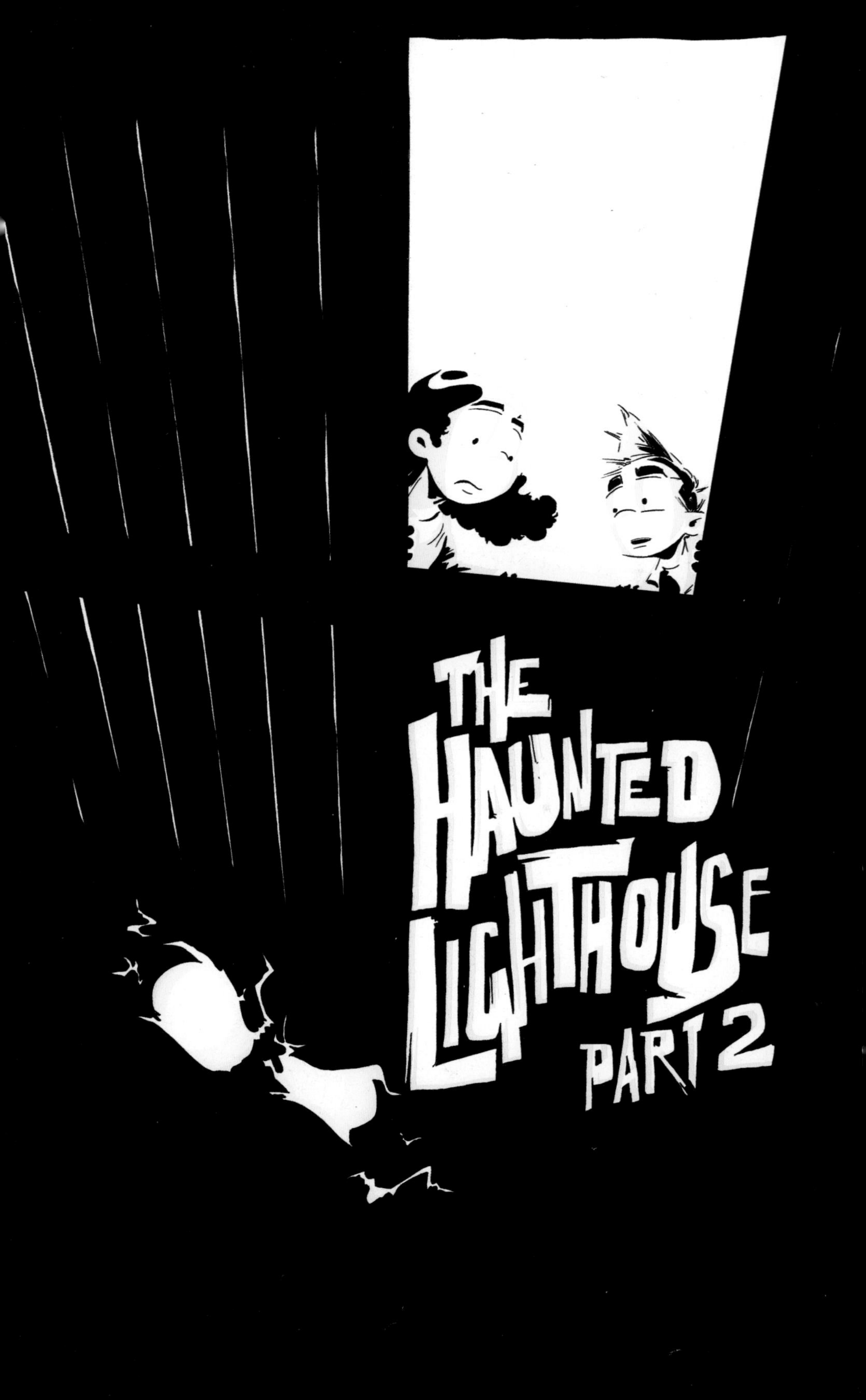

THE HAUNTED LIGHTHOUSE
PART 2

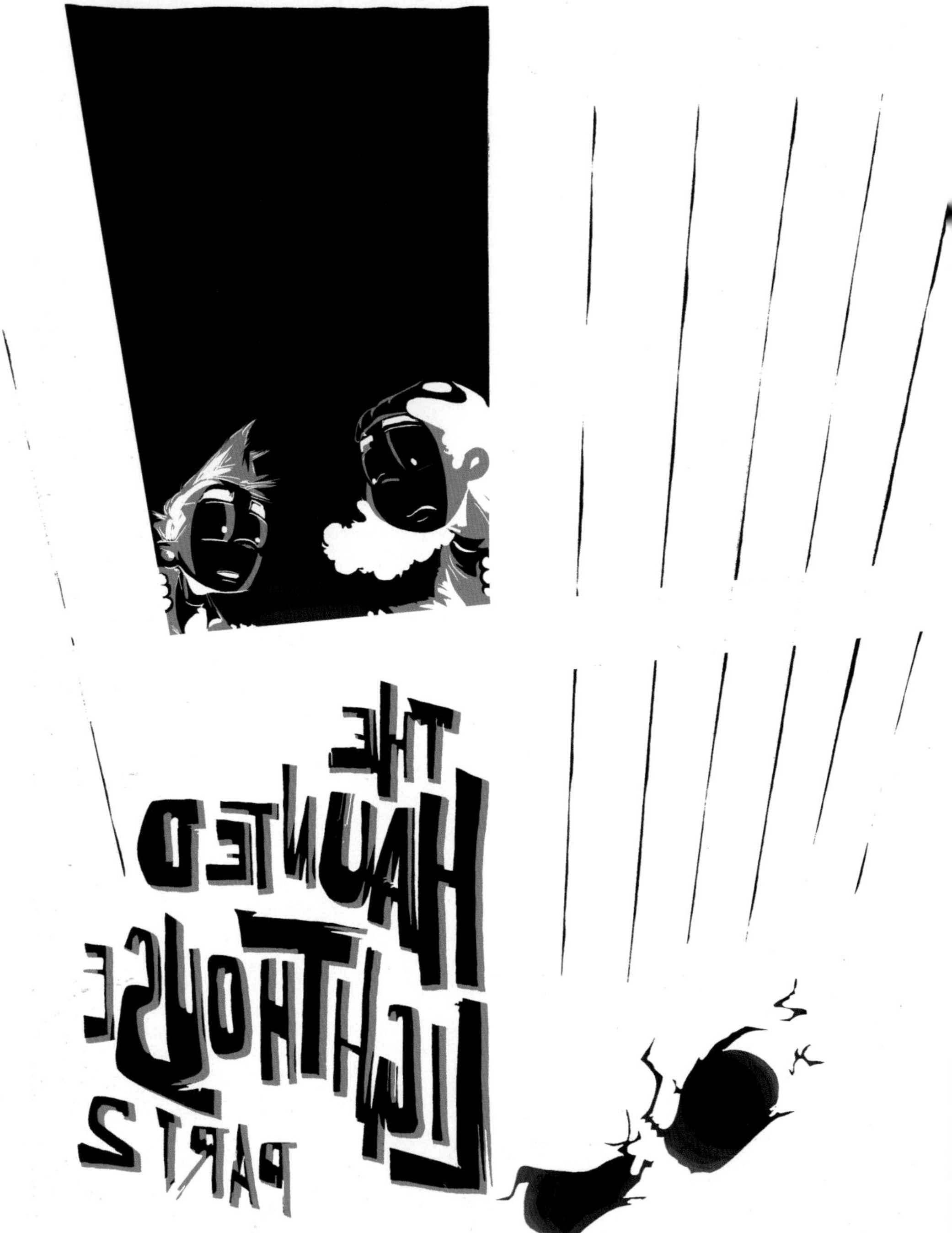
THE HAUNTED LIGHTHOUSE PART 2

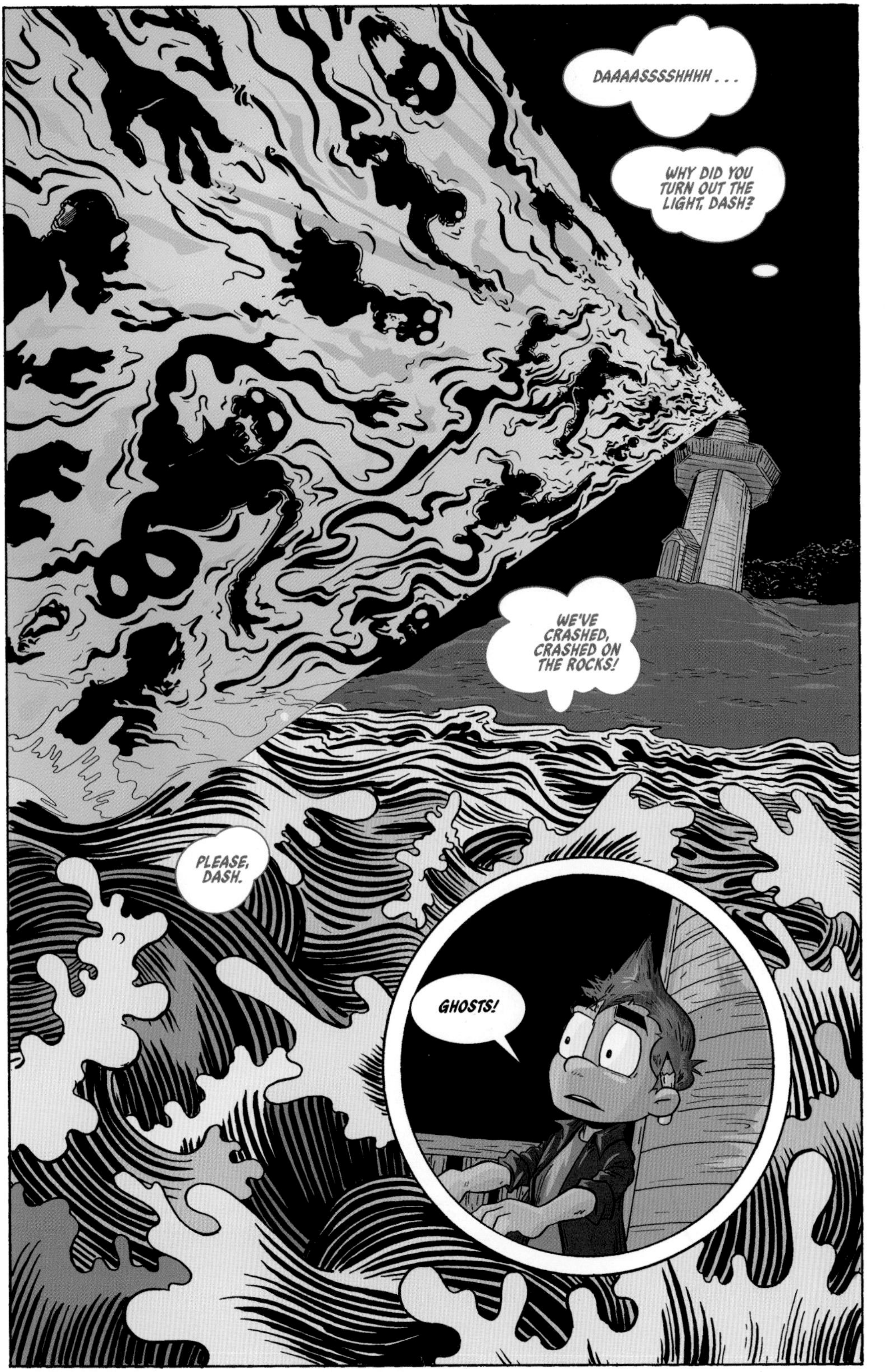
DAAAAASSSSHHHH . . .
WHY DID YOU TURN OUT THE LIGHT, DASH?
WE'VE CRASHED, CRASHED ON THE ROCKS!
PLEASE, DASH.
GHOSTS!

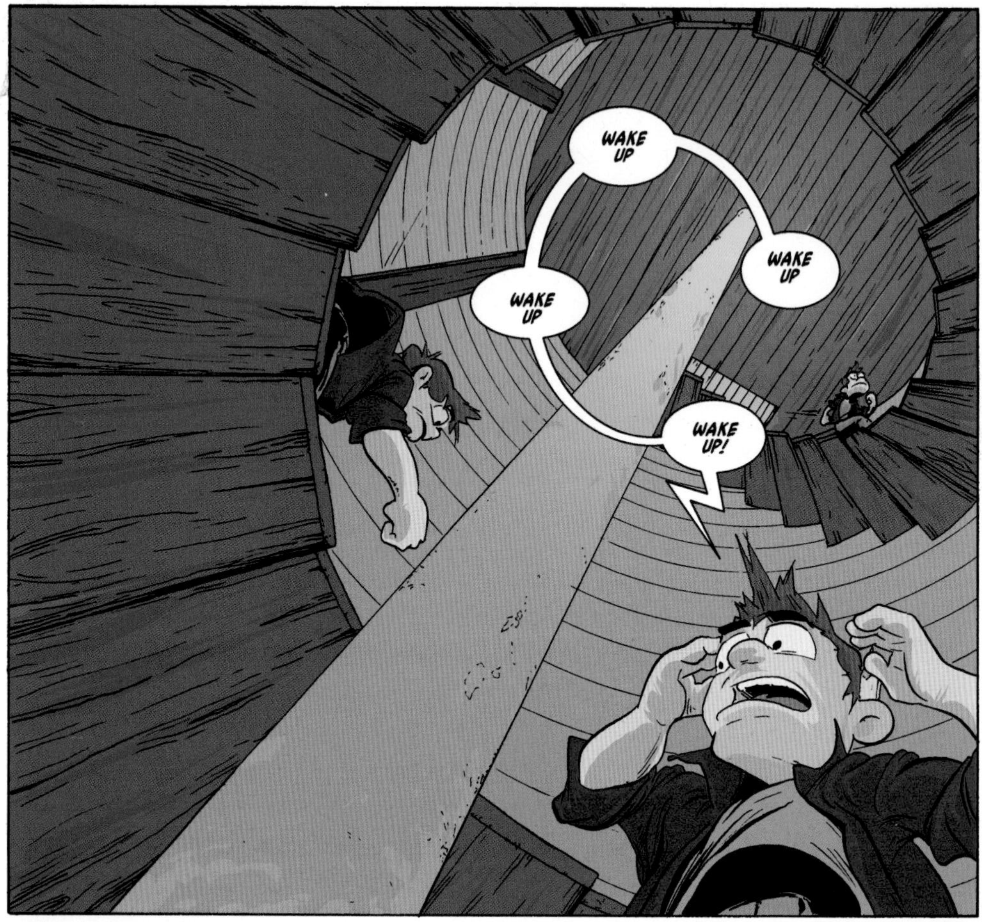
WAKE UP
WAKE UP
WAKE UP
WAKE UP!

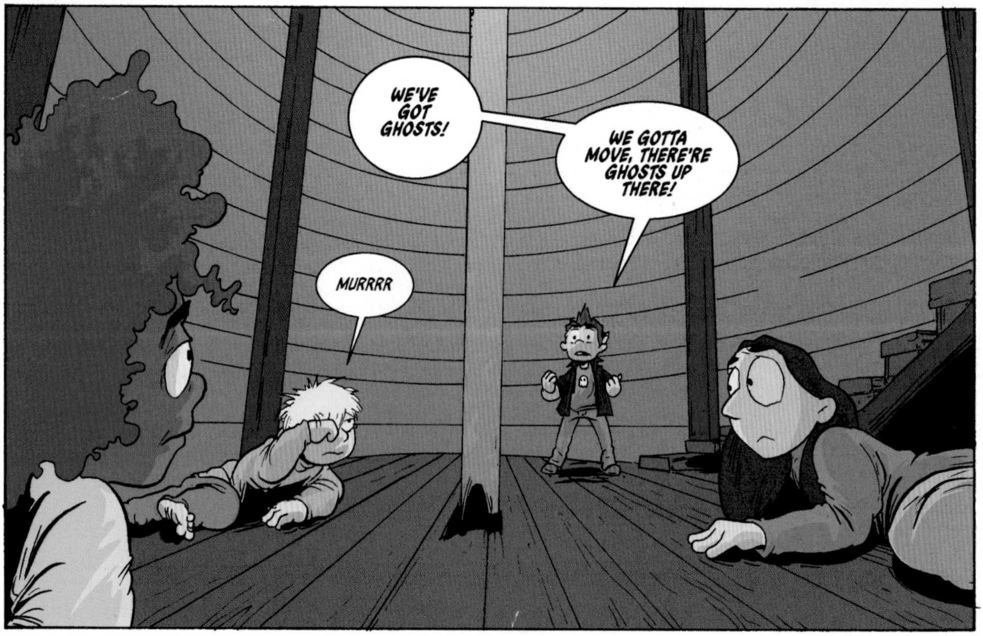
WE'VE GOT GHOSTS!
WE GOTTA MOVE, THERE'RE GHOSTS UP THERE!
MURRRR

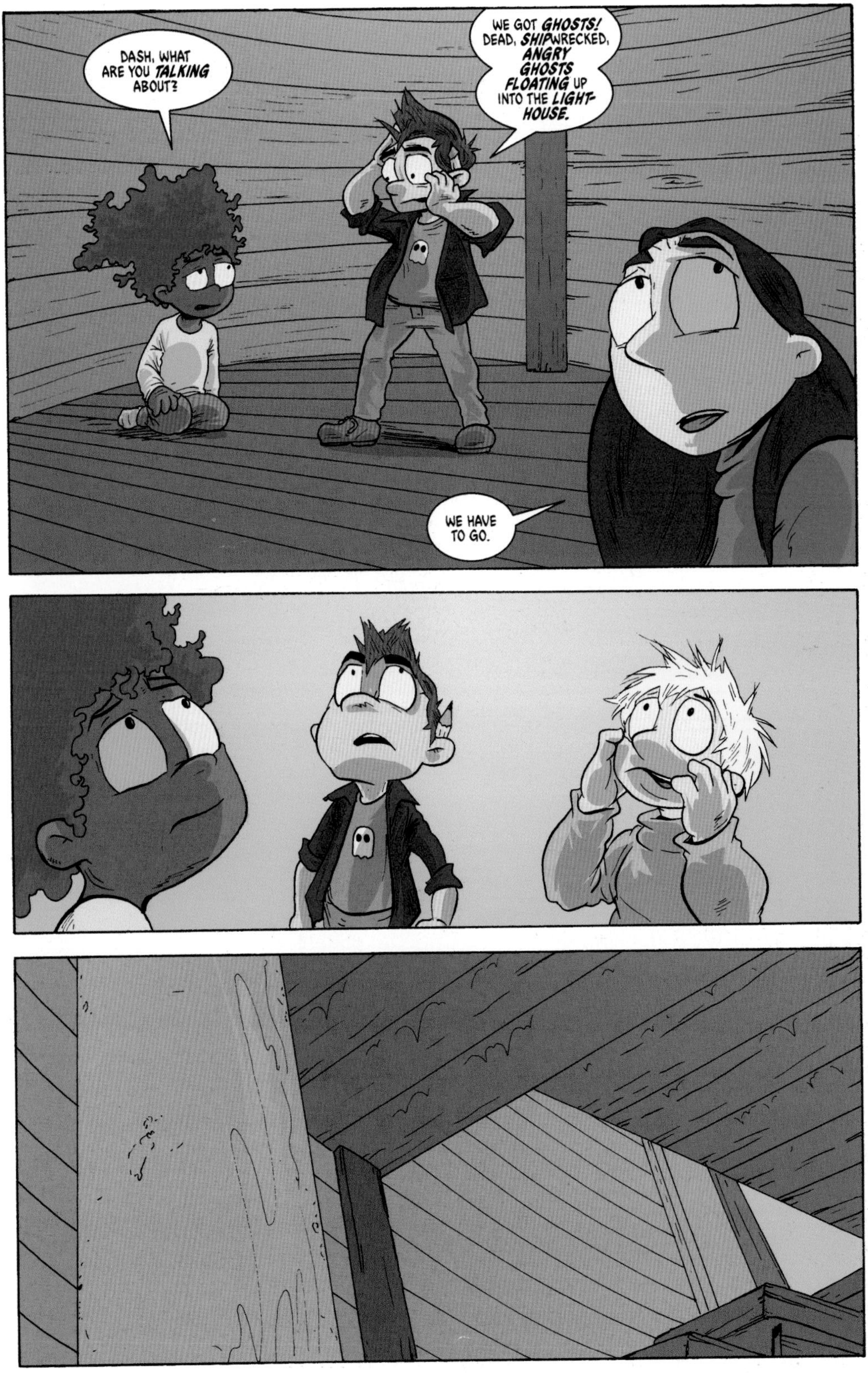
DASH, WHAT ARE YOU TALKING ABOUT?
WE GOT GHOSTS! DEAD, SHIPWRECKED, ANGRY GHOSTS FLOATING UP INTO THE LIGHT-HOUSE.
WE HAVE TO GO.

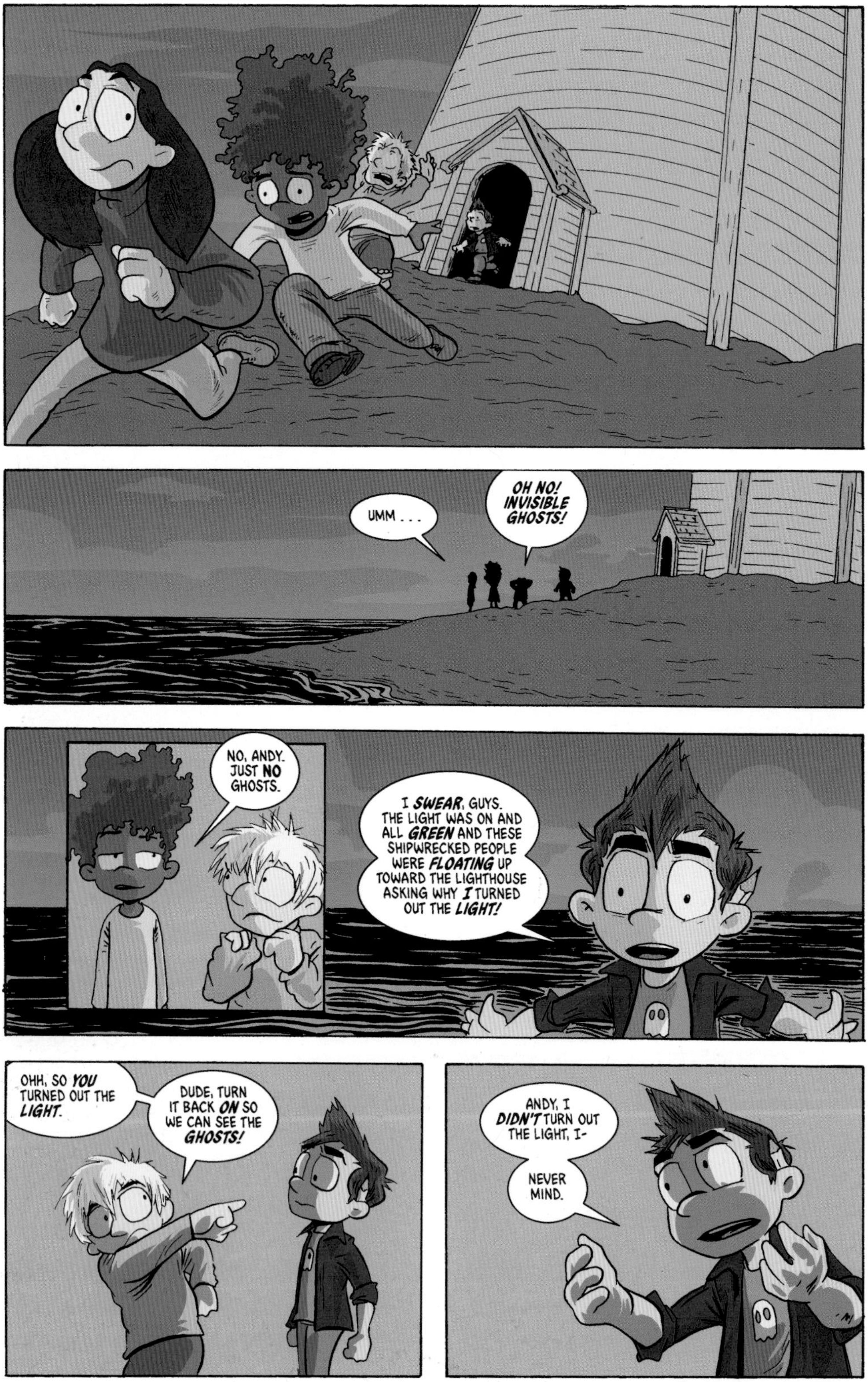
UMM . . .
OH NO! INVISIBLE GHOSTS!
NO, ANDY. JUST NO GHOSTS.
I SWEAR, GUYS. THE LIGHT WAS ON AND ALL GREEN AND THESE SHIPWRECKED PEOPLE WERE FLOATING UP TOWARD THE LIGHTHOUSE ASKING WHY I TURNED OUT THE LIGHT!
OHH, SO YOU TURNED OUT THE LIGHT.
DUDE, TURN IT BACK ON SO WE CAN SEE THE GHOSTS!
ANDY, I DIDN'T TURN OUT THE LIGHT, I-
NEVER MIND.

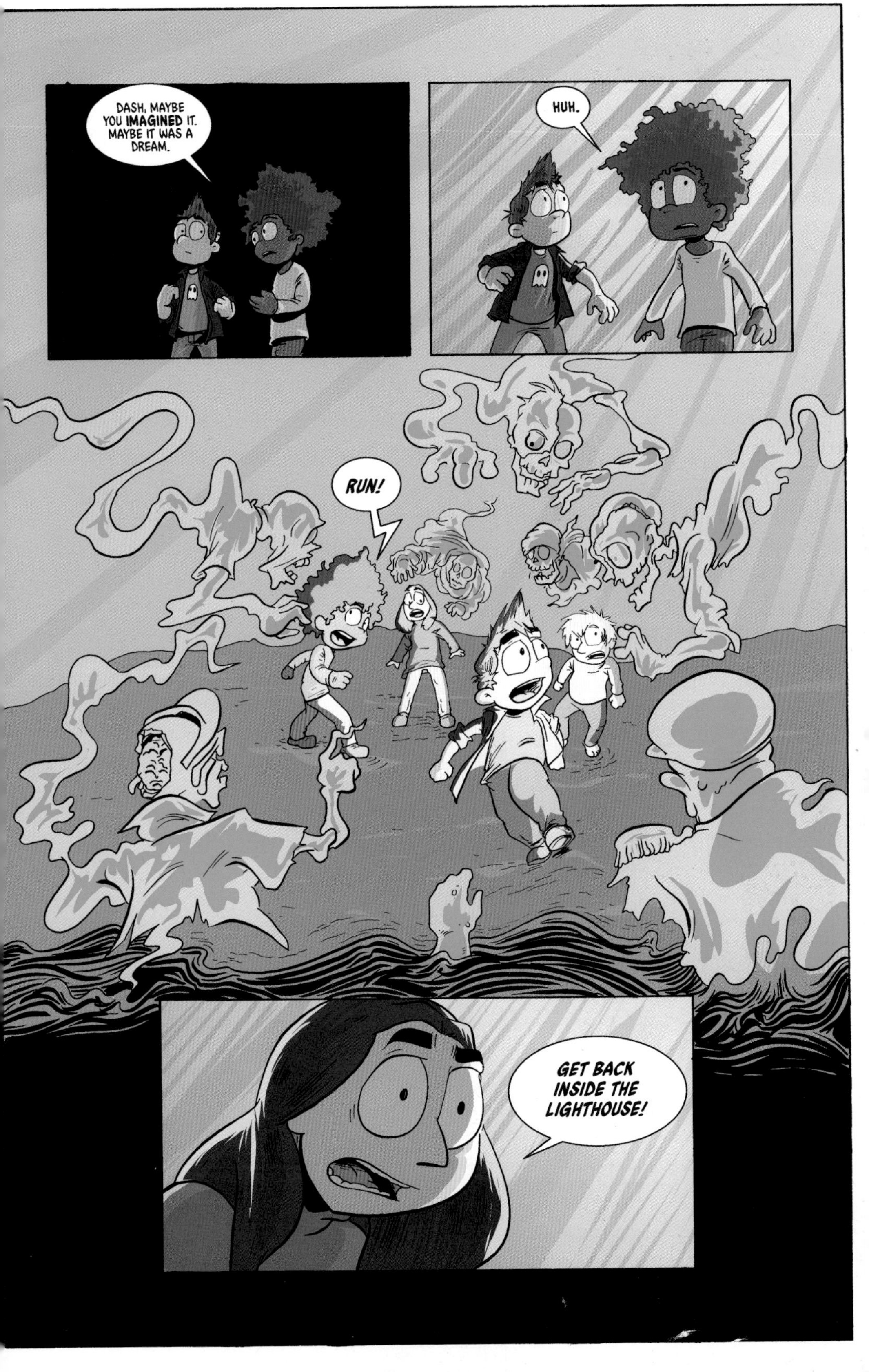
DASH, MAYBE YOU IMAGINED IT. MAYBE IT WAS A DREAM.
HUH.
RUN!
GET BACK INSIDE THE LIGHTHOUSE!

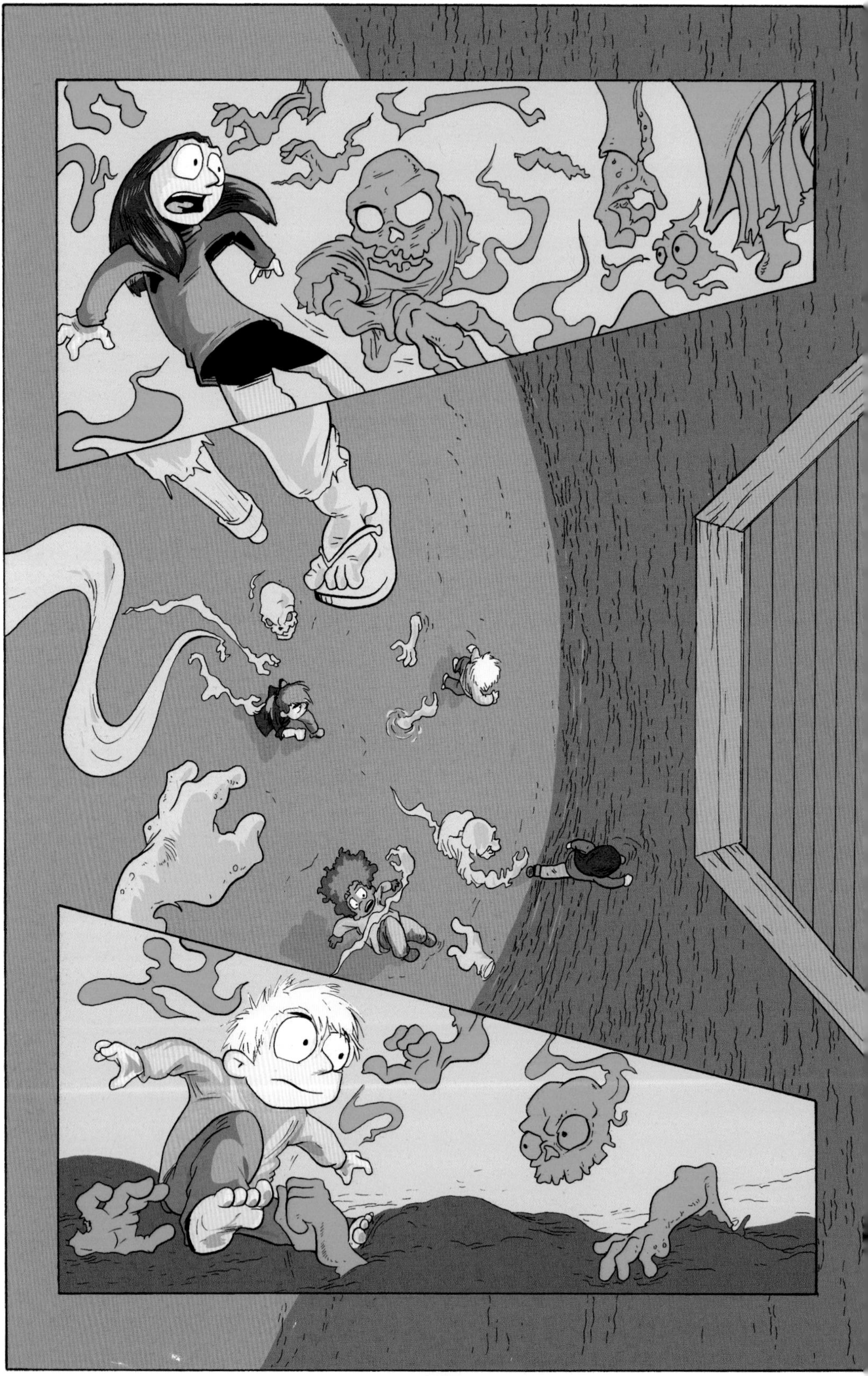

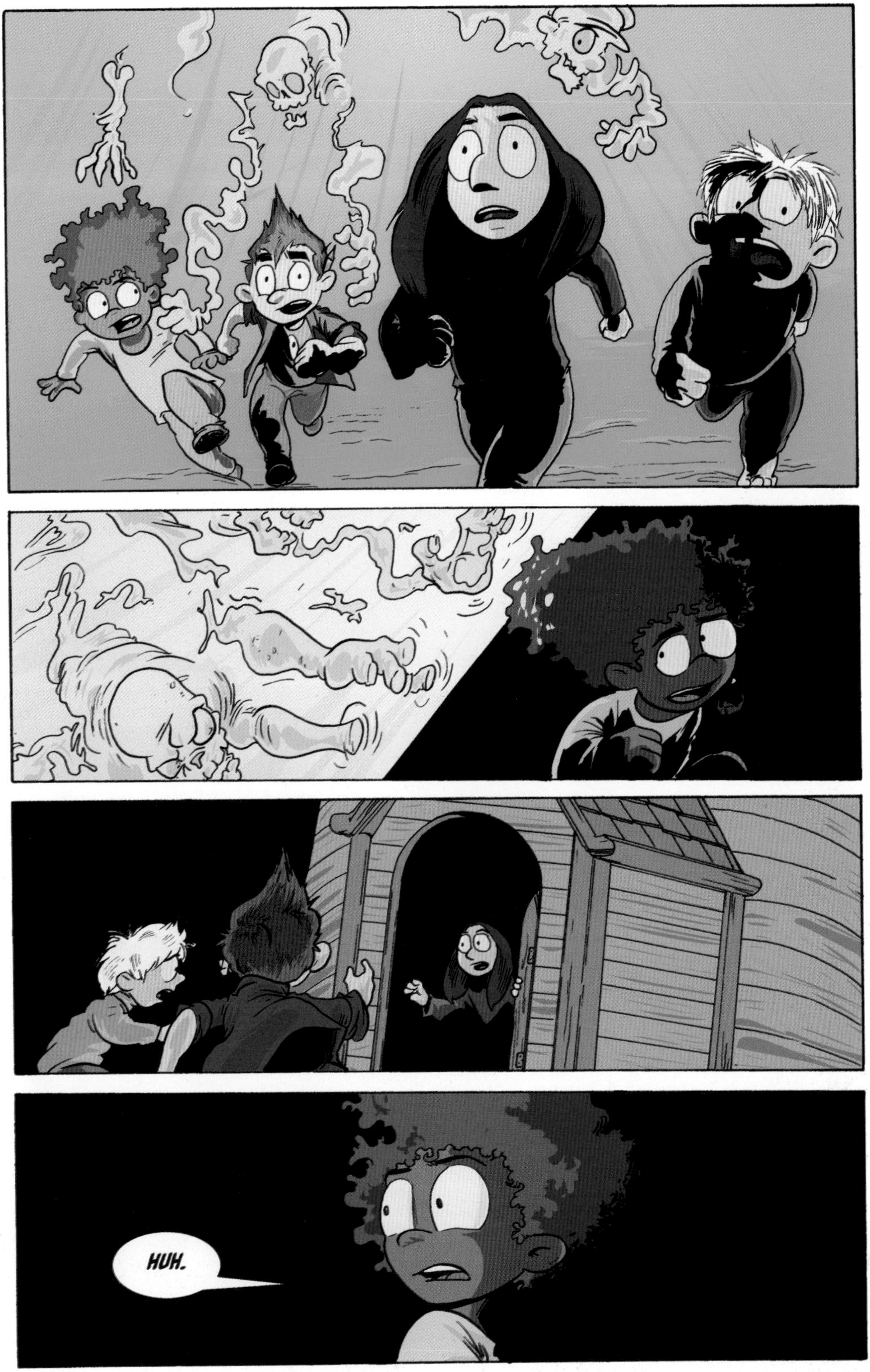
HUH.

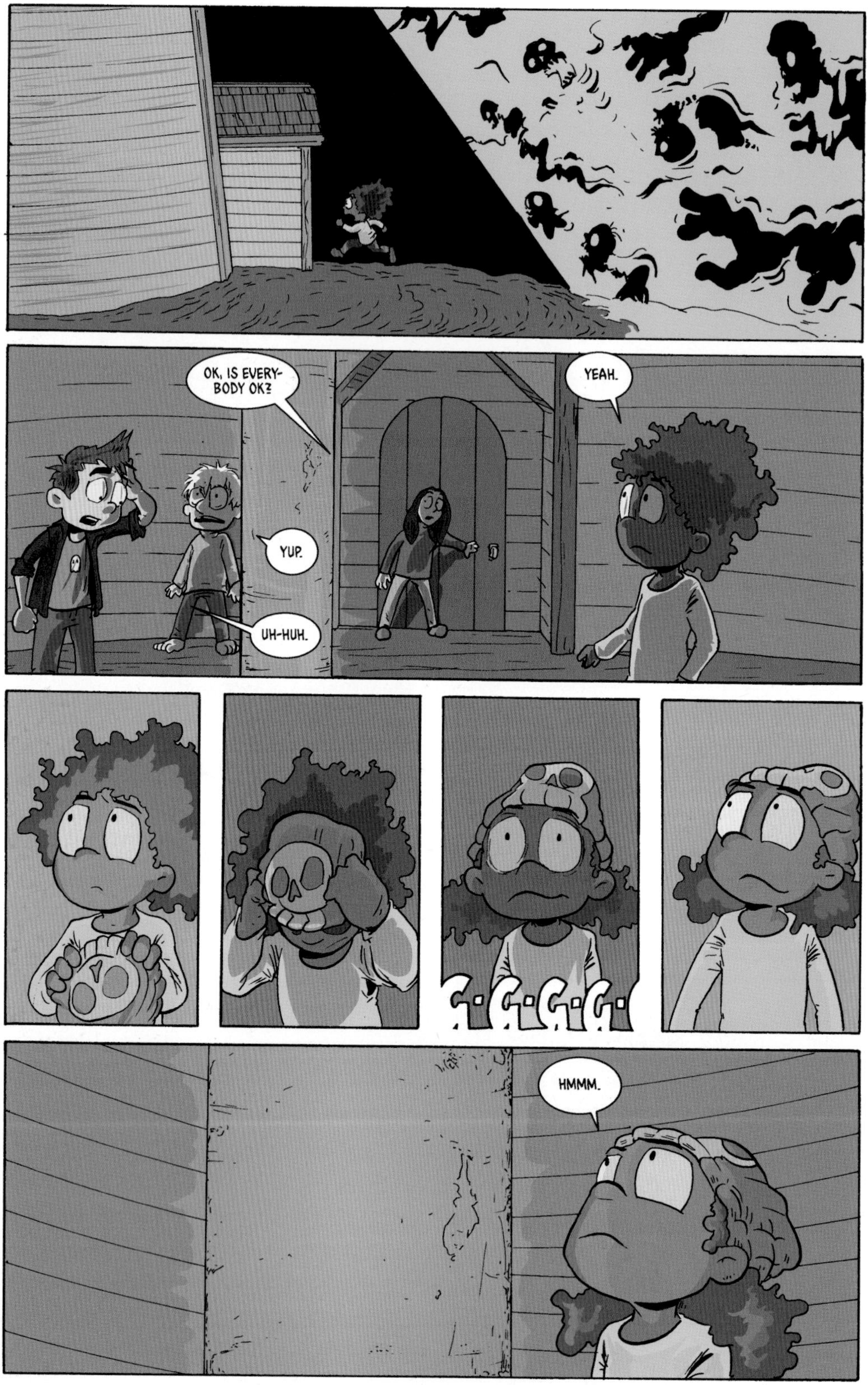
OK, IS EVERY-BODY OK?
YUP.
UH-HUH.
YEAH.
G-G-G-G-
HMMM.

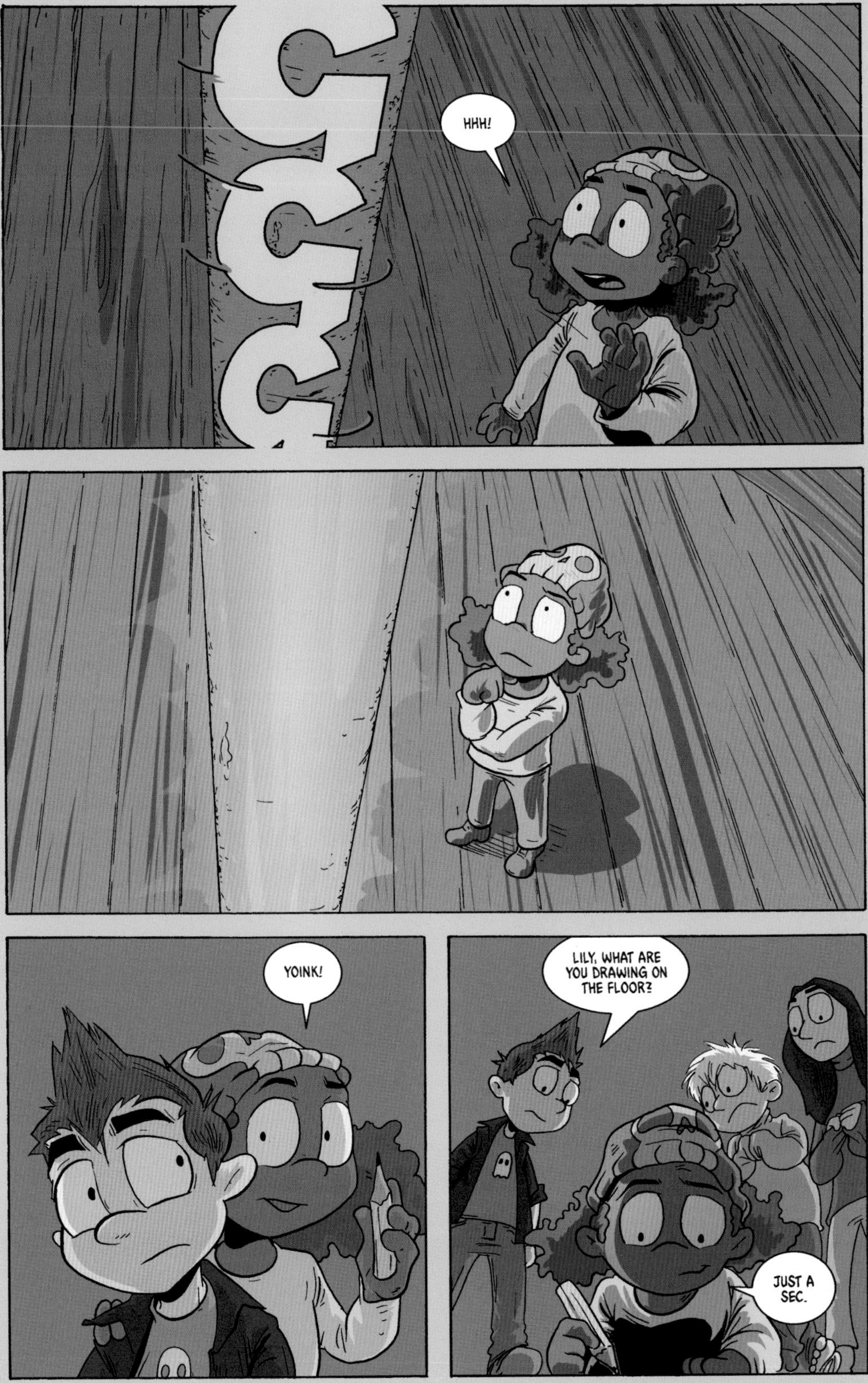
HHH!
YOINK!
LILY, WHAT ARE YOU DRAWING ON THE FLOOR?
JUST A SEC.

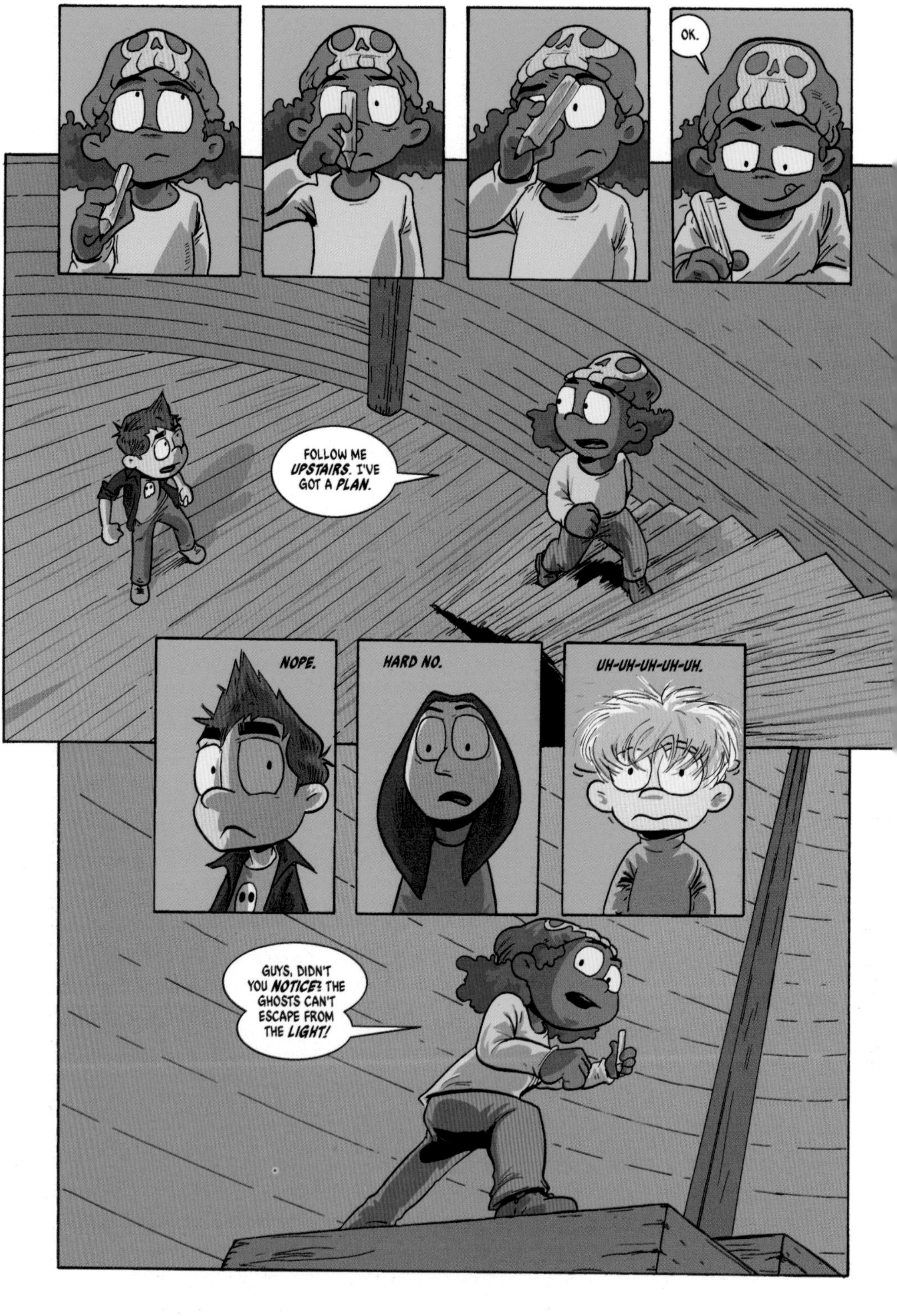
OK.
FOLLOW ME UPSTAIRS. I'VE GOT A PLAN.
NOPE.
HARD NO.
UH-UH-UH-UH-UH.
GUYS, DIDN'T YOU NOTICE? THE GHOSTS CAN'T ESCAPE FROM THE LIGHT!

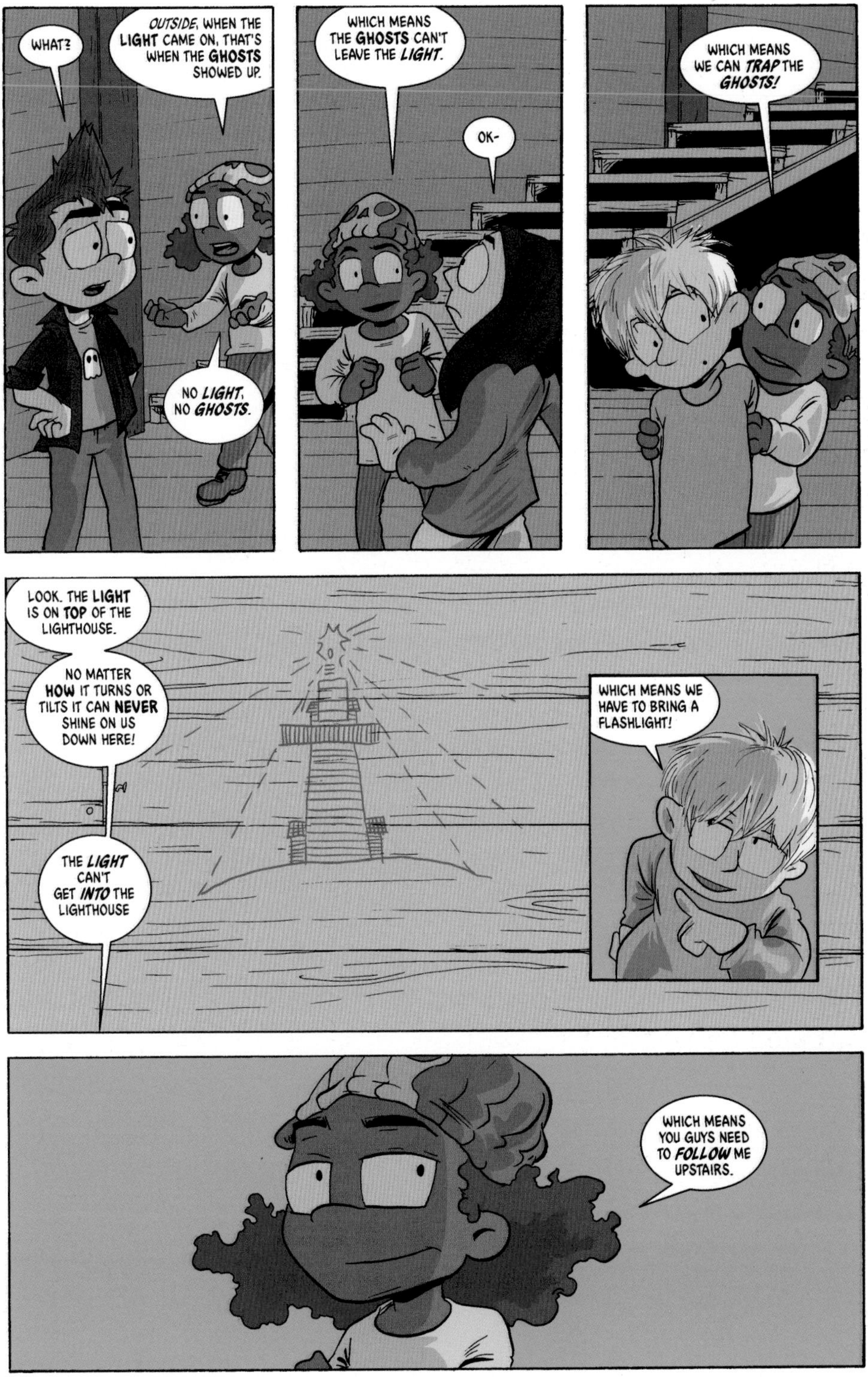
WHAT?
OUTSIDE, WHEN THE LIGHT CAME ON, THAT'S WHEN THE GHOSTS SHOWED UP.
NO LIGHT, NO GHOSTS.
WHICH MEANS THE GHOSTS CAN'T LEAVE THE LIGHT.
OK-
WHICH MEANS WE CAN TRAP THE GHOSTS!
LOOK. THE LIGHT IS ON TOP OF THE LIGHTHOUSE.
NO MATTER HOW IT TURNS OR TILTS IT CAN NEVER SHINE ON US DOWN HERE!
THE LIGHT CAN'T GET INTO THE LIGHTHOUSE
WHICH MEANS WE HAVE TO BRING A FLASHLIGHT!
WHICH MEANS YOU GUYS NEED TO FOLLOW ME UPSTAIRS.

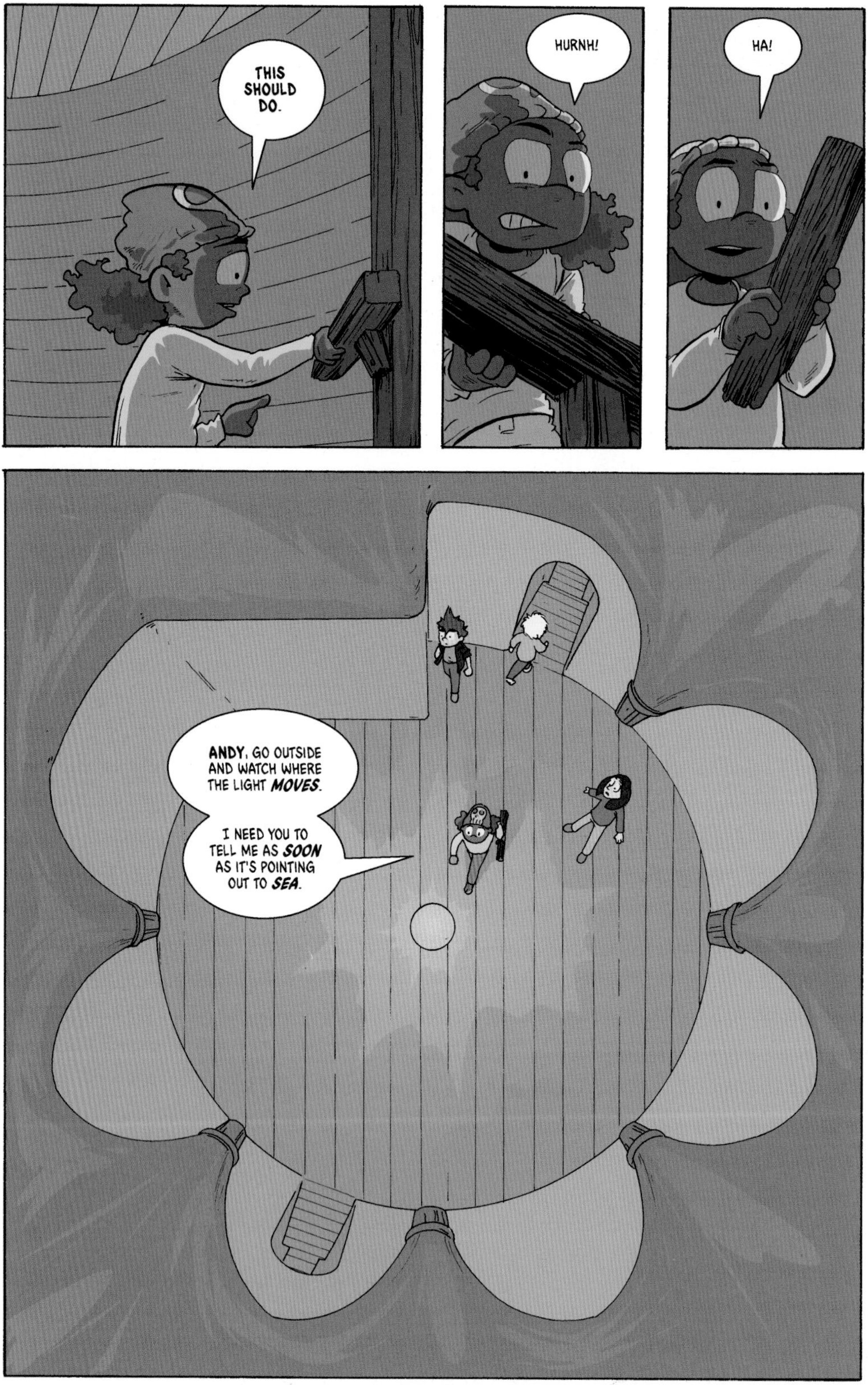
THIS SHOULD DO.
HURNH!
HA!
ANDY, GO OUTSIDE AND WATCH WHERE THE LIGHT MOVES.
I NEED YOU TO TELL ME AS SOON AS IT'S POINTING OUT TO SEA.

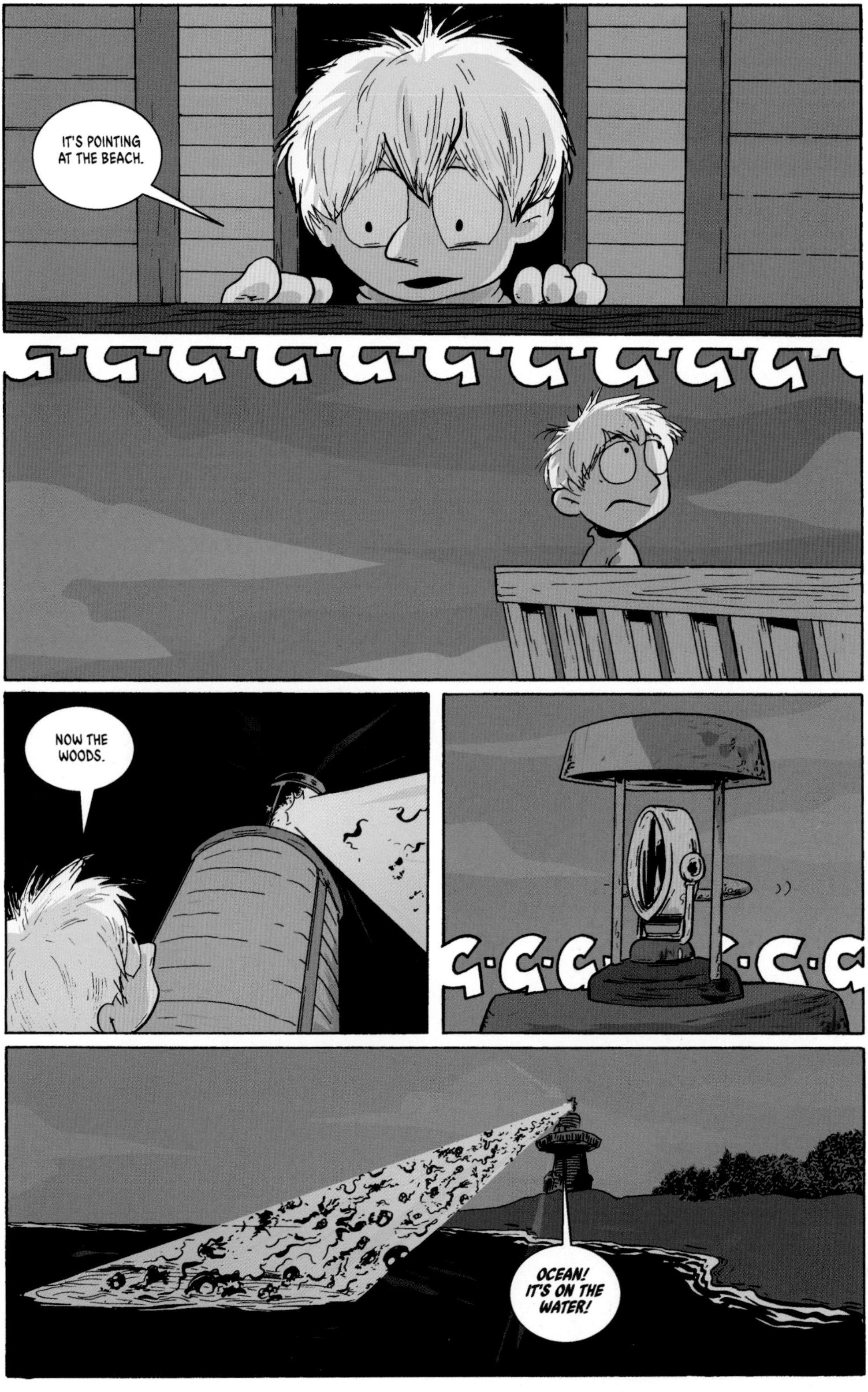
IT'S POINTING AT THE BEACH.
NOW THE WOODS.
OCEAN! IT'S ON THE WATER!

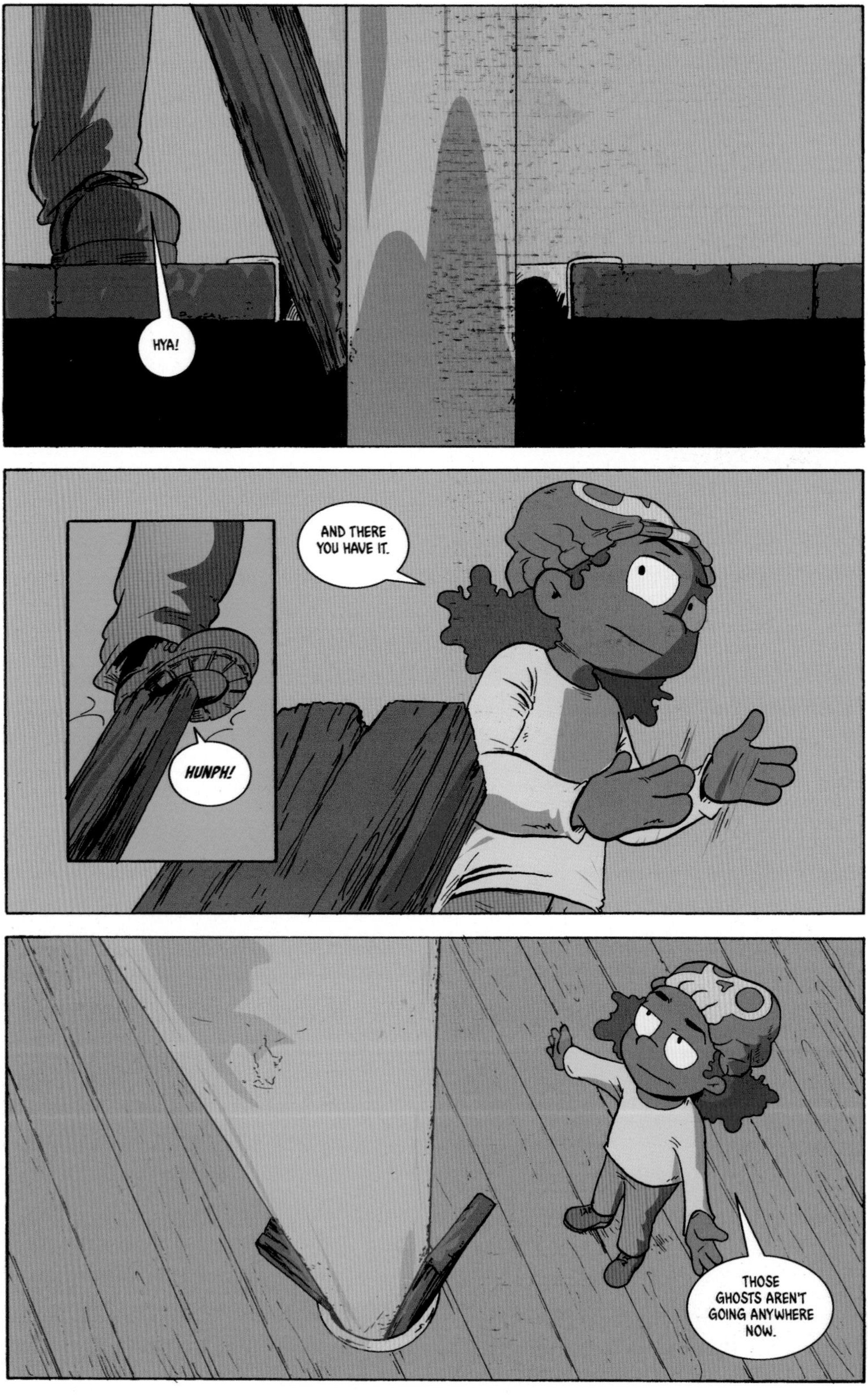
HYA!
HUNPH!
AND THERE YOU HAVE IT.
THOSE GHOSTS AREN'T GOING ANYWHERE NOW.

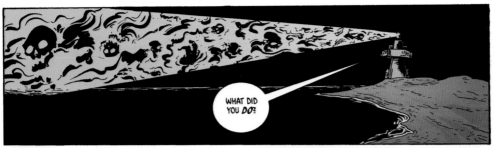

WHAT DID YOU *DO?*

CHECK IT *OUT.* THE LIGHT ONLY HITS THE OCEAN WAY OUT **THERE.**

THE POLE CAN'T **TURN** SO THE **LIGHT** CAN'T MOVE.

THANKS-

HEY!

LILY, I DON'T **CARE** WHAT EVERYBODY ELSE SAYS.

I THINK YOU'RE SMART.

SO, WHAT *NOW?* WAIT 'TIL MORNING AND WALK **HOME?**

ON SECOND THOUGHT-

LET'S STILL LEAVE RIGHT NOW.

100% AGREED.

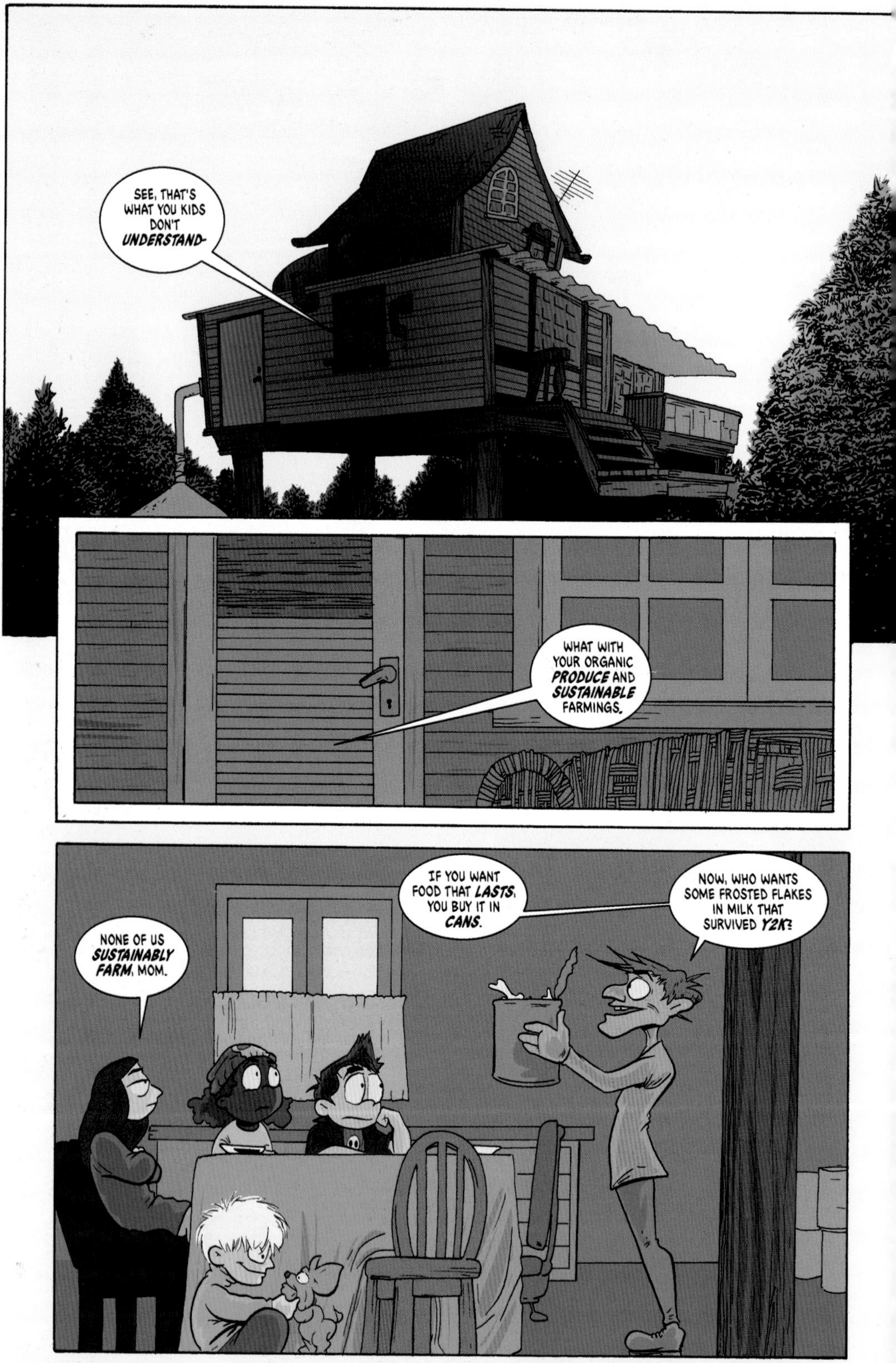

SEE, THAT'S WHAT YOU KIDS DON'T *UNDERSTAND*-
WHAT WITH YOUR ORGANIC *PRODUCE* AND *SUSTAINABLE* FARMINGS.
NONE OF US *SUSTAINABLY FARM*, MOM.
IF YOU WANT FOOD THAT *LASTS*, YOU BUY IT IN *CANS*.
NOW, WHO WANTS SOME FROSTED FLAKES IN MILK THAT SURVIVED *Y2K*?

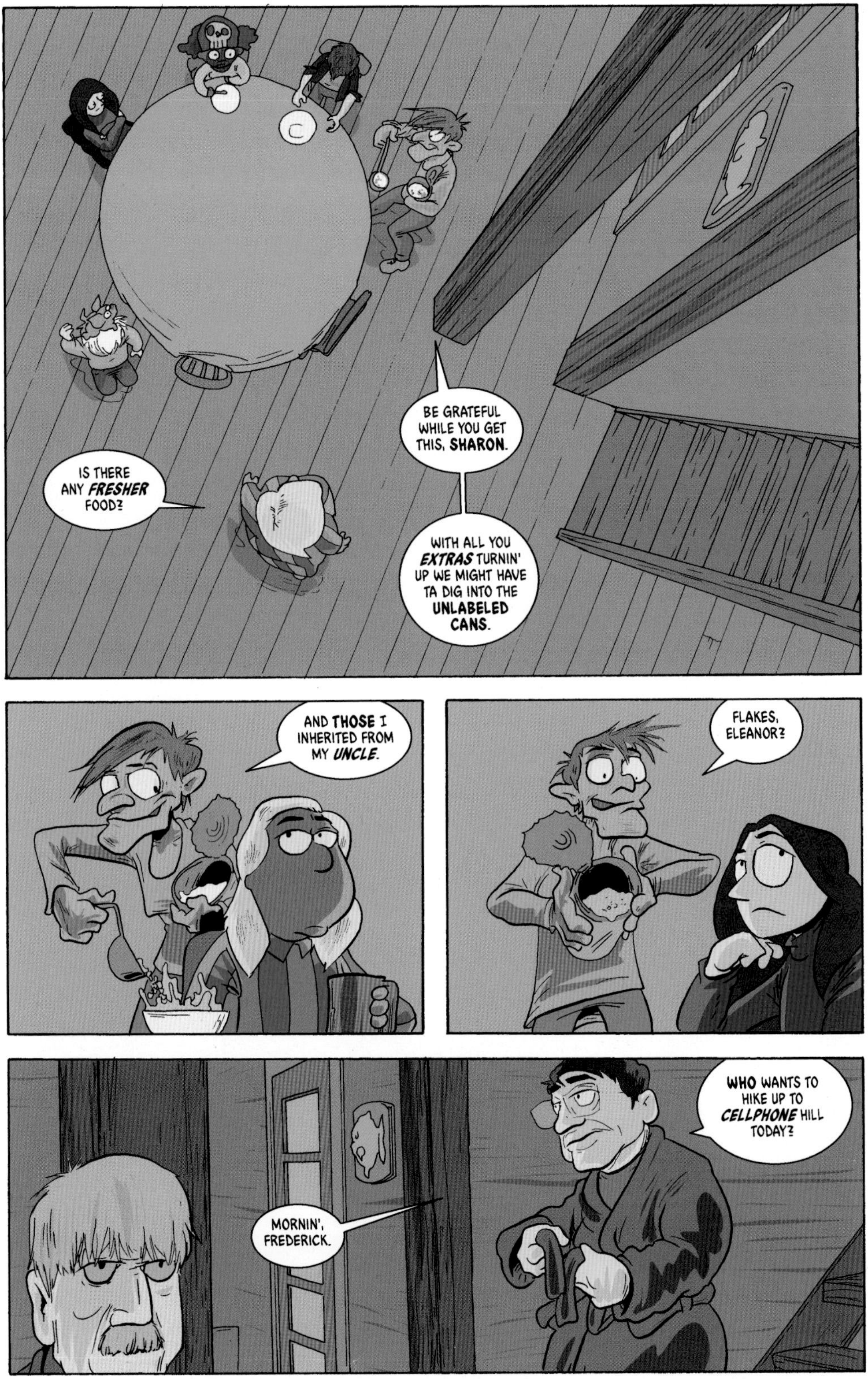
BE GRATEFUL WHILE YOU GET THIS, SHARON.
IS THERE ANY FRESHER FOOD?
WITH ALL YOU EXTRAS TURNIN' UP WE MIGHT HAVE TA DIG INTO THE UNLABELED CANS.
AND THOSE I INHERITED FROM MY UNCLE.
FLAKES, ELEANOR?
WHO WANTS TO HIKE UP TO CELLPHONE HILL TODAY?
MORNIN', FREDERICK.

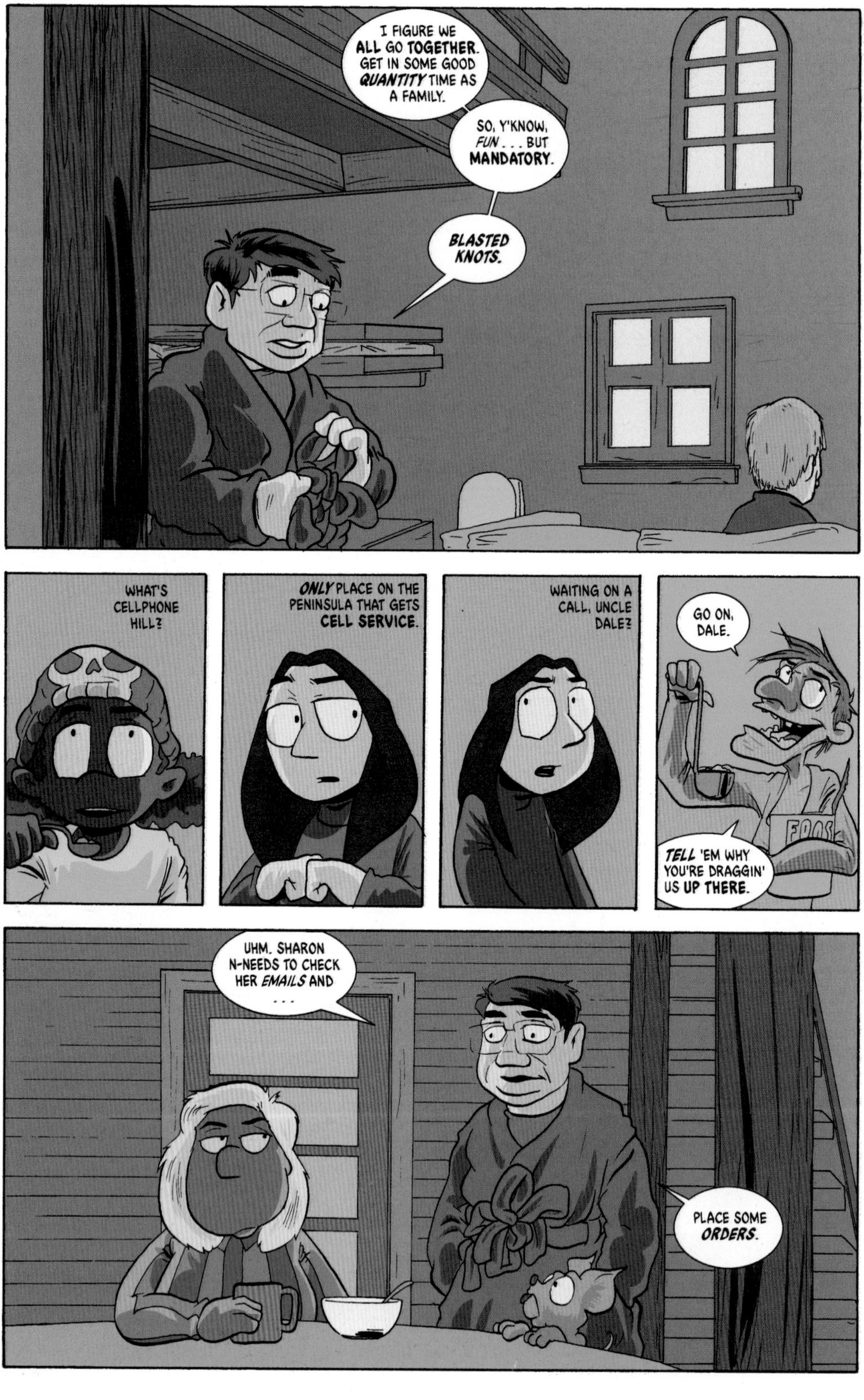
I FIGURE WE ALL GO TOGETHER. GET IN SOME GOOD QUANTITY TIME AS A FAMILY.
SO, Y'KNOW, FUN . . . BUT MANDATORY.
BLASTED KNOTS.
WHAT'S CELLPHONE HILL?
ONLY PLACE ON THE PENINSULA THAT GETS CELL SERVICE.
WAITING ON A CALL, UNCLE DALE?
GO ON, DALE.
FOOS
TELL 'EM WHY YOU'RE DRAGGIN' US UP THERE.
UHM. SHARON N-NEEDS TO CHECK HER EMAILS AND . . .
PLACE SOME ORDERS.

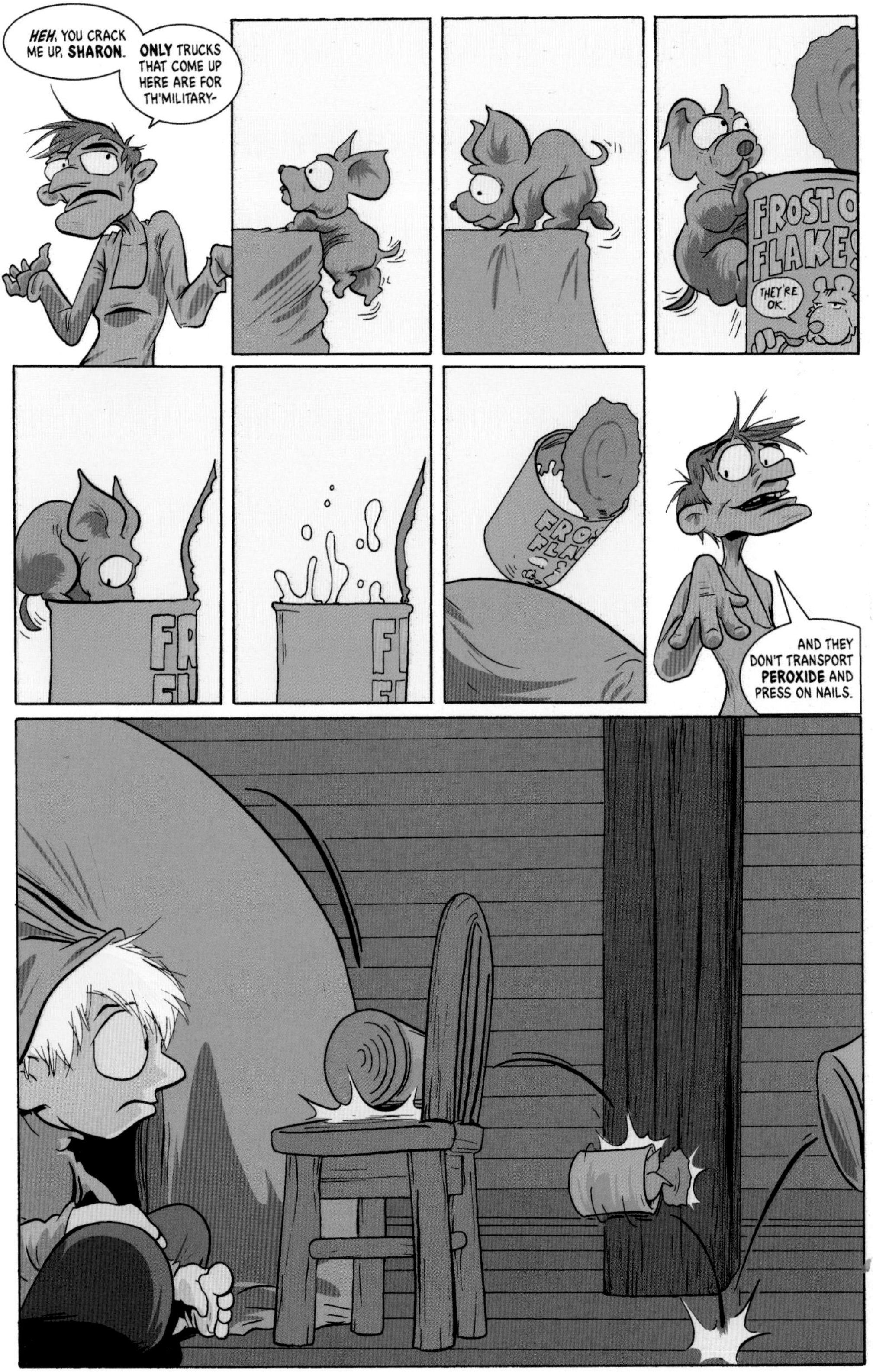

HEH, YOU CRACK ME UP, SHARON.
ONLY TRUCKS THAT COME UP HERE ARE FOR TH'MILITARY-
FROST O FLAKES
THEY'RE OK.
AND THEY DON'T TRANSPORT PEROXIDE AND PRESS ON NAILS.

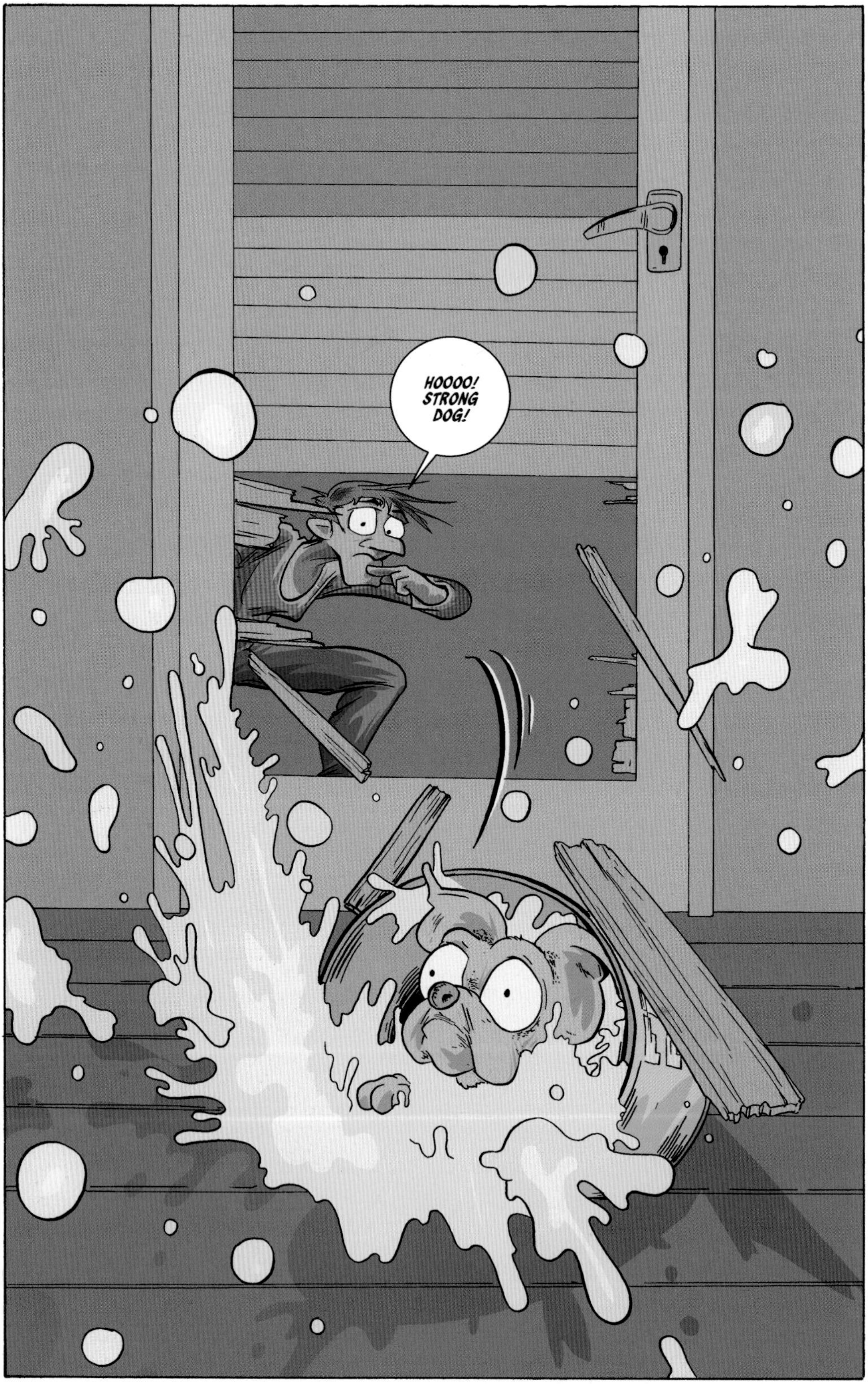
HOOOO! STRONG DOG!

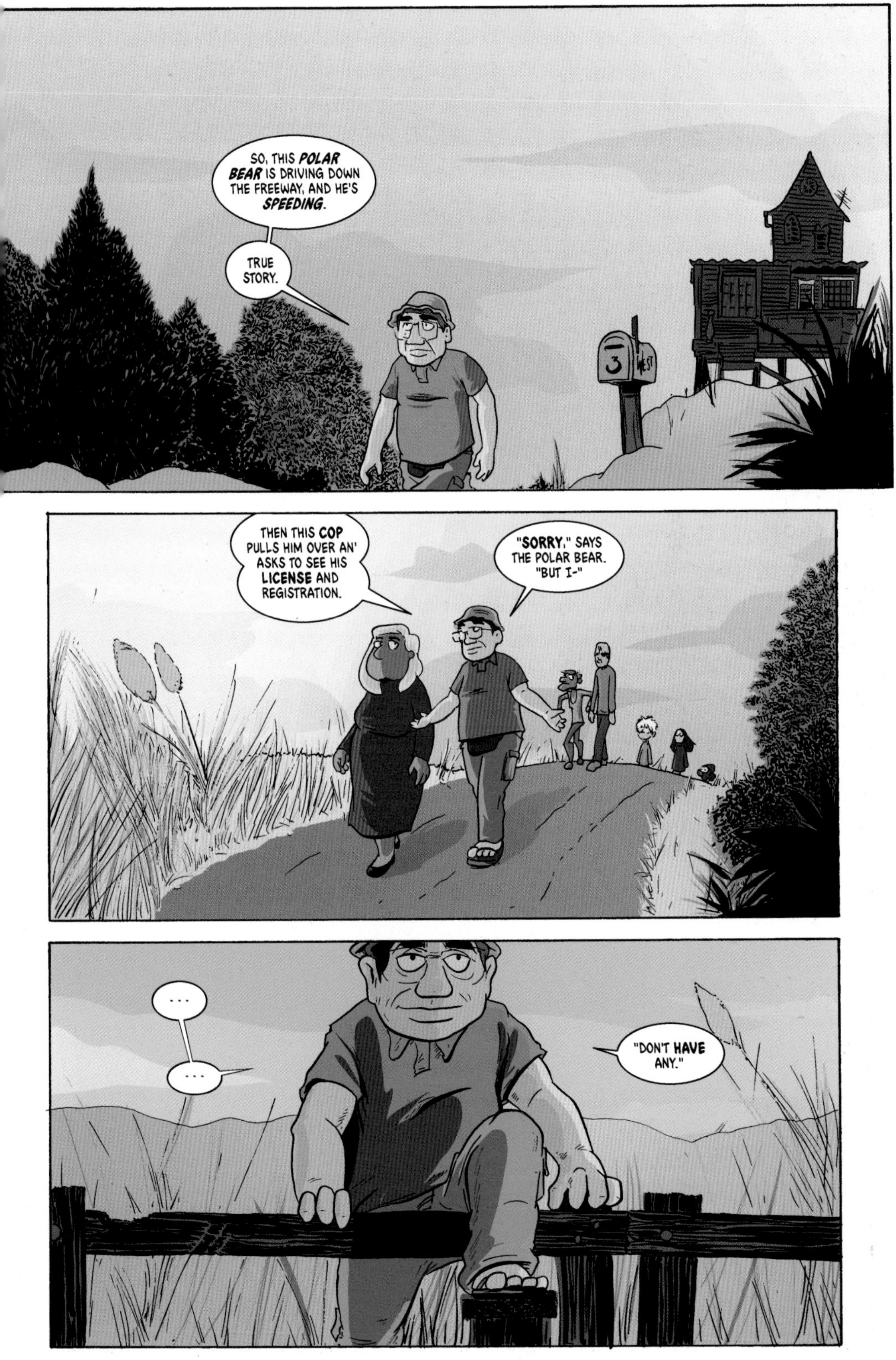
SO, THIS POLAR BEAR IS DRIVING DOWN THE FREEWAY, AND HE'S SPEEDING.
TRUE STORY.
3
WEST
THEN THIS COP PULLS HIM OVER AN' ASKS TO SEE HIS LICENSE AND REGISTRATION.
"SORRY," SAYS THE POLAR BEAR. "BUT I-"
...
...
"DON'T HAVE ANY."

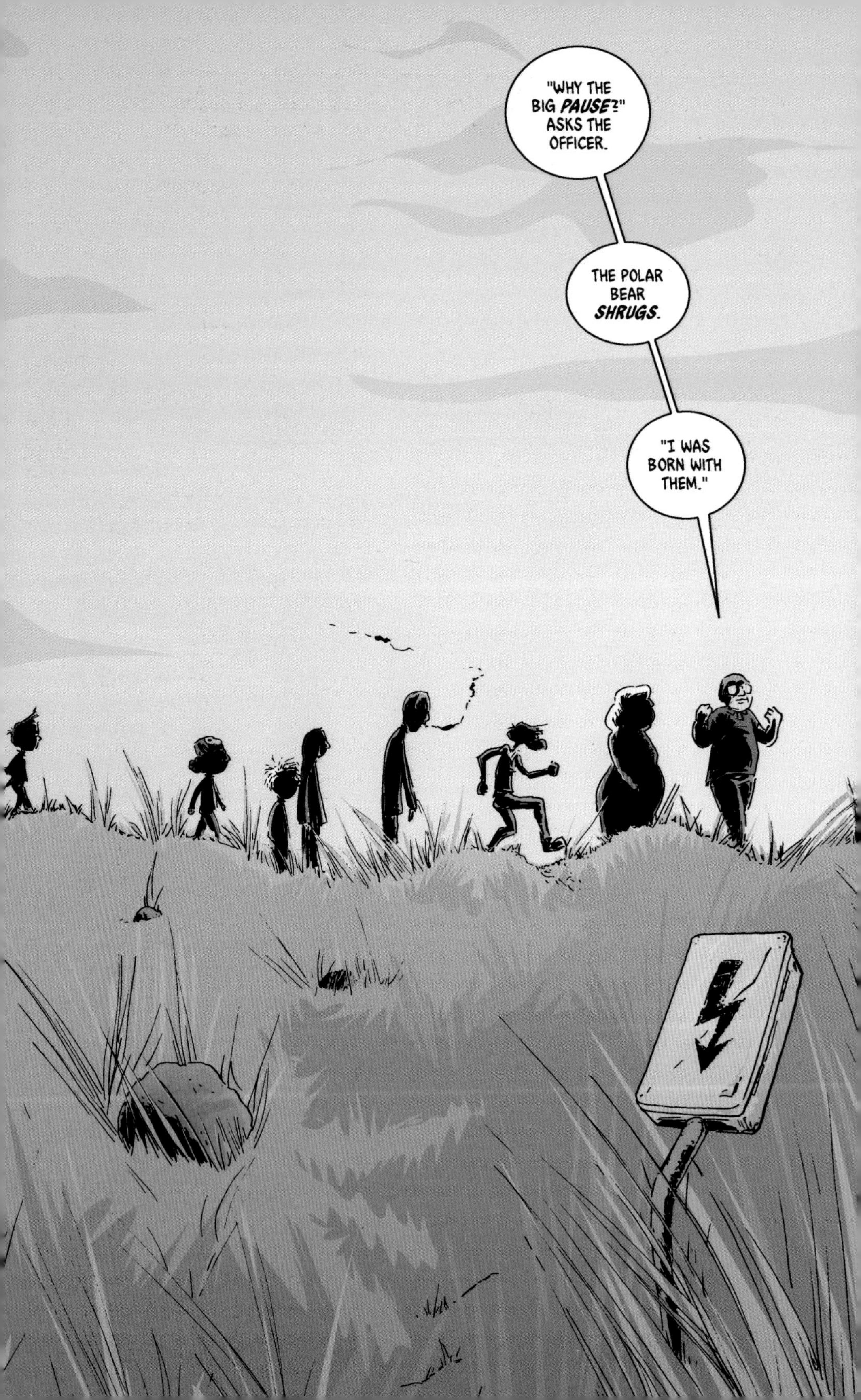
"WHY THE BIG PAUSE?" ASKS THE OFFICER.
THE POLAR BEAR SHRUGS.
"I WAS BORN WITH THEM."

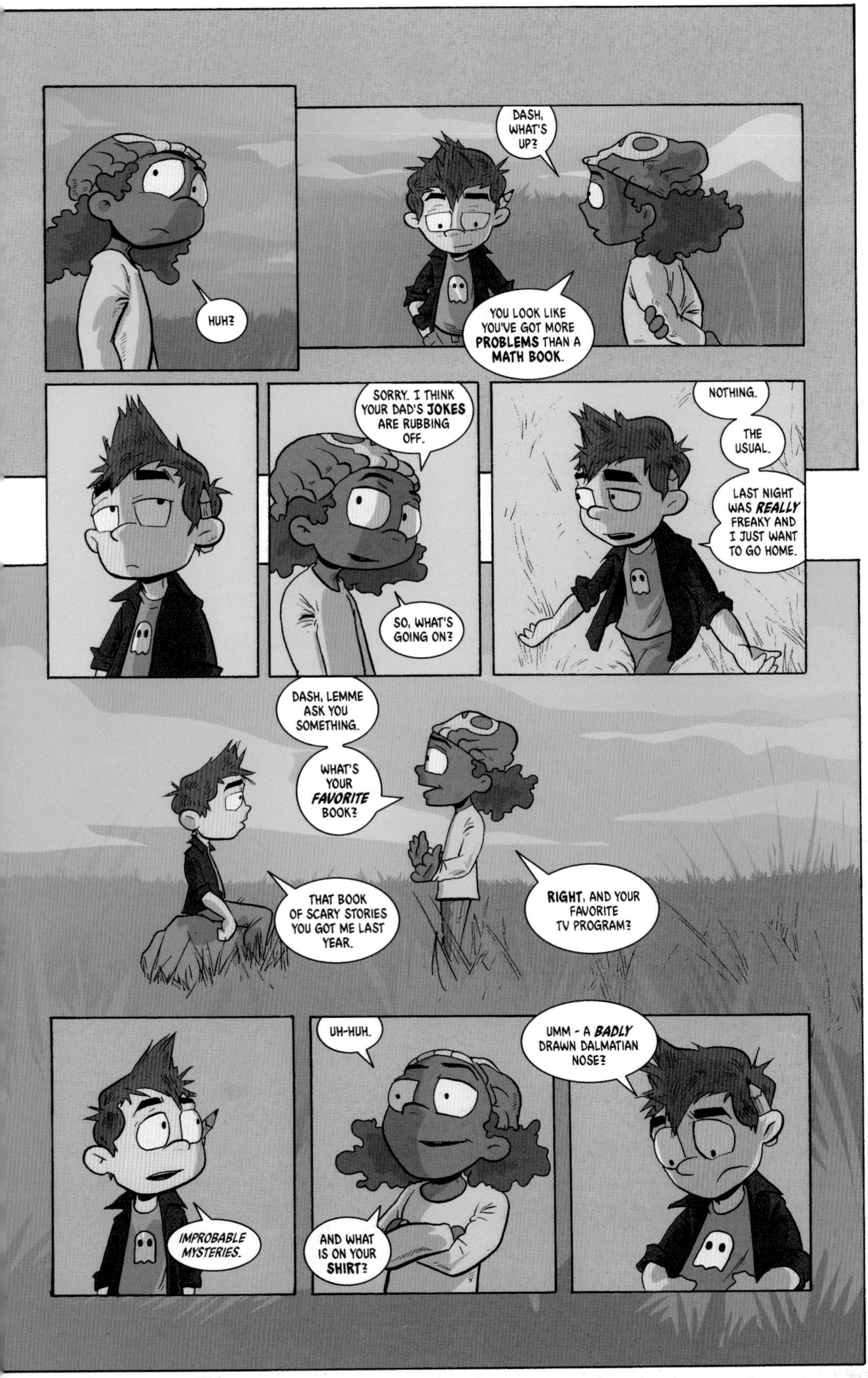
HUH?
DASH, WHAT'S UP?
YOU LOOK LIKE YOU'VE GOT MORE **PROBLEMS** THAN A **MATH BOOK**.
SORRY. I THINK YOUR DAD'S **JOKES** ARE RUBBING OFF.
SO, WHAT'S GOING ON?
NOTHING.
THE USUAL.
LAST NIGHT WAS ***REALLY*** FREAKY AND I JUST WANT TO GO HOME.
DASH, LEMME ASK YOU SOMETHING.
WHAT'S YOUR ***FAVORITE*** BOOK?
THAT BOOK OF SCARY STORIES YOU GOT ME LAST YEAR.
RIGHT, AND YOUR FAVORITE TV PROGRAM?
IMPROBABLE MYSTERIES.
UH-HUH.
AND WHAT IS ON YOUR **SHIRT**?
UMM - A ***BADLY*** DRAWN DALMATIAN NOSE?

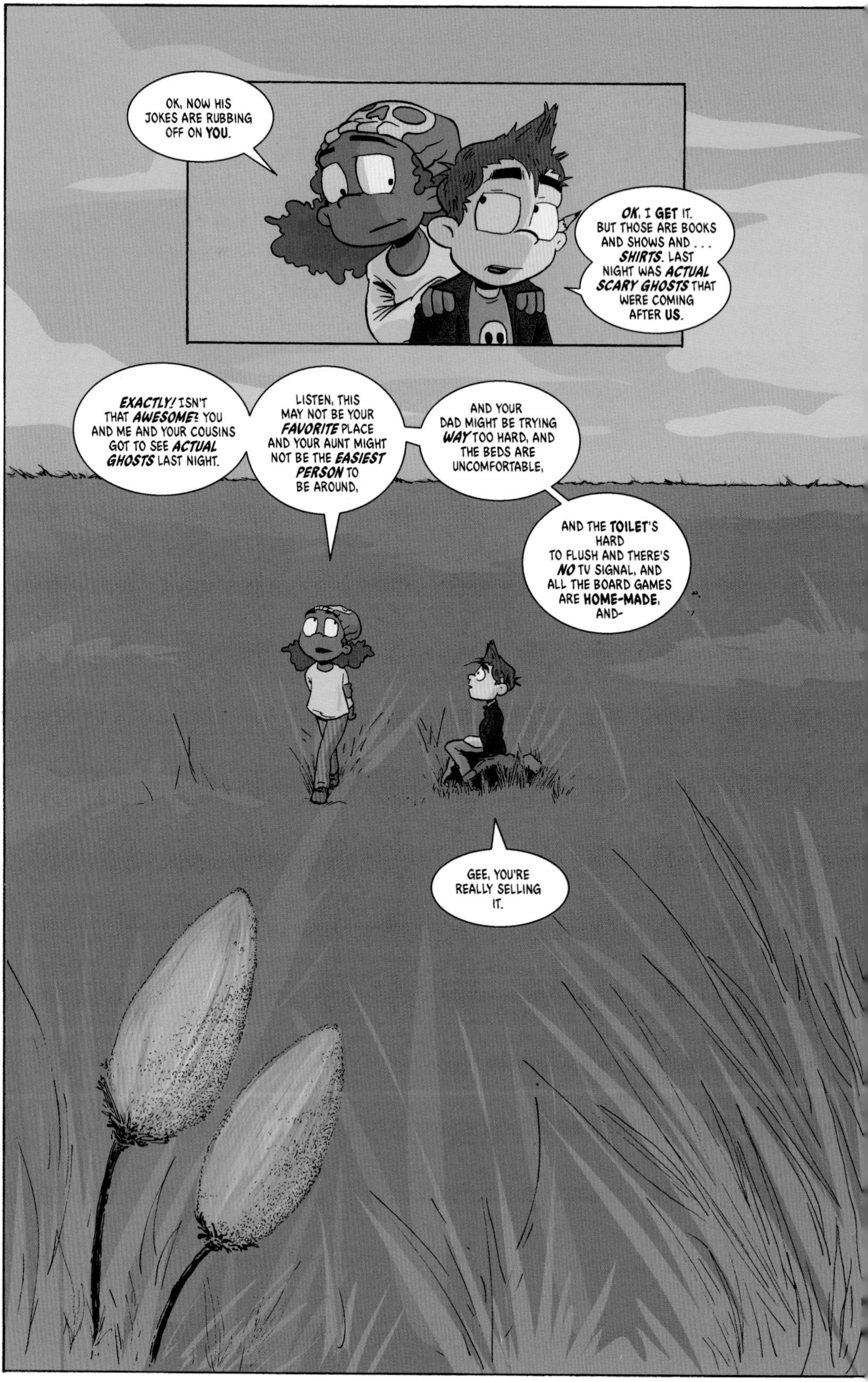
OK, NOW HIS JOKES ARE RUBBING OFF ON YOU.
OK, I GET IT. BUT THOSE ARE BOOKS AND SHOWS AND . . . SHIRTS. LAST NIGHT WAS ACTUAL SCARY GHOSTS THAT WERE COMING AFTER US.
EXACTLY! ISN'T THAT AWESOME? YOU AND ME AND YOUR COUSINS GOT TO SEE ACTUAL GHOSTS LAST NIGHT.
LISTEN, THIS MAY NOT BE YOUR FAVORITE PLACE AND YOUR AUNT MIGHT NOT BE THE EASIEST PERSON TO BE AROUND,
AND YOUR DAD MIGHT BE TRYING WAY TOO HARD, AND THE BEDS ARE UNCOMFORTABLE,
AND THE TOILET'S HARD TO FLUSH AND THERE'S NO TV SIGNAL, AND ALL THE BOARD GAMES ARE HOME-MADE, AND-
GEE, YOU'RE REALLY SELLING IT.

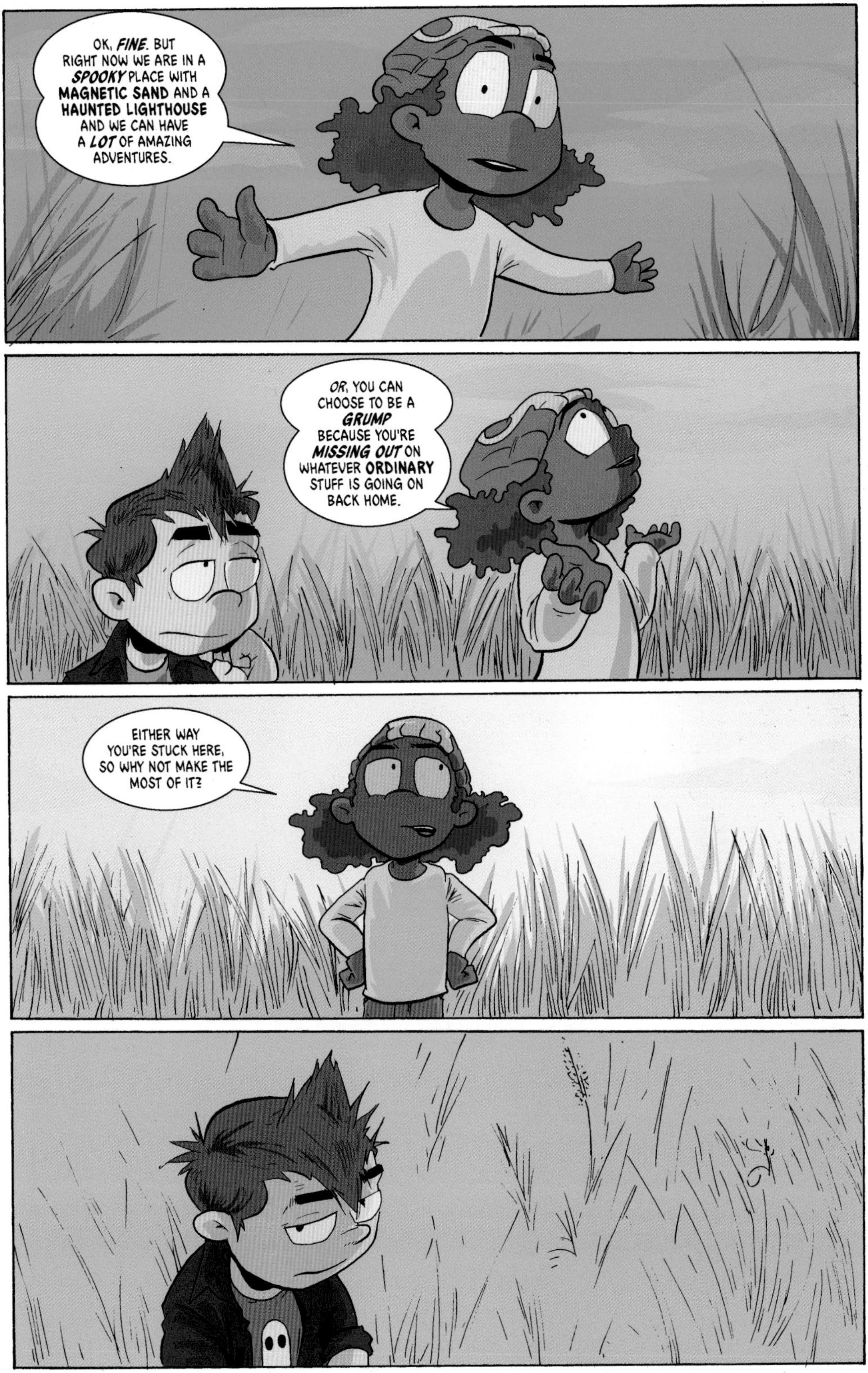
OK, *FINE*. BUT RIGHT NOW WE ARE IN A *SPOOKY* PLACE WITH **MAGNETIC SAND** AND A **HAUNTED LIGHTHOUSE** AND WE CAN HAVE A *LOT* OF AMAZING ADVENTURES.
OR, YOU CAN CHOOSE TO BE A ***GRUMP*** BECAUSE YOU'RE ***MISSING OUT*** ON WHATEVER **ORDINARY** STUFF IS GOING ON BACK HOME.
EITHER WAY YOU'RE STUCK HERE, SO WHY NOT MAKE THE MOST OF IT?

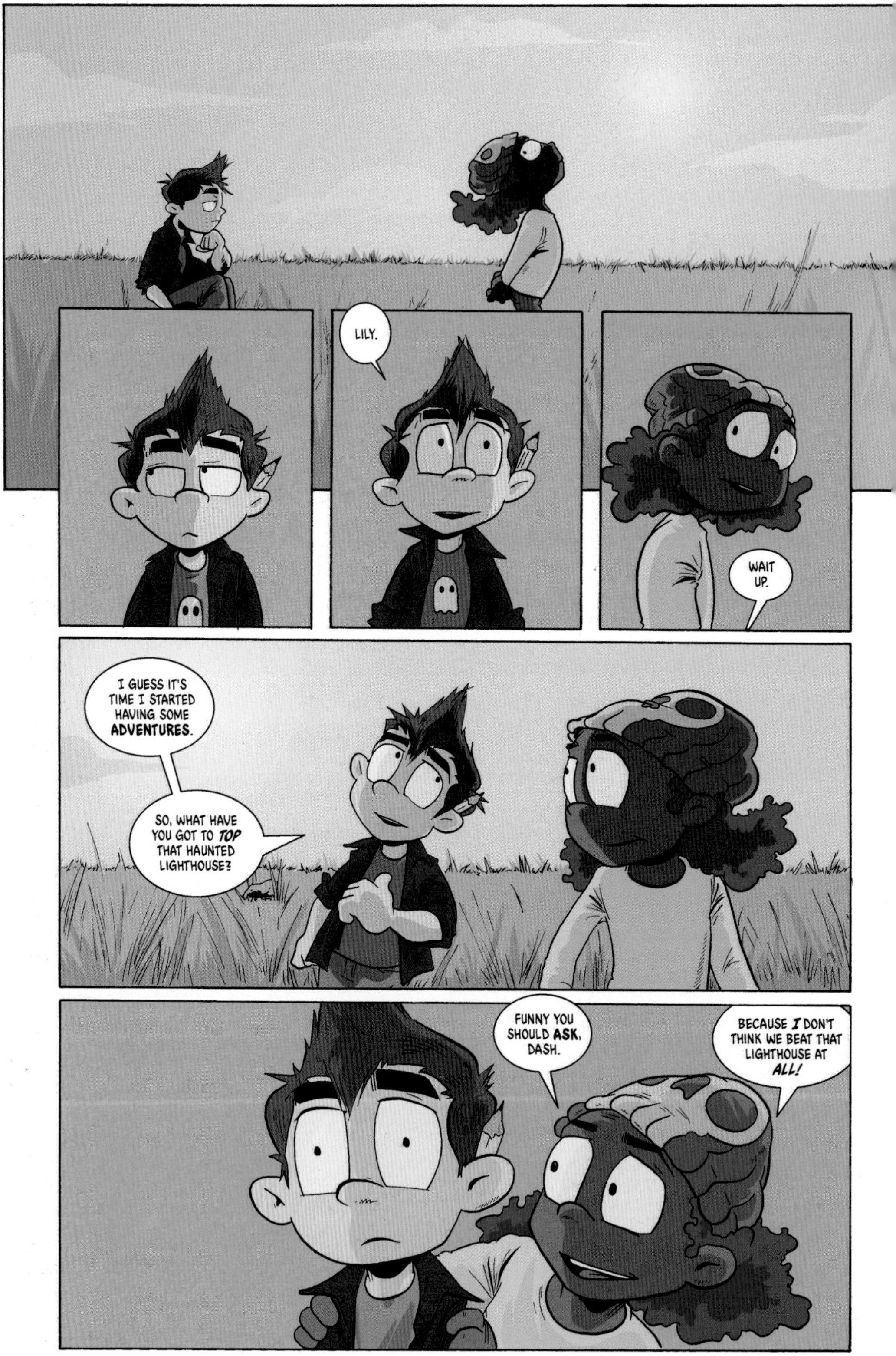
LILY.
WAIT UP.
I GUESS IT'S TIME I STARTED HAVING SOME **ADVENTURES**.
SO, WHAT HAVE YOU GOT TO ***TOP*** THAT HAUNTED LIGHTHOUSE?
FUNNY YOU SHOULD **ASK**, DASH.
BECAUSE ***I*** DON'T THINK WE BEAT THAT LIGHTHOUSE AT ***ALL!***

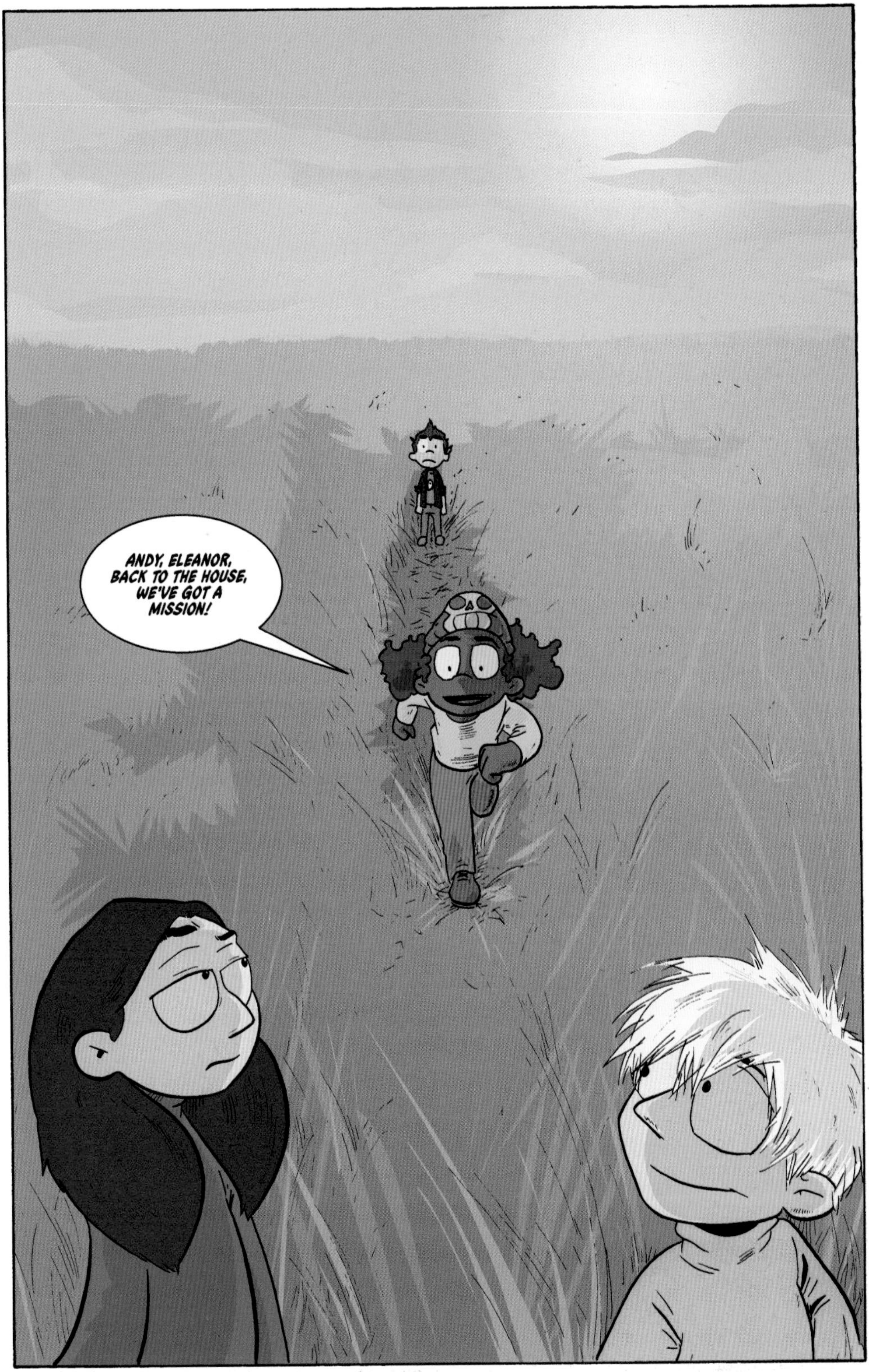
ANDY, ELEANOR, BACK TO THE HOUSE, WE'VE GOT A MISSION!

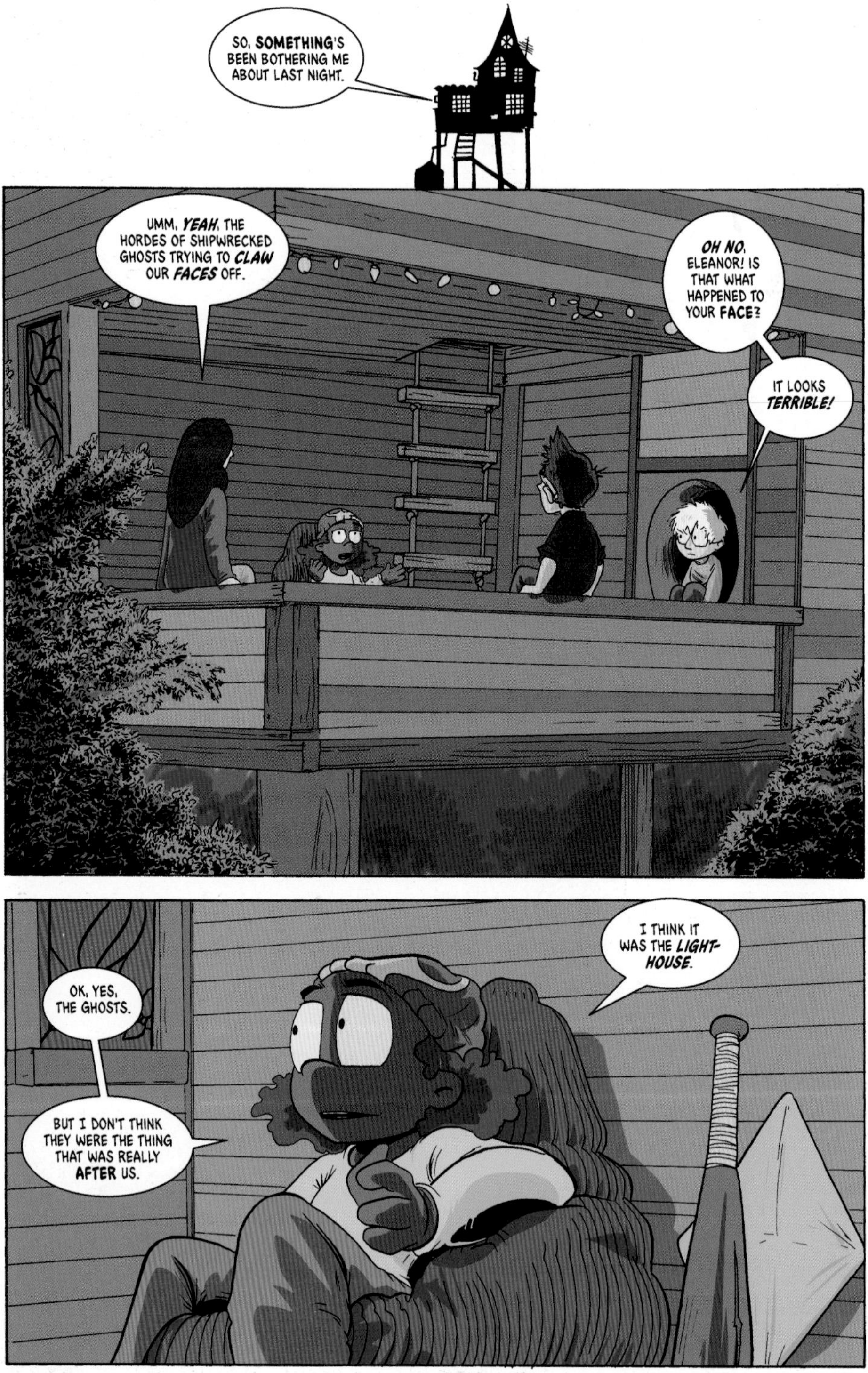
SO, SOMETHING'S BEEN BOTHERING ME ABOUT LAST NIGHT.
UMM, YEAH, THE HORDES OF SHIPWRECKED GHOSTS TRYING TO CLAW OUR FACES OFF.
OH NO, ELEANOR! IS THAT WHAT HAPPENED TO YOUR FACE?
IT LOOKS TERRIBLE!
OK, YES, THE GHOSTS.
BUT I DON'T THINK THEY WERE THE THING THAT WAS REALLY AFTER US.
I THINK IT WAS THE LIGHT-HOUSE.

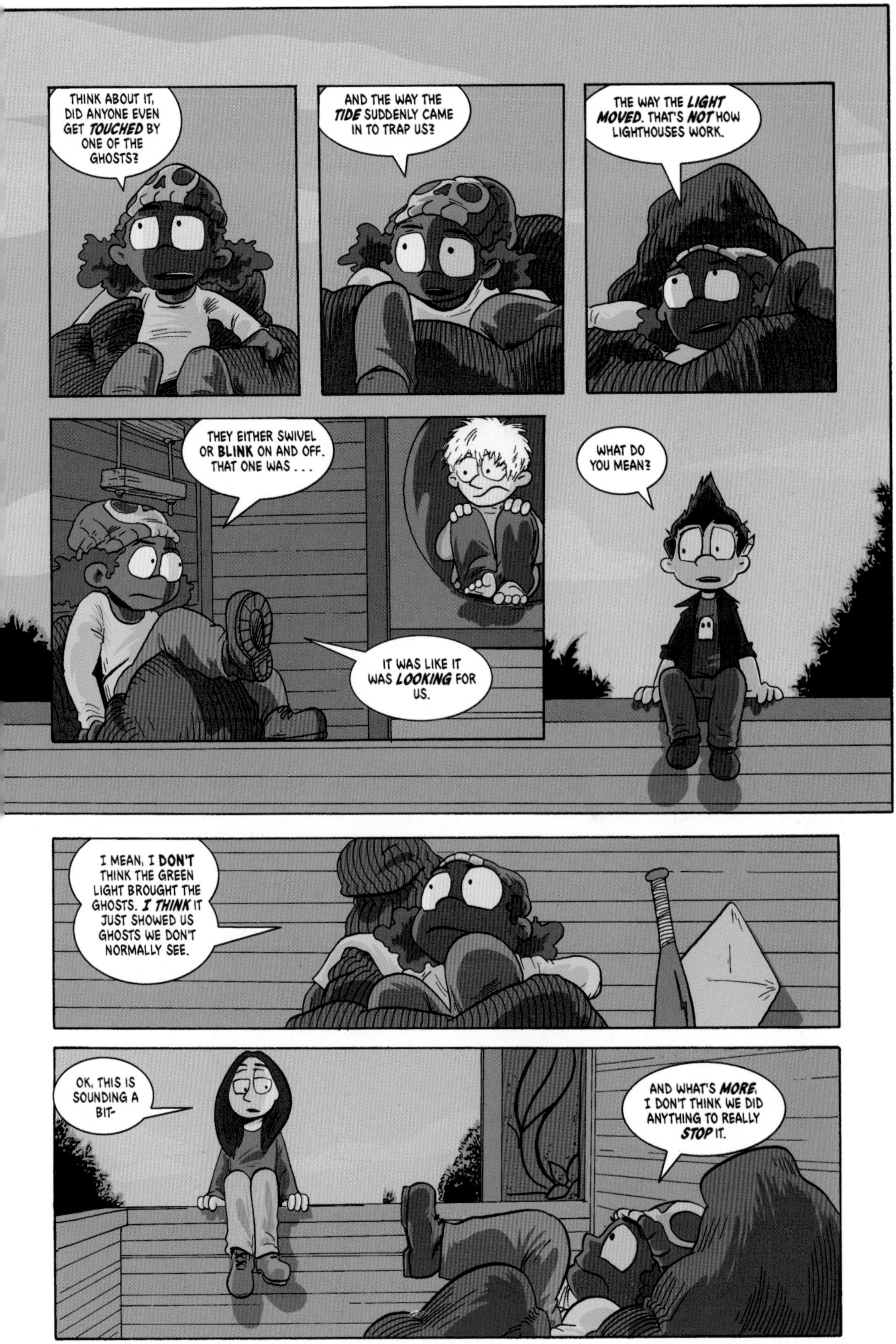
THINK ABOUT IT, DID ANYONE EVEN GET TOUCHED BY ONE OF THE GHOSTS?
AND THE WAY THE TIDE SUDDENLY CAME IN TO TRAP US?
THE WAY THE LIGHT MOVED. THAT'S NOT HOW LIGHTHOUSES WORK.
THEY EITHER SWIVEL OR BLINK ON AND OFF. THAT ONE WAS . . .
WHAT DO YOU MEAN?
IT WAS LIKE IT WAS LOOKING FOR US.
I MEAN, I DON'T THINK THE GREEN LIGHT BROUGHT THE GHOSTS. I THINK IT JUST SHOWED US GHOSTS WE DON'T NORMALLY SEE.
OK, THIS IS SOUNDING A BIT-
AND WHAT'S MORE, I DON'T THINK WE DID ANYTHING TO REALLY STOP IT.

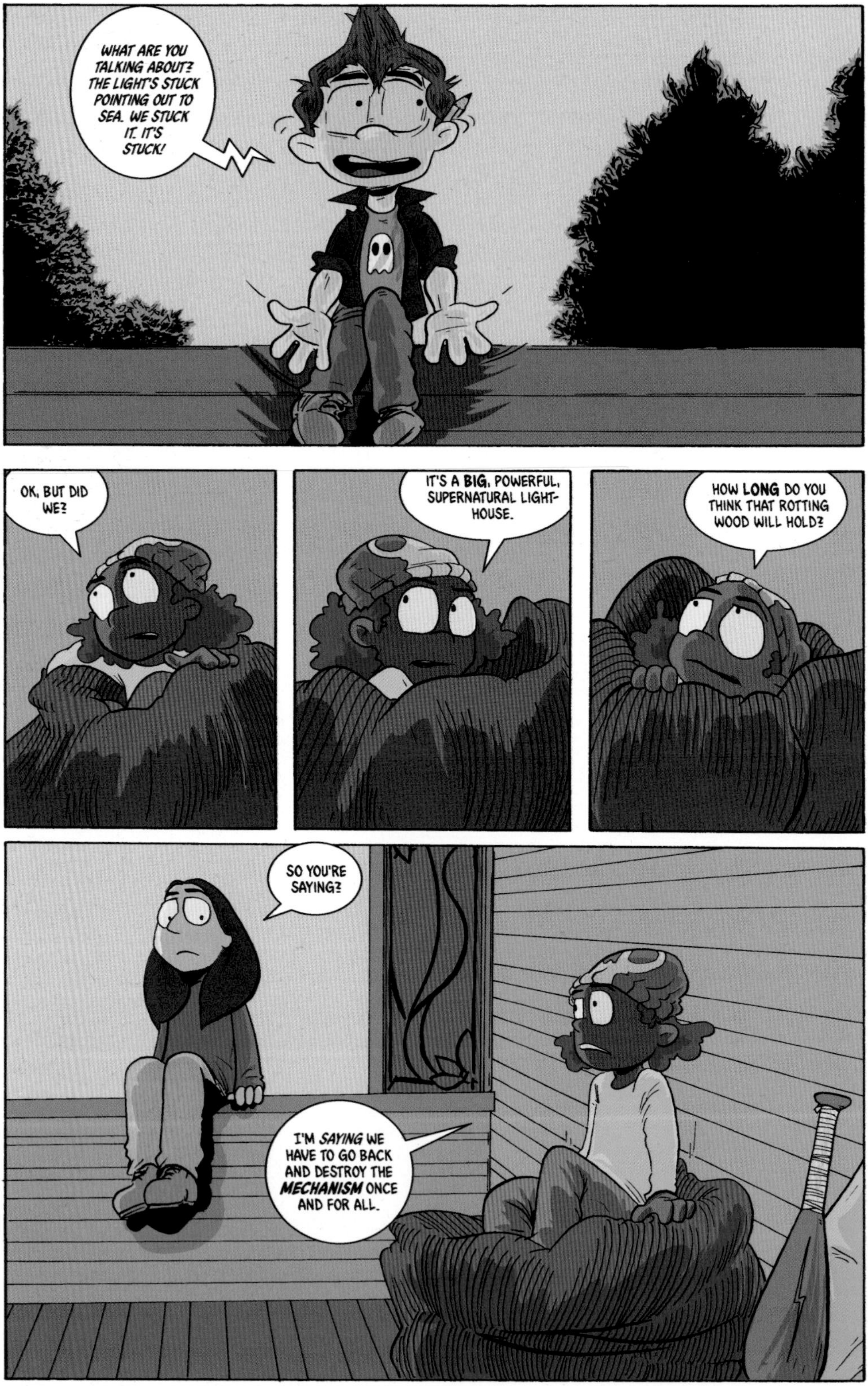
WHAT ARE YOU TALKING ABOUT? THE LIGHT'S STUCK POINTING OUT TO SEA. WE STUCK IT. IT'S STUCK!
OK, BUT DID WE?
IT'S A **BIG**, POWERFUL, SUPERNATURAL LIGHT-HOUSE.
HOW **LONG** DO YOU THINK THAT ROTTING WOOD WILL HOLD?
SO YOU'RE SAYING?
I'M *SAYING* WE HAVE TO GO BACK AND DESTROY THE ***MECHANISM*** ONCE AND FOR ALL.

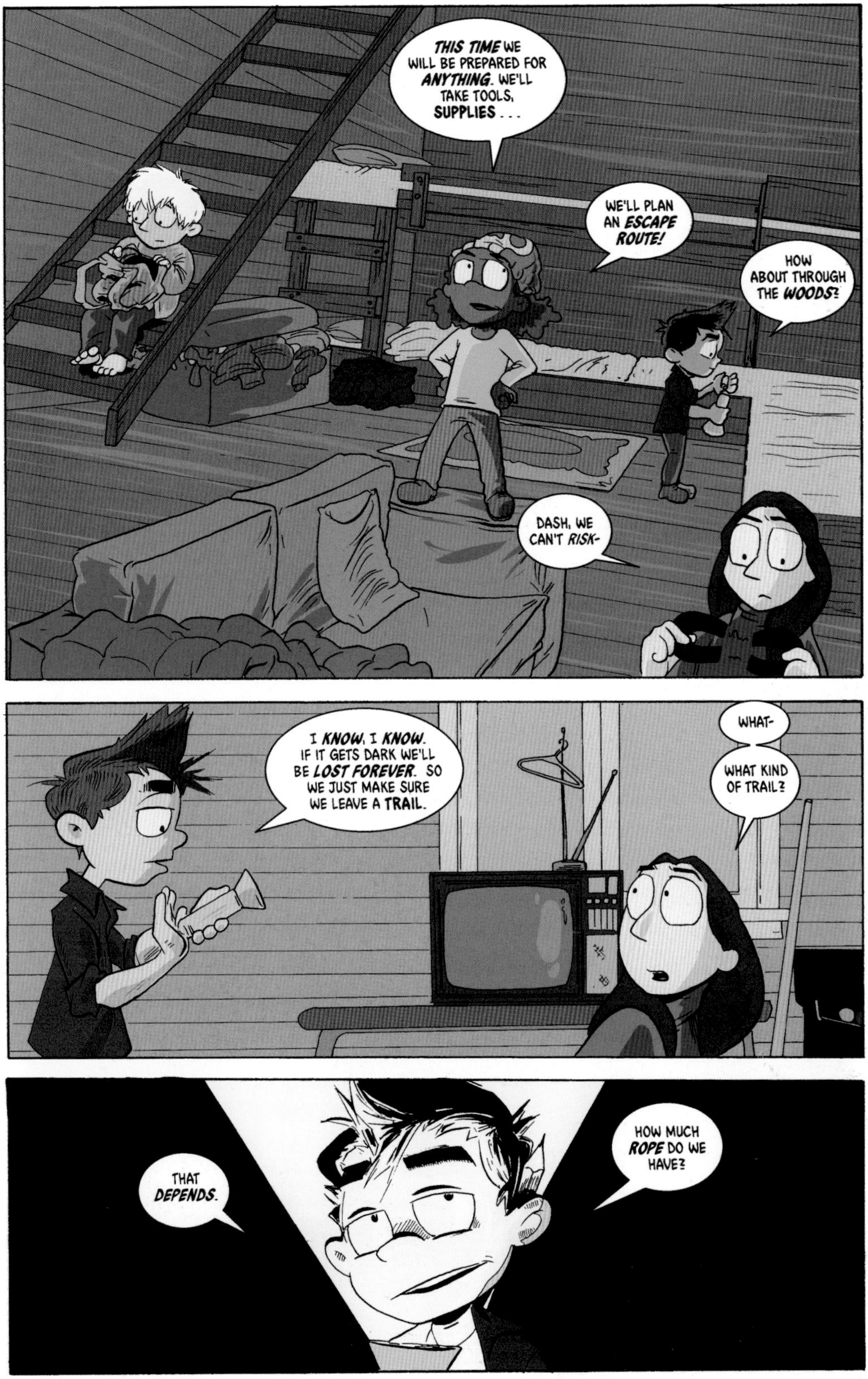
THIS TIME WE WILL BE PREPARED FOR ANYTHING. WE'LL TAKE TOOLS, SUPPLIES . . .
WE'LL PLAN AN ESCAPE ROUTE!
HOW ABOUT THROUGH THE WOODS?
DASH, WE CAN'T RISK-
I KNOW, I KNOW. IF IT GETS DARK WE'LL BE LOST FOREVER. SO WE JUST MAKE SURE WE LEAVE A TRAIL.
WHAT-
WHAT KIND OF TRAIL?
THAT DEPENDS.
HOW MUCH ROPE DO WE HAVE?

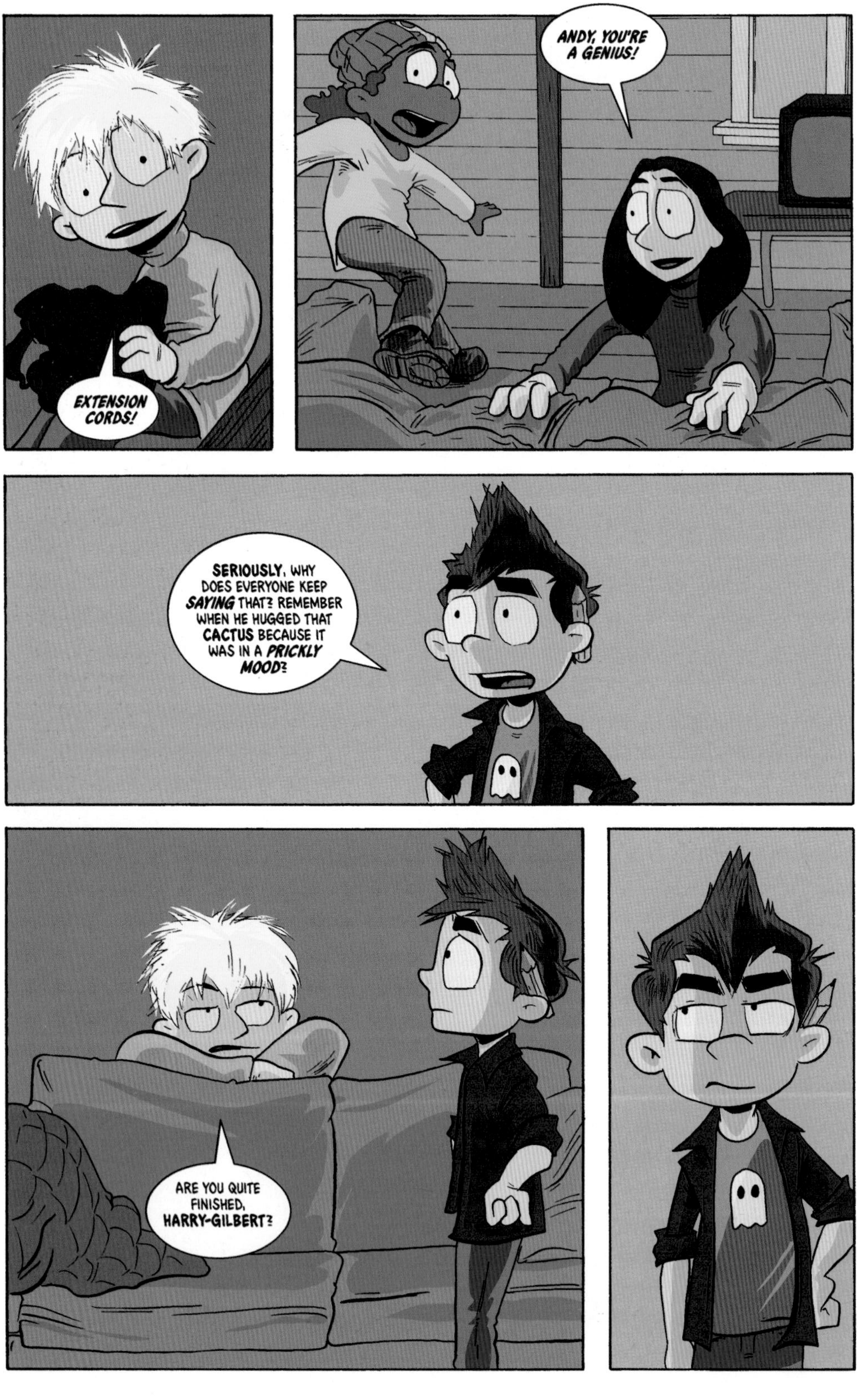
EXTENSION CORDS!
ANDY, YOU'RE A GENIUS!
SERIOUSLY, WHY DOES EVERYONE KEEP SAYING THAT? REMEMBER WHEN HE HUGGED THAT CACTUS BECAUSE IT WAS IN A PRICKLY MOOD?
ARE YOU QUITE FINISHED, HARRY-GILBERT?

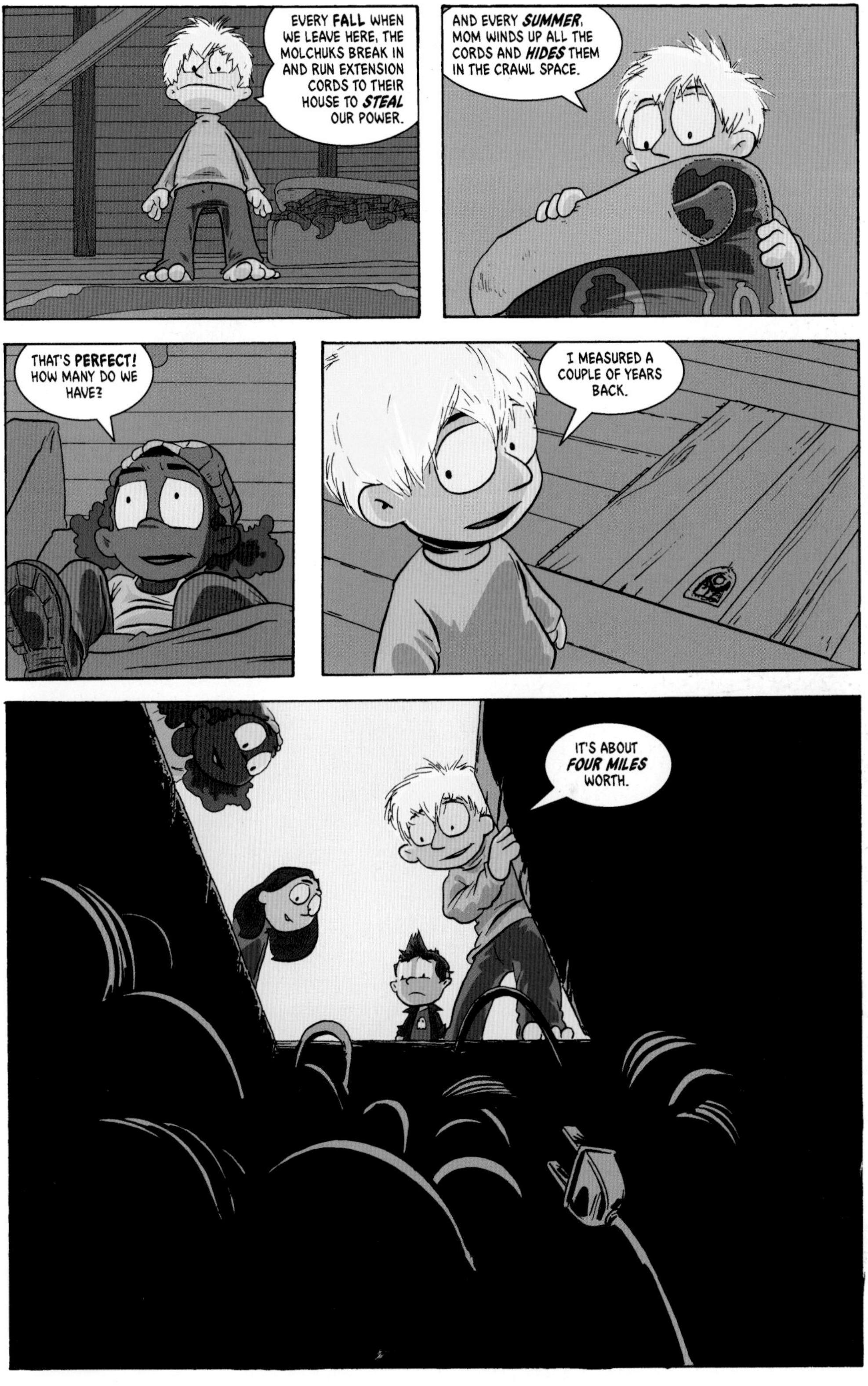
EVERY FALL WHEN WE LEAVE HERE, THE MOLCHUKS BREAK IN AND RUN EXTENSION CORDS TO THEIR HOUSE TO STEAL OUR POWER.
AND EVERY SUMMER, MOM WINDS UP ALL THE CORDS AND HIDES THEM IN THE CRAWL SPACE.
THAT'S PERFECT! HOW MANY DO WE HAVE?
I MEASURED A COUPLE OF YEARS BACK.
IT'S ABOUT FOUR MILES WORTH.

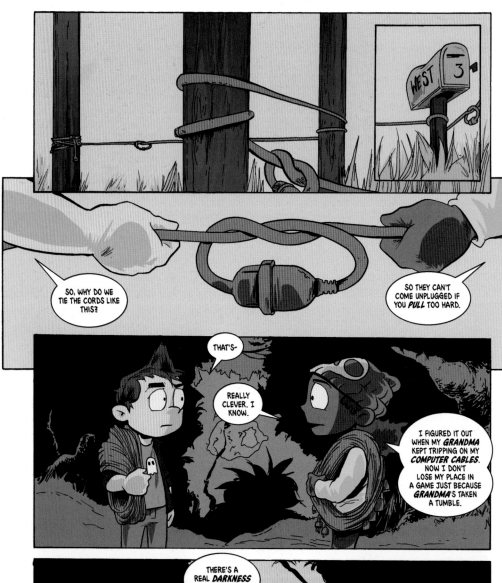

SO, WHY DO WE TIE THE CORDS LIKE THIS?

SO THEY CAN'T COME UNPLUGGED IF YOU *PULL* TOO HARD.

THAT'S-

REALLY CLEVER. I KNOW.

I FIGURED IT OUT WHEN MY *GRANDMA* KEPT TRIPPING ON MY *COMPUTER CABLES*. NOW I DON'T LOSE MY PLACE IN A GAME JUST BECAUSE *GRANDMA*'S TAKEN A TUMBLE.

THERE'S A REAL *DARKNESS* TO YOU, LILY.

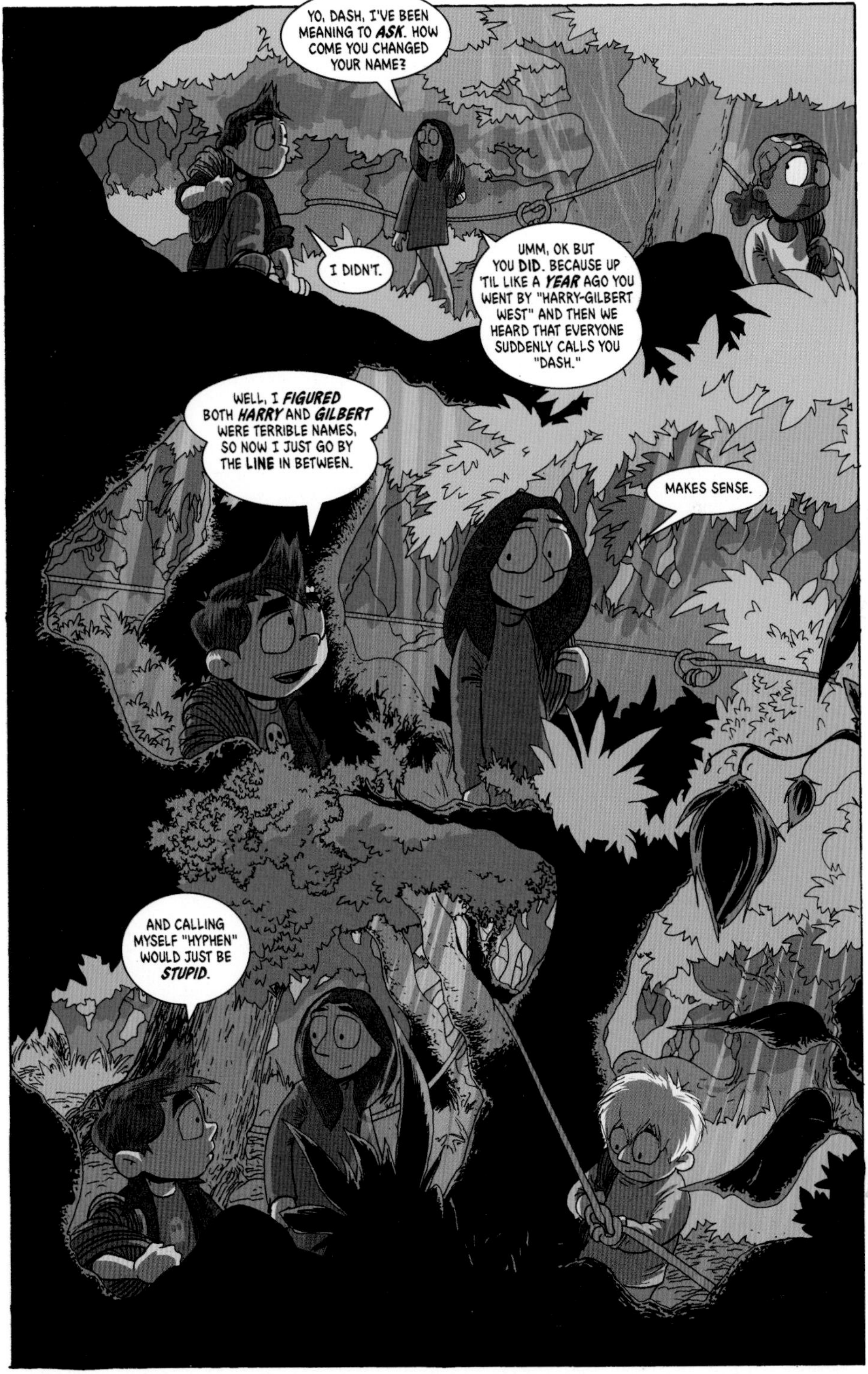
YO, DASH, I'VE BEEN MEANING TO ASK. HOW COME YOU CHANGED YOUR NAME?
I DIDN'T.
UMM, OK BUT YOU DID. BECAUSE UP 'TIL LIKE A YEAR AGO YOU WENT BY "HARRY-GILBERT WEST" AND THEN WE HEARD THAT EVERYONE SUDDENLY CALLS YOU "DASH."
WELL, I FIGURED BOTH HARRY AND GILBERT WERE TERRIBLE NAMES, SO NOW I JUST GO BY THE LINE IN BETWEEN.
MAKES SENSE.
AND CALLING MYSELF "HYPHEN" WOULD JUST BE STUPID.

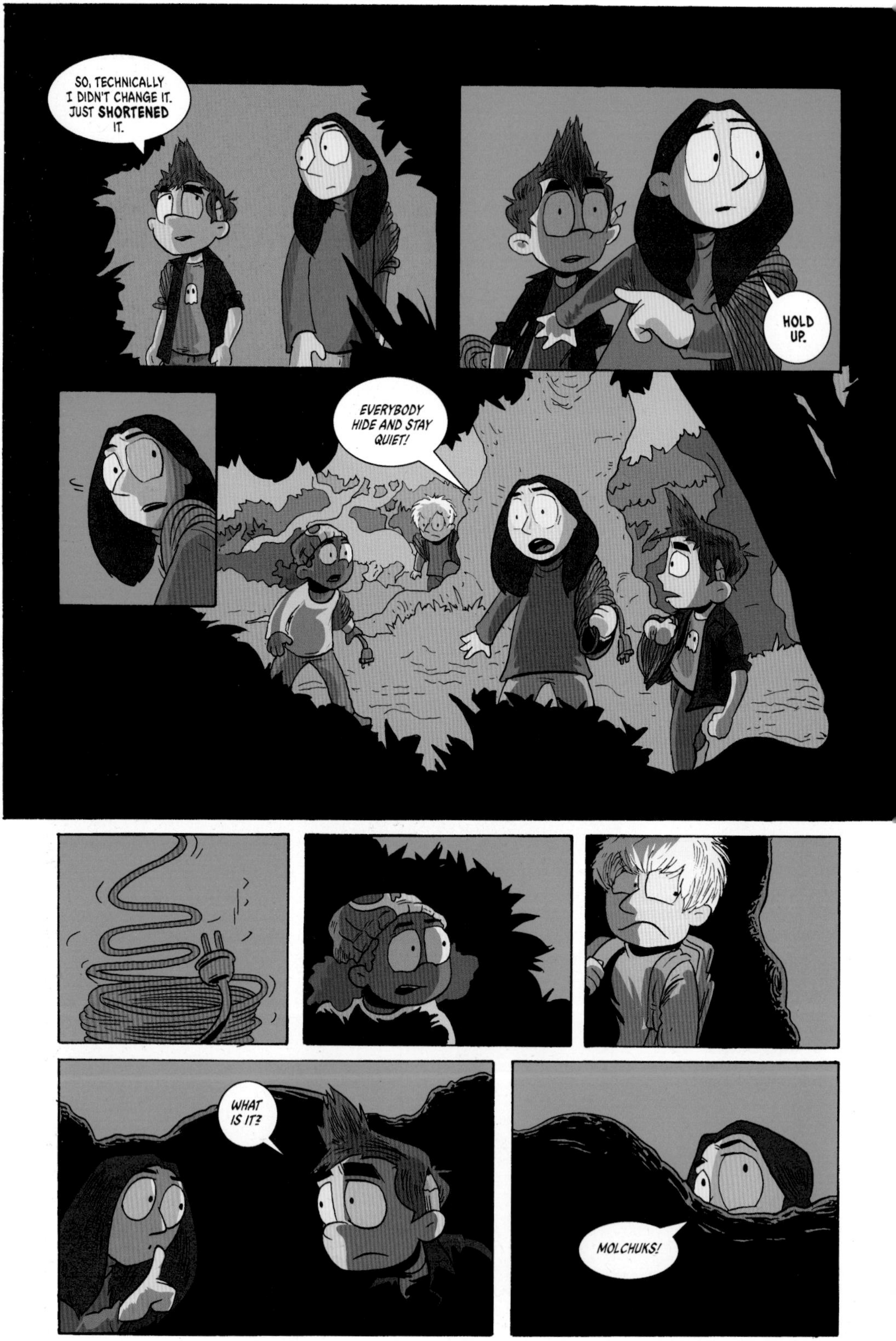
SO, TECHNICALLY I DIDN'T CHANGE IT. JUST SHORTENED IT.
HOLD UP.
EVERYBODY HIDE AND STAY QUIET!
WHAT IS IT?
MOLCHUKS!

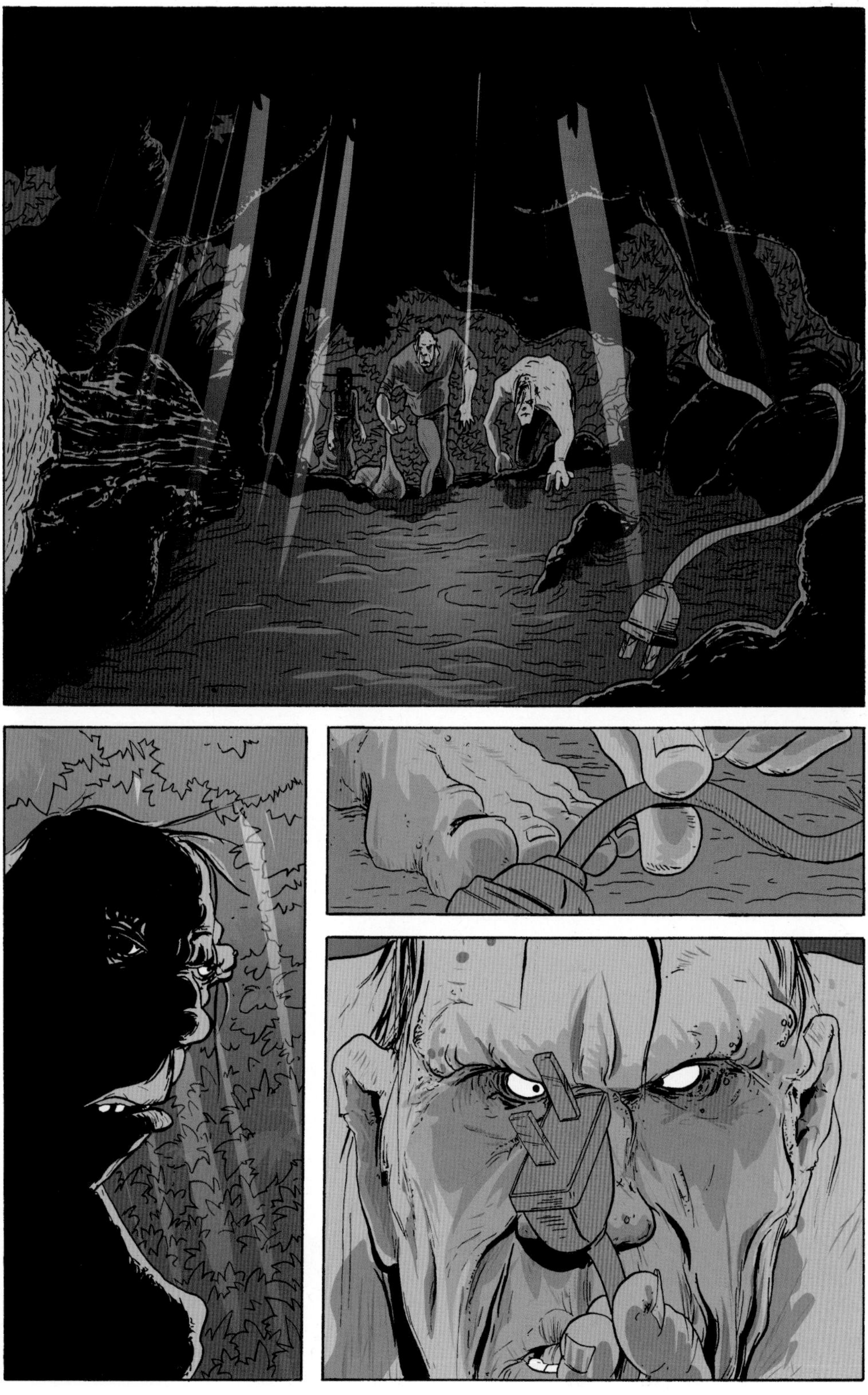

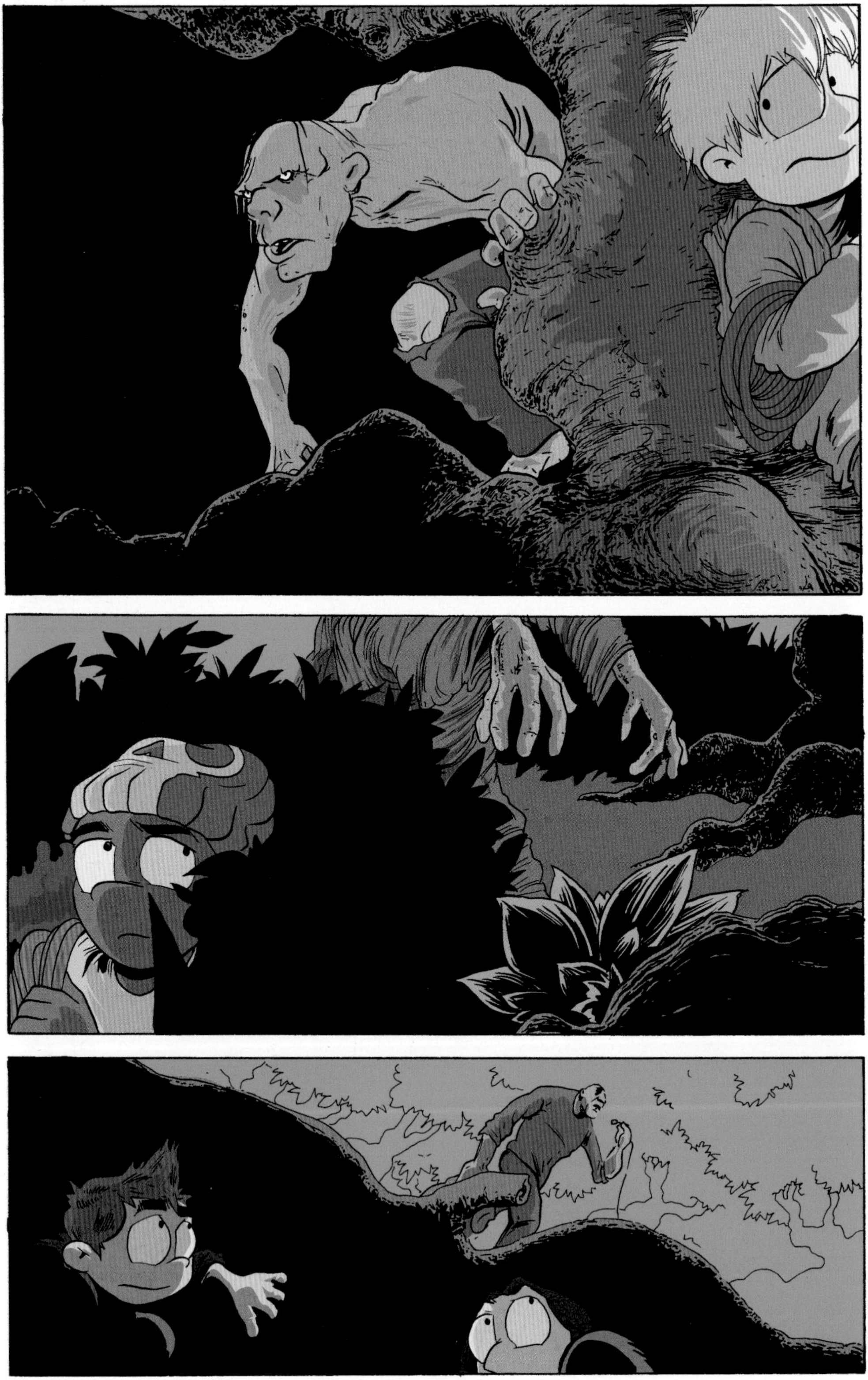

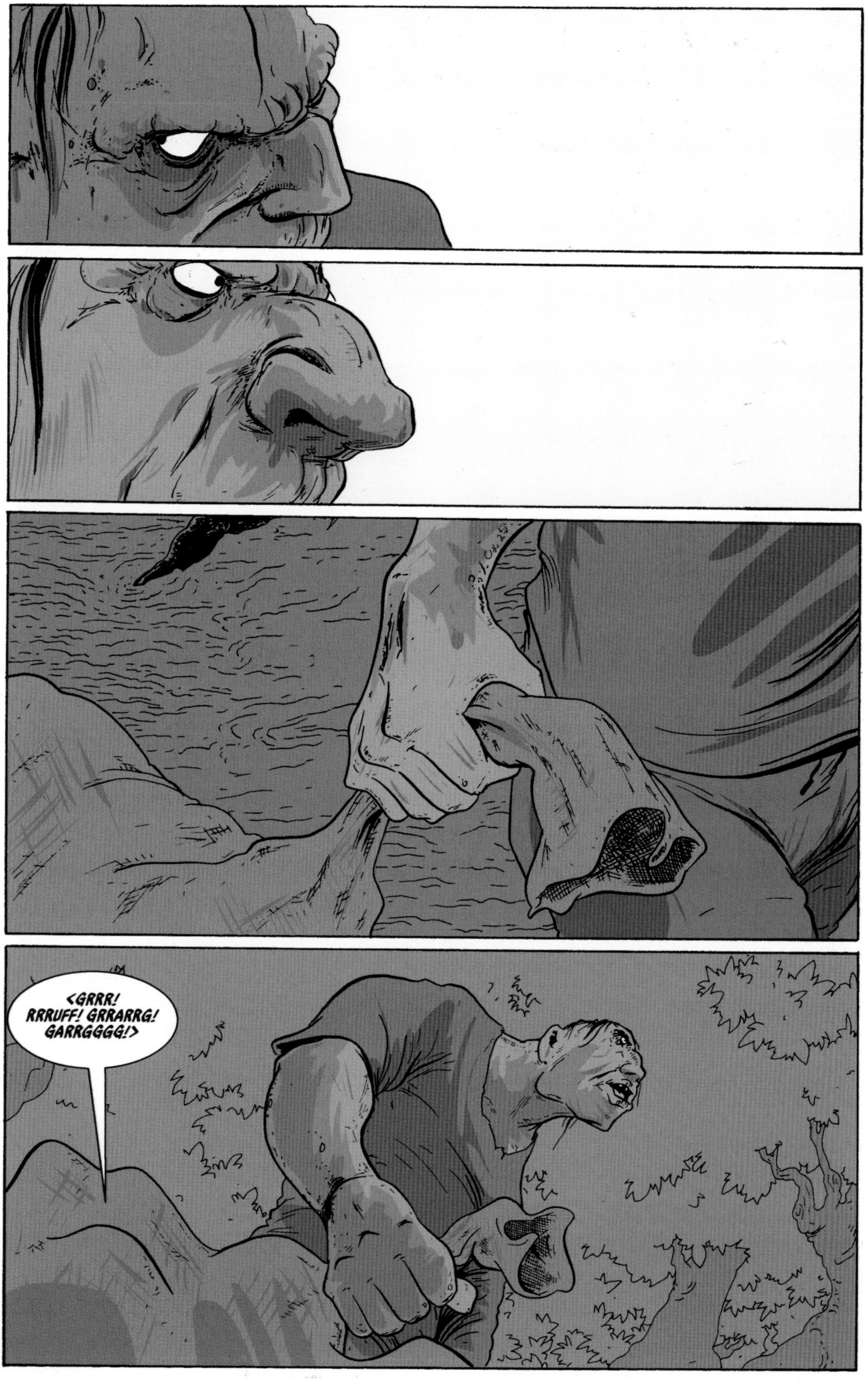
<GRRR! RRRUFF! GRRARRG! GARRGGGG!>

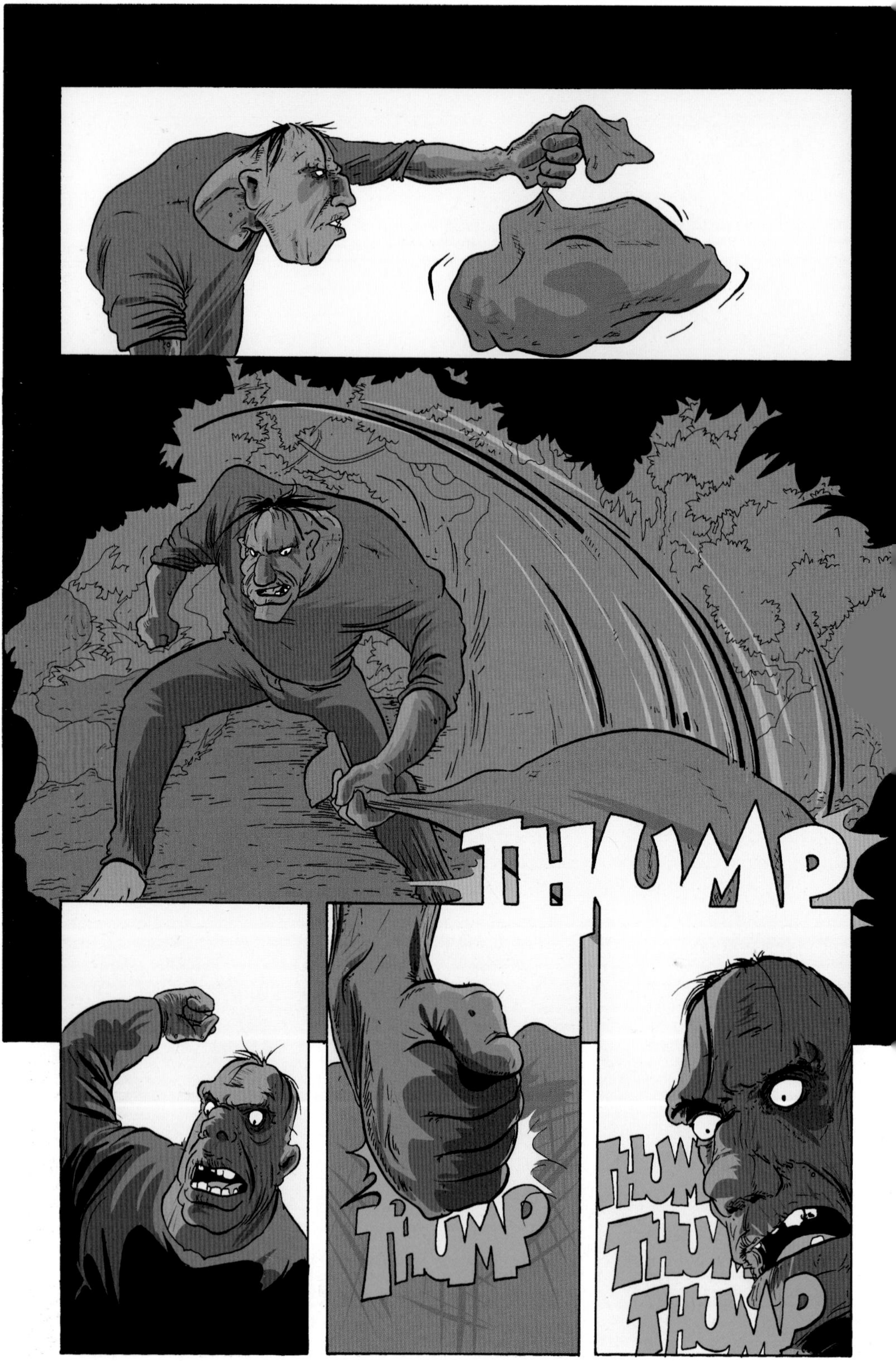
THUMP
THUMP
THUM
THUM
THUMP

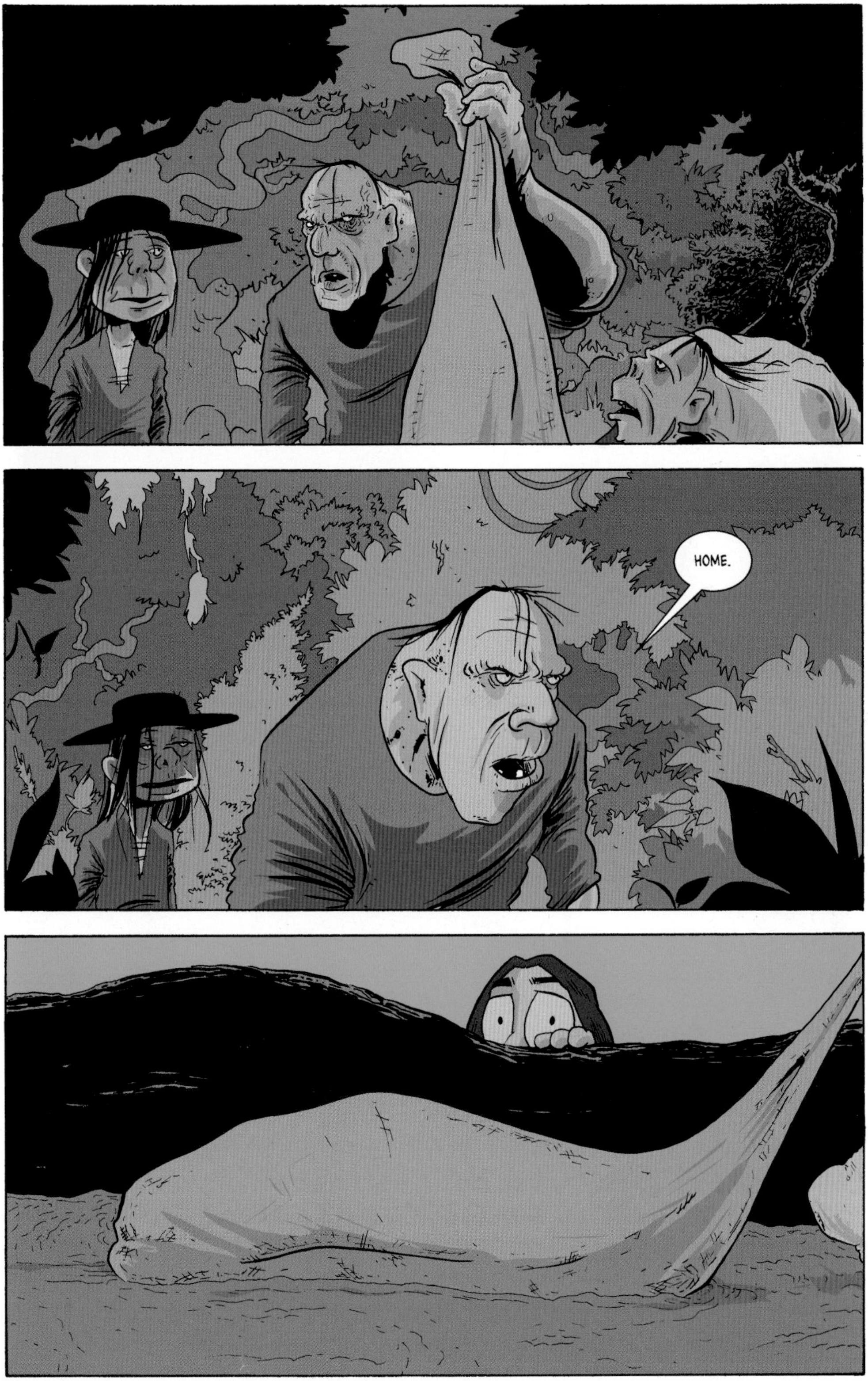
HOME.

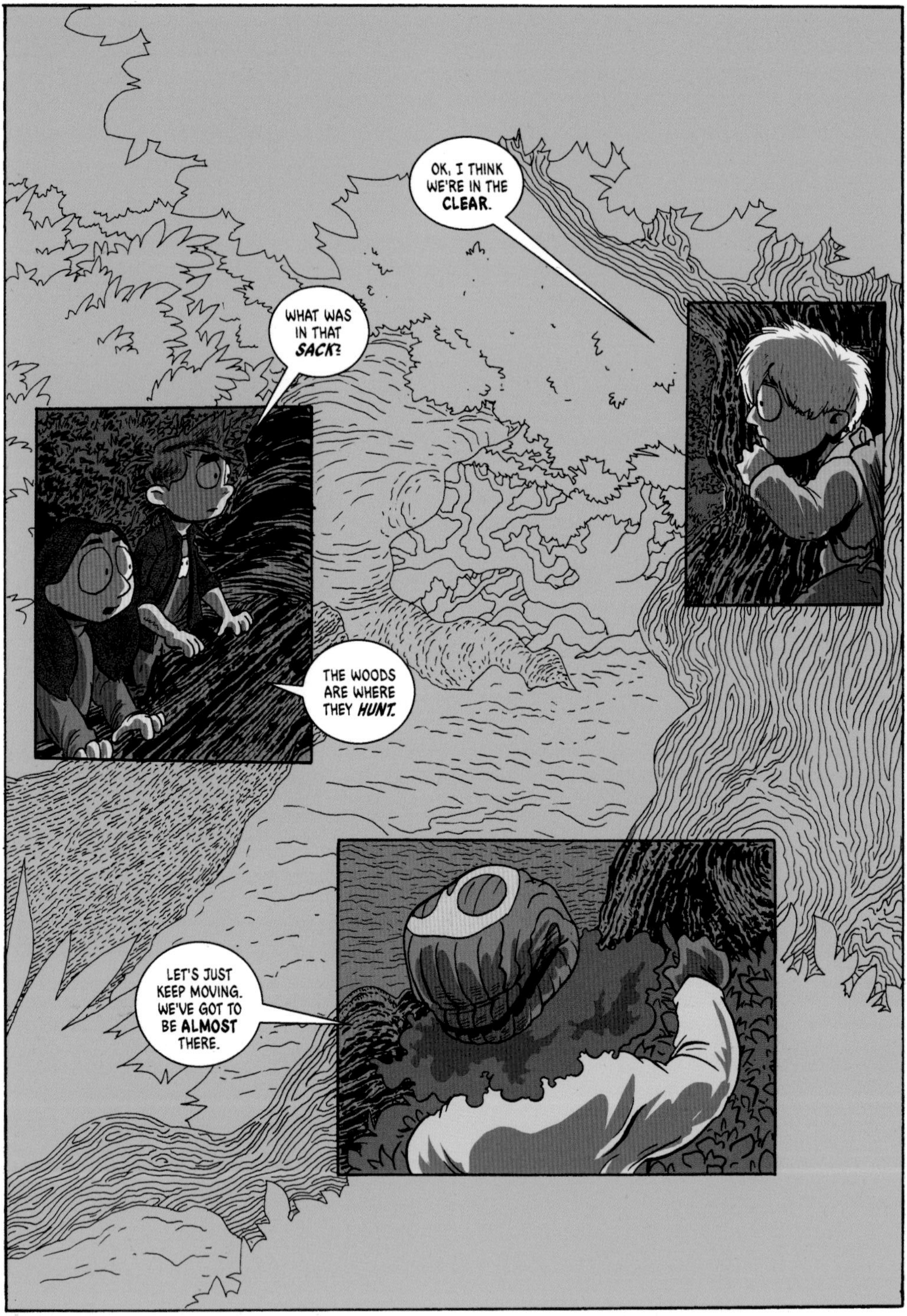
OK, I THINK WE'RE IN THE CLEAR.
WHAT WAS IN THAT SACK?
THE WOODS ARE WHERE THEY HUNT.
LET'S JUST KEEP MOVING. WE'VE GOT TO BE ALMOST THERE.

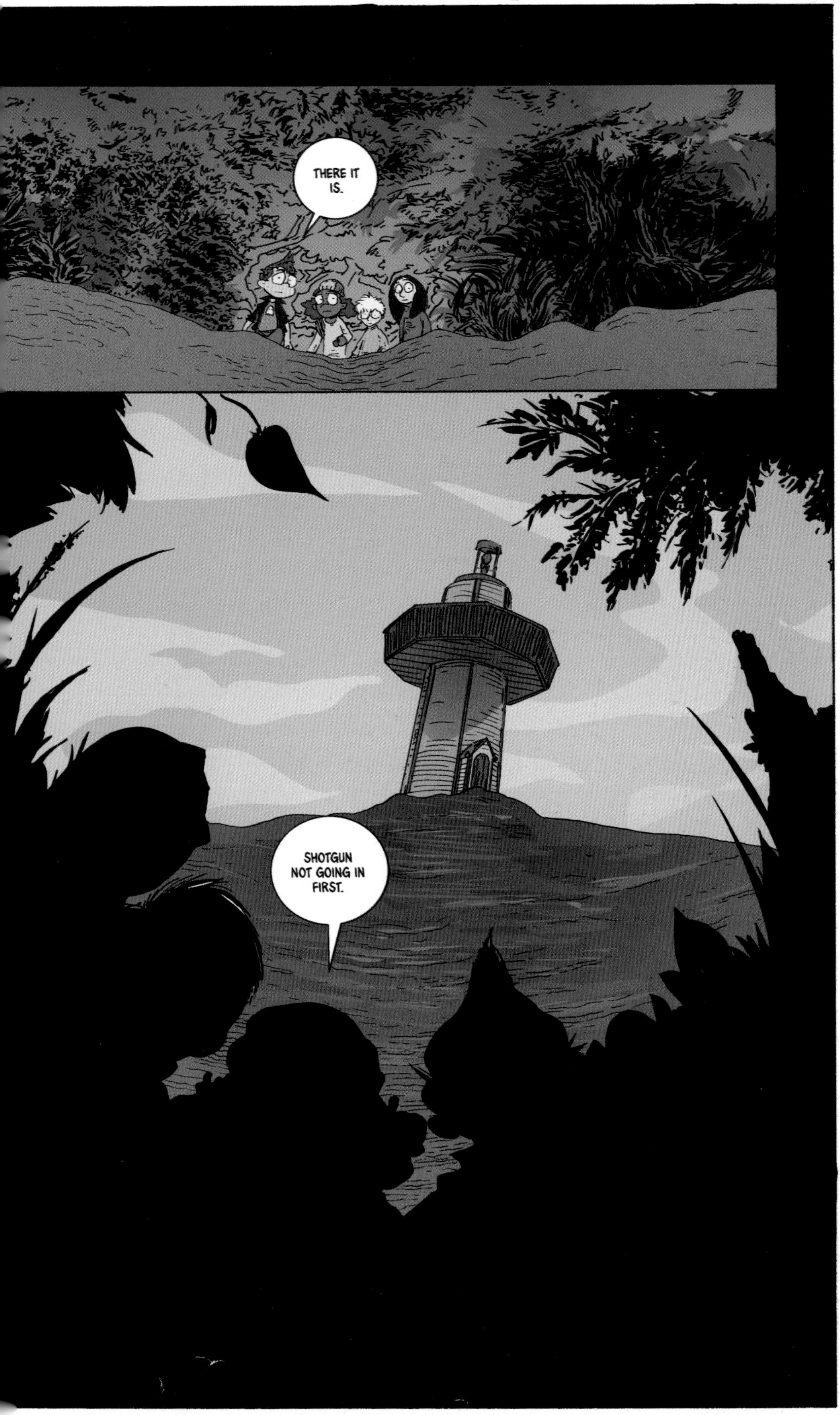
THERE IT IS.
SHOTGUN NOT GOING IN FIRST.

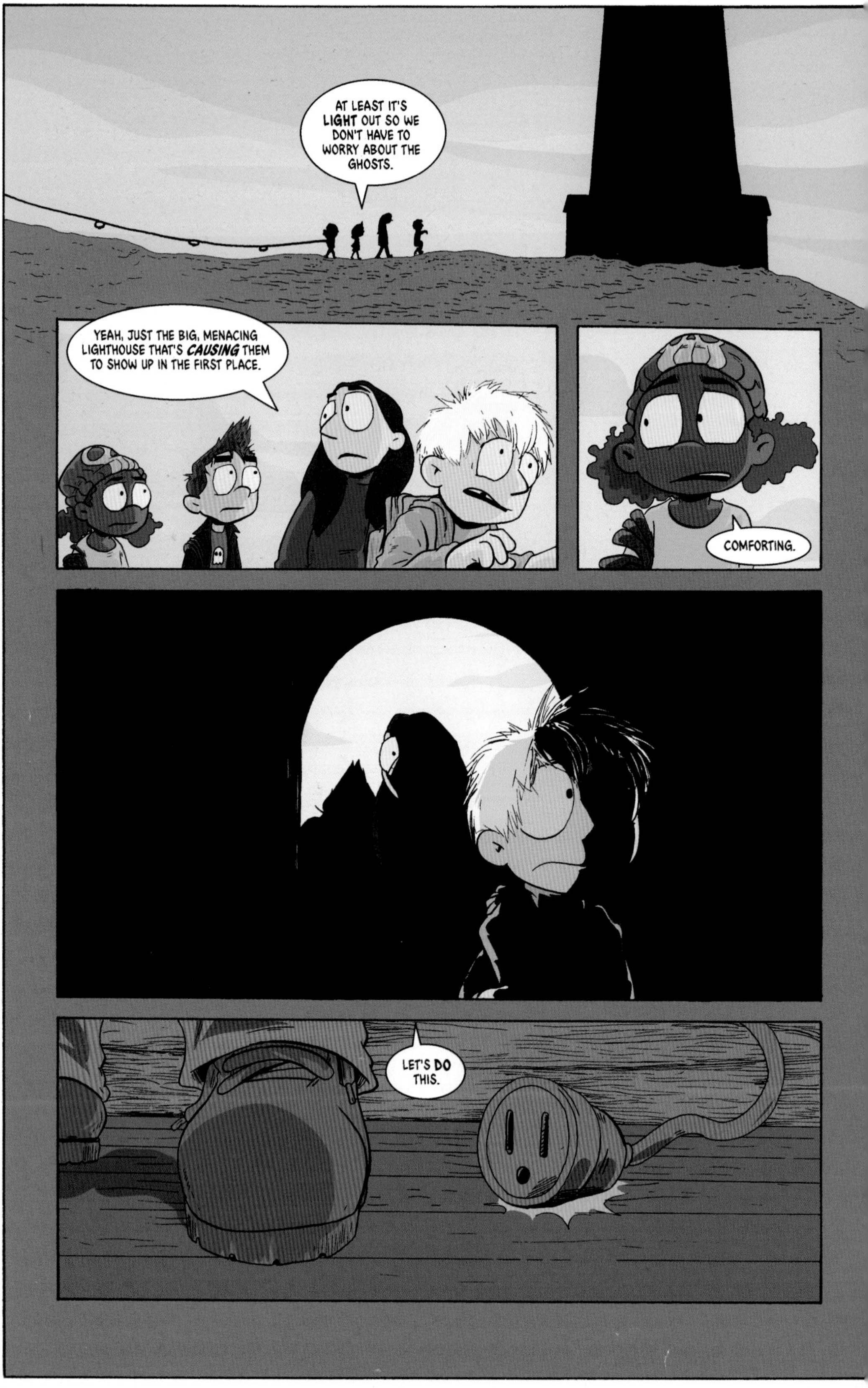
AT LEAST IT'S LIGHT OUT SO WE DON'T HAVE TO WORRY ABOUT THE GHOSTS.
YEAH, JUST THE BIG, MENACING LIGHTHOUSE THAT'S CAUSING THEM TO SHOW UP IN THE FIRST PLACE.
COMFORTING.
LET'S DO THIS.

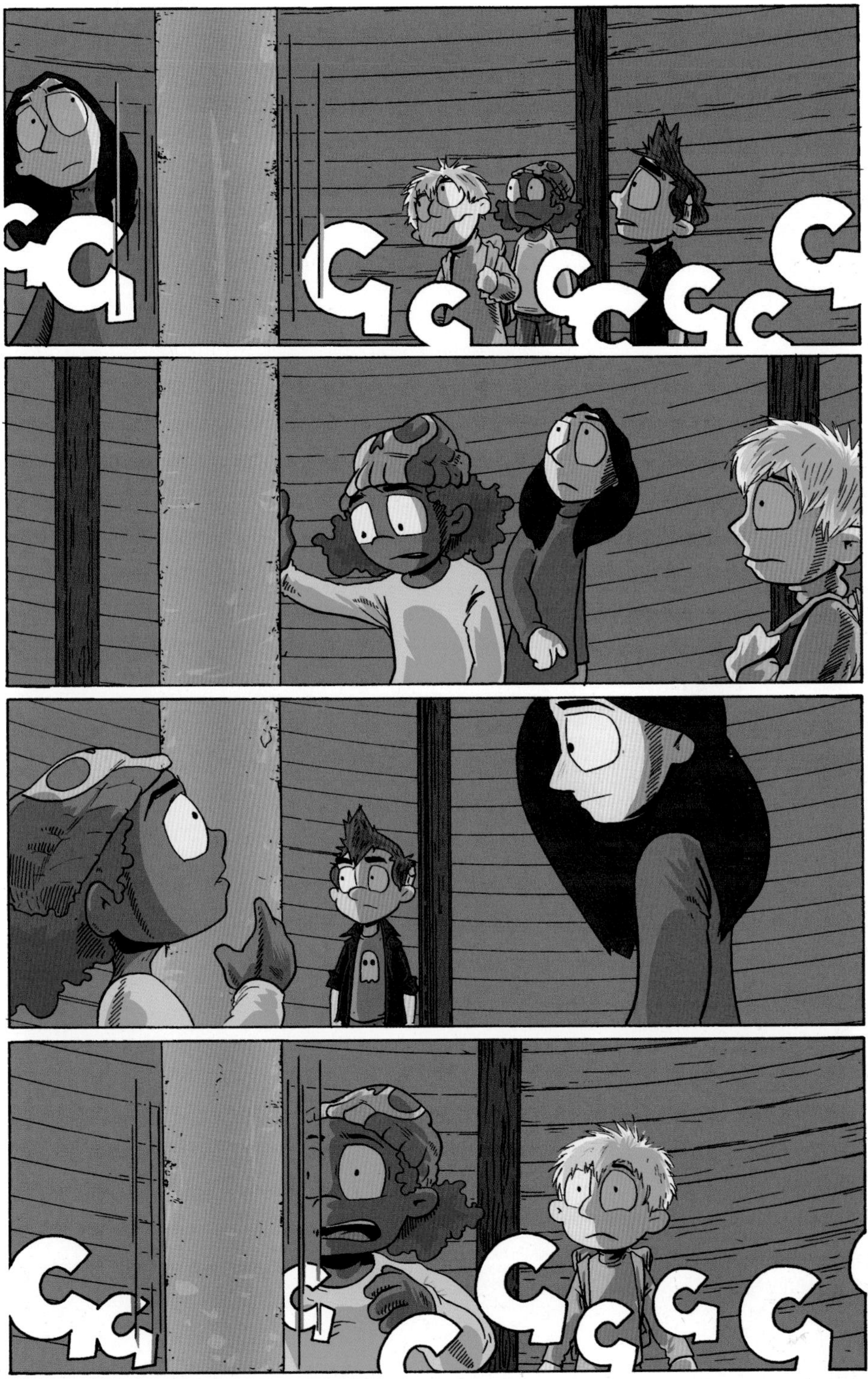

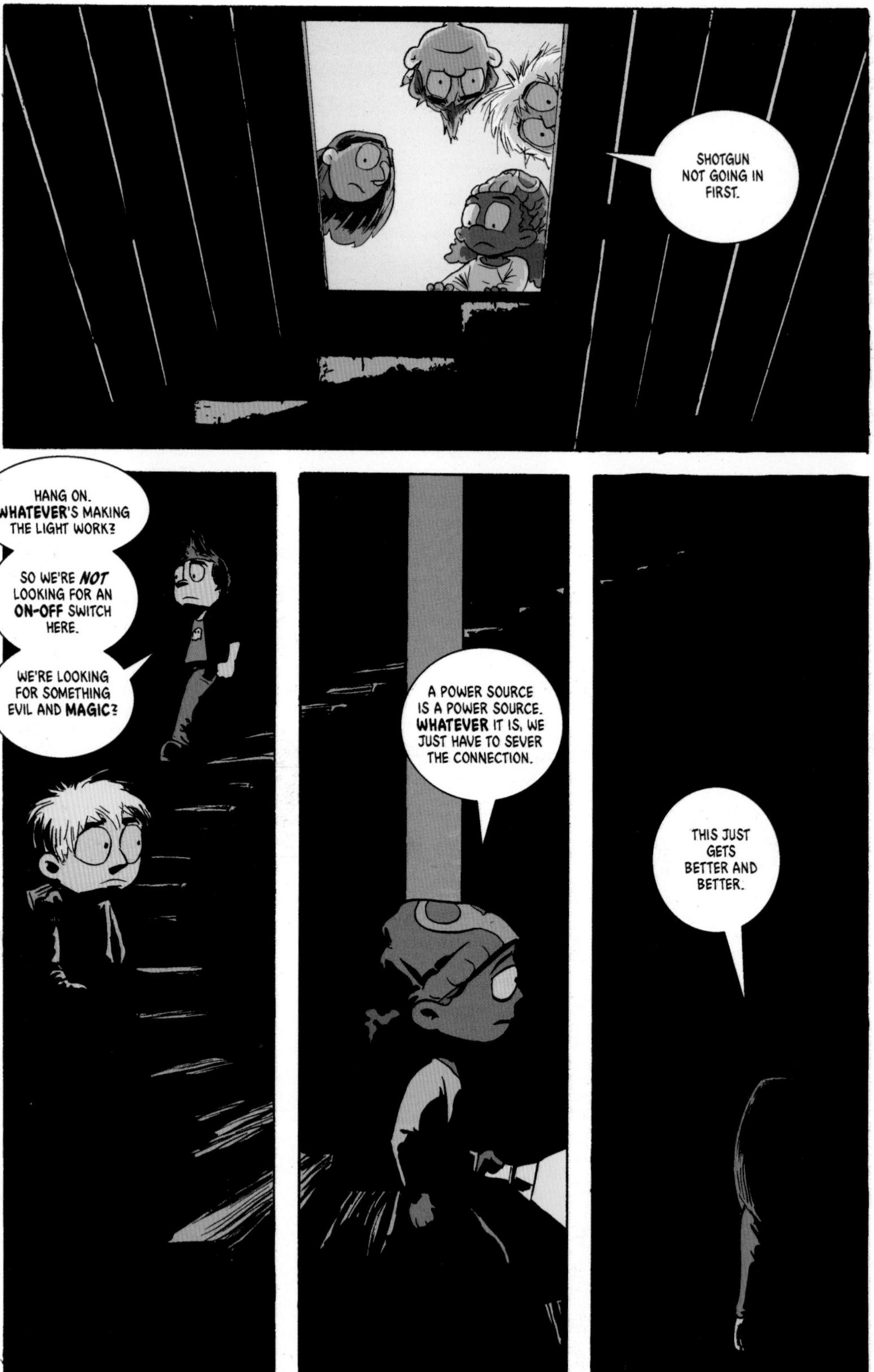
SHOTGUN NOT GOING IN FIRST.
HANG ON. WHATEVER'S MAKING THE LIGHT WORK?
SO WE'RE NOT LOOKING FOR AN ON-OFF SWITCH HERE.
WE'RE LOOKING FOR SOMETHING EVIL AND MAGIC?
A POWER SOURCE IS A POWER SOURCE. WHATEVER IT IS, WE JUST HAVE TO SEVER THE CONNECTION.
THIS JUST GETS BETTER AND BETTER.

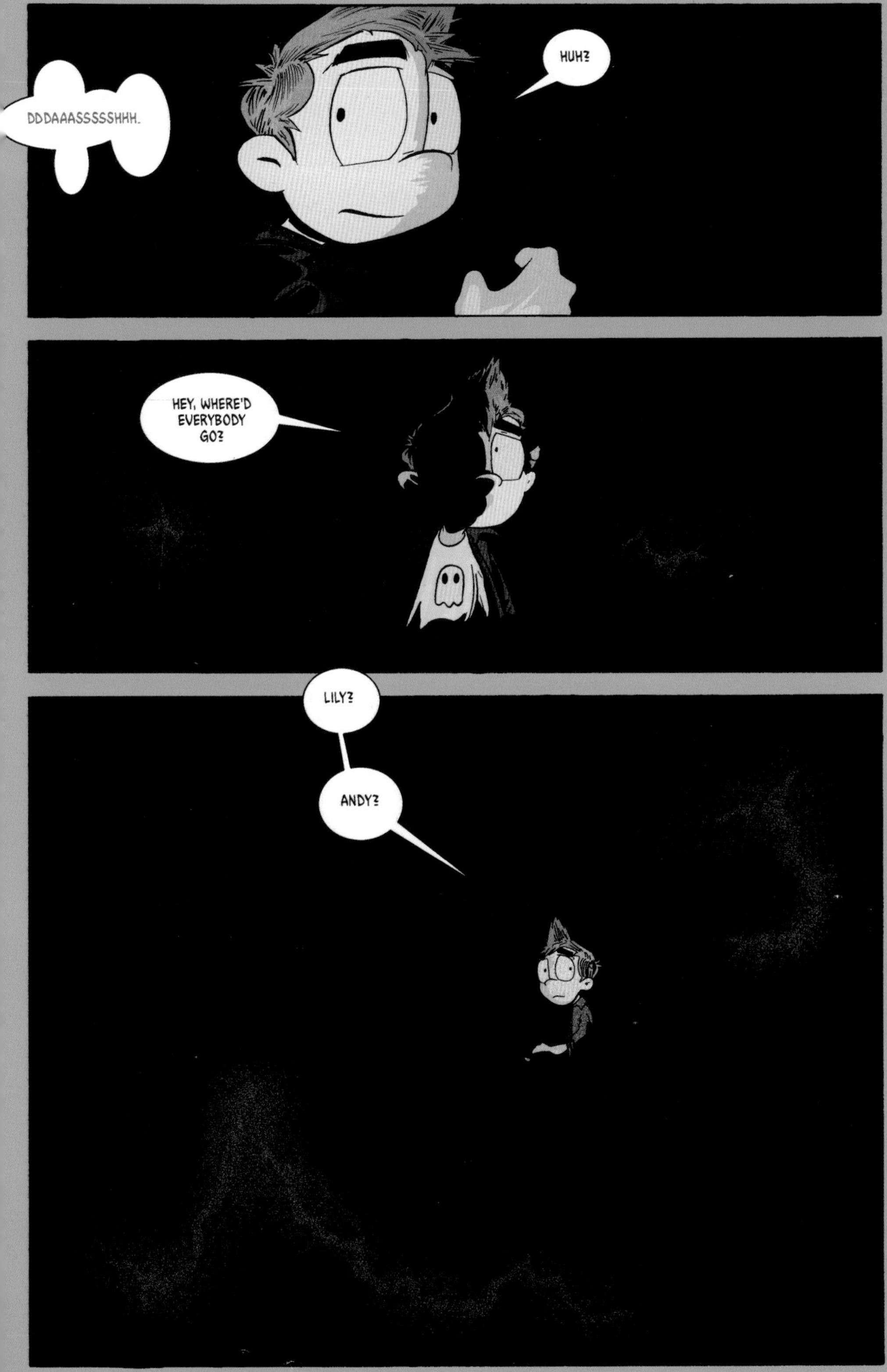
DDDAAASSSSSHHH.
HUH?
HEY, WHERE'D EVERYBODY GO?
LILY?
ANDY?

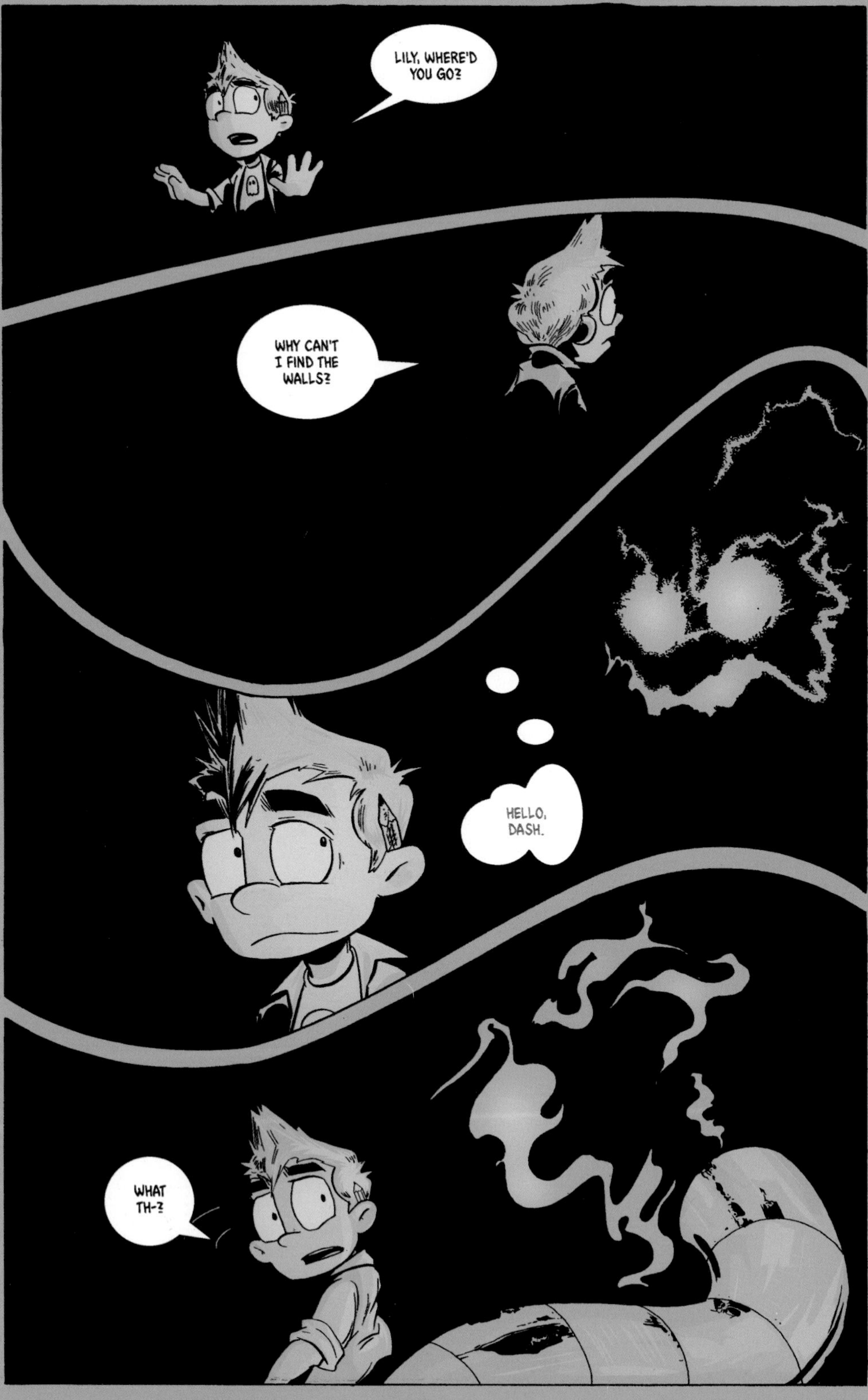
LILY, WHERE'D YOU GO?
WHY CAN'T I FIND THE WALLS?
HELLO, DASH.
WHAT TH-?

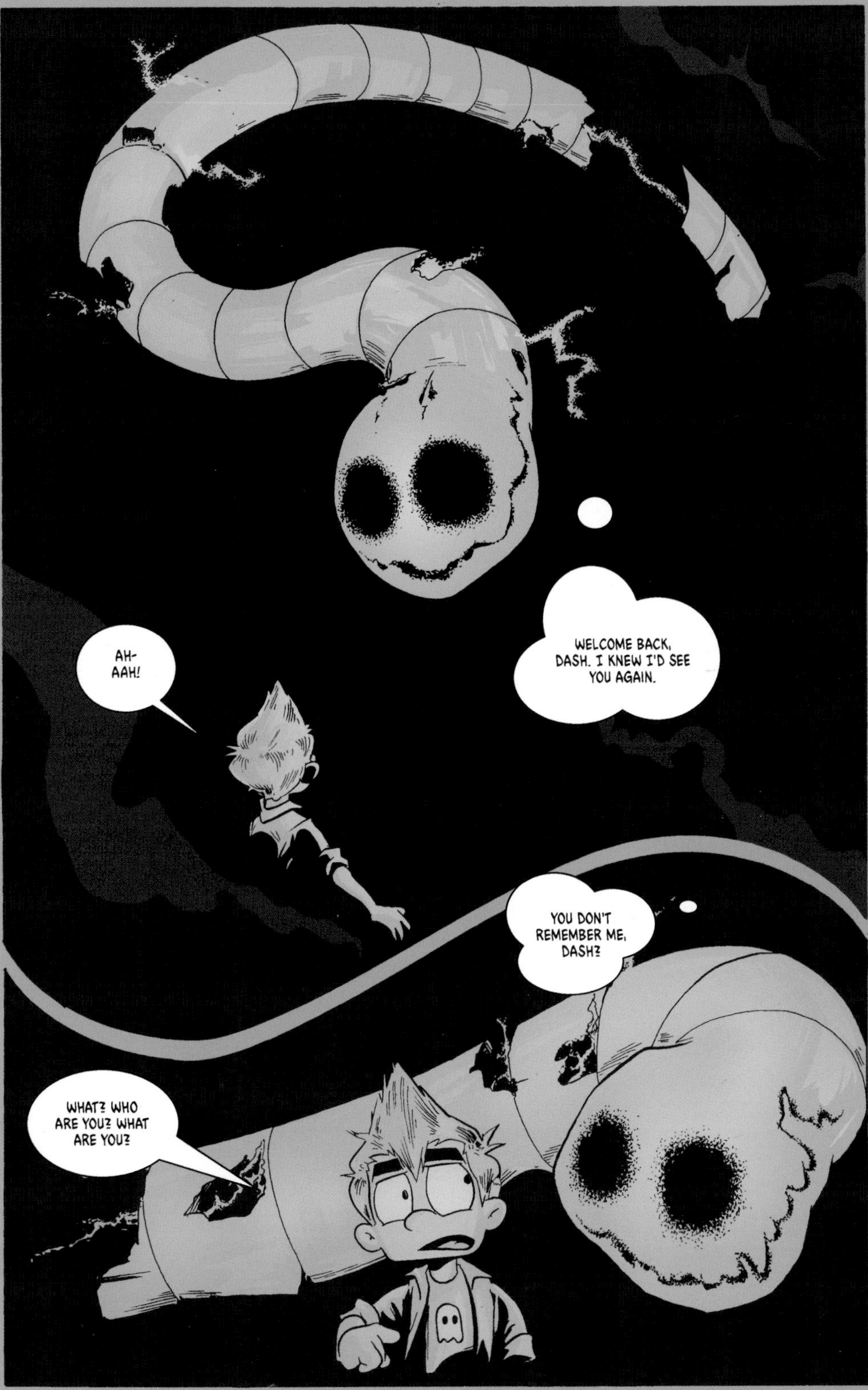
WELCOME BACK, DASH. I KNEW I'D SEE YOU AGAIN.
AH-AAH!
YOU DON'T REMEMBER ME, DASH?
WHAT? WHO ARE YOU? WHAT ARE YOU?

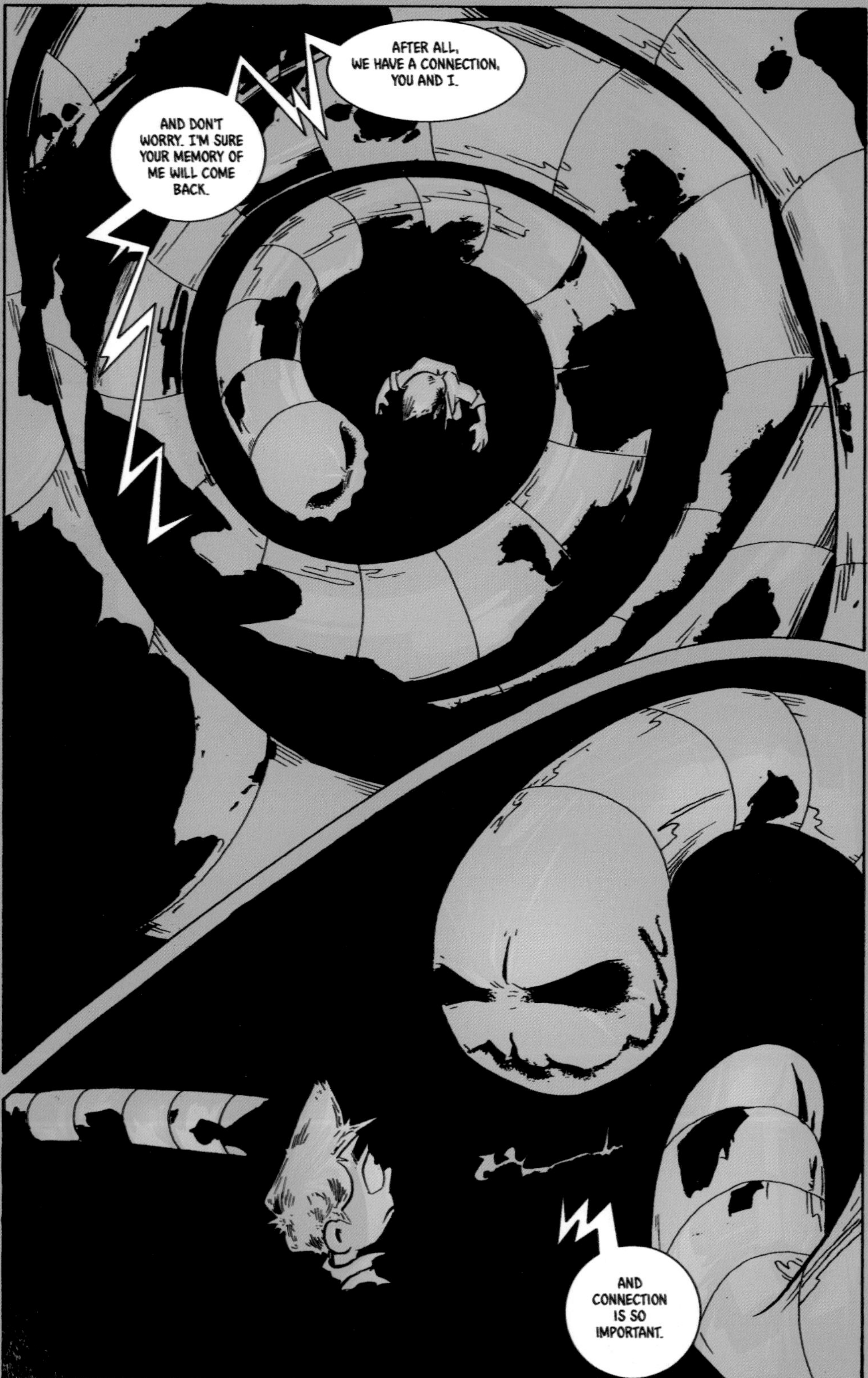
AFTER ALL, WE HAVE A CONNECTION, YOU AND I.
AND DON'T WORRY. I'M SURE YOUR MEMORY OF ME WILL COME BACK.
AND CONNECTION IS SO IMPORTANT.

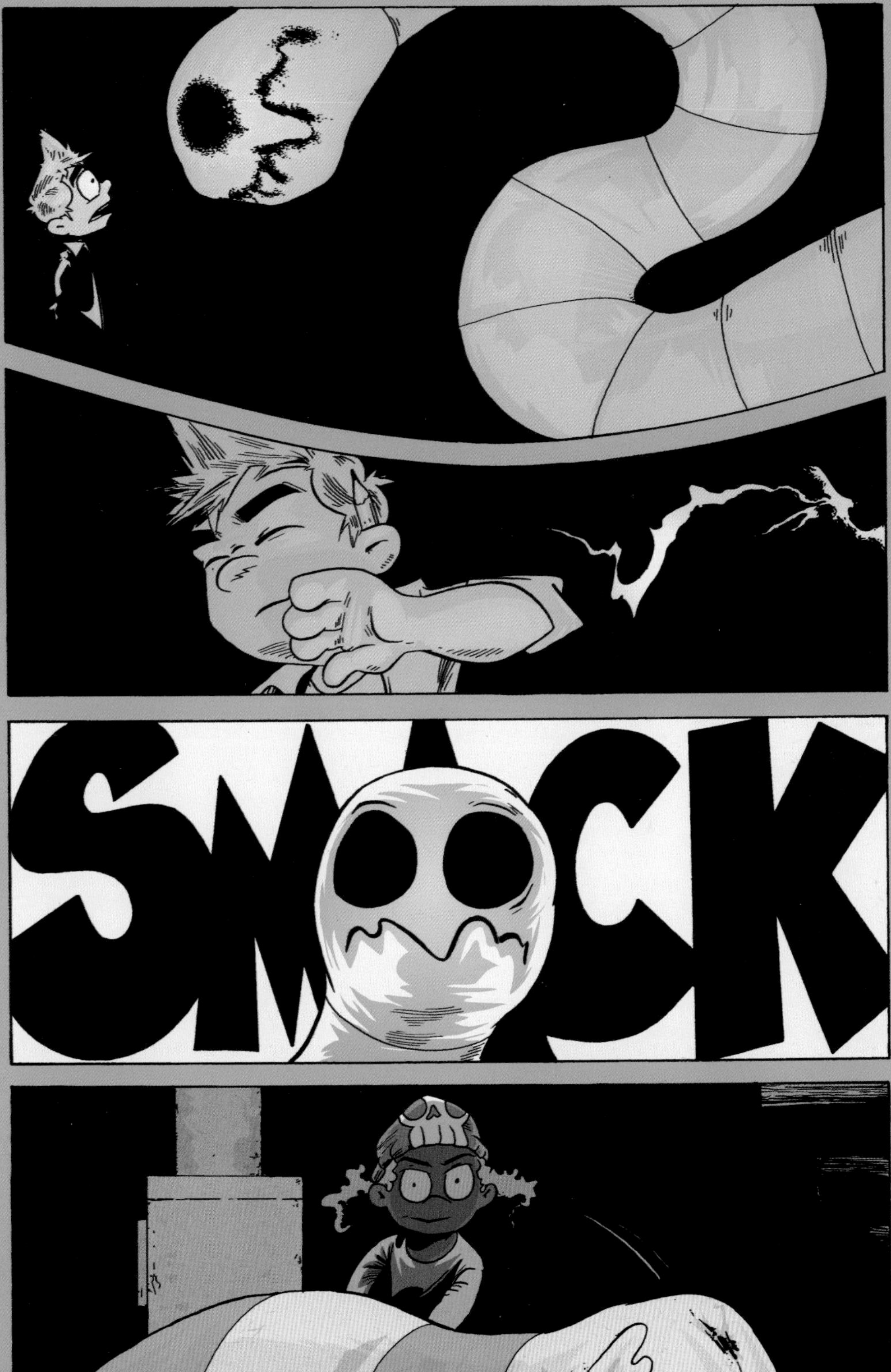
SMACK

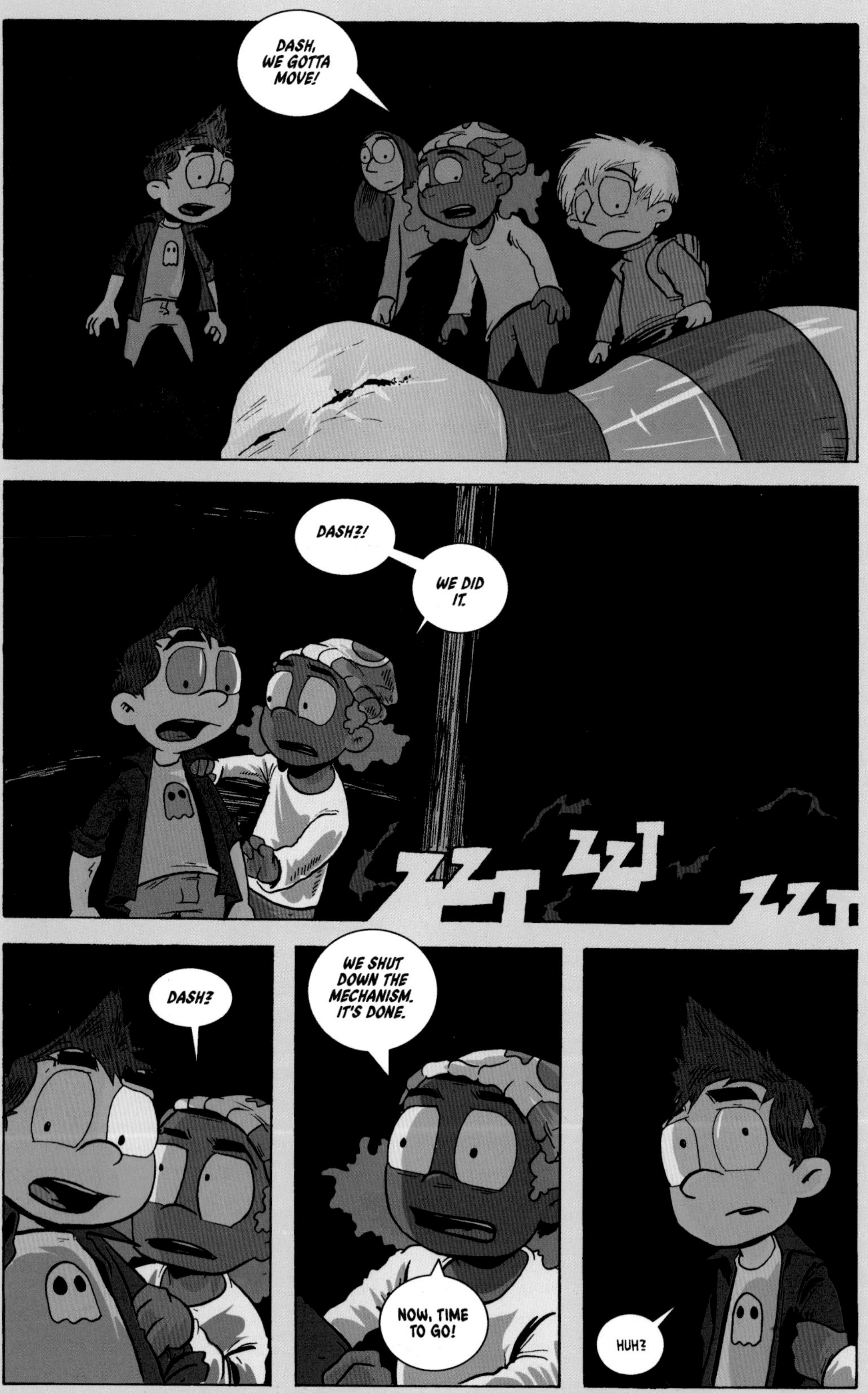
DASH, WE GOTTA MOVE!
DASH?!
WE DID IT.
ZZZT ZZZT ZZZT
DASH?
WE SHUT DOWN THE MECHANISM. IT'S DONE.
NOW, TIME TO GO!
HUH?

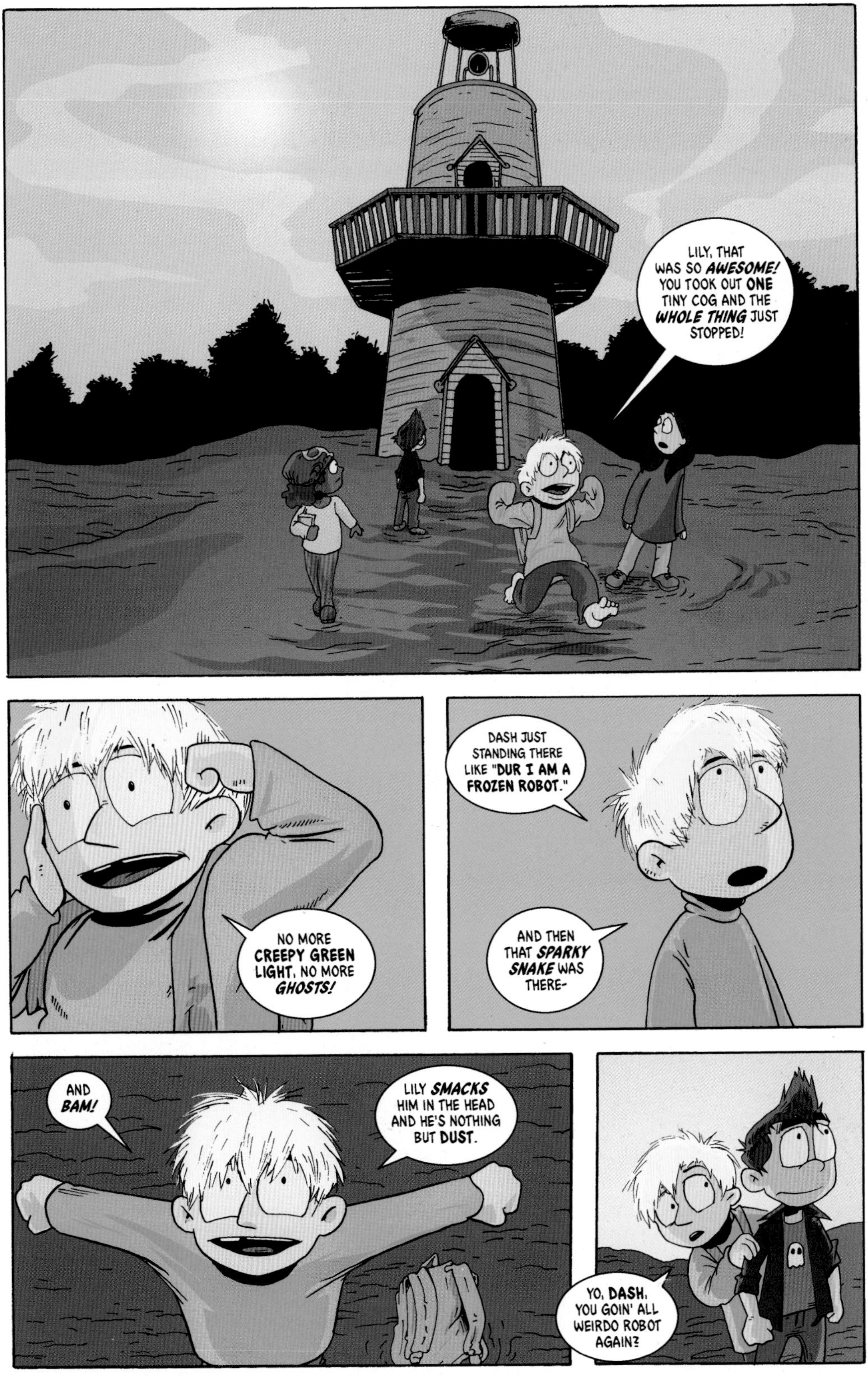

LILY, THAT WAS SO AWESOME! YOU TOOK OUT ONE TINY COG AND THE WHOLE THING JUST STOPPED!
NO MORE CREEPY GREEN LIGHT, NO MORE GHOSTS!
DASH JUST STANDING THERE LIKE "DUR I AM A FROZEN ROBOT."
AND THEN THAT SPARKY SNAKE WAS THERE-
AND BAM!
LILY SMACKS HIM IN THE HEAD AND HE'S NOTHING BUT DUST.
YO, DASH, YOU GOIN' ALL WEIRDO ROBOT AGAIN?

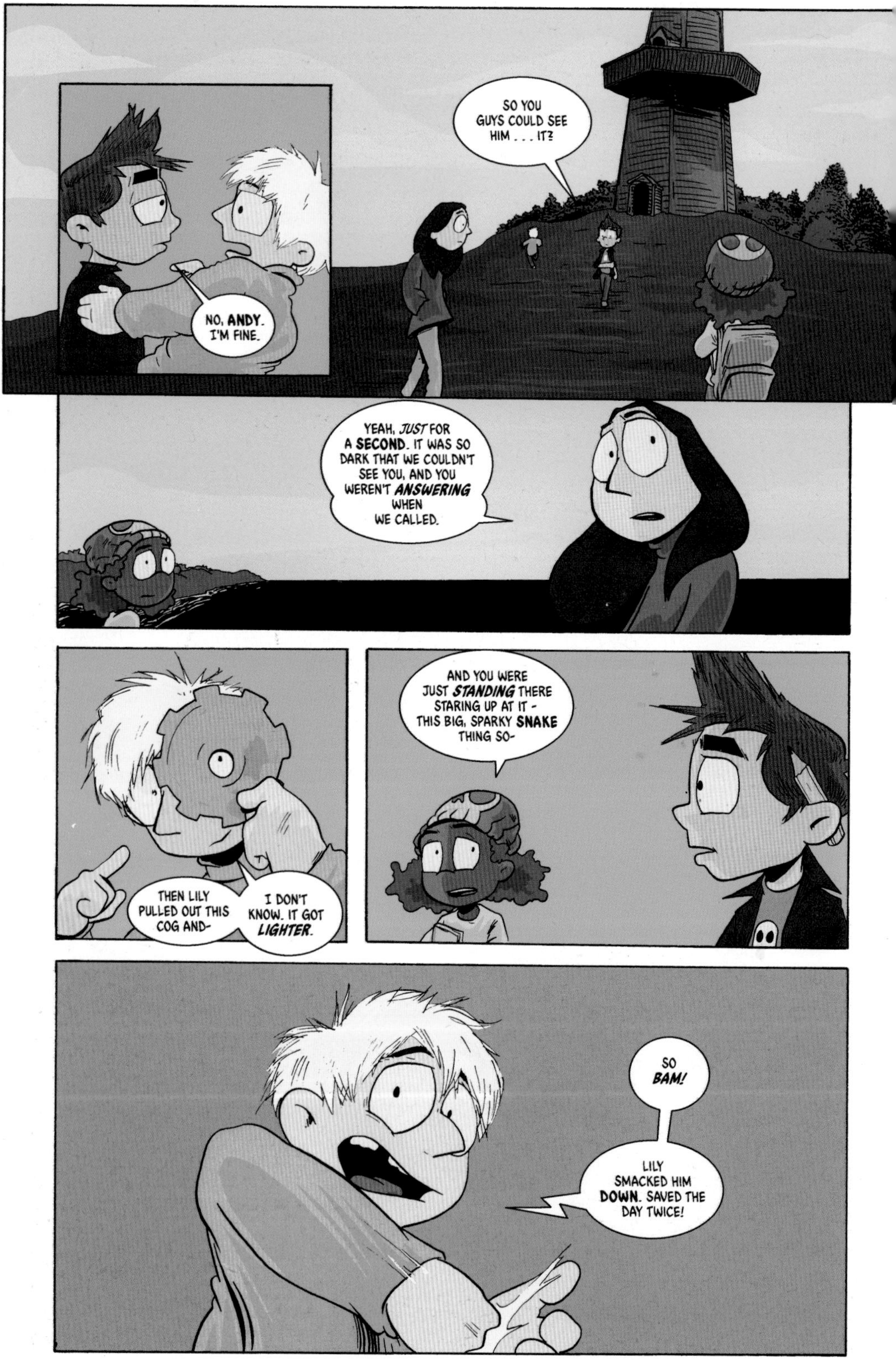

SO YOU GUYS COULD SEE HIM . . . IT?
NO, ANDY. I'M FINE.
YEAH, JUST FOR A SECOND. IT WAS SO DARK THAT WE COULDN'T SEE YOU, AND YOU WEREN'T ANSWERING WHEN WE CALLED.
THEN LILY PULLED OUT THIS COG AND-
I DON'T KNOW. IT GOT LIGHTER.
AND YOU WERE JUST STANDING THERE STARING UP AT IT - THIS BIG, SPARKY SNAKE THING SO-
SO BAM!
LILY SMACKED HIM DOWN. SAVED THE DAY TWICE!

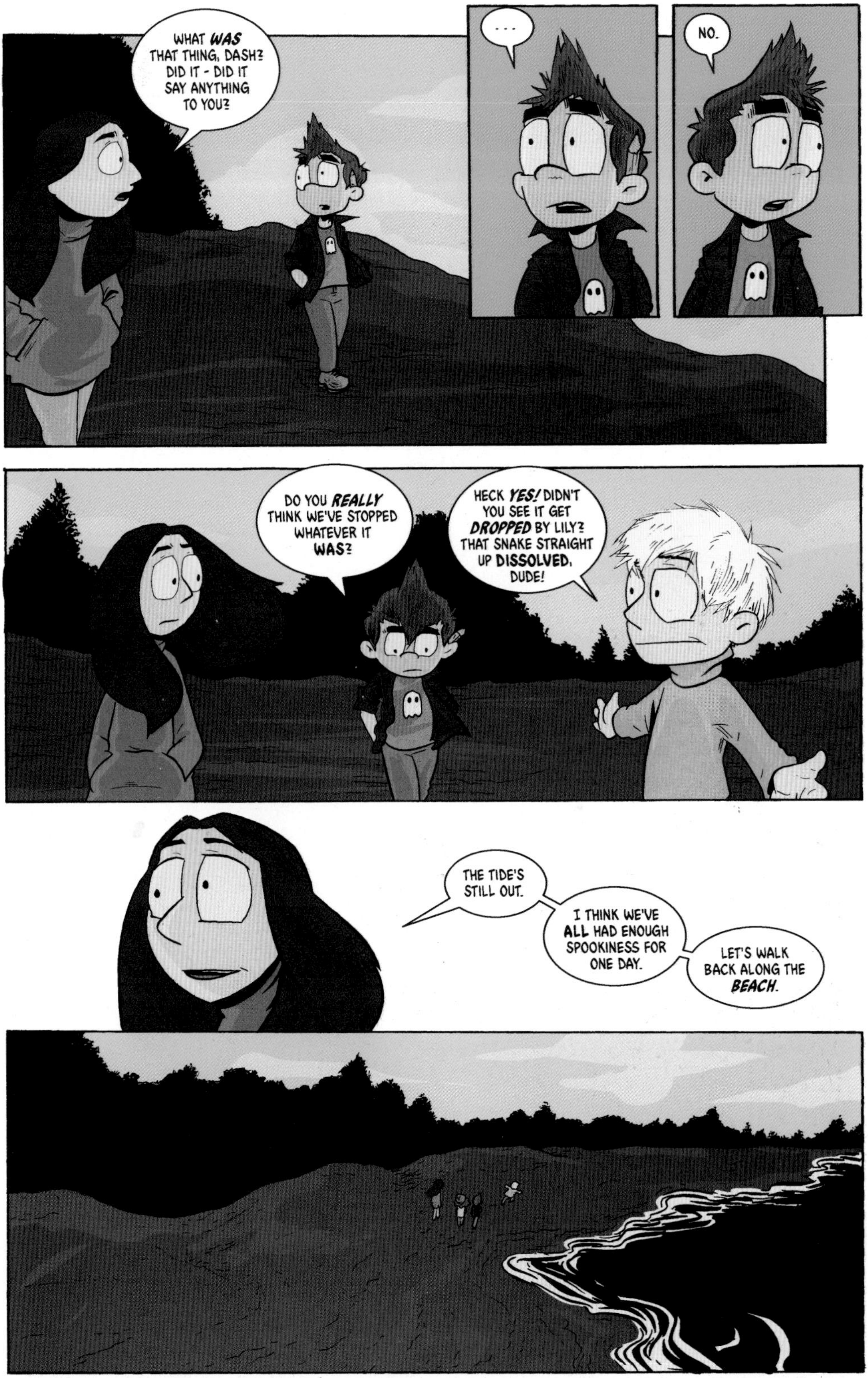
WHAT WAS THAT THING, DASH? DID IT - DID IT SAY ANYTHING TO YOU?
...
NO.
DO YOU REALLY THINK WE'VE STOPPED WHATEVER IT WAS?
HECK YES! DIDN'T YOU SEE IT GET DROPPED BY LILY? THAT SNAKE STRAIGHT UP DISSOLVED, DUDE!
THE TIDE'S STILL OUT.
I THINK WE'VE ALL HAD ENOUGH SPOOKINESS FOR ONE DAY.
LET'S WALK BACK ALONG THE BEACH.

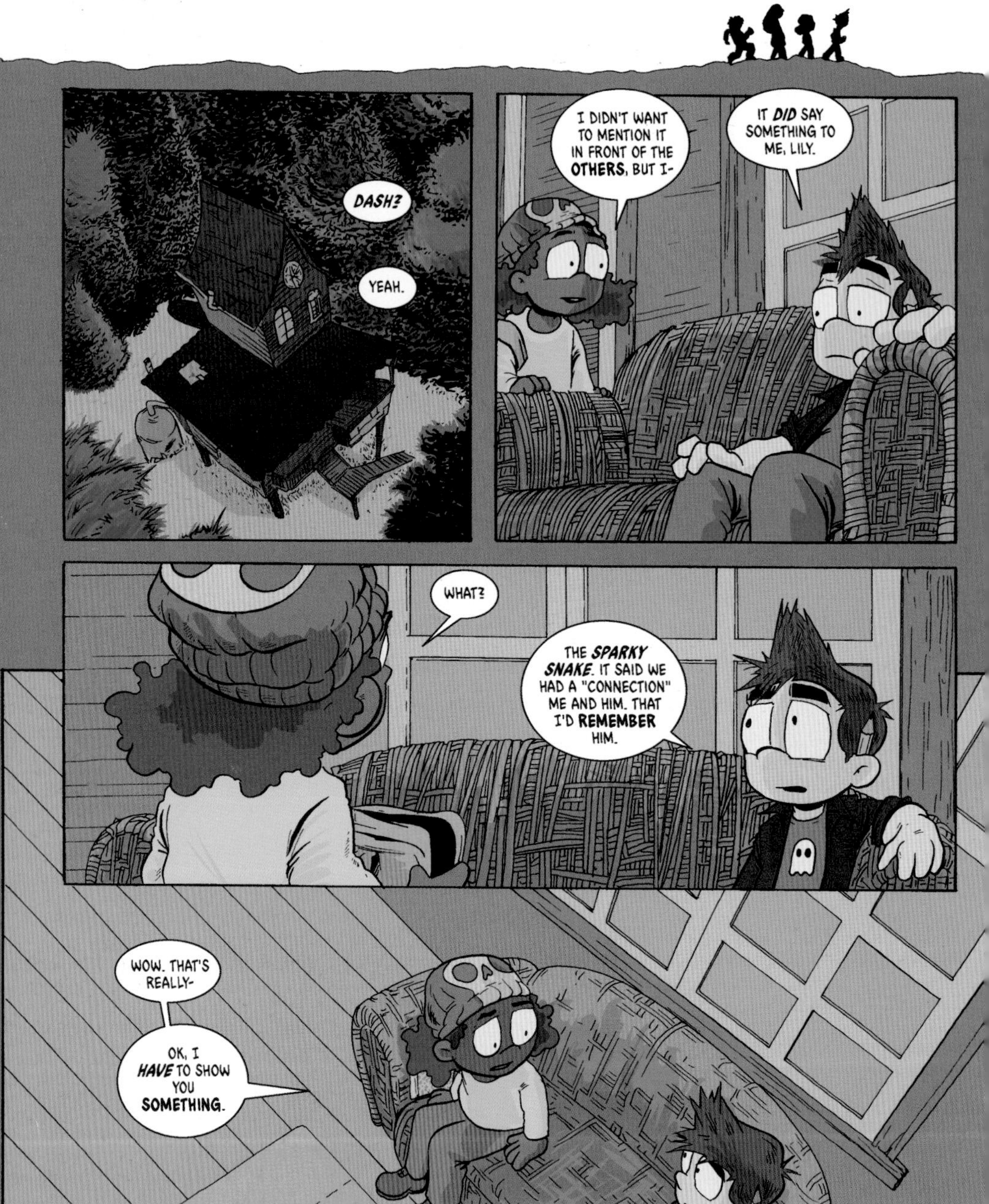
DASH?
YEAH.
I DIDN'T WANT TO MENTION IT IN FRONT OF THE OTHERS, BUT I-
IT DID SAY SOMETHING TO ME, LILY.
WHAT?
THE SPARKY SNAKE. IT SAID WE HAD A "CONNECTION" ME AND HIM. THAT I'D REMEMBER HIM.
WOW. THAT'S REALLY-
OK, I HAVE TO SHOW YOU SOMETHING.
WHAT IS IT?

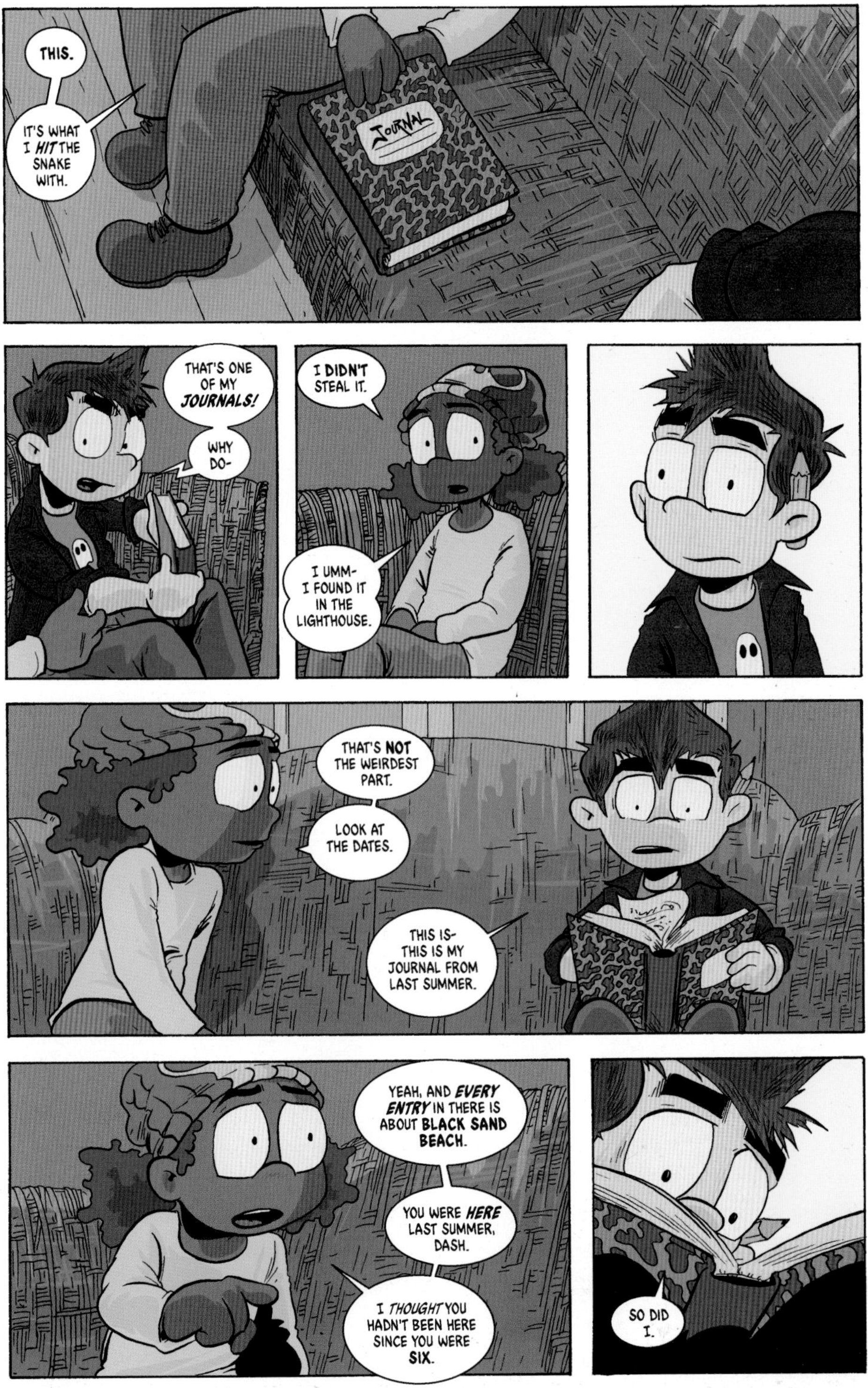
THIS.
IT'S WHAT I *HIT* THE SNAKE WITH.
JOURNAL
THAT'S ONE OF MY *JOURNALS!*
WHY DO-
I **DIDN'T** STEAL IT.
I UMM- I FOUND IT IN THE LIGHTHOUSE.
THAT'S **NOT** THE WEIRDEST PART.
LOOK AT THE DATES.
THIS IS- THIS IS MY JOURNAL FROM LAST SUMMER.
YEAH, AND ***EVERY ENTRY*** IN THERE IS ABOUT **BLACK SAND BEACH**.
YOU WERE *HERE* LAST SUMMER, DASH.
I *THOUGHT* YOU HADN'T BEEN HERE SINCE YOU WERE **SIX**.
SO DID I.

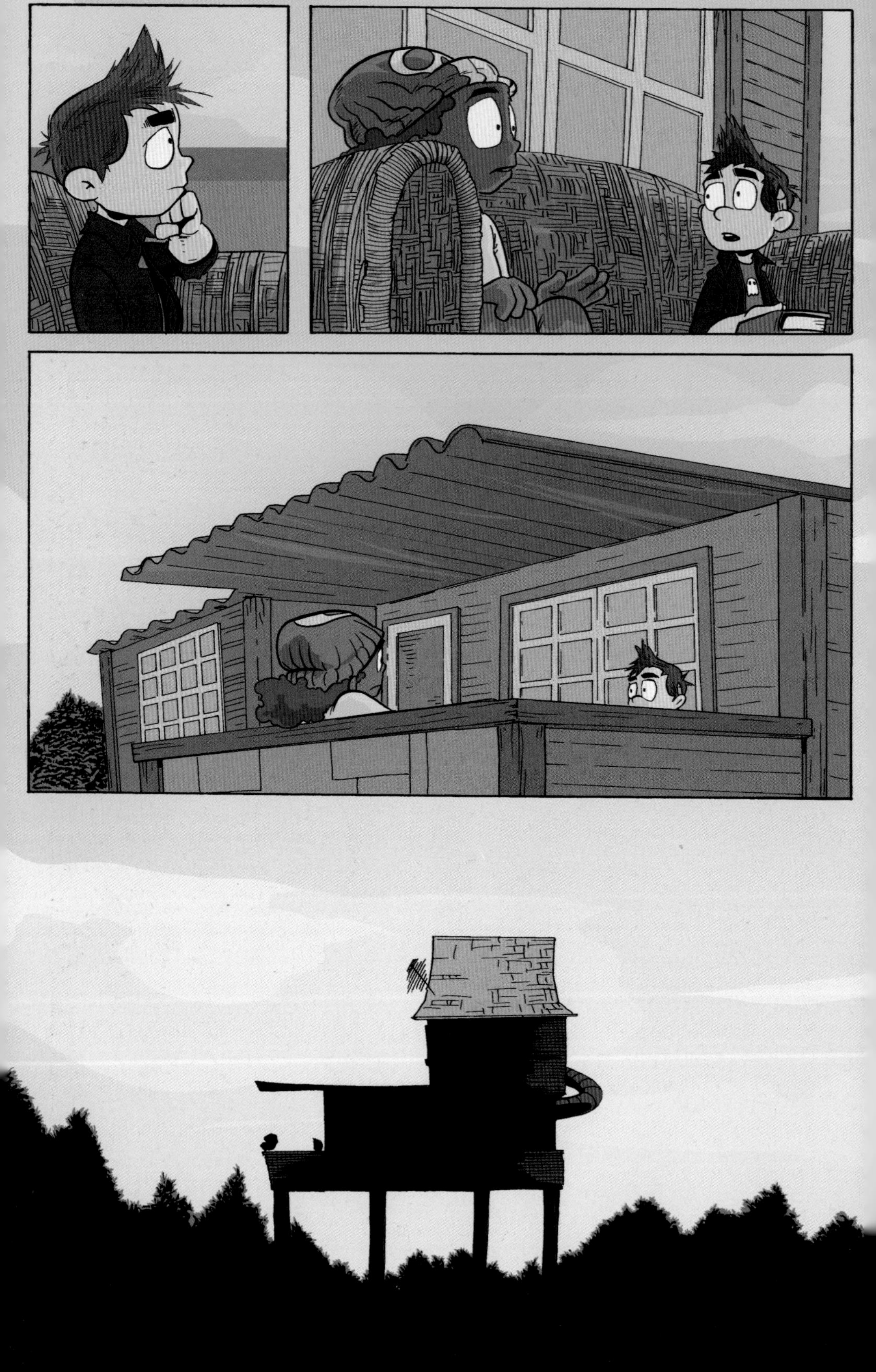

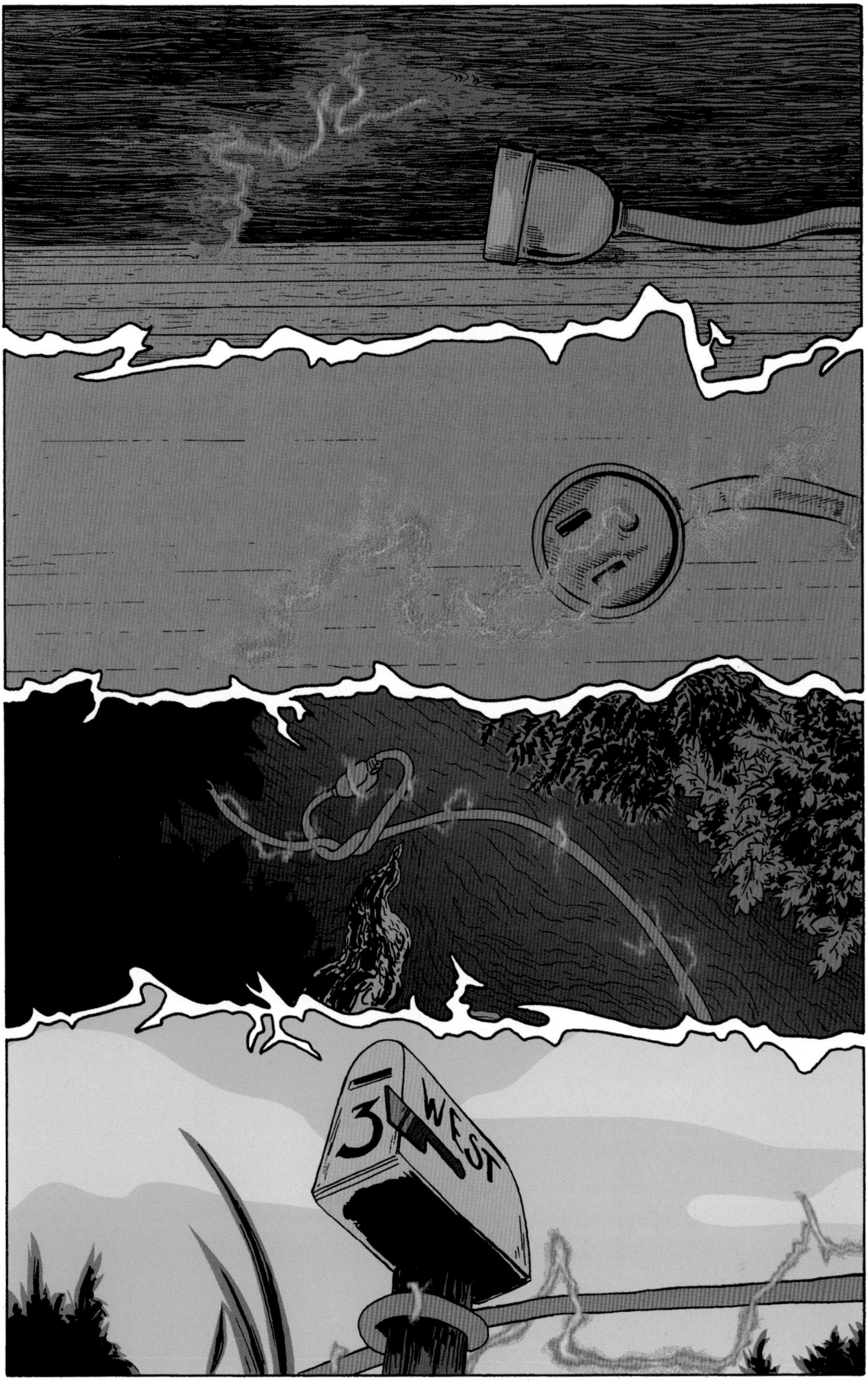
3 WEST

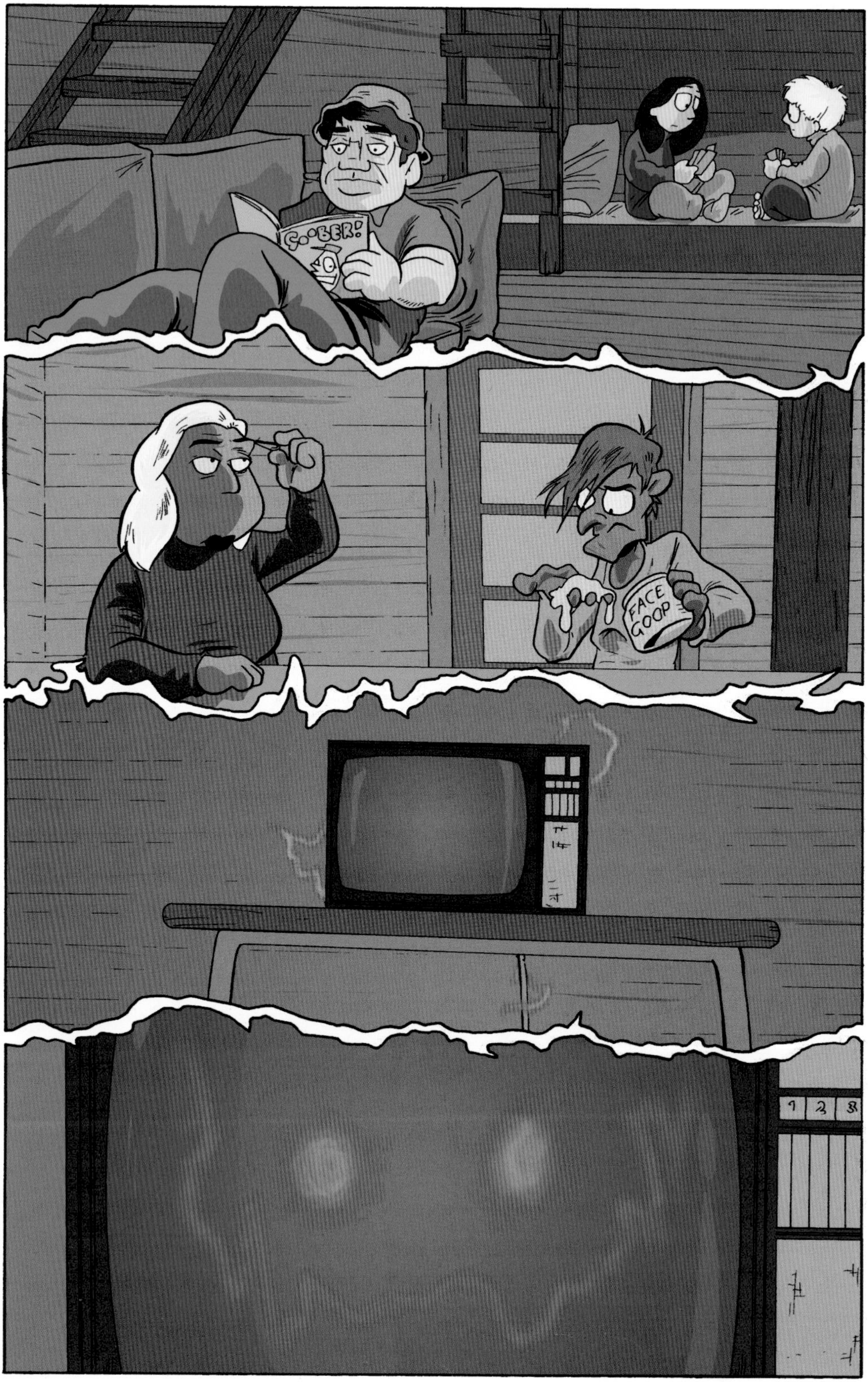
FACE
GOOP

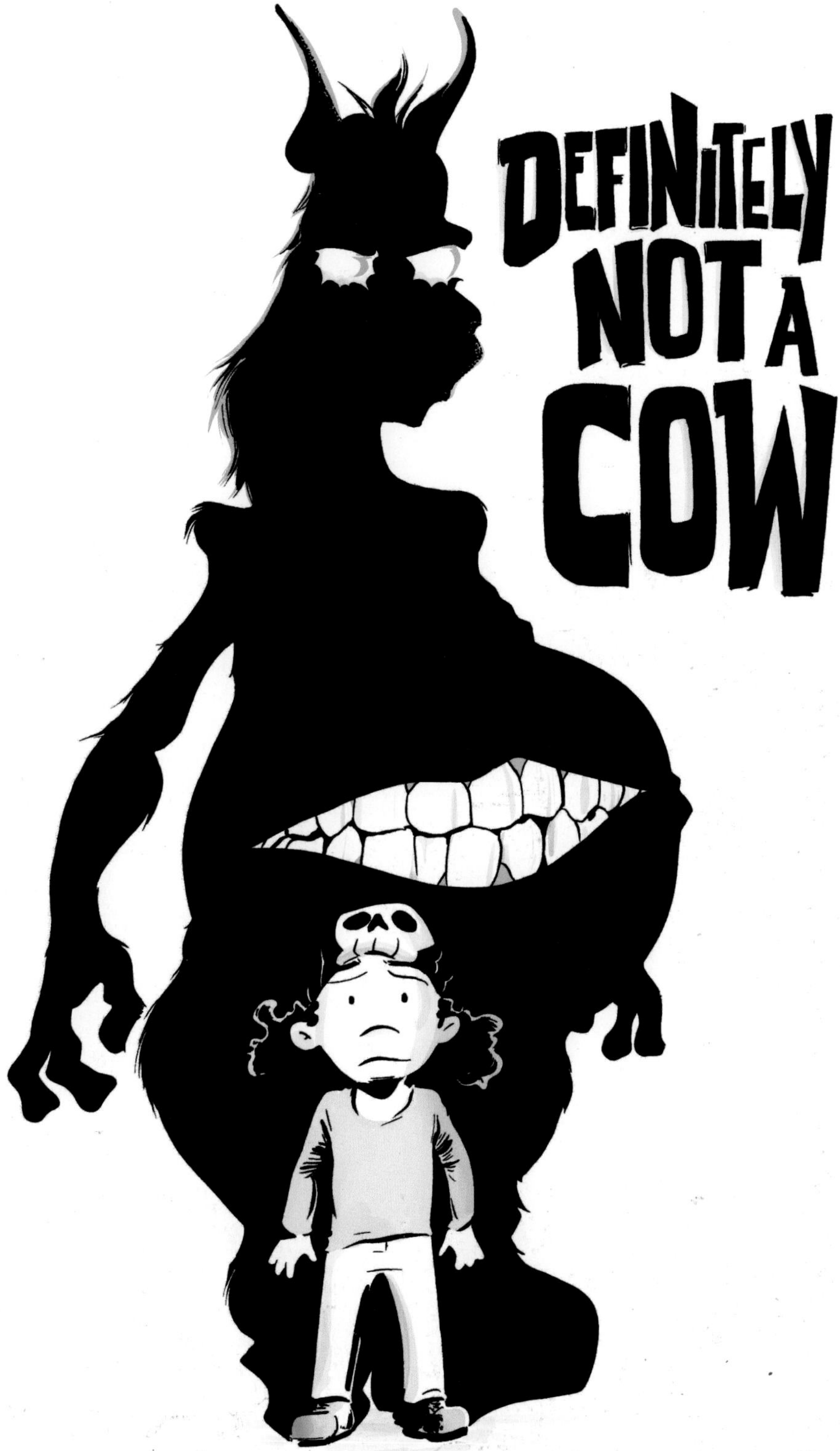
DEFINITELY NOT A COW

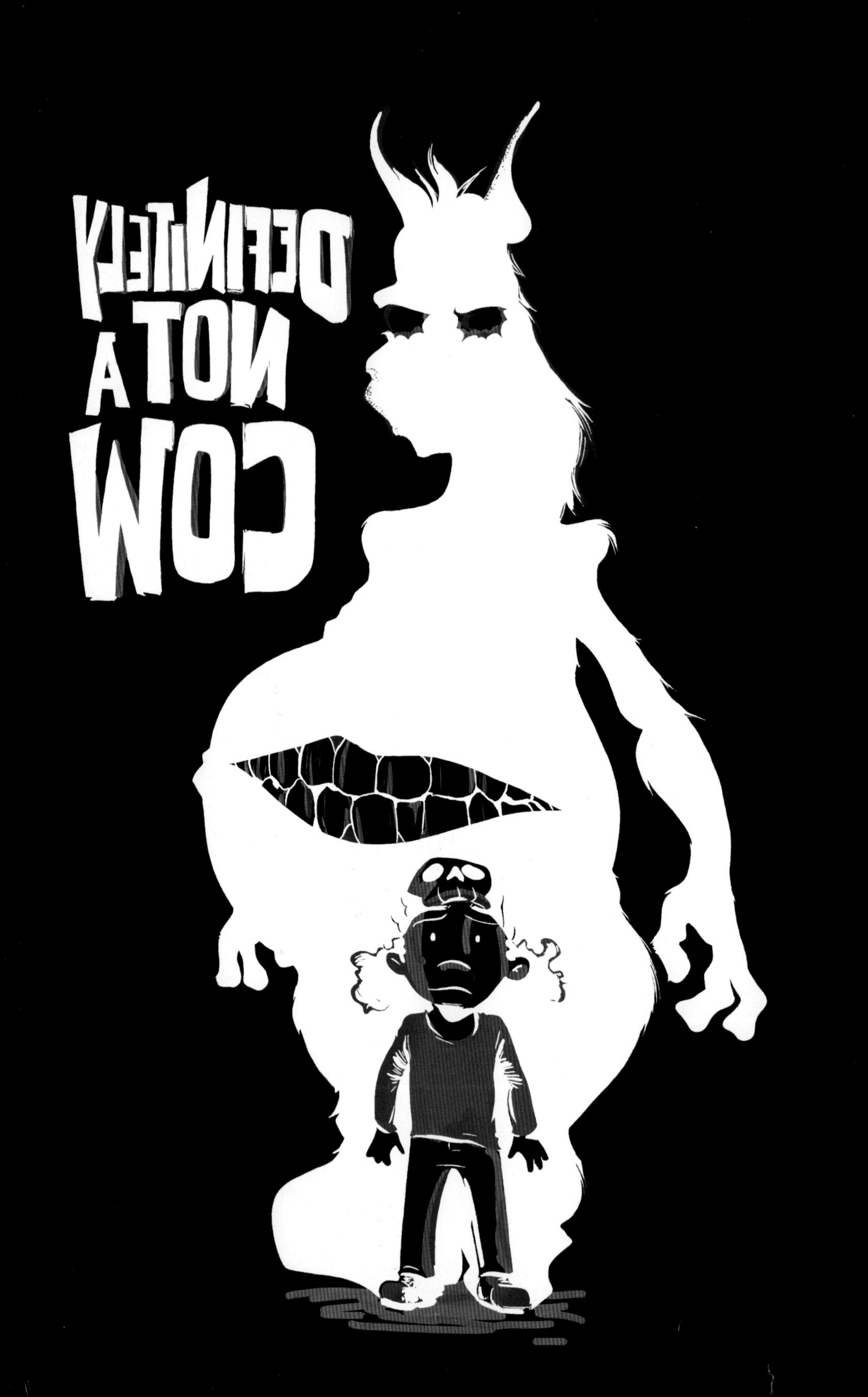
DEFINITELY NOT A COW

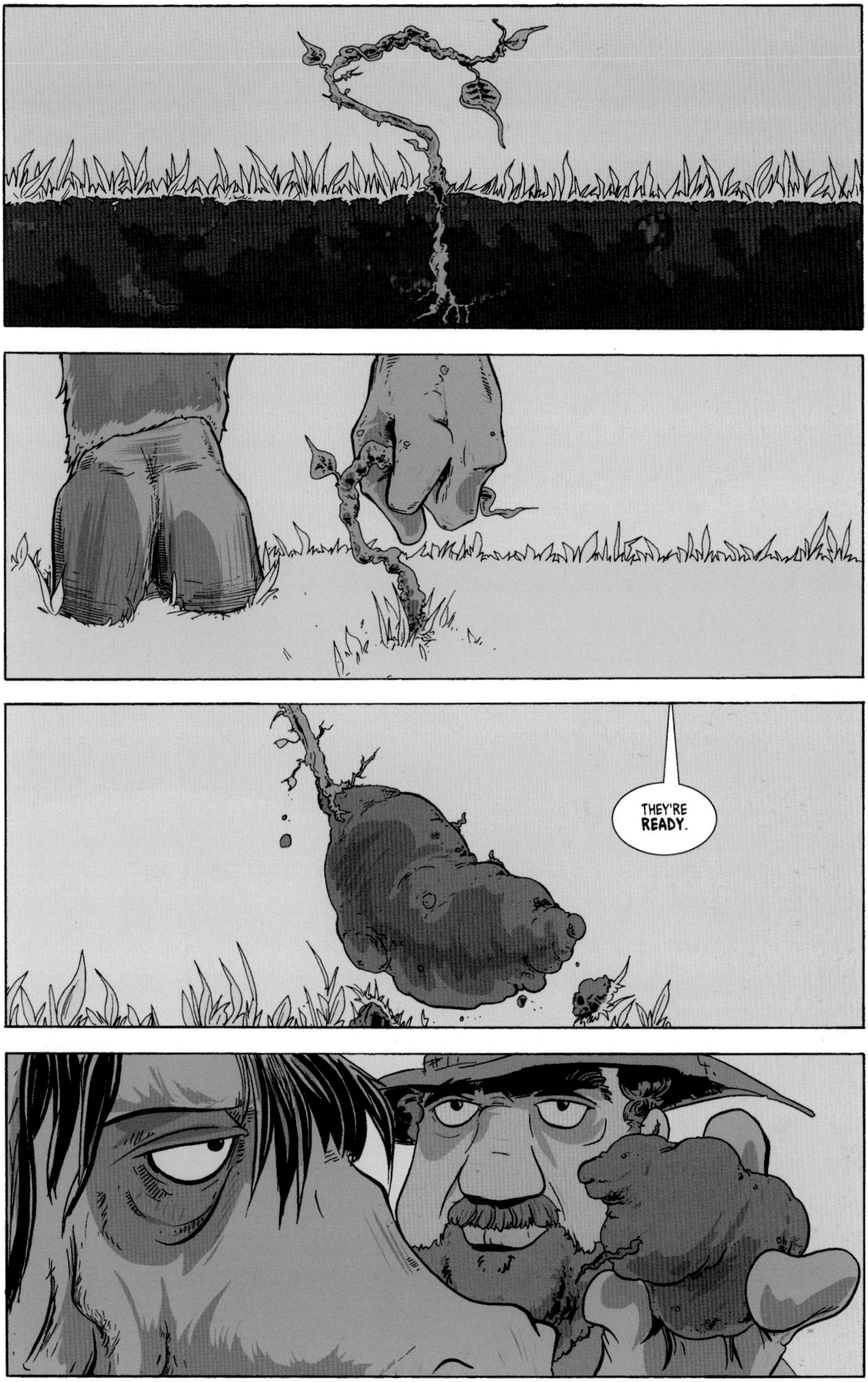
THEY'RE READY.

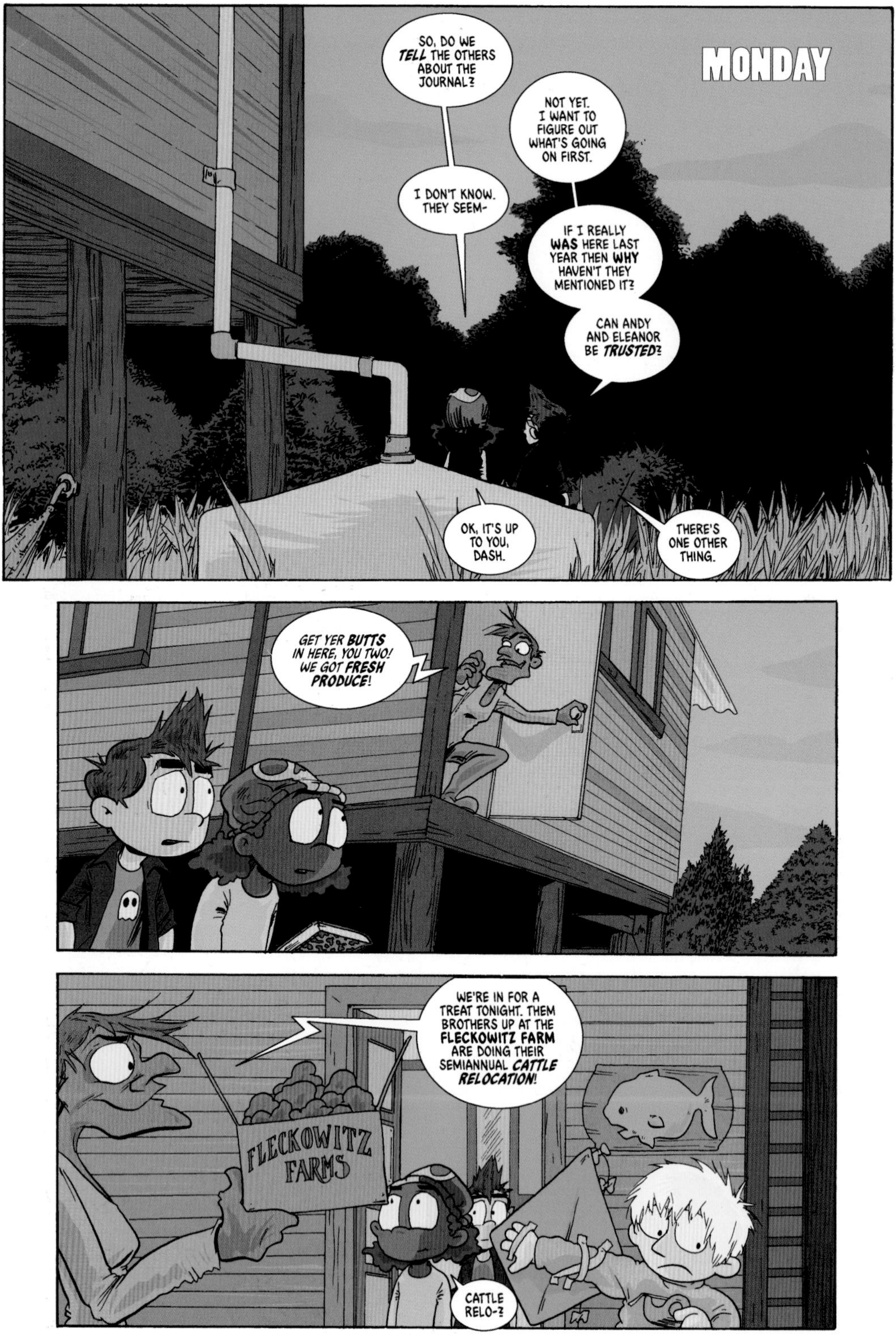
MONDAY
SO, DO WE TELL THE OTHERS ABOUT THE JOURNAL?
NOT YET. I WANT TO FIGURE OUT WHAT'S GOING ON FIRST.
I DON'T KNOW. THEY SEEM-
IF I REALLY WAS HERE LAST YEAR THEN WHY HAVEN'T THEY MENTIONED IT?
CAN ANDY AND ELEANOR BE TRUSTED?
OK, IT'S UP TO YOU, DASH.
THERE'S ONE OTHER THING.
GET YER BUTTS IN HERE, YOU TWO! WE GOT FRESH PRODUCE!
WE'RE IN FOR A TREAT TONIGHT. THEM BROTHERS UP AT THE FLECKOWITZ FARM ARE DOING THEIR SEMIANNUAL CATTLE RELOCATION!
FLECKOWITZ FARMS
CATTLE RELO-?

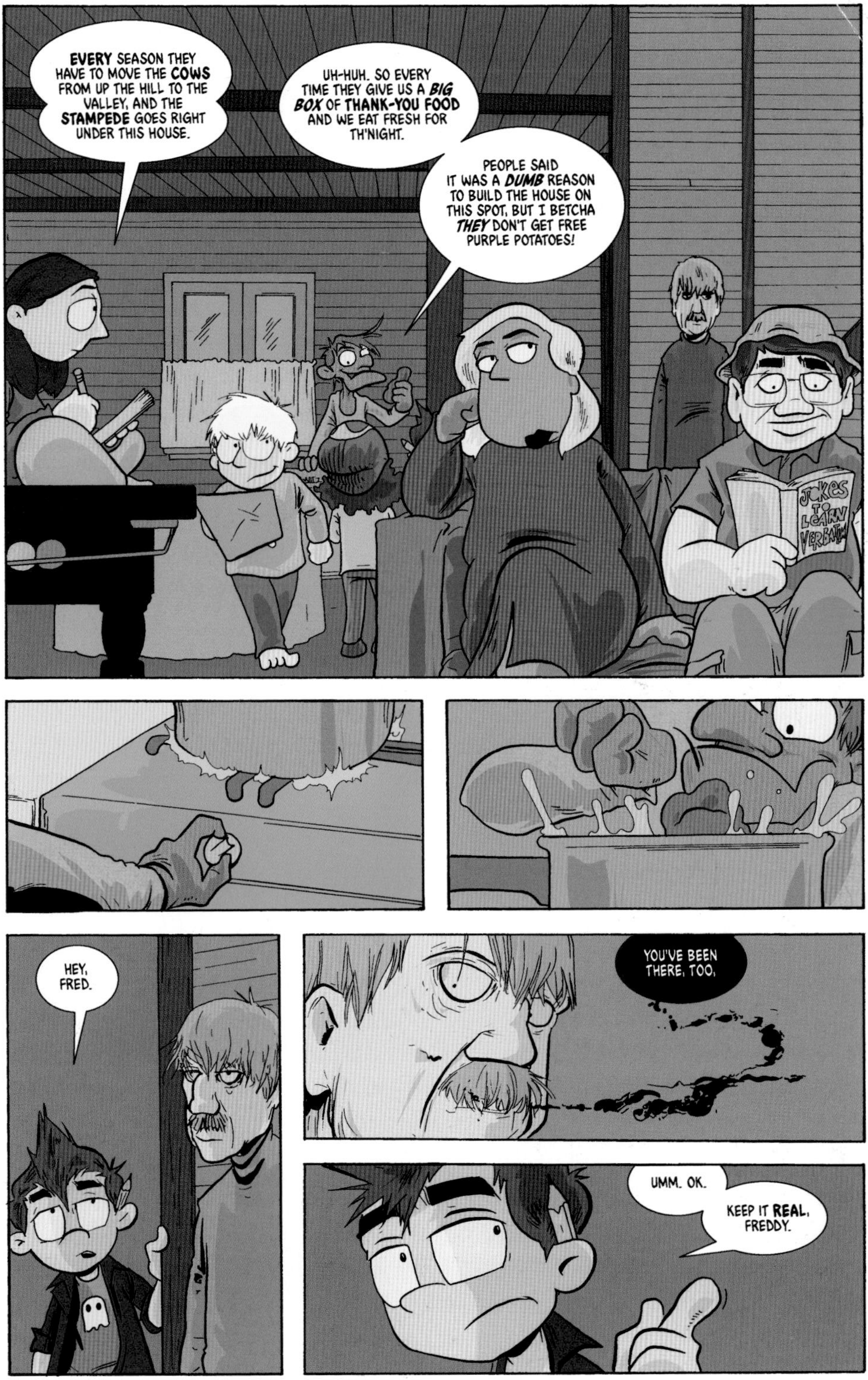
EVERY SEASON THEY HAVE TO MOVE THE COWS FROM UP THE HILL TO THE VALLEY, AND THE STAMPEDE GOES RIGHT UNDER THIS HOUSE.
UH-HUH. SO EVERY TIME THEY GIVE US A BIG BOX OF THANK-YOU FOOD AND WE EAT FRESH FOR TH'NIGHT.
PEOPLE SAID IT WAS A DUMB REASON TO BUILD THE HOUSE ON THIS SPOT, BUT I BETCHA THEY DON'T GET FREE PURPLE POTATOES!
JOKES TO LEARN VERBATIM
HEY, FRED.
YOU'VE BEEN THERE, TOO,
UMM. OK.
KEEP IT REAL, FREDDY.

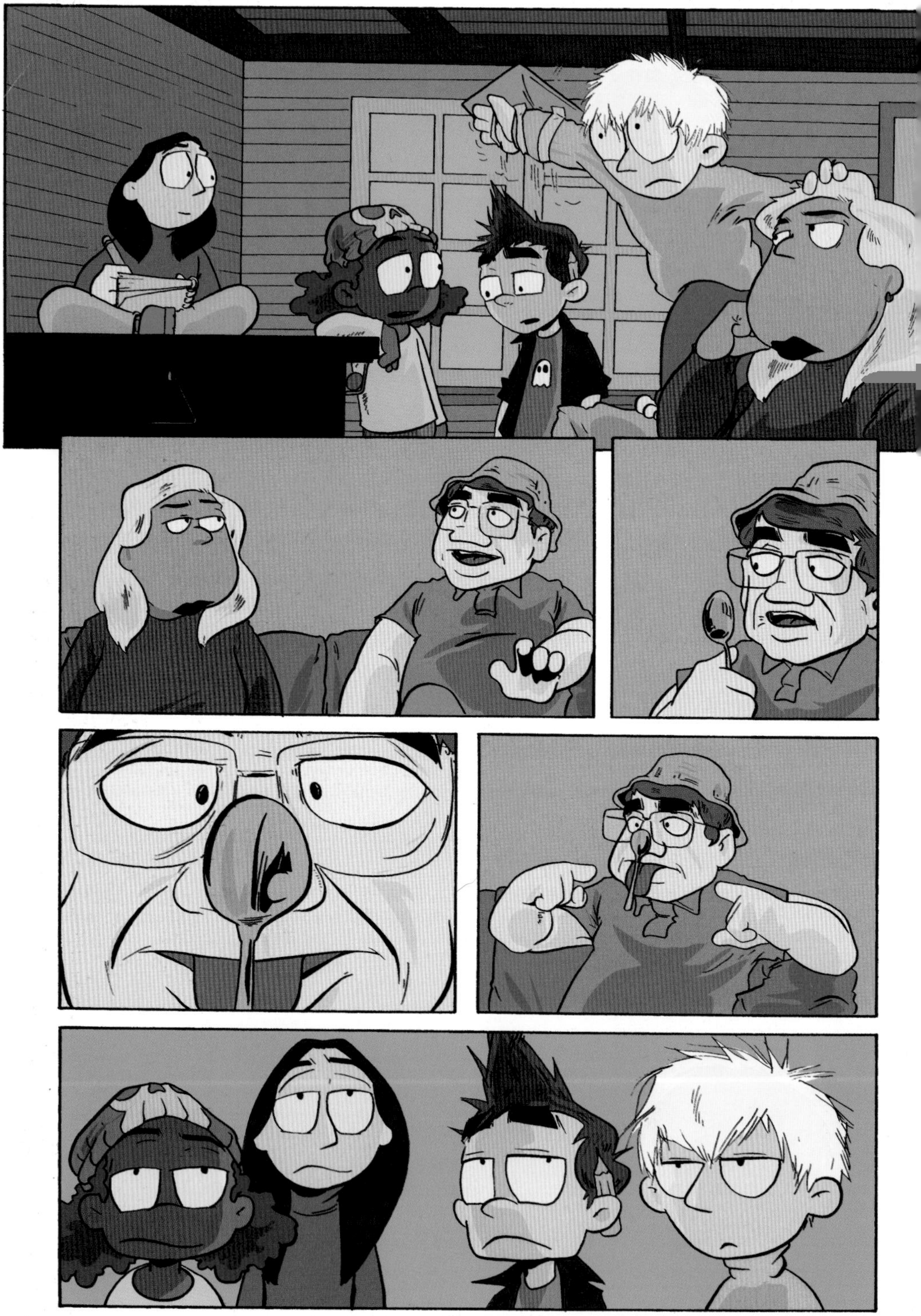

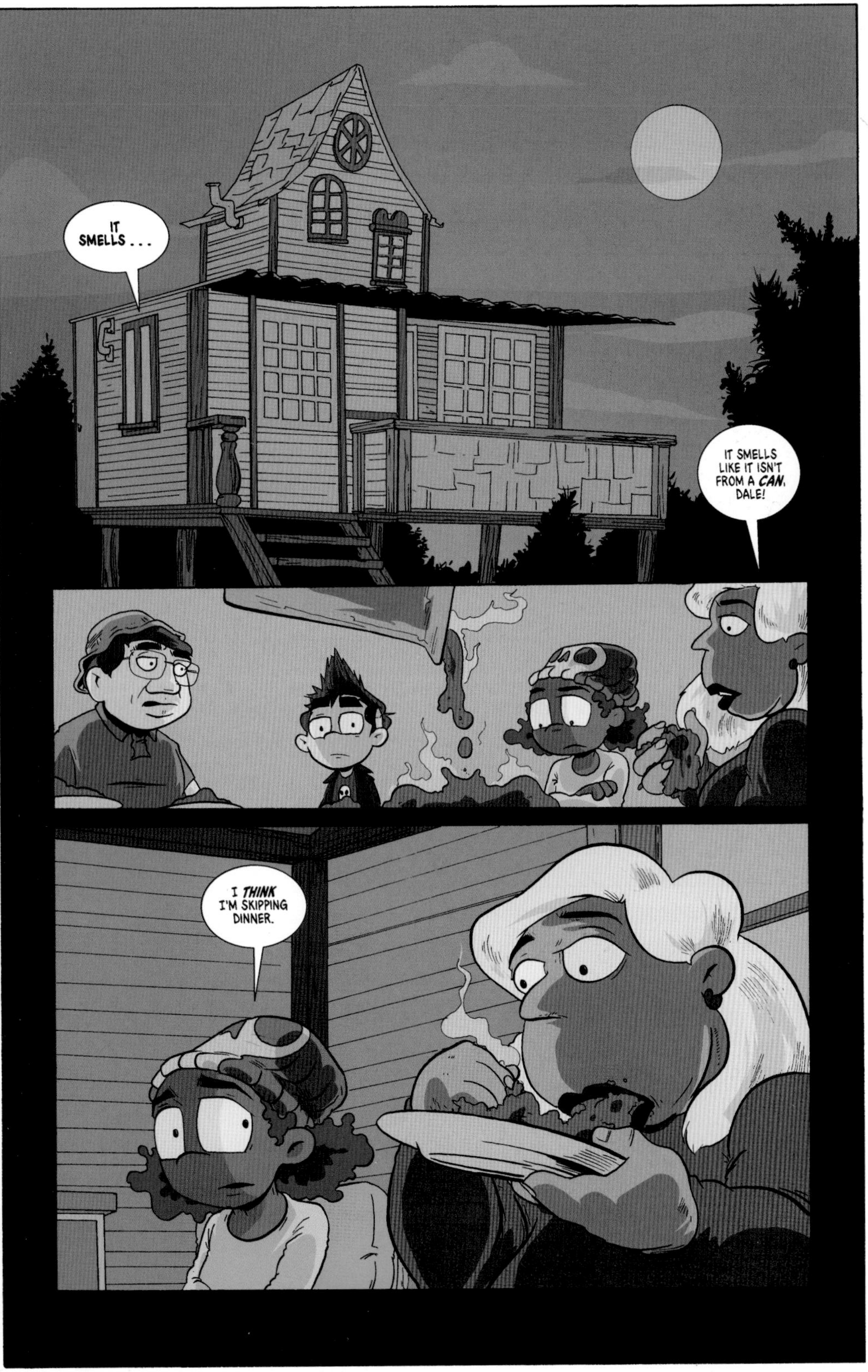
IT SMELLS . . .
IT SMELLS LIKE IT ISN'T FROM A *CAN*, DALE!
I *THINK* I'M SKIPPING DINNER.

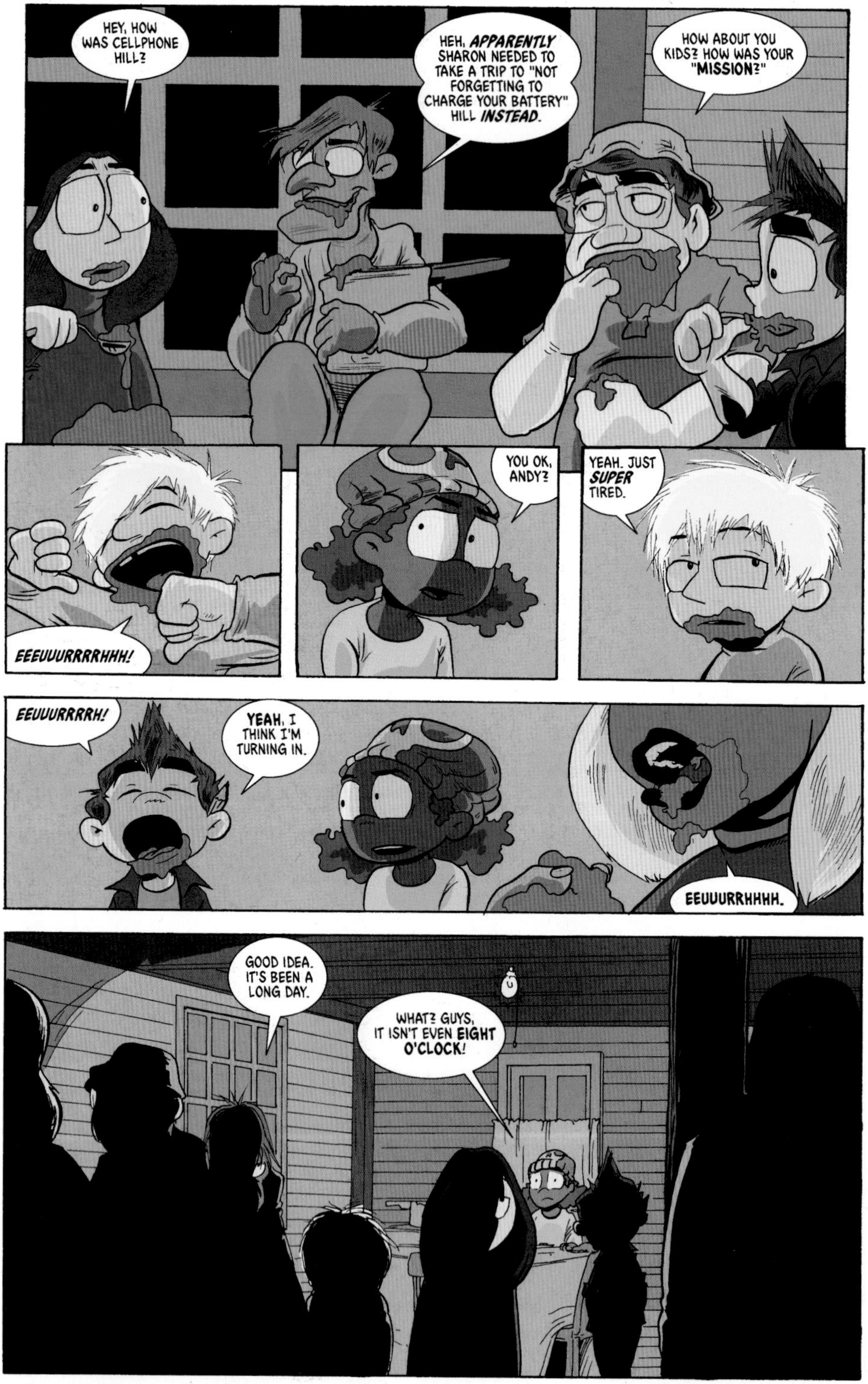
HEY, HOW WAS CELLPHONE HILL?
HEH, APPARENTLY SHARON NEEDED TO TAKE A TRIP TO "NOT FORGETTING TO CHARGE YOUR BATTERY" HILL INSTEAD.
HOW ABOUT YOU KIDS? HOW WAS YOUR "MISSION?"
EEEUUURRRRHHH!
YOU OK, ANDY?
YEAH. JUST SUPER TIRED.
EEUUURRRRH!
YEAH, I THINK I'M TURNING IN.
EEUUURRHHHH.
GOOD IDEA. IT'S BEEN A LONG DAY.
WHAT? GUYS, IT ISN'T EVEN EIGHT O'CLOCK!

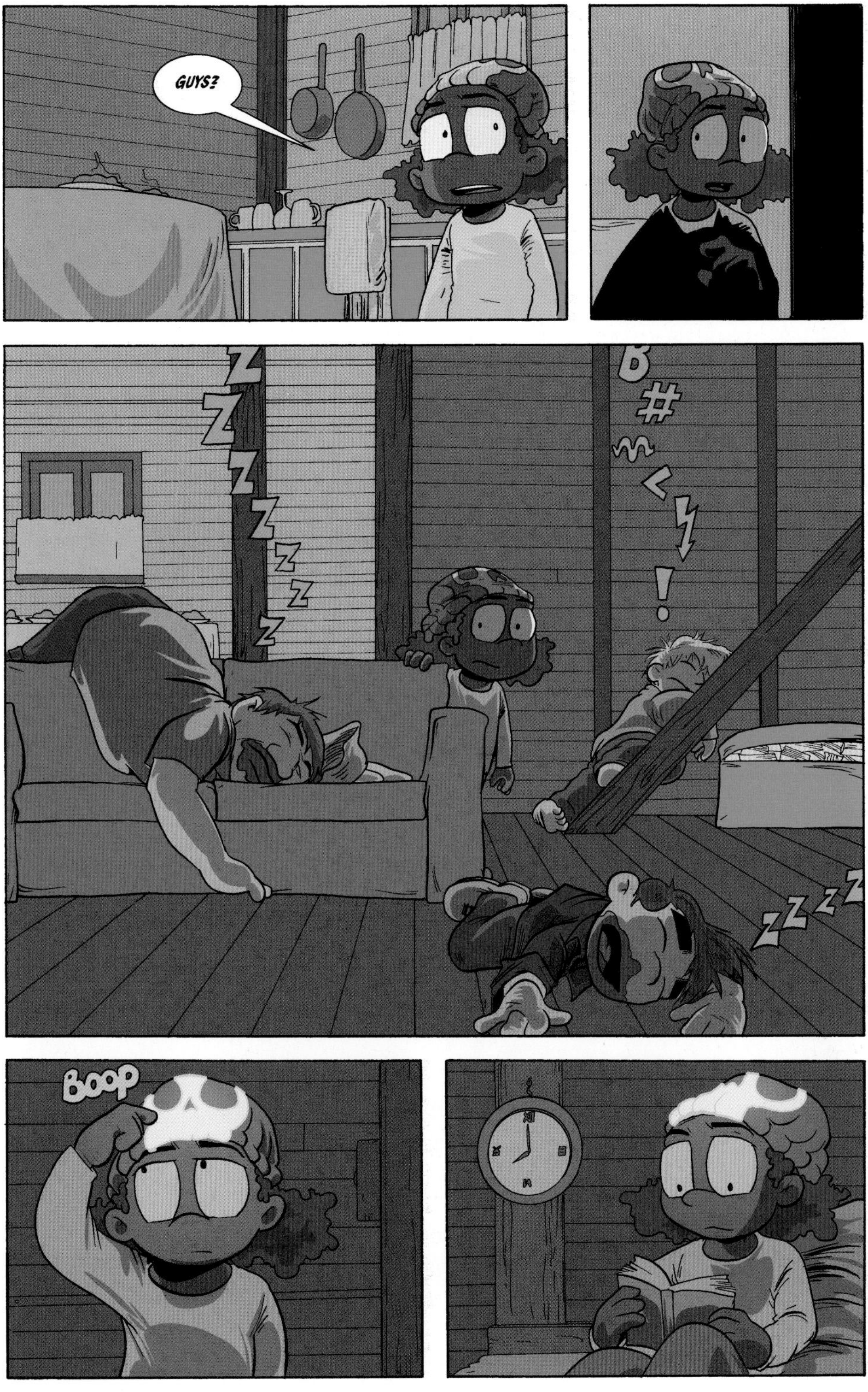
GUYS?
BOOP

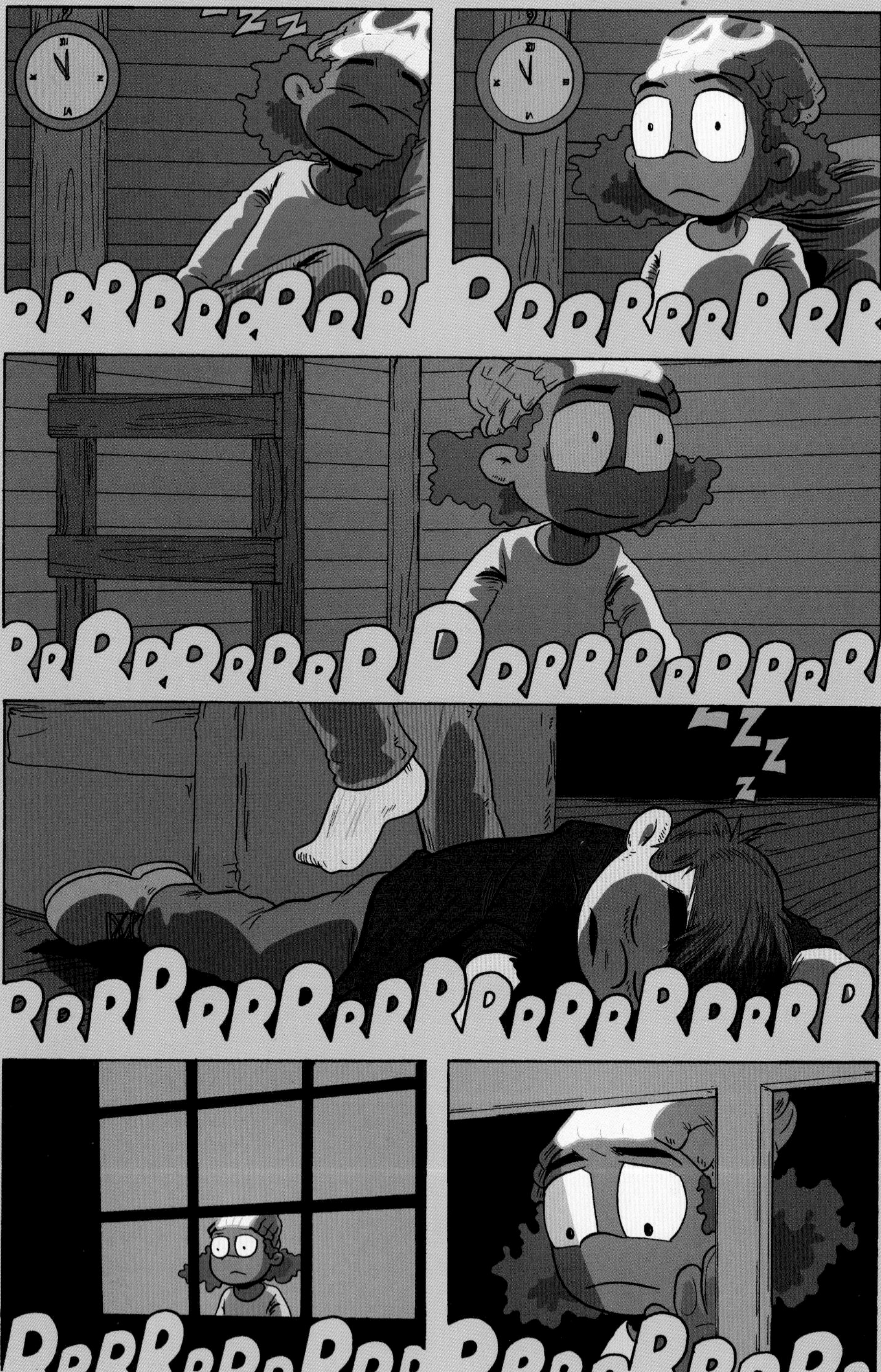

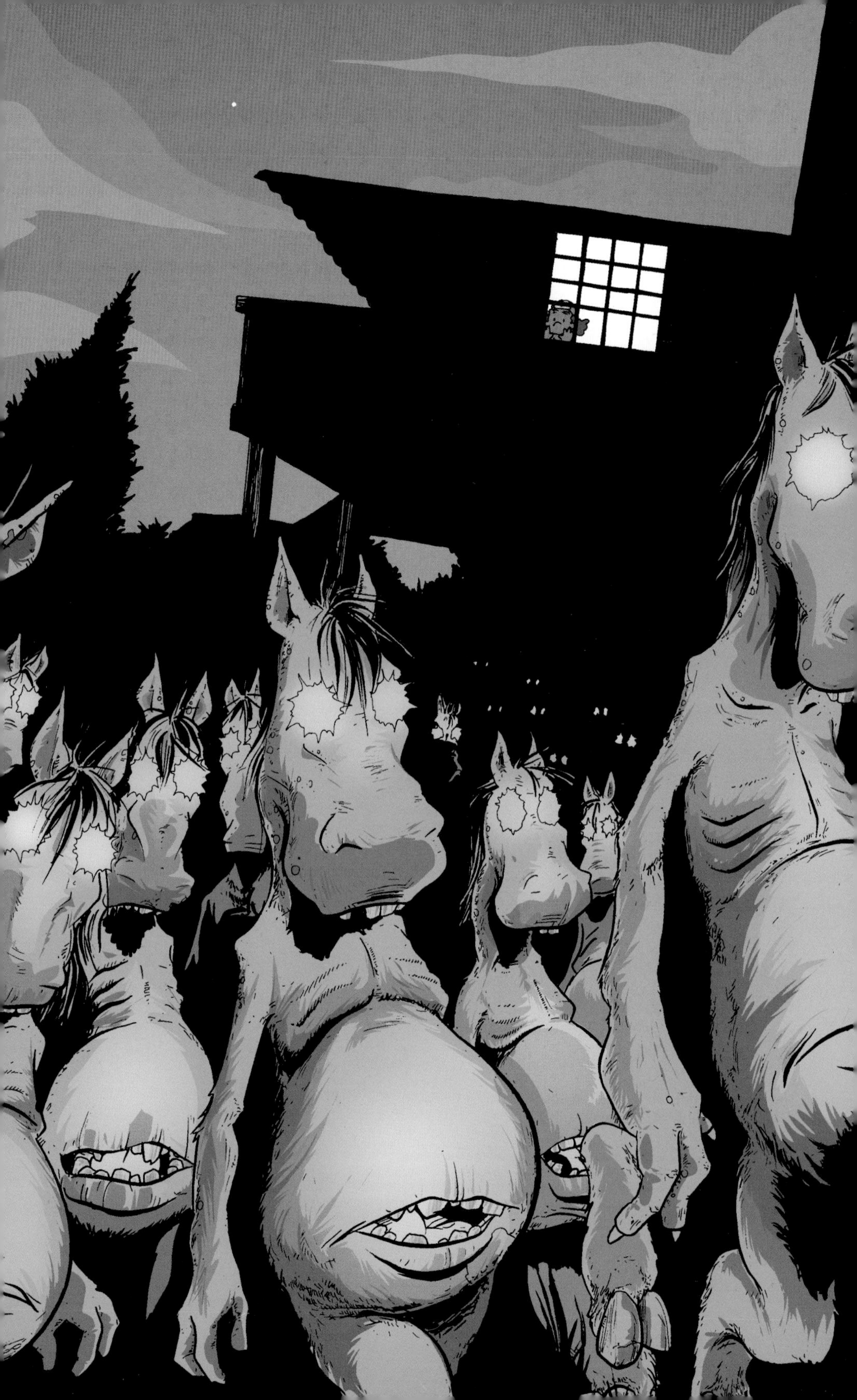

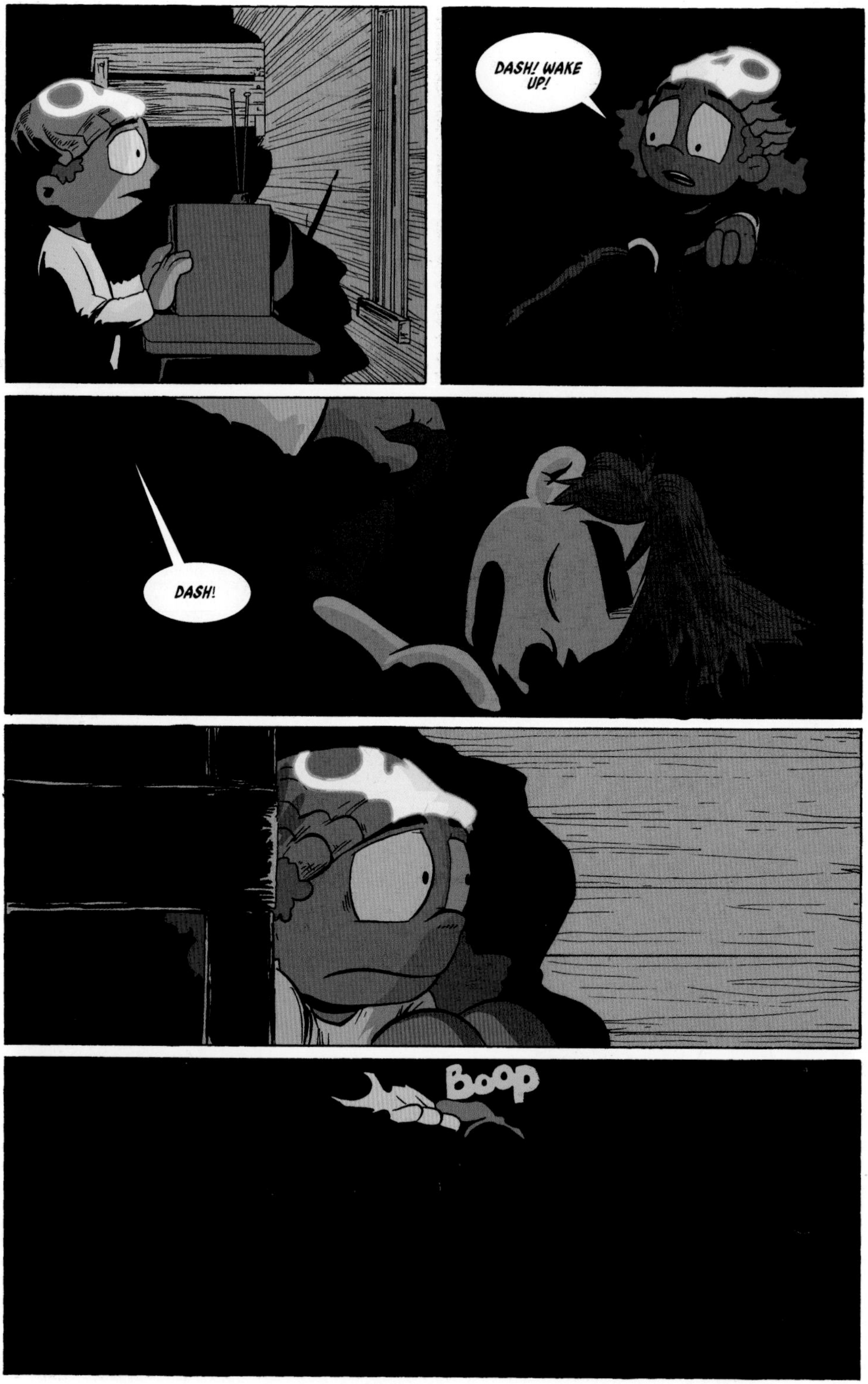
DASH! WAKE UP!
DASH!
Boop

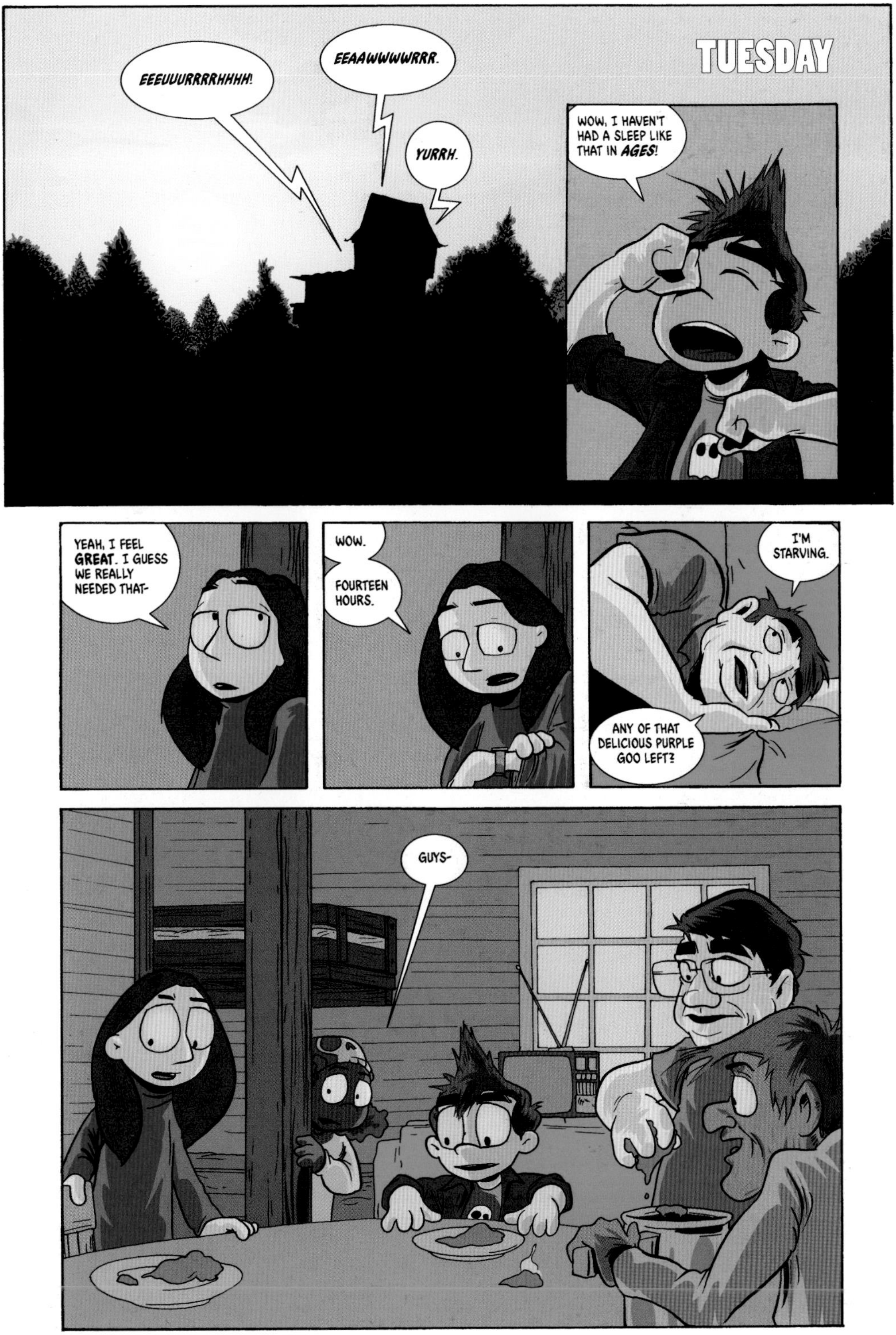
TUESDAY
EEEUUURRRRHHHH!
EEAAWWWWRRR.
YURRH.
WOW, I HAVEN'T HAD A SLEEP LIKE THAT IN AGES!
YEAH, I FEEL GREAT. I GUESS WE REALLY NEEDED THAT-
WOW.
FOURTEEN HOURS.
I'M STARVING.
ANY OF THAT DELICIOUS PURPLE GOO LEFT?
GUYS-

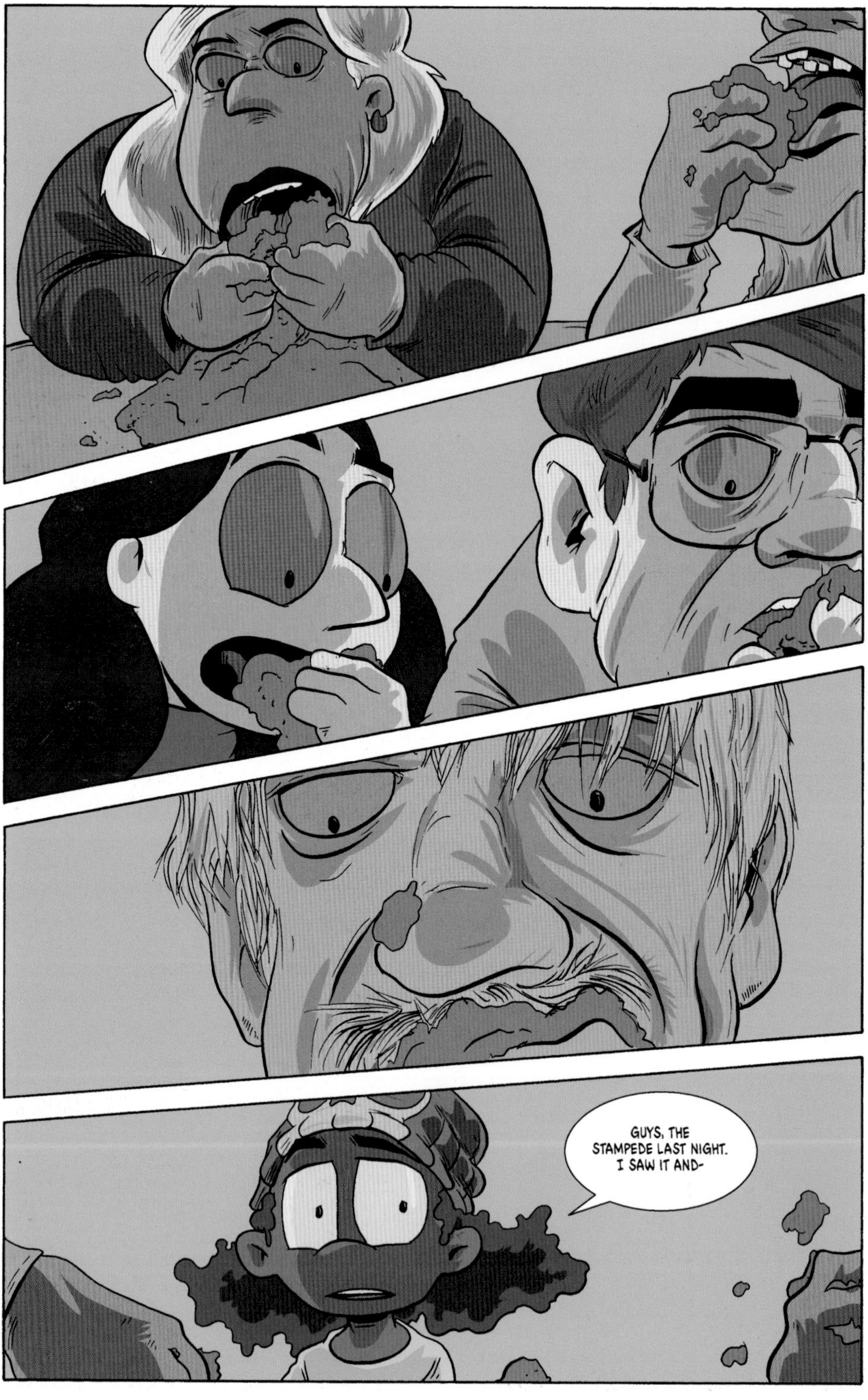
GUYS, THE STAMPEDE LAST NIGHT. I SAW IT AND-

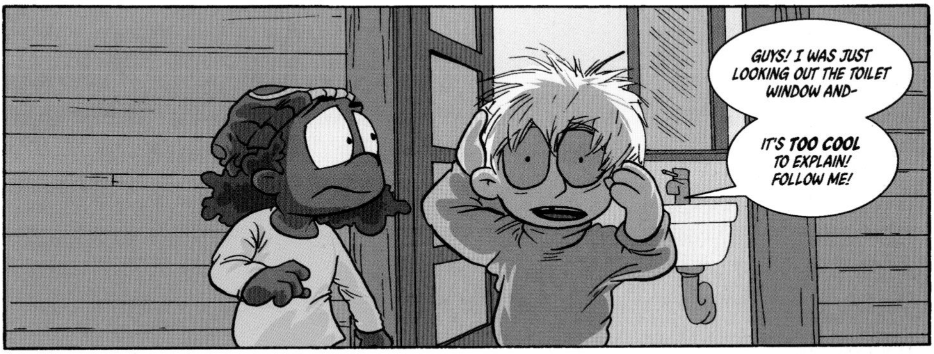
GUYS! I WAS JUST LOOKING OUT THE TOILET WINDOW AND-
IT'S TOO COOL TO EXPLAIN! FOLLOW ME!

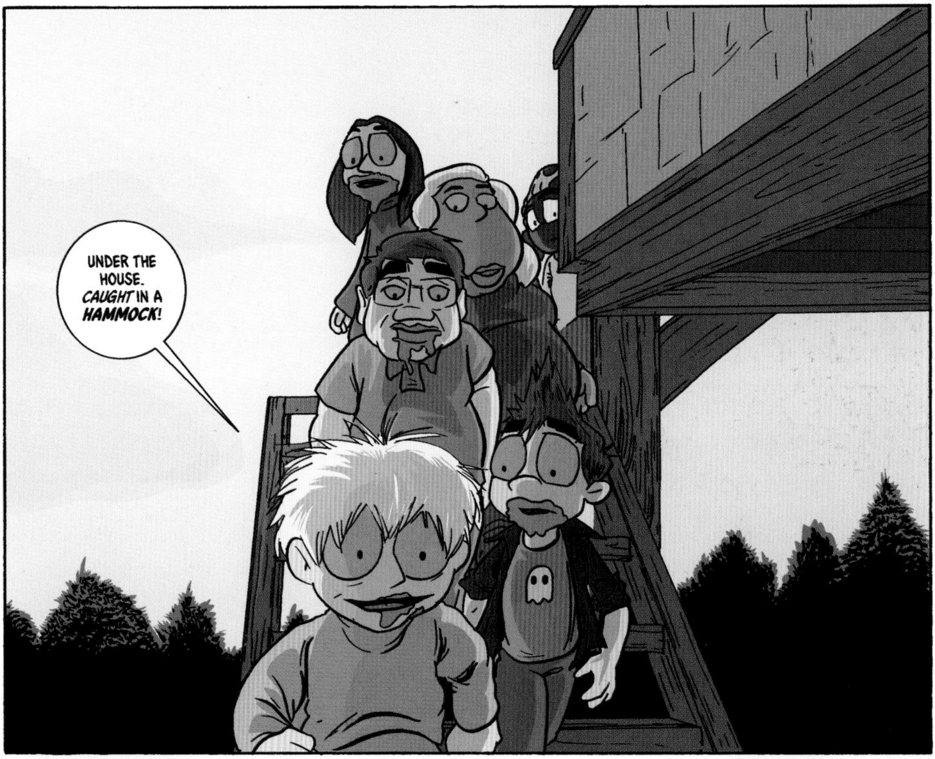
UNDER THE HOUSE. CAUGHT IN A HAMMOCK!

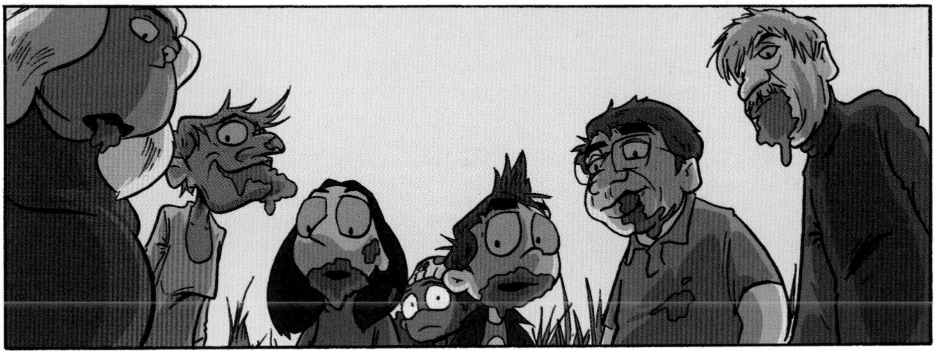

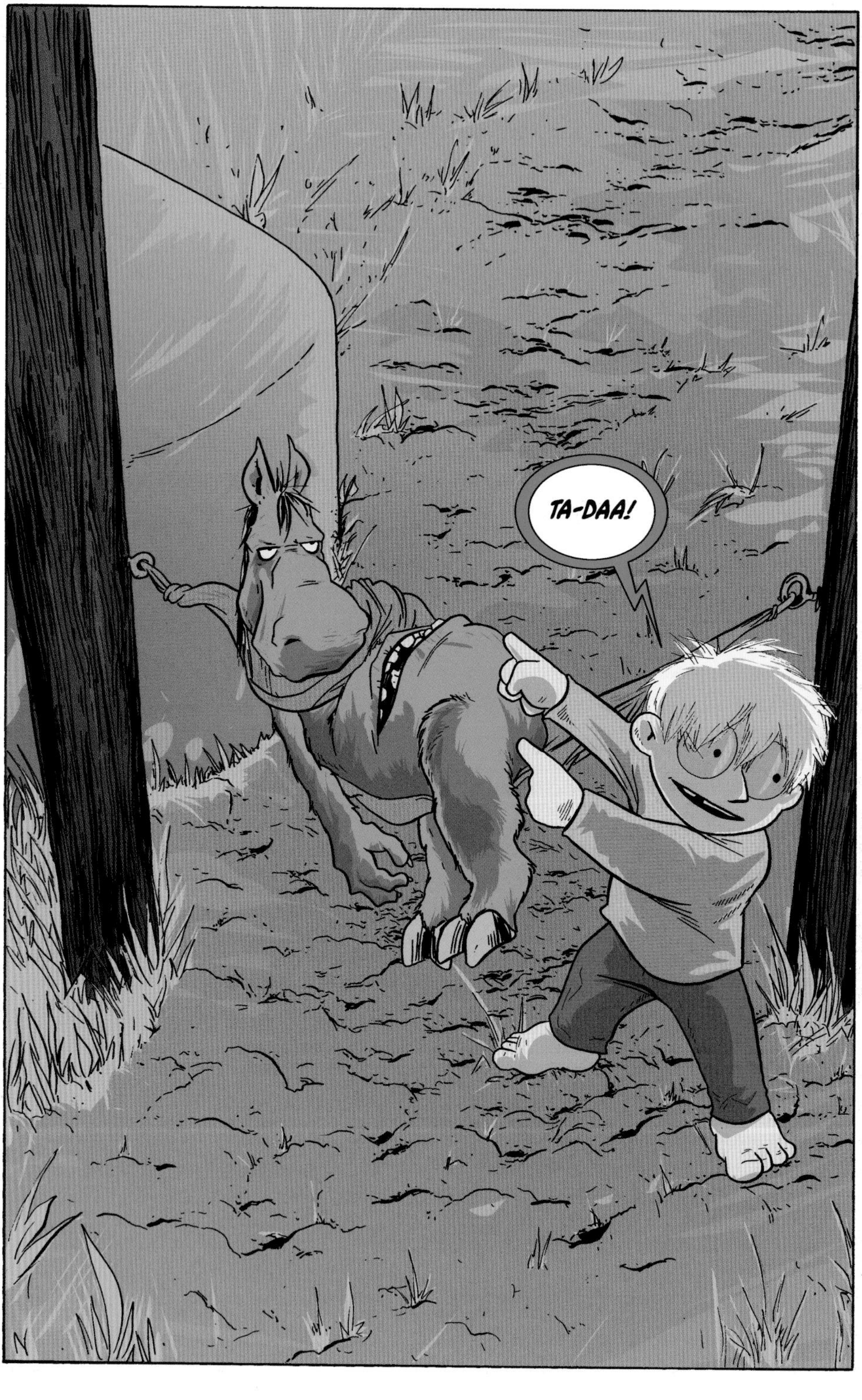
TA-DAA!

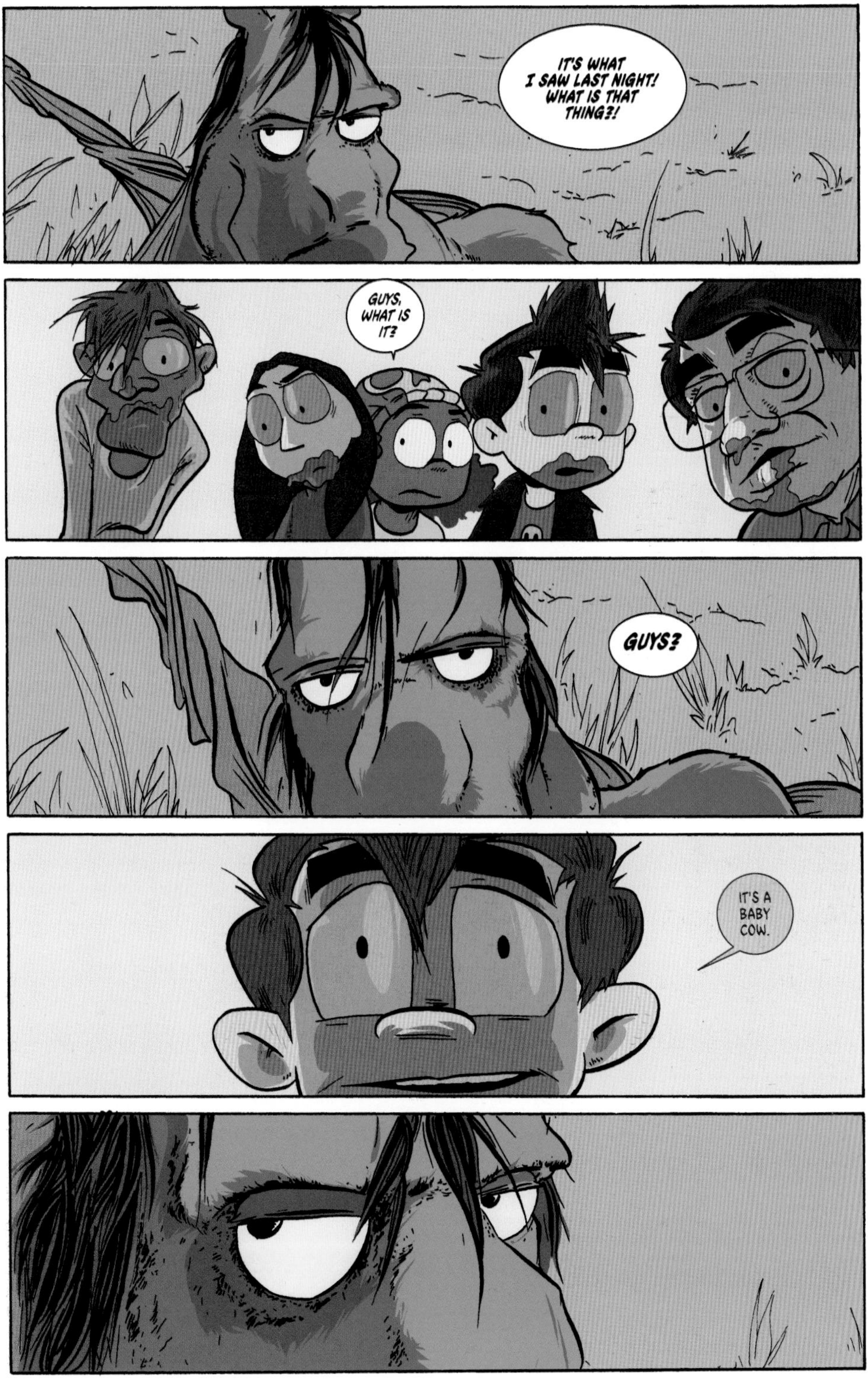
IT'S WHAT I SAW LAST NIGHT! WHAT IS THAT THING?!
GUYS, WHAT IS IT?
GUYS?
IT'S A BABY COW.

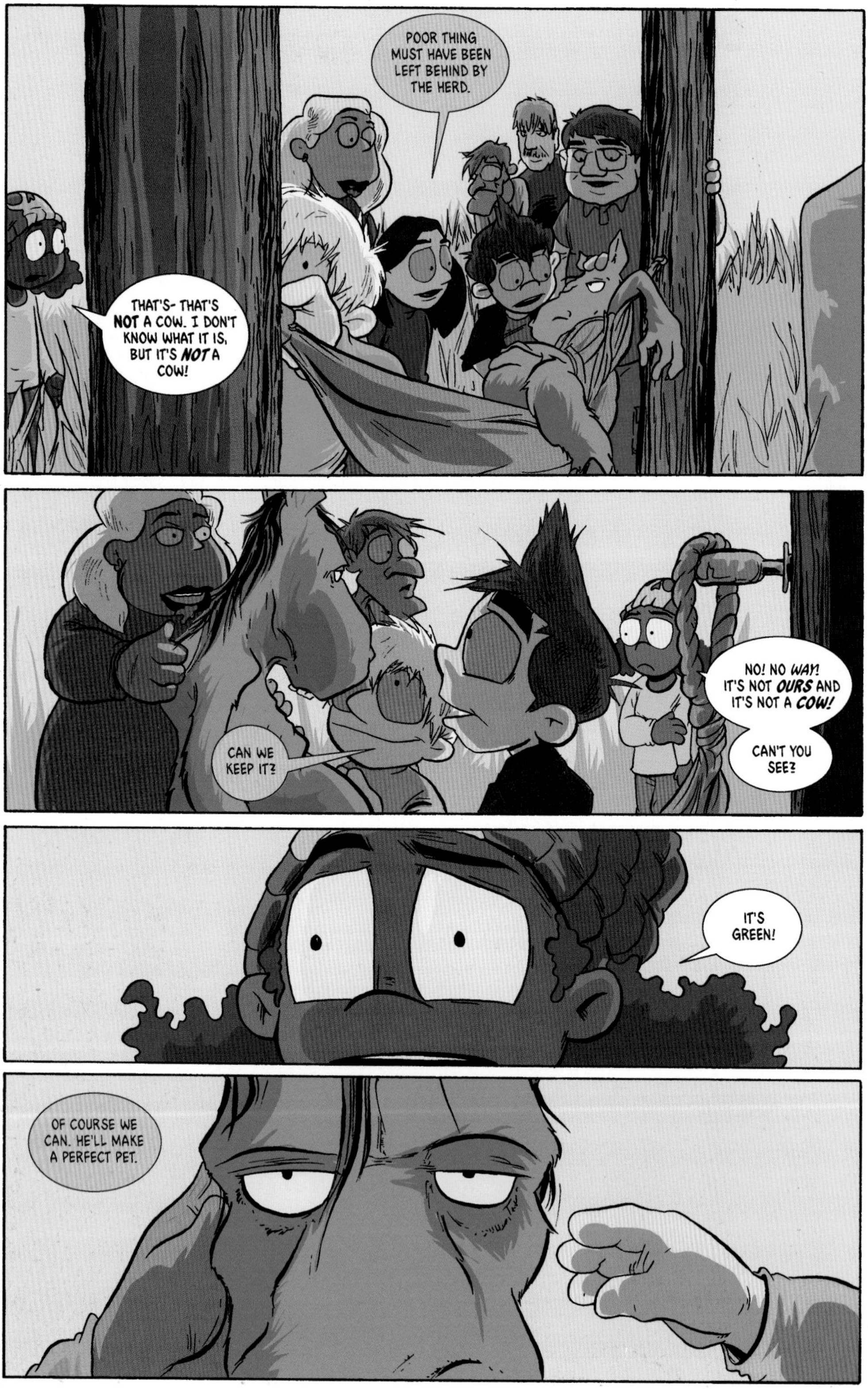
POOR THING MUST HAVE BEEN LEFT BEHIND BY THE HERD.
THAT'S- THAT'S NOT A COW. I DON'T KNOW WHAT IT IS, BUT IT'S NOT A COW!
CAN WE KEEP IT?
NO! NO WAY! IT'S NOT OURS AND IT'S NOT A COW!
CAN'T YOU SEE?
IT'S GREEN!
OF COURSE WE CAN. HE'LL MAKE A PERFECT PET.

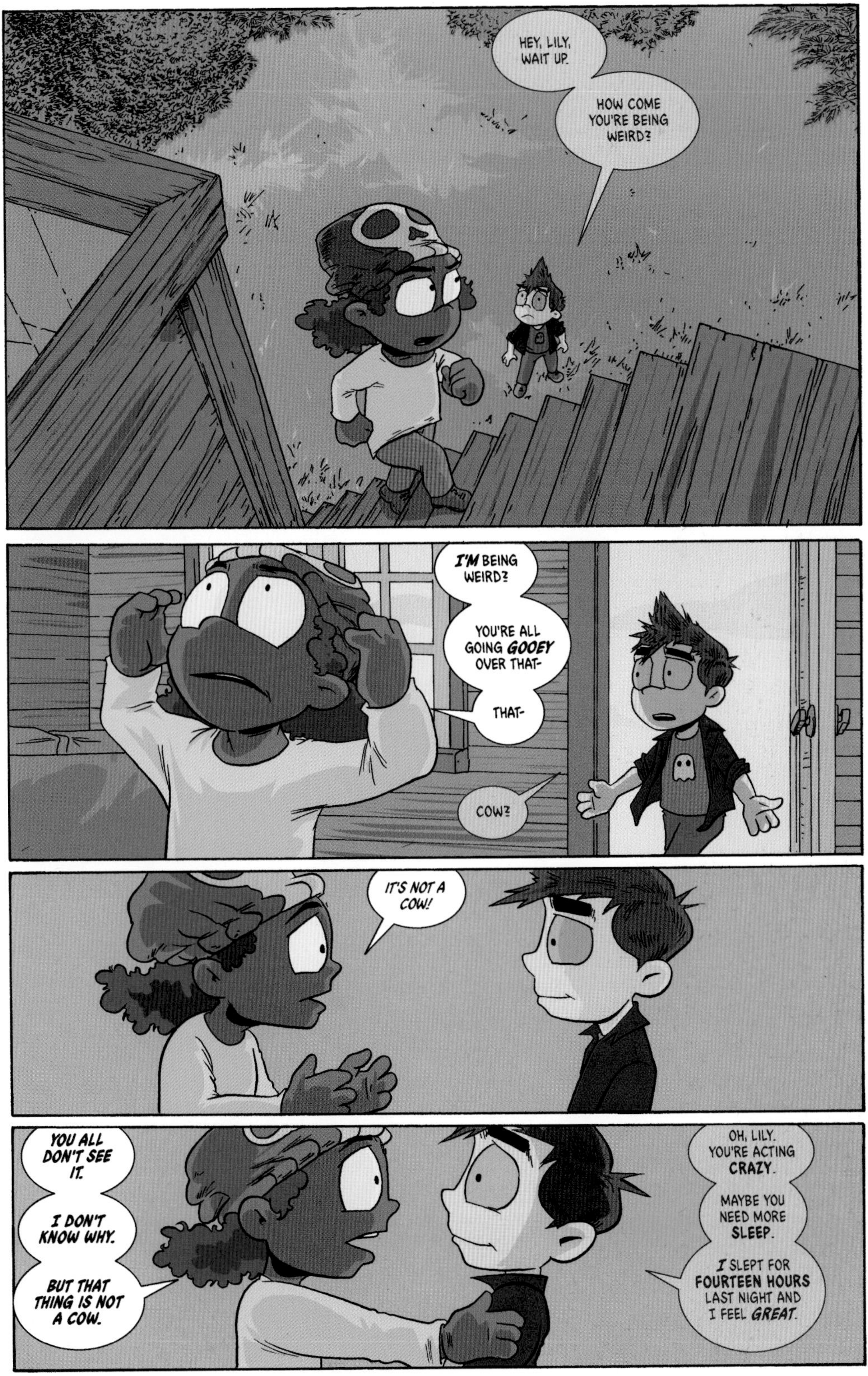
HEY, LILY, WAIT UP.
HOW COME YOU'RE BEING WEIRD?
I'M BEING WEIRD?
YOU'RE ALL GOING GOOEY OVER THAT-
THAT-
COW?
IT'S NOT A COW!
YOU ALL DON'T SEE IT.
I DON'T KNOW WHY.
BUT THAT THING IS NOT A COW.
OH, LILY. YOU'RE ACTING CRAZY.
MAYBE YOU NEED MORE SLEEP.
I SLEPT FOR FOURTEEN HOURS LAST NIGHT AND I FEEL GREAT.

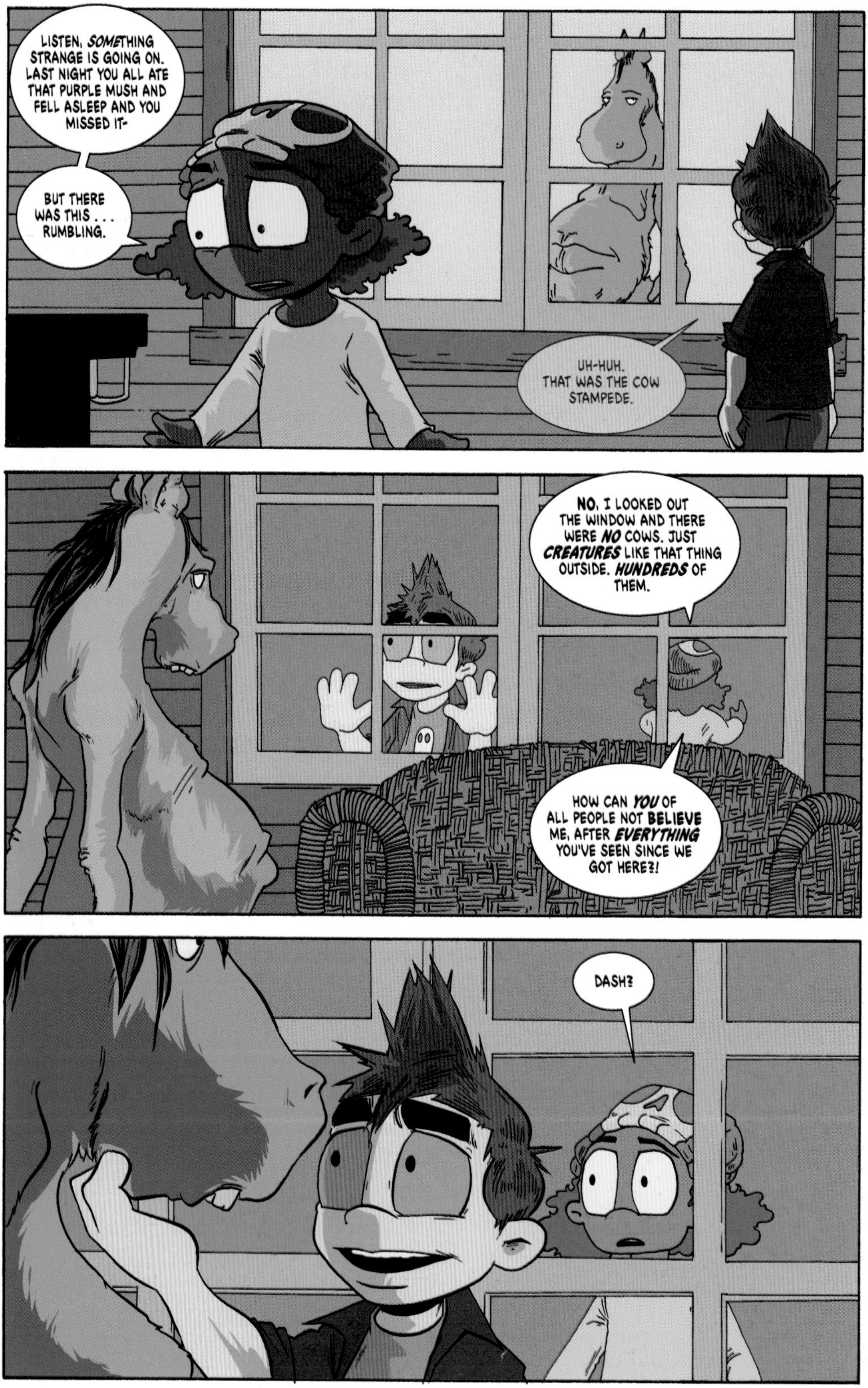
LISTEN, *SOME*THING STRANGE IS GOING ON. LAST NIGHT YOU ALL ATE THAT PURPLE MUSH AND FELL ASLEEP AND YOU MISSED IT-
BUT THERE WAS THIS . . . RUMBLING.
UH-HUH. THAT WAS THE COW STAMPEDE.
NO, I LOOKED OUT THE WINDOW AND THERE WERE ***NO*** COWS. JUST ***CREATURES*** LIKE THAT THING OUTSIDE. ***HUNDREDS*** OF THEM.
HOW CAN ***YOU*** OF ALL PEOPLE NOT **BELIEVE** ME, AFTER ***EVERYTHING*** YOU'VE SEEN SINCE WE GOT HERE?!
DASH?

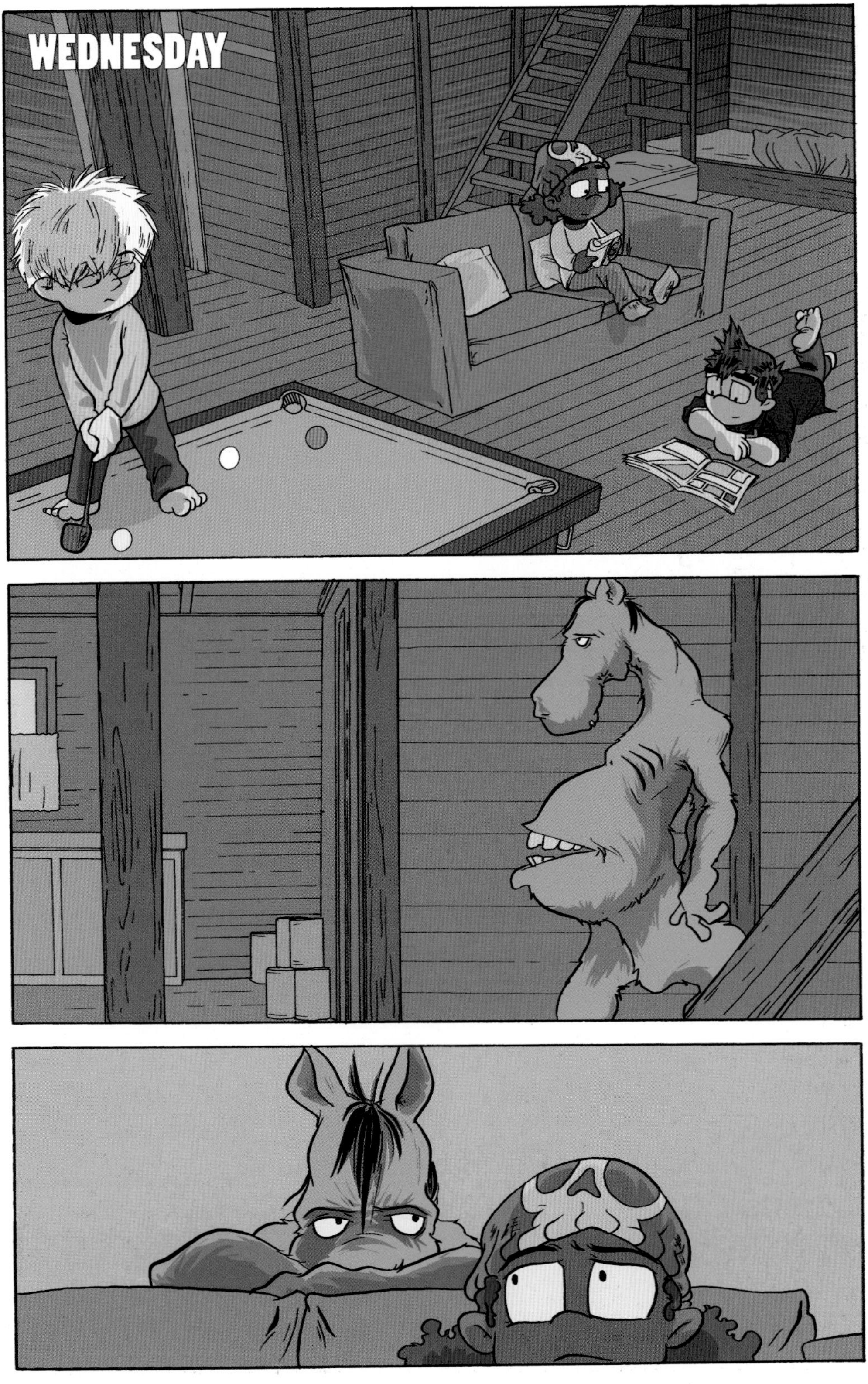
WEDNESDAY

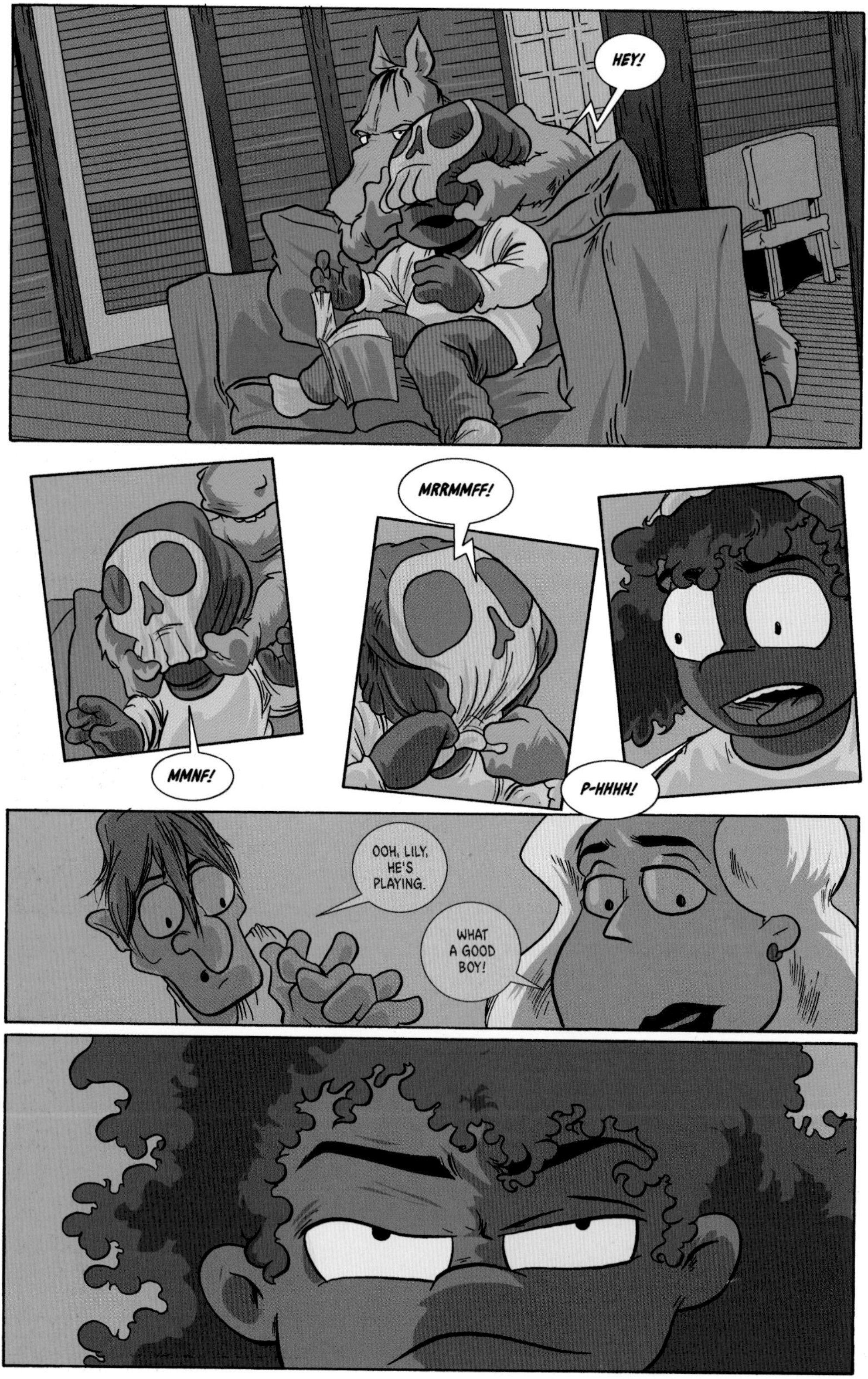
HEY!
MMNF!
MRRMMFF!
P-HHHH!
OOH, LILY, HE'S PLAYING.
WHAT A GOOD BOY!

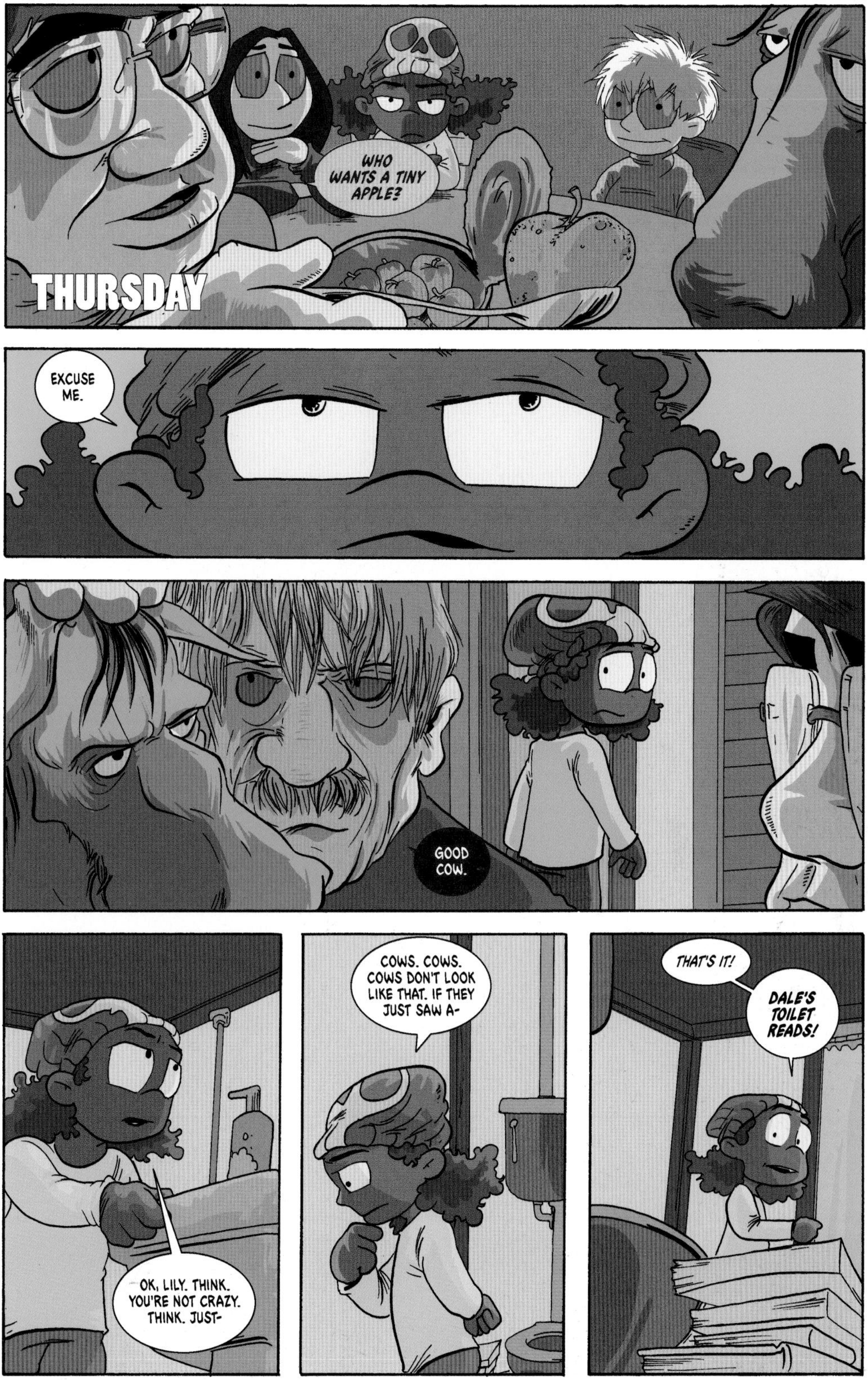
THURSDAY
WHO WANTS A TINY APPLE?
EXCUSE ME.
GOOD COW.
OK, LILY. THINK. YOU'RE NOT CRAZY. THINK. JUST-
COWS. COWS. COWS DON'T LOOK LIKE THAT. IF THEY JUST SAW A-
THAT'S IT!
DALE'S TOILET READS!

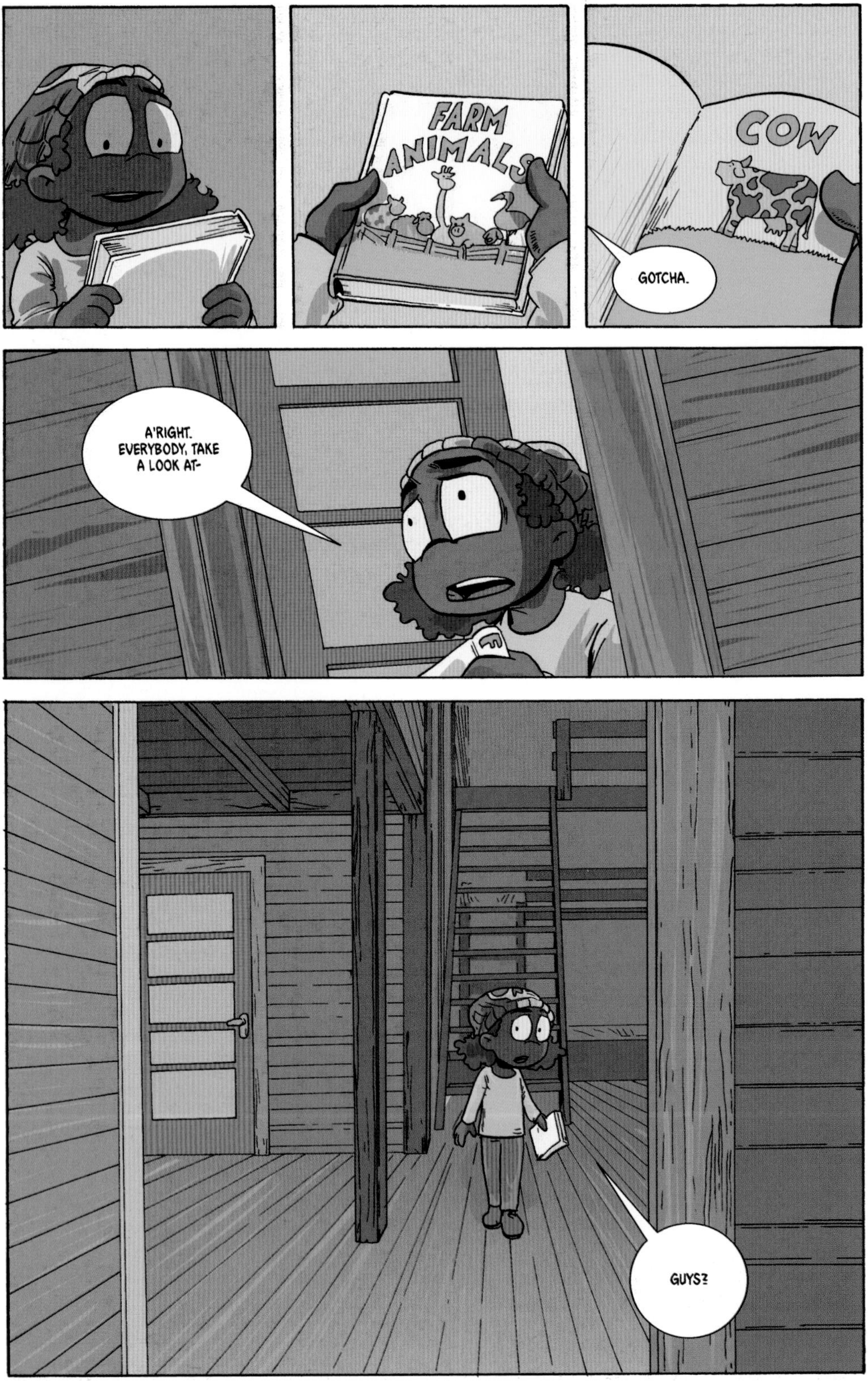
FARM ANIMALS
COW
GOTCHA.
A'RIGHT. EVERYBODY, TAKE A LOOK AT-
GUYS?

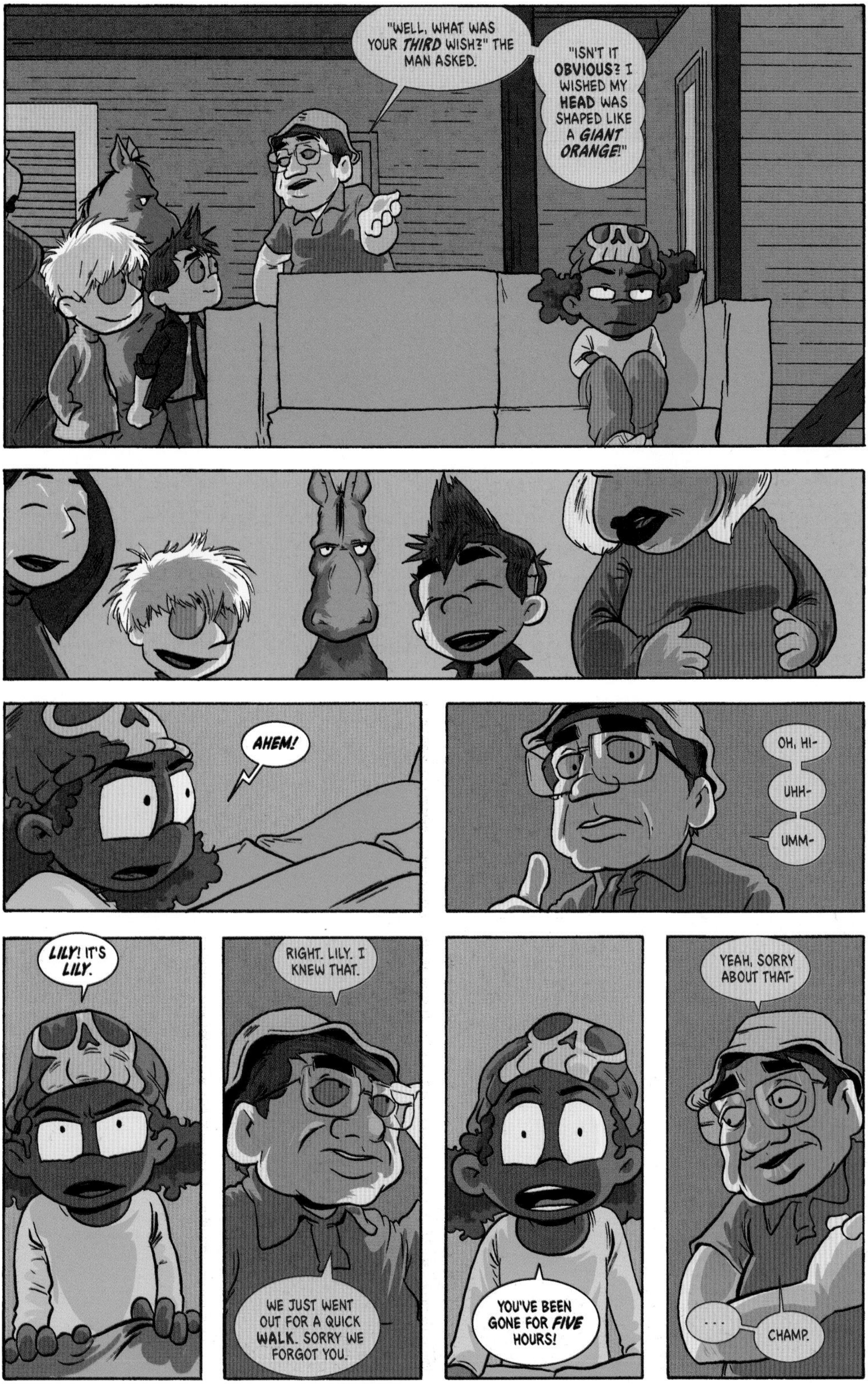
"WELL, WHAT WAS YOUR THIRD WISH?" THE MAN ASKED.
"ISN'T IT OBVIOUS? I WISHED MY HEAD WAS SHAPED LIKE A GIANT ORANGE!"
AHEM!
OH, HI-
UHH-
UMM-
LILY! IT'S LILY.
RIGHT. LILY. I KNEW THAT.
WE JUST WENT OUT FOR A QUICK WALK. SORRY WE FORGOT YOU.
YOU'VE BEEN GONE FOR FIVE HOURS!
YEAH, SORRY ABOUT THAT-
...
CHAMP.

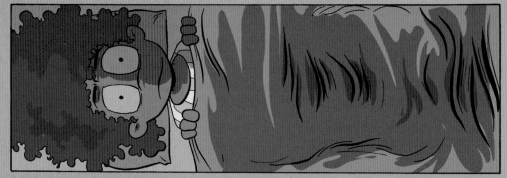

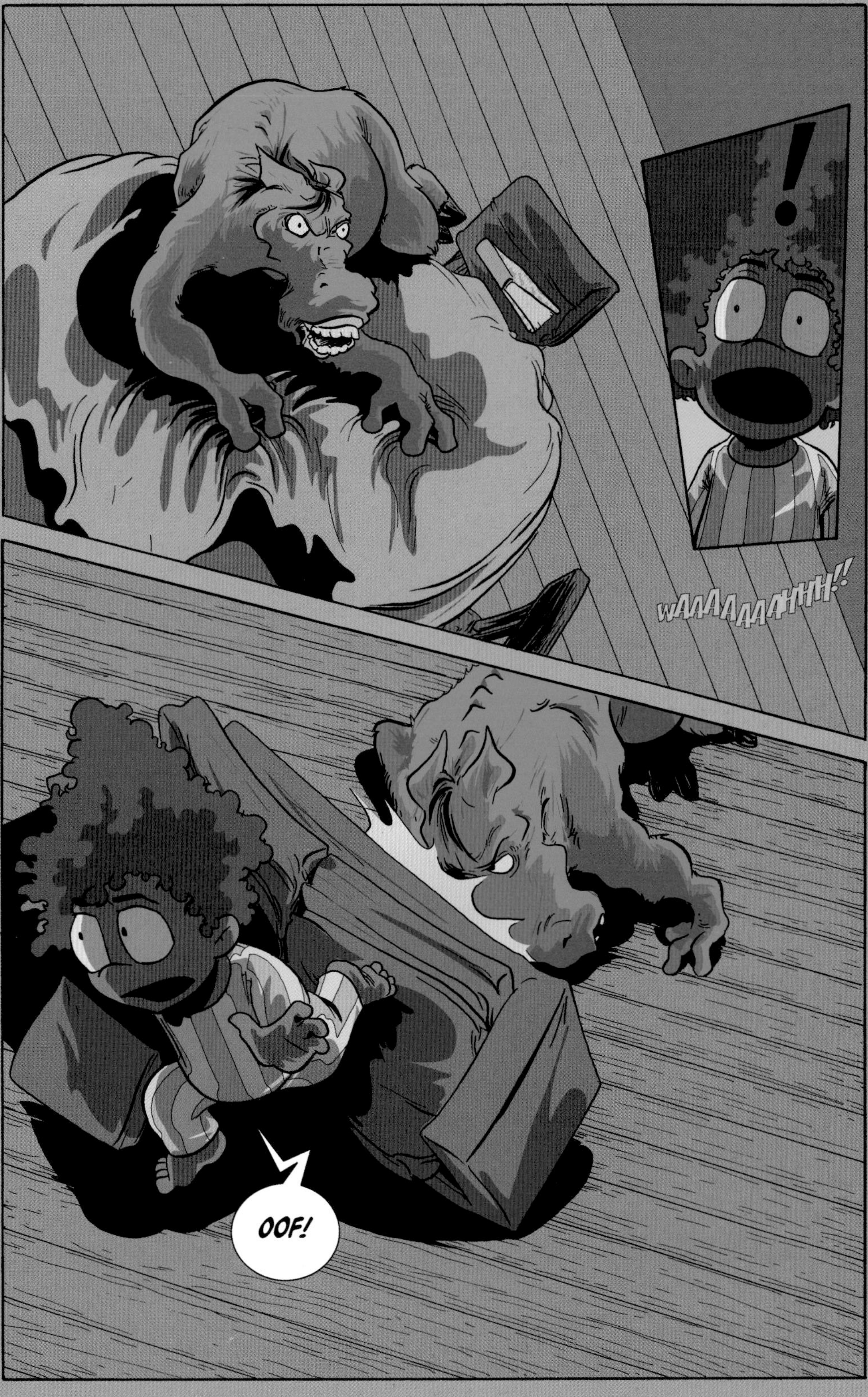
!
WAAAAAAAHHHH!!
OOF!

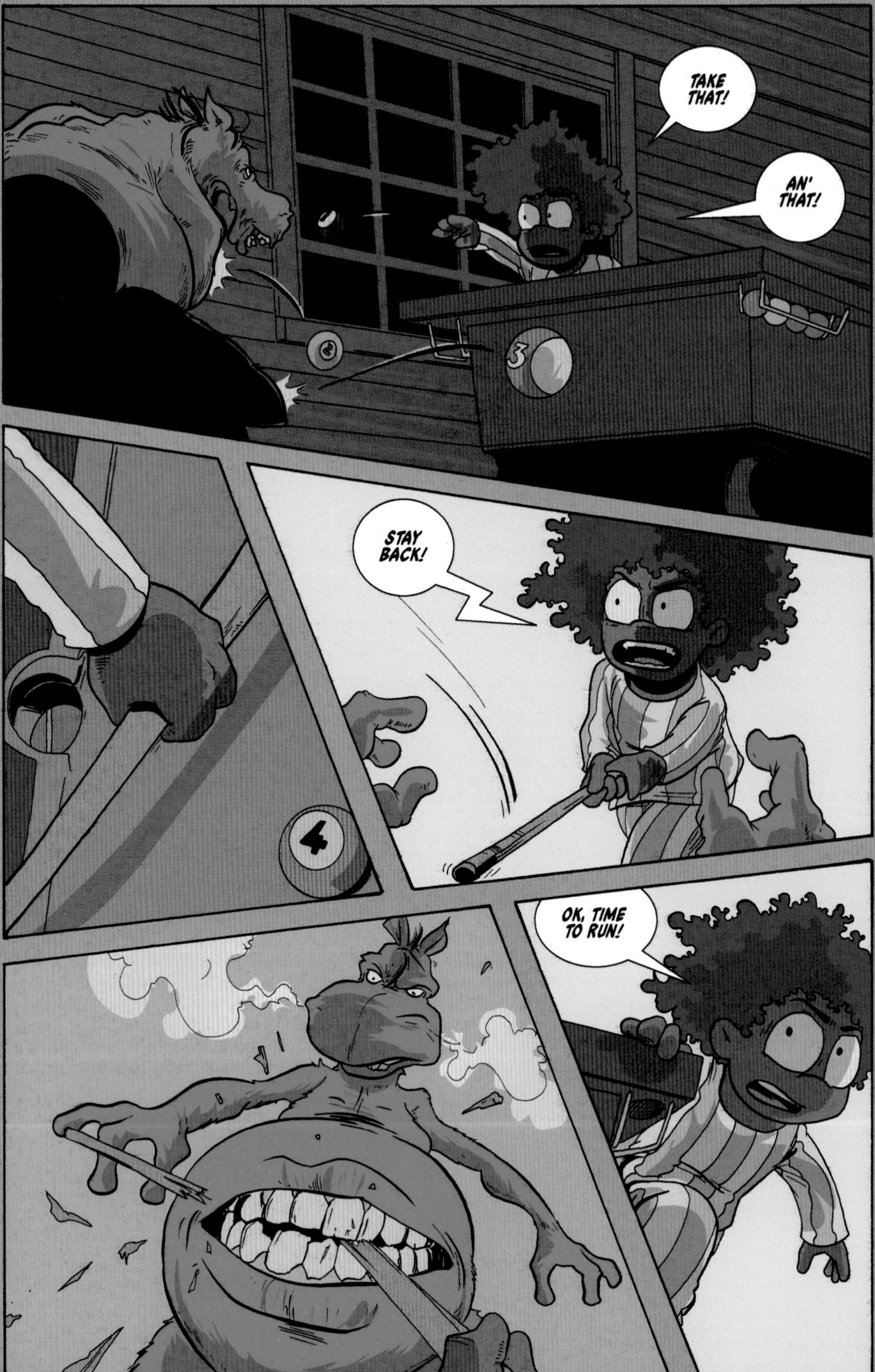
TAKE THAT!
AN' THAT!
STAY BACK!
OK, TIME TO RUN!

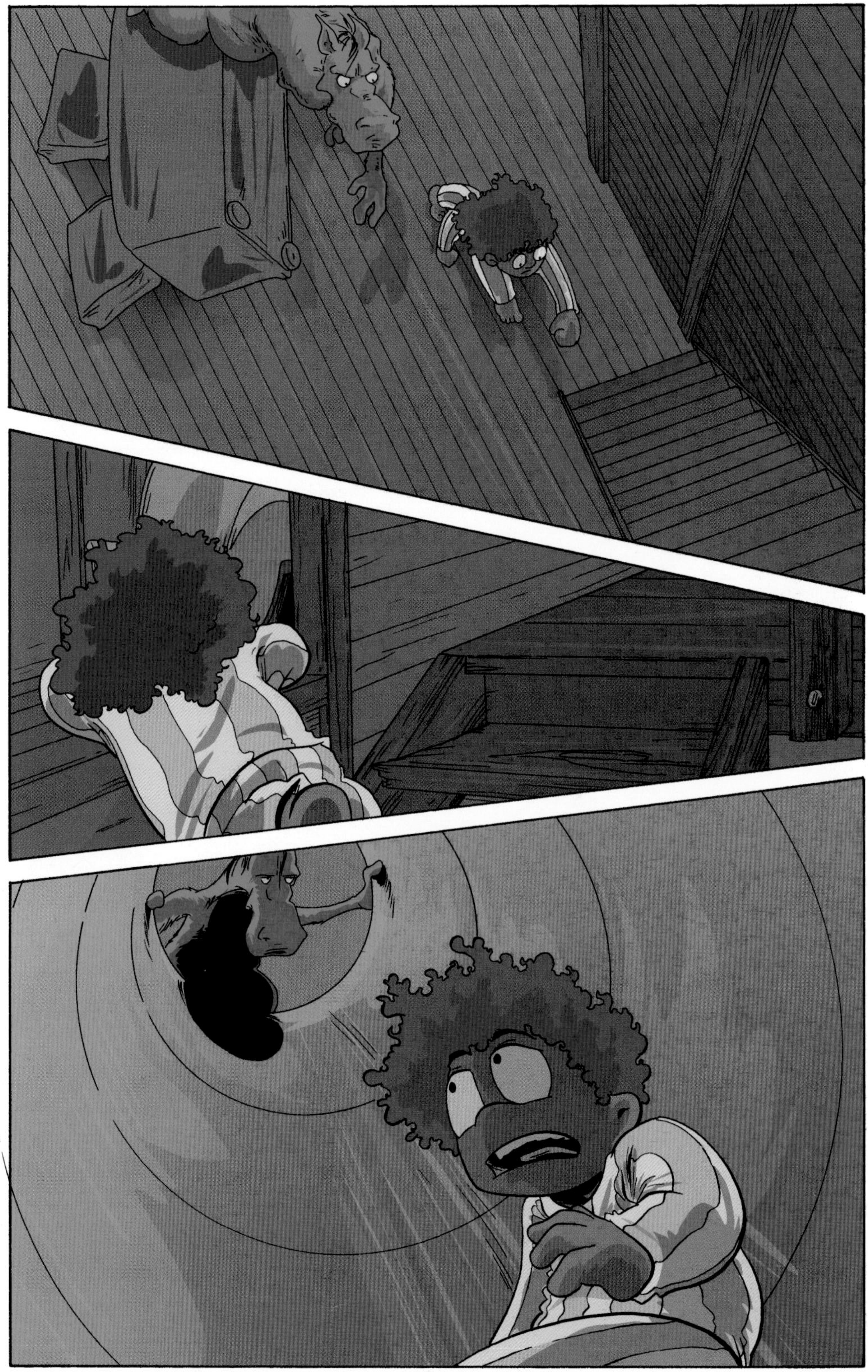

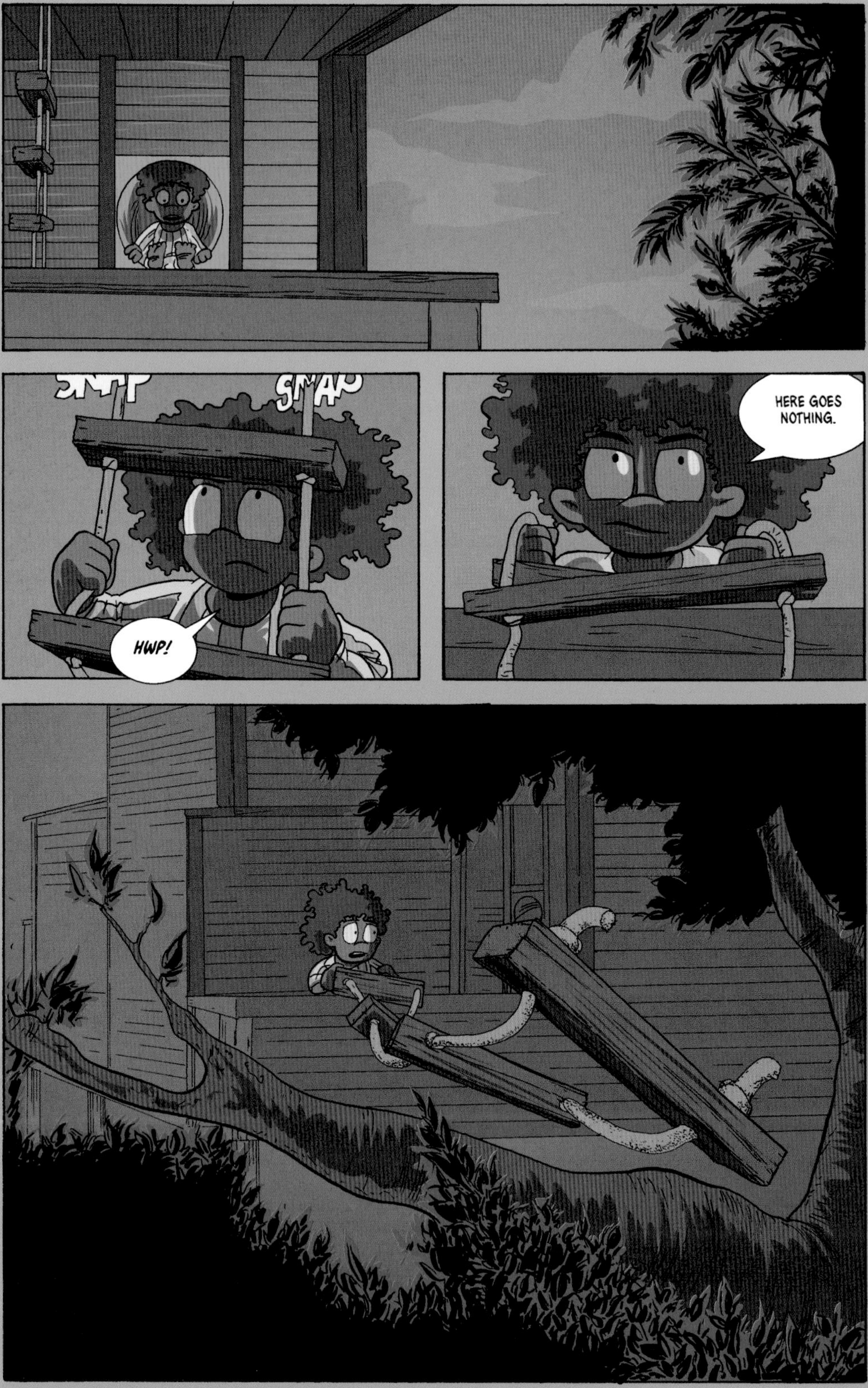
HWP!
HERE GOES NOTHING.

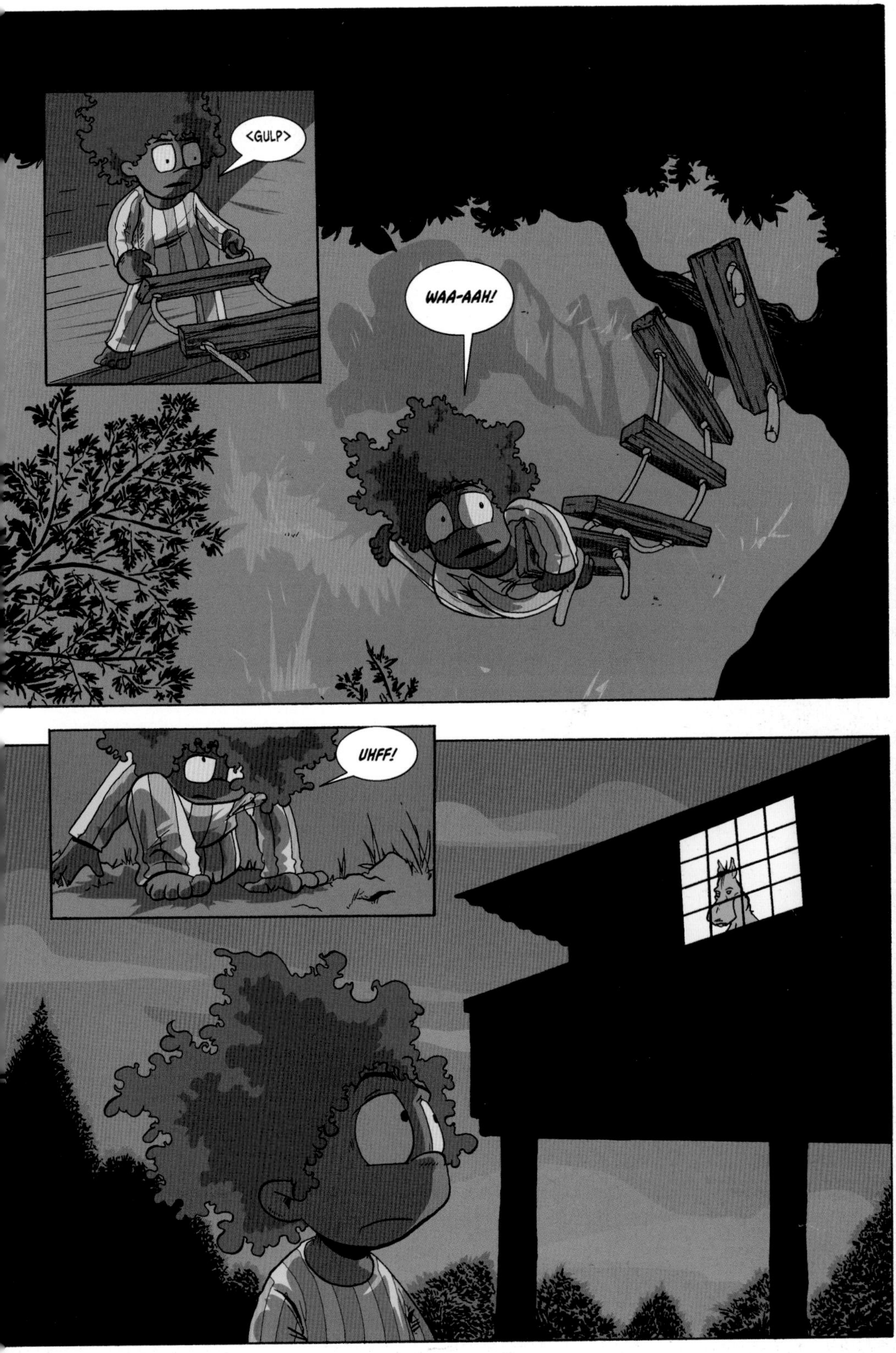
<GULP>
WAA-AAH!
UHFF!

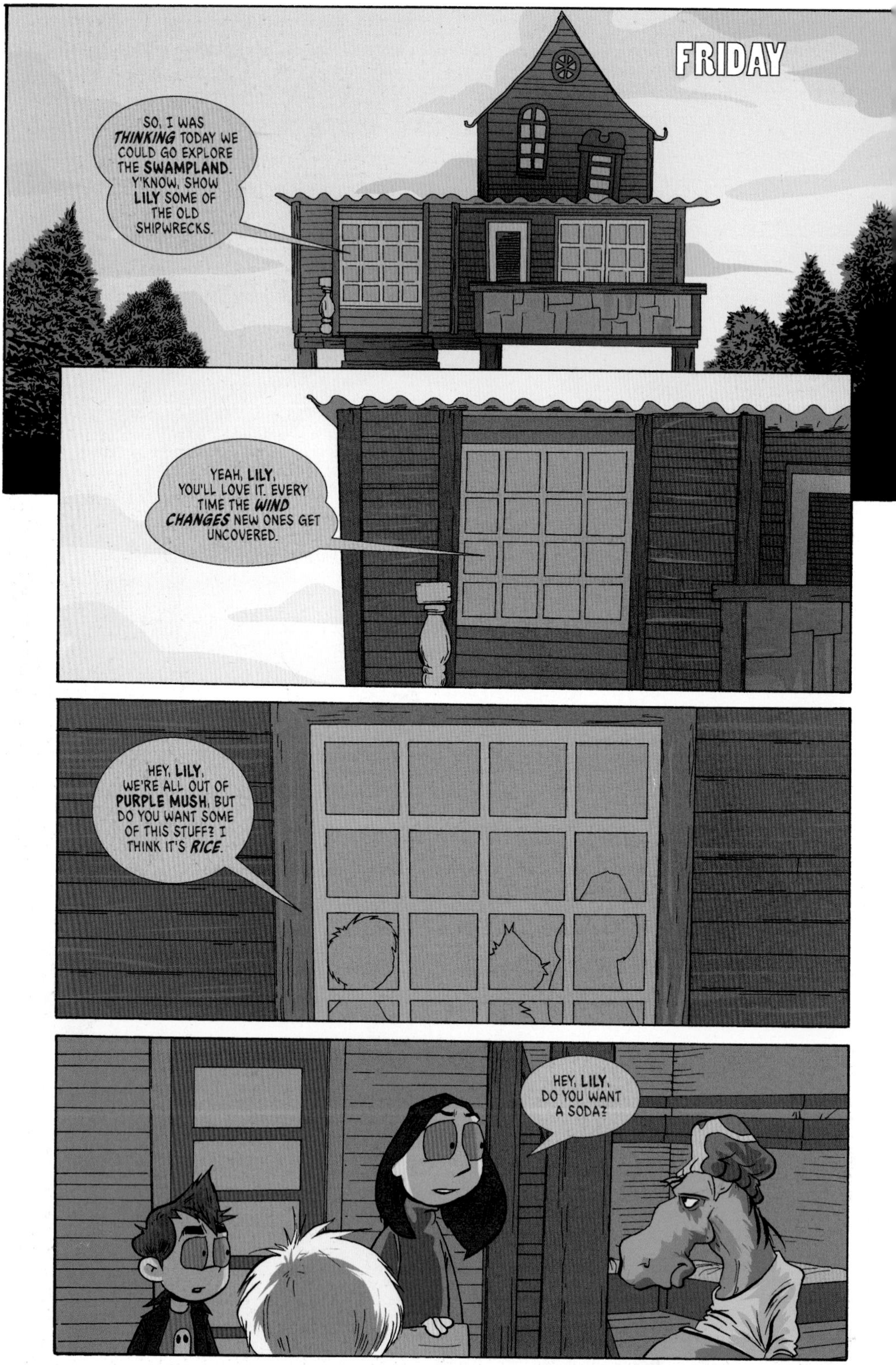
FRIDAY
SO, I WAS THINKING TODAY WE COULD GO EXPLORE THE SWAMPLAND. Y'KNOW, SHOW LILY SOME OF THE OLD SHIPWRECKS.
YEAH, LILY, YOU'LL LOVE IT. EVERY TIME THE WIND CHANGES NEW ONES GET UNCOVERED.
HEY, LILY, WE'RE ALL OUT OF PURPLE MUSH, BUT DO YOU WANT SOME OF THIS STUFF? I THINK IT'S RICE.
HEY, LILY, DO YOU WANT A SODA?

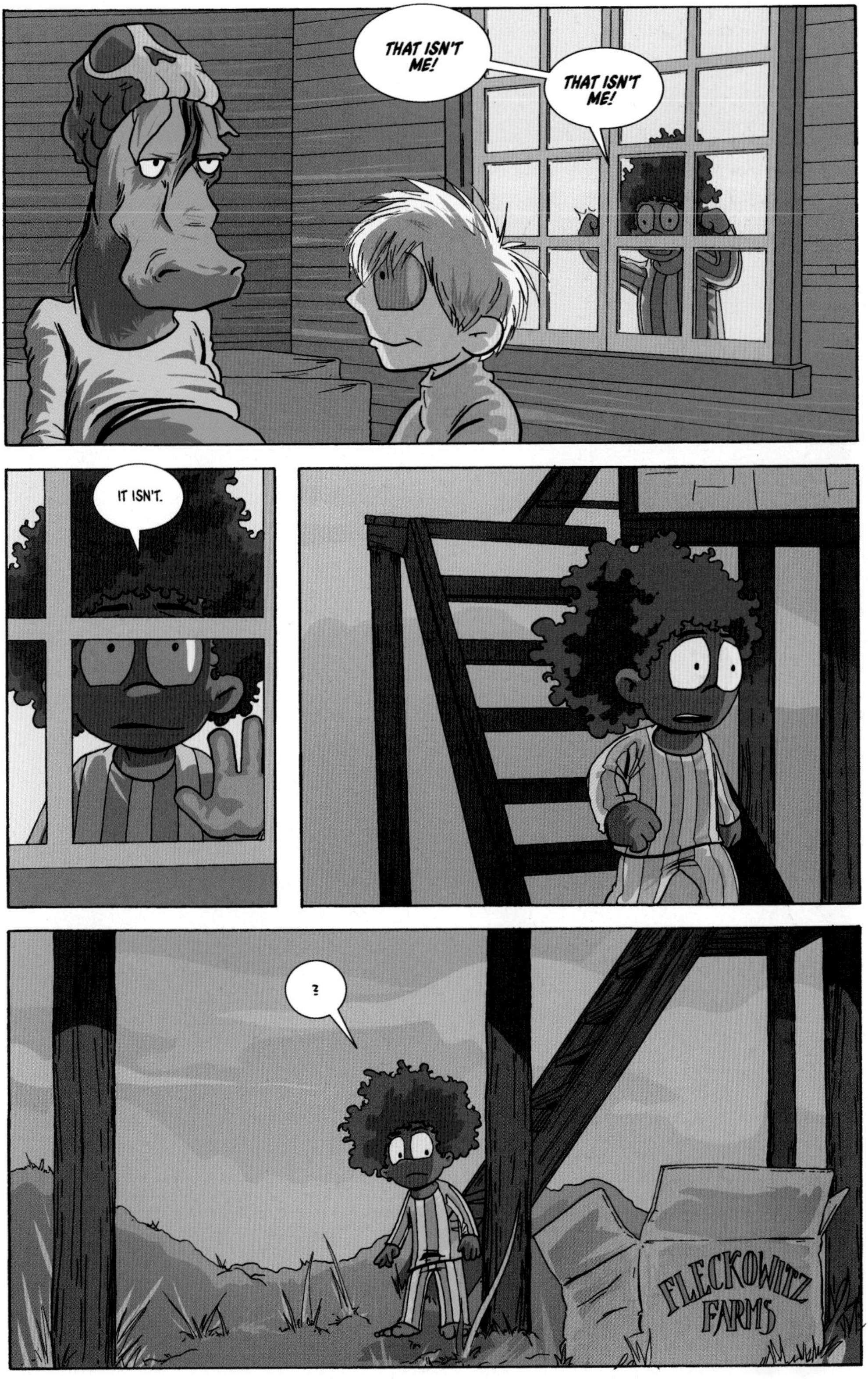
THAT ISN'T ME!
THAT ISN'T ME!
IT ISN'T.
?
FLECKOWITZ FARMS

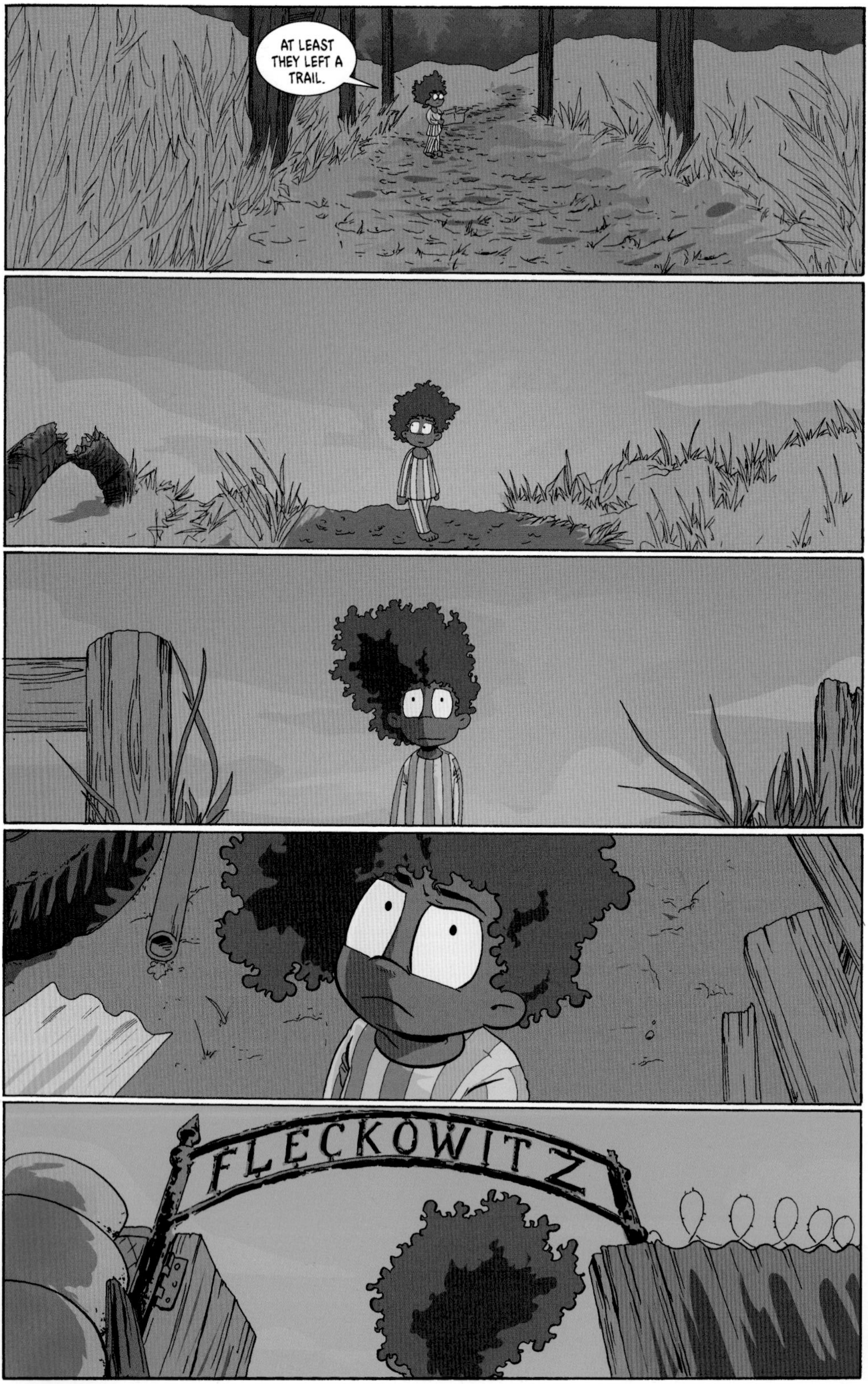
AT LEAST THEY LEFT A TRAIL.
FLECKOWITZ

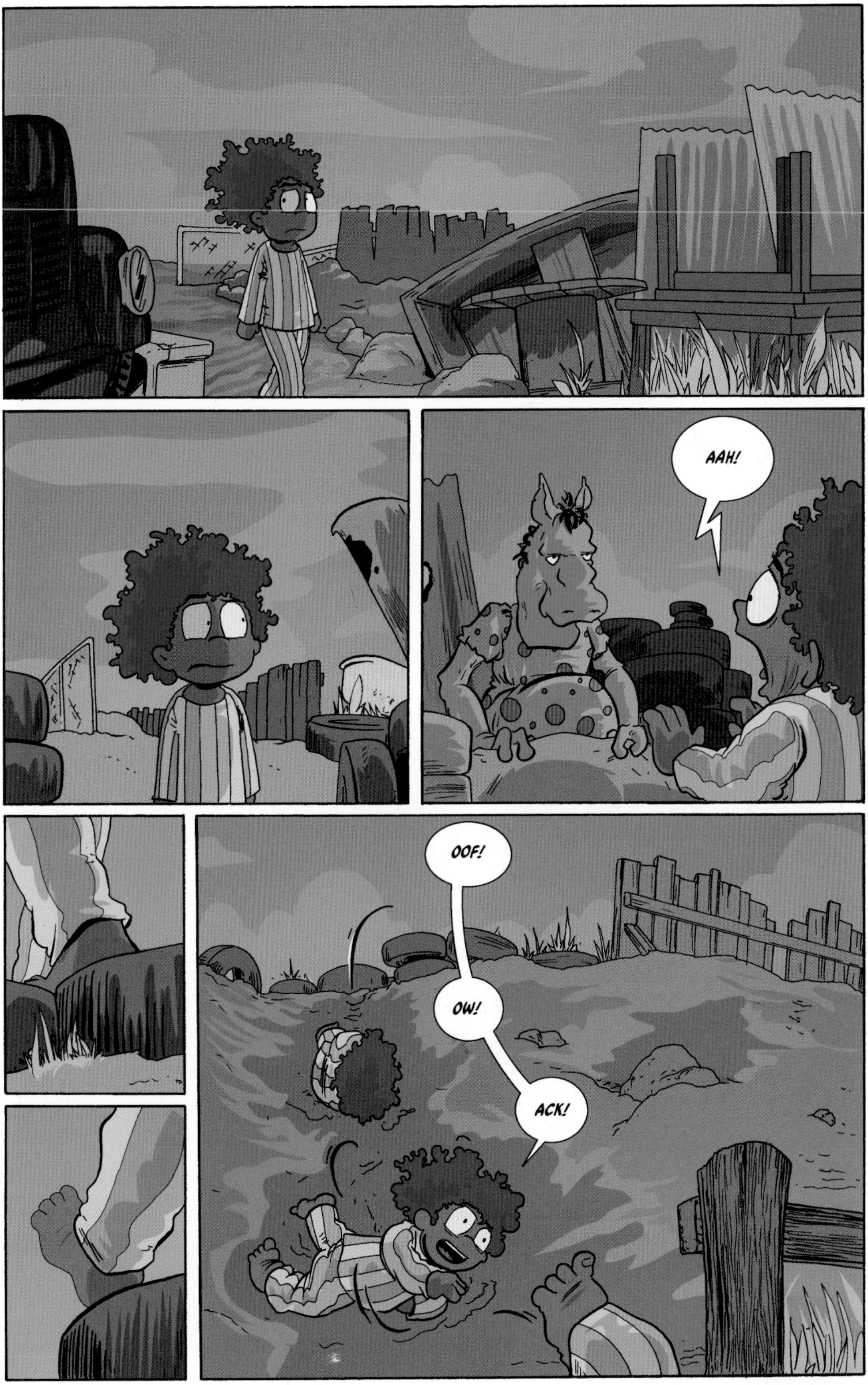
AAH!
OOF!
OW!
ACK!

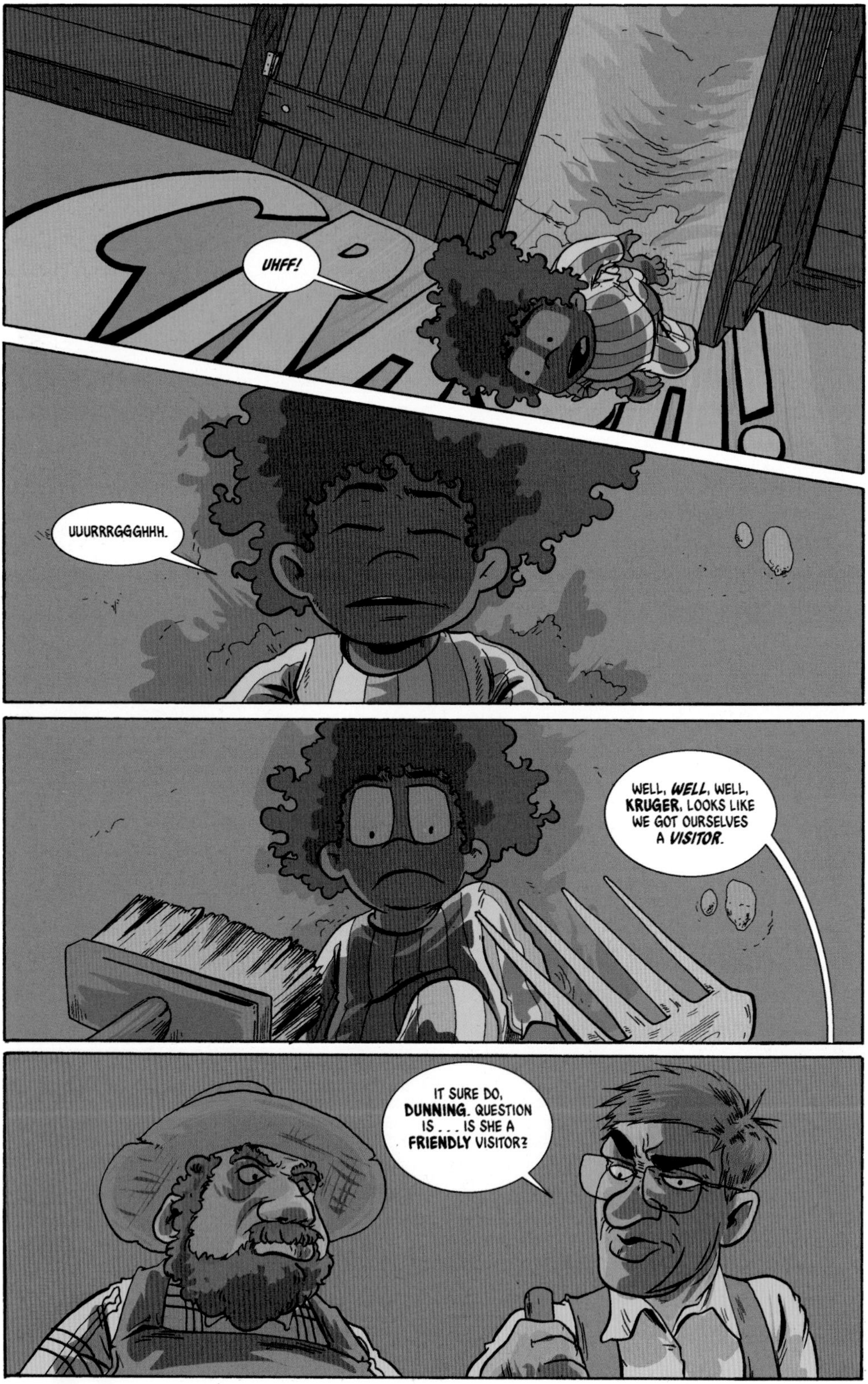
UHFF!
UUURRRGGGHHH.
WELL, WELL, WELL, KRUGER, LOOKS LIKE WE GOT OURSELVES A VISITOR.
IT SURE DO, DUNNING. QUESTION IS . . . IS SHE A FRIENDLY VISITOR?

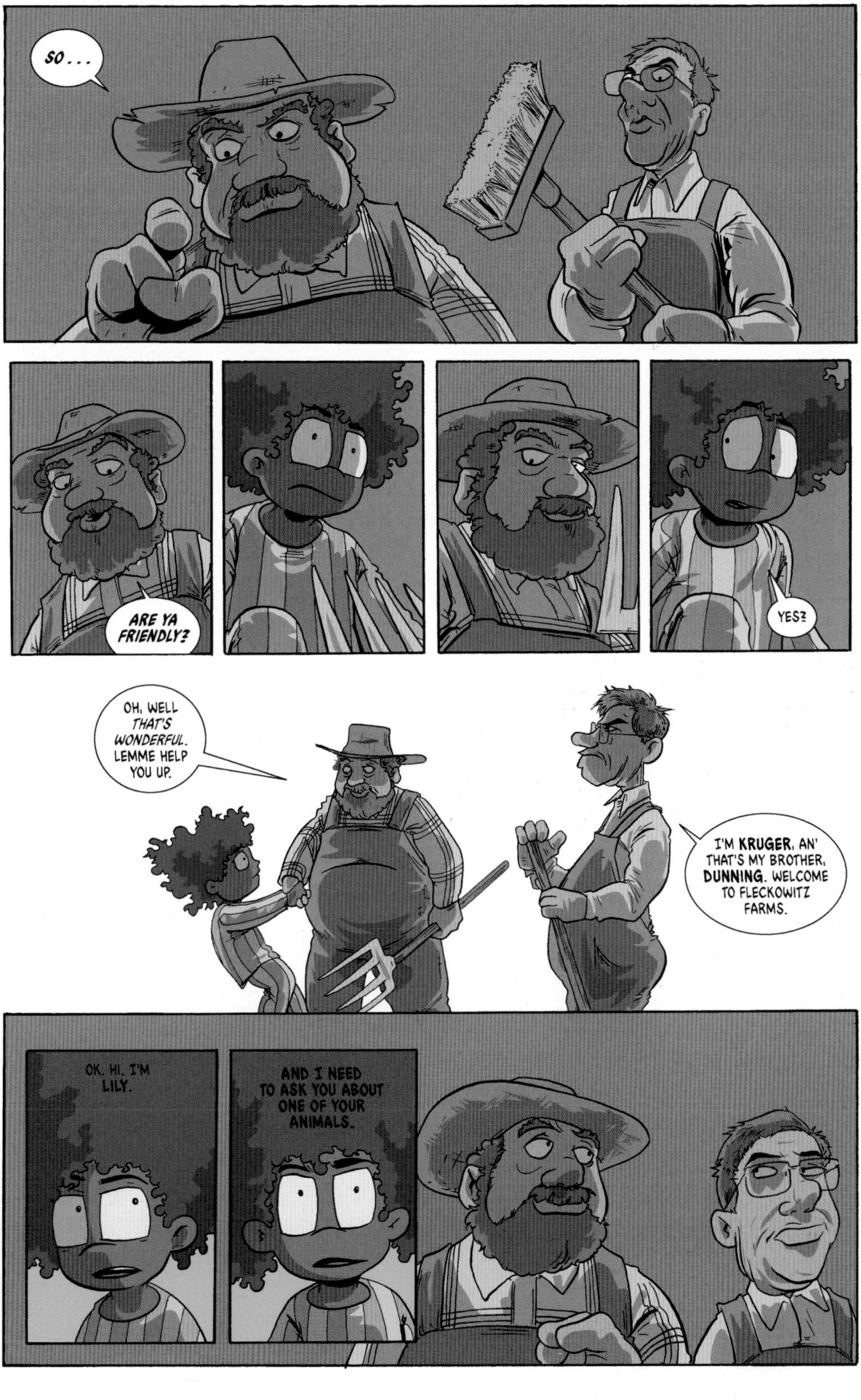
SO...
ARE YA FRIENDLY?
YES?
OH, WELL THAT'S WONDERFUL. LEMME HELP YOU UP.
I'M KRUGER, AN' THAT'S MY BROTHER, DUNNING. WELCOME TO FLECKOWITZ FARMS.
OK. HI. I'M LILY.
AND I NEED TO ASK YOU ABOUT ONE OF YOUR ANIMALS.

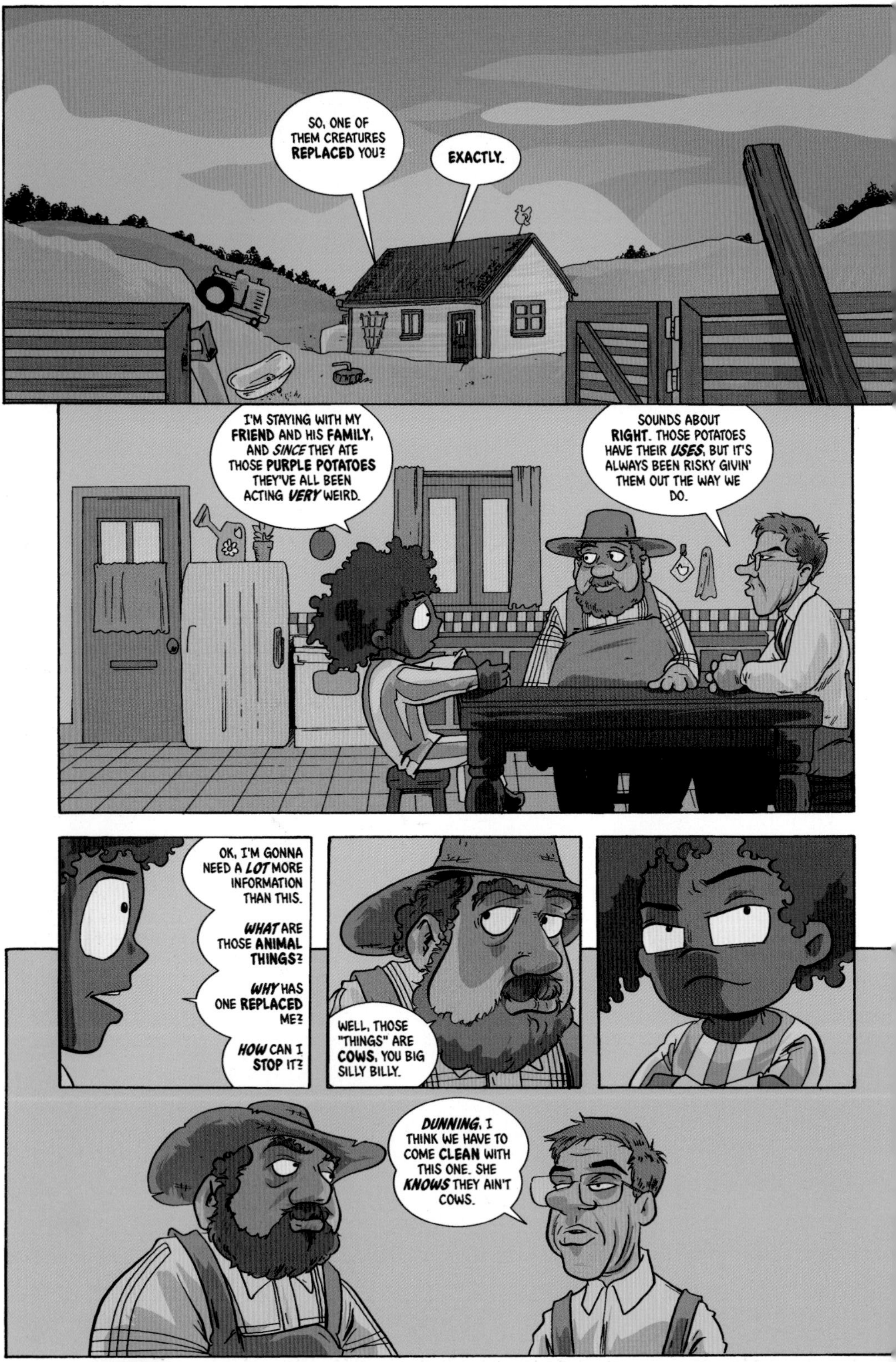
SO, ONE OF THEM CREATURES REPLACED YOU?
EXACTLY.
I'M STAYING WITH MY FRIEND AND HIS FAMILY, AND SINCE THEY ATE THOSE PURPLE POTATOES THEY'VE ALL BEEN ACTING VERY WEIRD.
SOUNDS ABOUT RIGHT. THOSE POTATOES HAVE THEIR USES, BUT IT'S ALWAYS BEEN RISKY GIVIN' THEM OUT THE WAY WE DO.
OK, I'M GONNA NEED A LOT MORE INFORMATION THAN THIS.
WHAT ARE THOSE ANIMAL THINGS?
WHY HAS ONE REPLACED ME?
HOW CAN I STOP IT?
WELL, THOSE "THINGS" ARE COWS, YOU BIG SILLY BILLY.
DUNNING, I THINK WE HAVE TO COME CLEAN WITH THIS ONE. SHE KNOWS THEY AIN'T COWS.

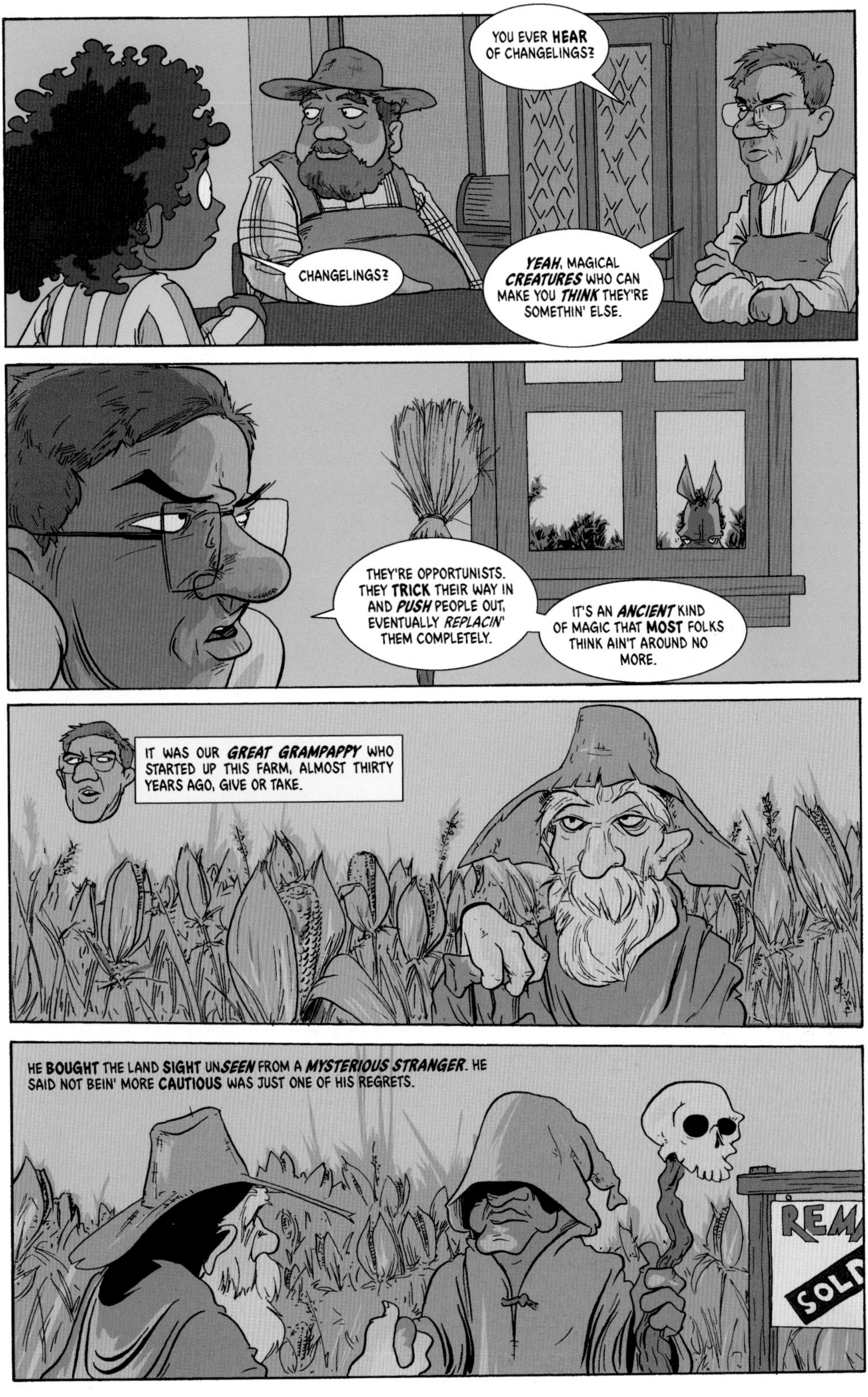
YOU EVER HEAR OF CHANGELINGS?
CHANGELINGS?
YEAH, MAGICAL CREATURES WHO CAN MAKE YOU THINK THEY'RE SOMETHIN' ELSE.
THEY'RE OPPORTUNISTS. THEY TRICK THEIR WAY IN AND PUSH PEOPLE OUT, EVENTUALLY REPLACIN' THEM COMPLETELY.
IT'S AN ANCIENT KIND OF MAGIC THAT MOST FOLKS THINK AIN'T AROUND NO MORE.
IT WAS OUR GREAT GRAMPAPPY WHO STARTED UP THIS FARM, ALMOST THIRTY YEARS AGO, GIVE OR TAKE.
HE BOUGHT THE LAND SIGHT UNSEEN FROM A MYSTERIOUS STRANGER. HE SAID NOT BEIN' MORE CAUTIOUS WAS JUST ONE OF HIS REGRETS.

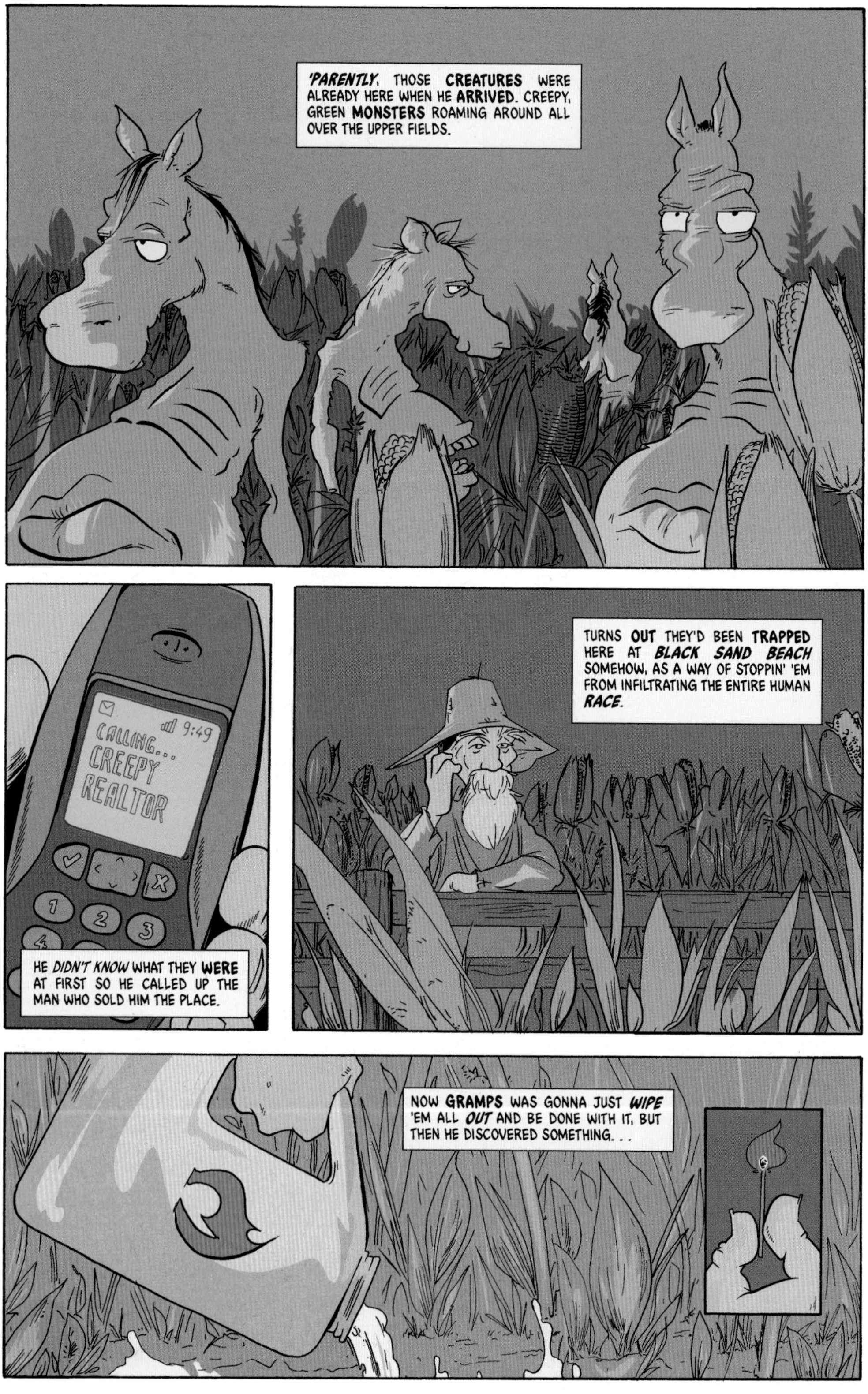
'PARENTLY, THOSE CREATURES WERE ALREADY HERE WHEN HE ARRIVED. CREEPY, GREEN MONSTERS ROAMING AROUND ALL OVER THE UPPER FIELDS.
9:49
CALLING... CREEPY REALTOR
HE DIDN'T KNOW WHAT THEY WERE AT FIRST SO HE CALLED UP THE MAN WHO SOLD HIM THE PLACE.
TURNS OUT THEY'D BEEN TRAPPED HERE AT BLACK SAND BEACH SOMEHOW, AS A WAY OF STOPPIN' 'EM FROM INFILTRATING THE ENTIRE HUMAN RACE.
NOW GRAMPS WAS GONNA JUST WIPE 'EM ALL OUT AND BE DONE WITH IT, BUT THEN HE DISCOVERED SOMETHING. . .

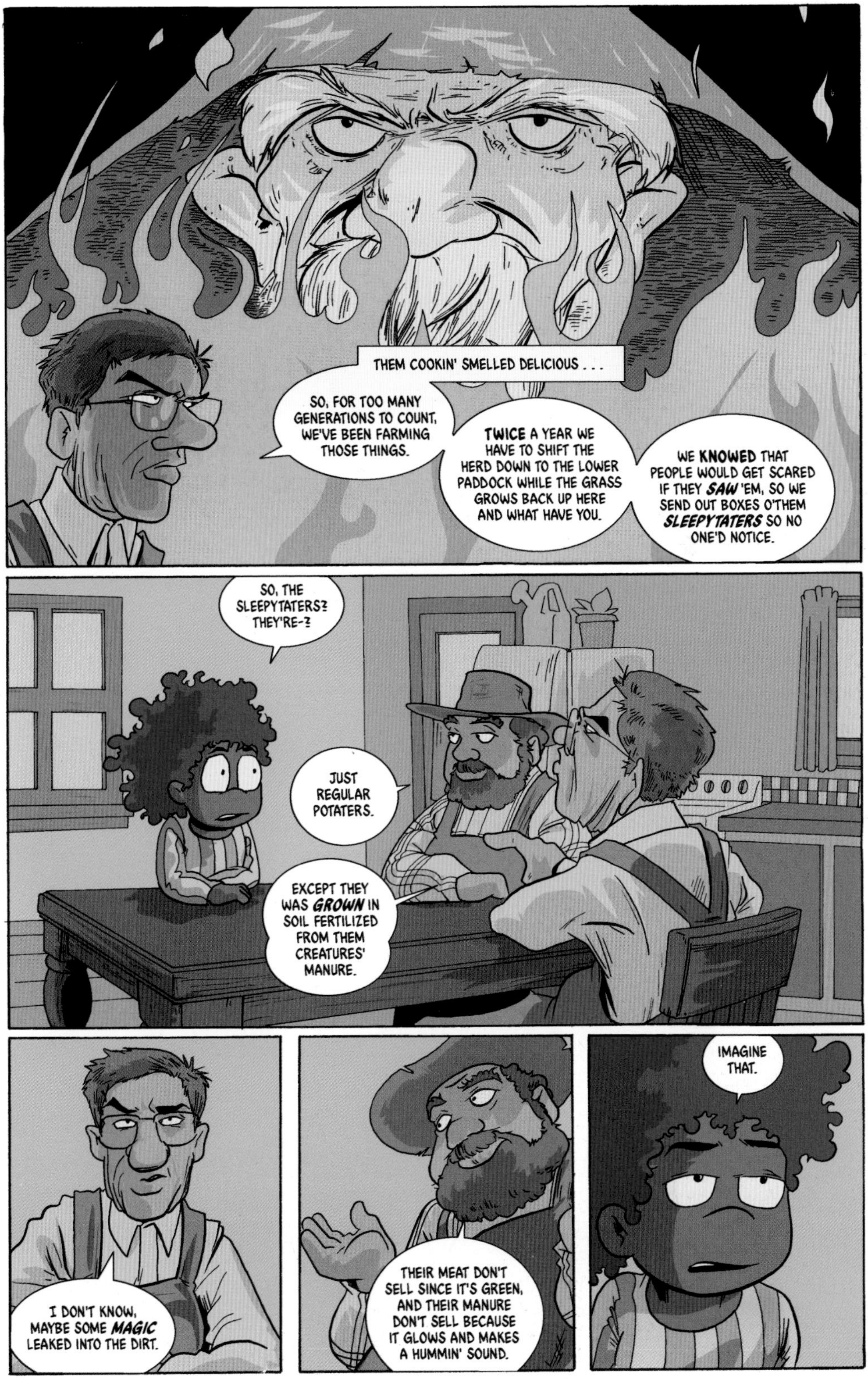

THEM COOKIN' SMELLED DELICIOUS . . .
SO, FOR TOO MANY GENERATIONS TO COUNT, WE'VE BEEN FARMING THOSE THINGS.
TWICE A YEAR WE HAVE TO SHIFT THE HERD DOWN TO THE LOWER PADDOCK WHILE THE GRASS GROWS BACK UP HERE AND WHAT HAVE YOU.
WE KNOWED THAT PEOPLE WOULD GET SCARED IF THEY SAW 'EM, SO WE SEND OUT BOXES O'THEM SLEEPYTATERS SO NO ONE'D NOTICE.
SO, THE SLEEPYTATERS?! THEY'RE-?!
JUST REGULAR POTATERS.
EXCEPT THEY WAS GROWN IN SOIL FERTILIZED FROM THEM CREATURES' MANURE.
I DON'T KNOW, MAYBE SOME MAGIC LEAKED INTO THE DIRT.
THEIR MEAT DON'T SELL SINCE IT'S GREEN, AND THEIR MANURE DON'T SELL BECAUSE IT GLOWS AND MAKES A HUMMIN' SOUND.
IMAGINE THAT.

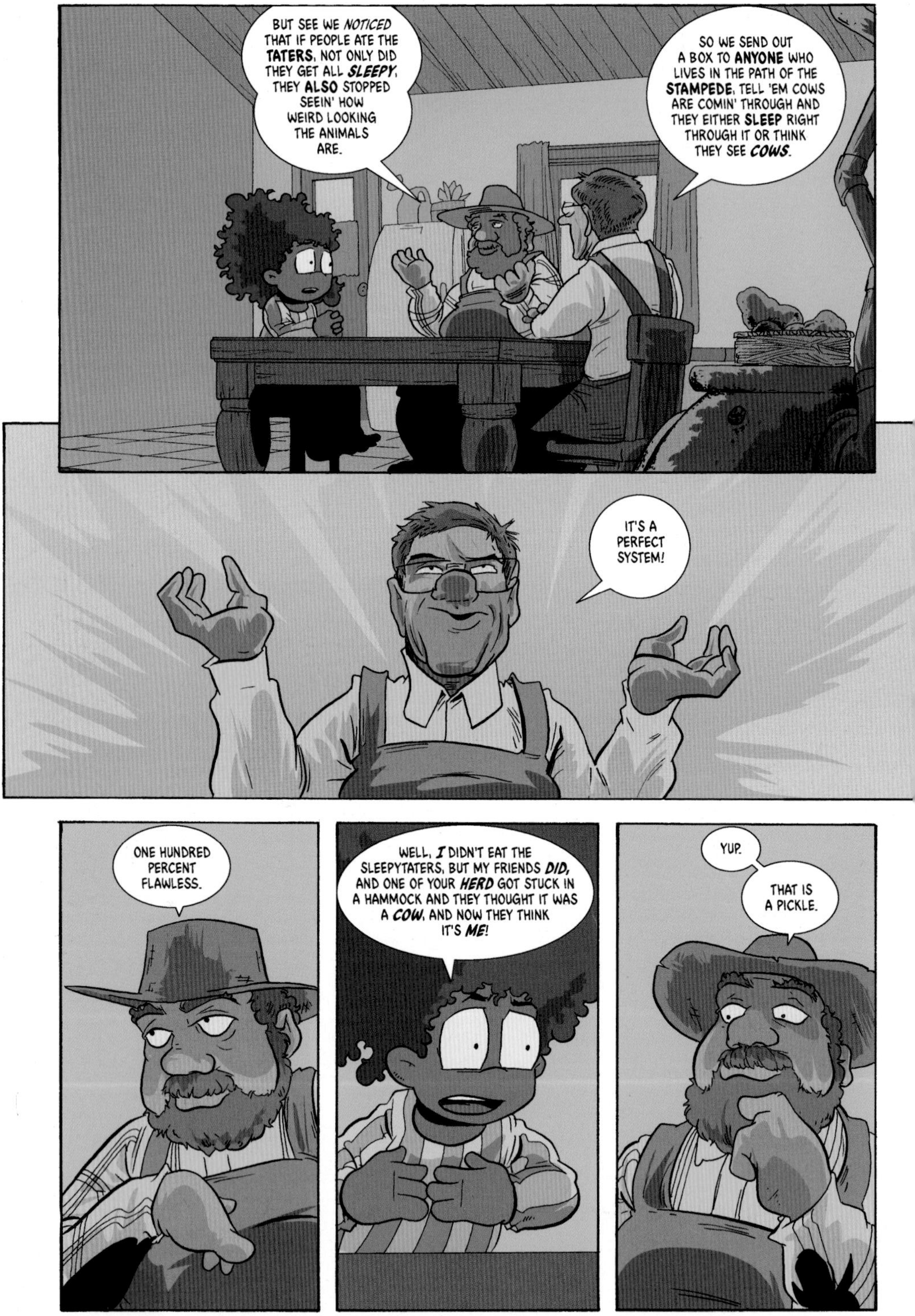
BUT SEE WE NOTICED THAT IF PEOPLE ATE THE TATERS, NOT ONLY DID THEY GET ALL SLEEPY, THEY ALSO STOPPED SEEIN' HOW WEIRD LOOKING THE ANIMALS ARE.
SO WE SEND OUT A BOX TO ANYONE WHO LIVES IN THE PATH OF THE STAMPEDE, TELL 'EM COWS ARE COMIN' THROUGH AND THEY EITHER SLEEP RIGHT THROUGH IT OR THINK THEY SEE COWS.
IT'S A PERFECT SYSTEM!
ONE HUNDRED PERCENT FLAWLESS.
WELL, I DIDN'T EAT THE SLEEPYTATERS, BUT MY FRIENDS DID, AND ONE OF YOUR HERD GOT STUCK IN A HAMMOCK AND THEY THOUGHT IT WAS A COW, AND NOW THEY THINK IT'S ME!
YUP.
THAT IS A PICKLE.

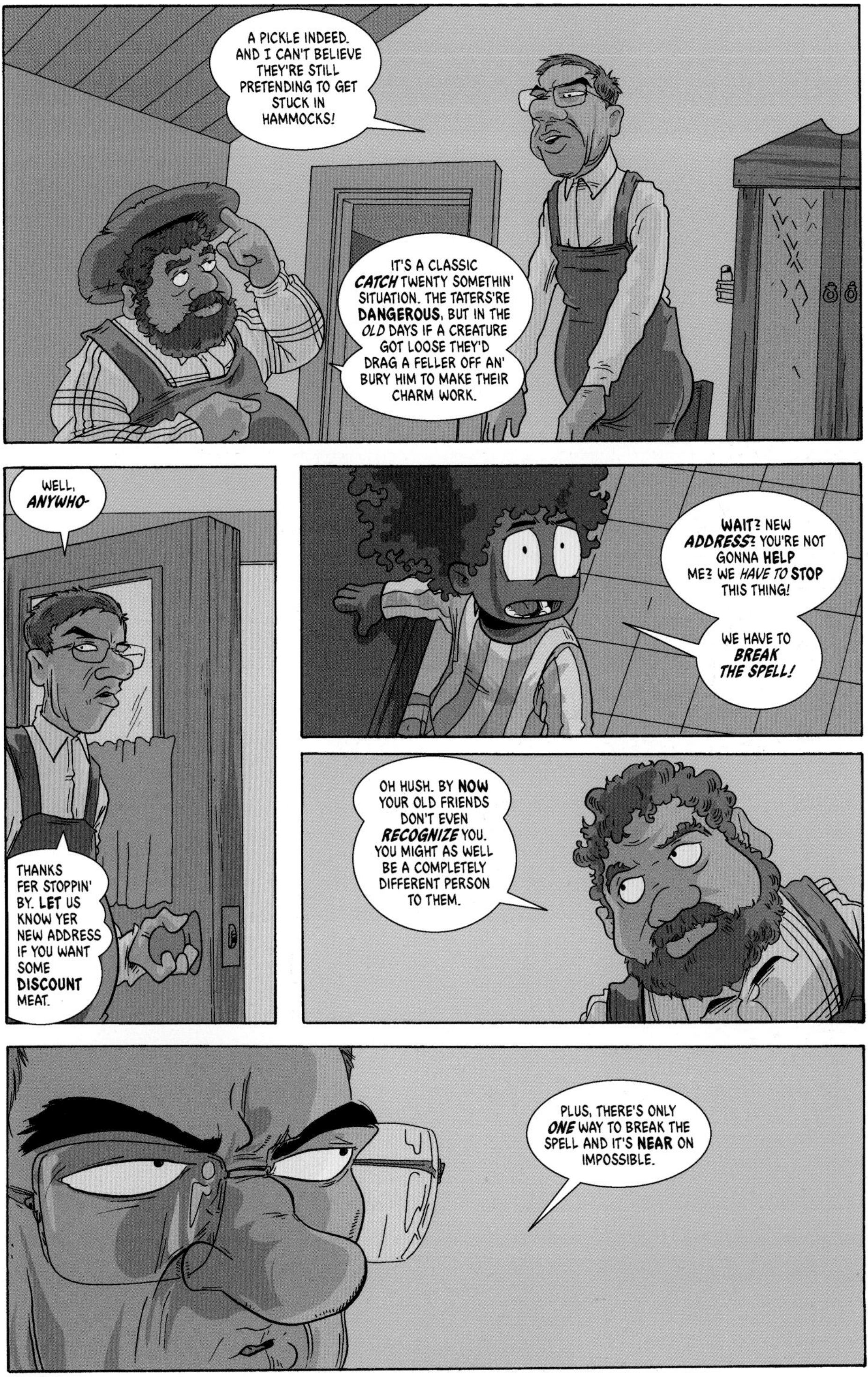
A PICKLE INDEED. AND I CAN'T BELIEVE THEY'RE STILL PRETENDING TO GET STUCK IN HAMMOCKS!
IT'S A CLASSIC CATCH TWENTY SOMETHIN' SITUATION. THE TATERS'RE DANGEROUS, BUT IN THE OLD DAYS IF A CREATURE GOT LOOSE THEY'D DRAG A FELLER OFF AN' BURY HIM TO MAKE THEIR CHARM WORK.
WELL, ANYWHO-
THANKS FER STOPPIN' BY. LET US KNOW YER NEW ADDRESS IF YOU WANT SOME DISCOUNT MEAT.
WAIT? NEW ADDRESS? YOU'RE NOT GONNA HELP ME? WE HAVE TO STOP THIS THING!
WE HAVE TO BREAK THE SPELL!
OH HUSH. BY NOW YOUR OLD FRIENDS DON'T EVEN RECOGNIZE YOU. YOU MIGHT AS WELL BE A COMPLETELY DIFFERENT PERSON TO THEM.
PLUS, THERE'S ONLY ONE WAY TO BREAK THE SPELL AND IT'S NEAR ON IMPOSSIBLE.

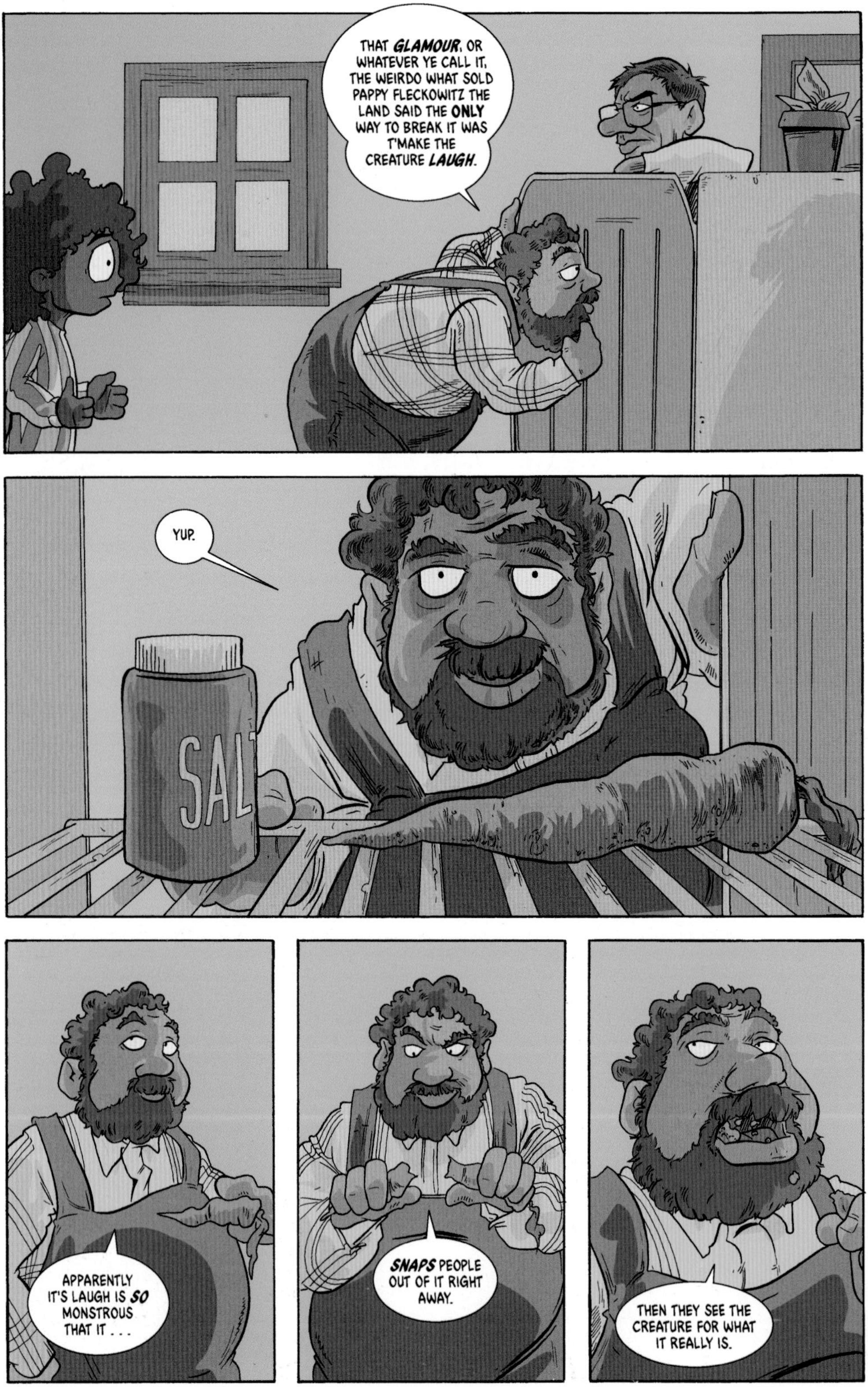
THAT **GLAMOUR**, OR WHATEVER YE CALL IT, THE WEIRDO WHAT SOLD PAPPY FLECKOWITZ THE LAND SAID THE **ONLY** WAY TO BREAK IT WAS T'MAKE THE CREATURE **LAUGH**.
YUP.
SALT
APPARENTLY IT'S LAUGH IS **SO** MONSTROUS THAT IT . . .
SNAPS PEOPLE OUT OF IT RIGHT AWAY.
THEN THEY SEE THE CREATURE FOR WHAT IT REALLY IS.

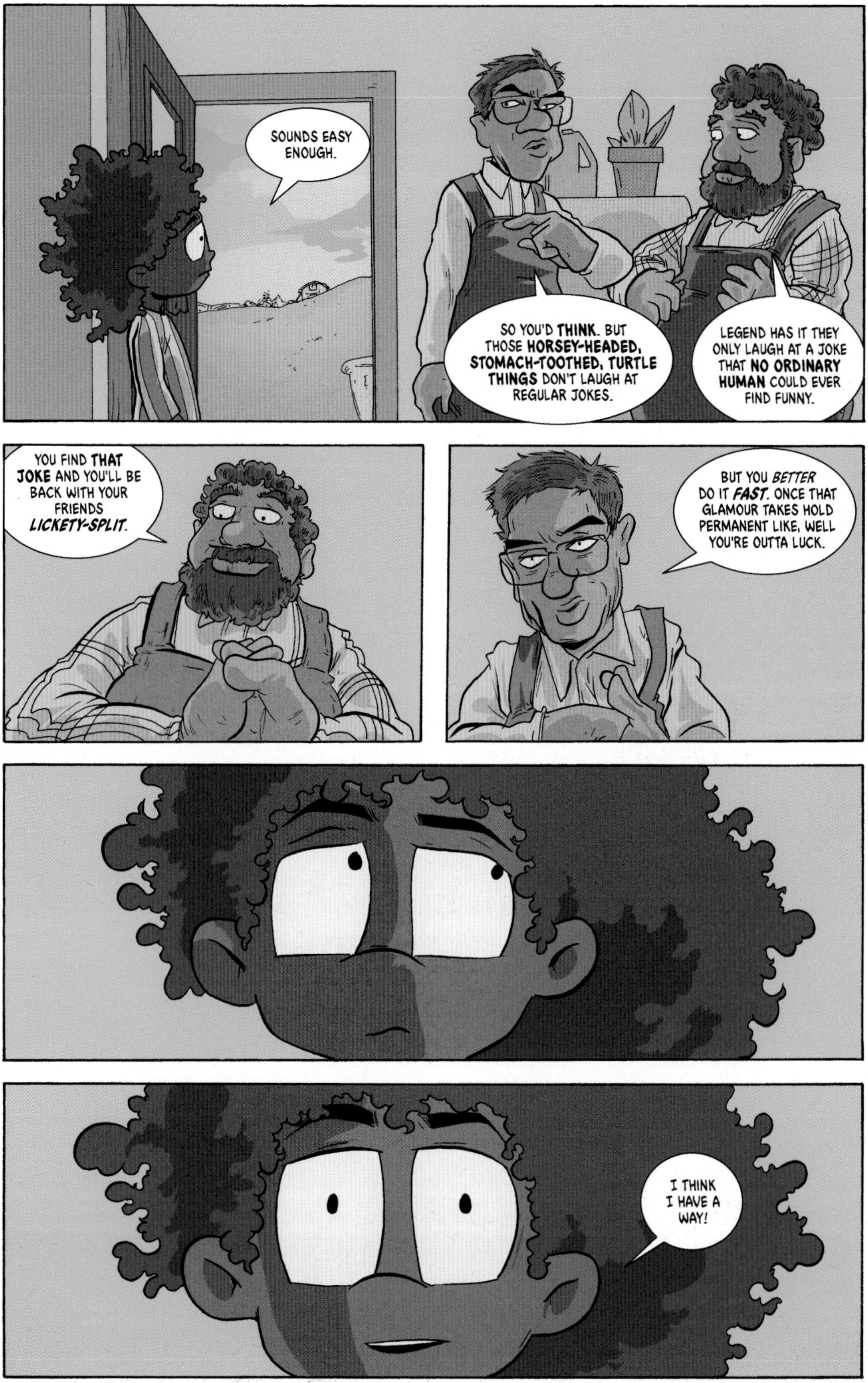
SOUNDS EASY ENOUGH.
SO YOU'D **THINK**. BUT THOSE **HORSEY-HEADED, STOMACH-TOOTHED, TURTLE THINGS** DON'T LAUGH AT REGULAR JOKES.
LEGEND HAS IT THEY ONLY LAUGH AT A JOKE THAT **NO ORDINARY HUMAN** COULD EVER FIND FUNNY.
YOU FIND **THAT JOKE** AND YOU'LL BE BACK WITH YOUR FRIENDS ***LICKETY-SPLIT***.
BUT YOU *BETTER* DO IT ***FAST***. ONCE THAT GLAMOUR TAKES HOLD PERMANENT LIKE, WELL YOU'RE OUTTA LUCK.
I THINK I HAVE A WAY!

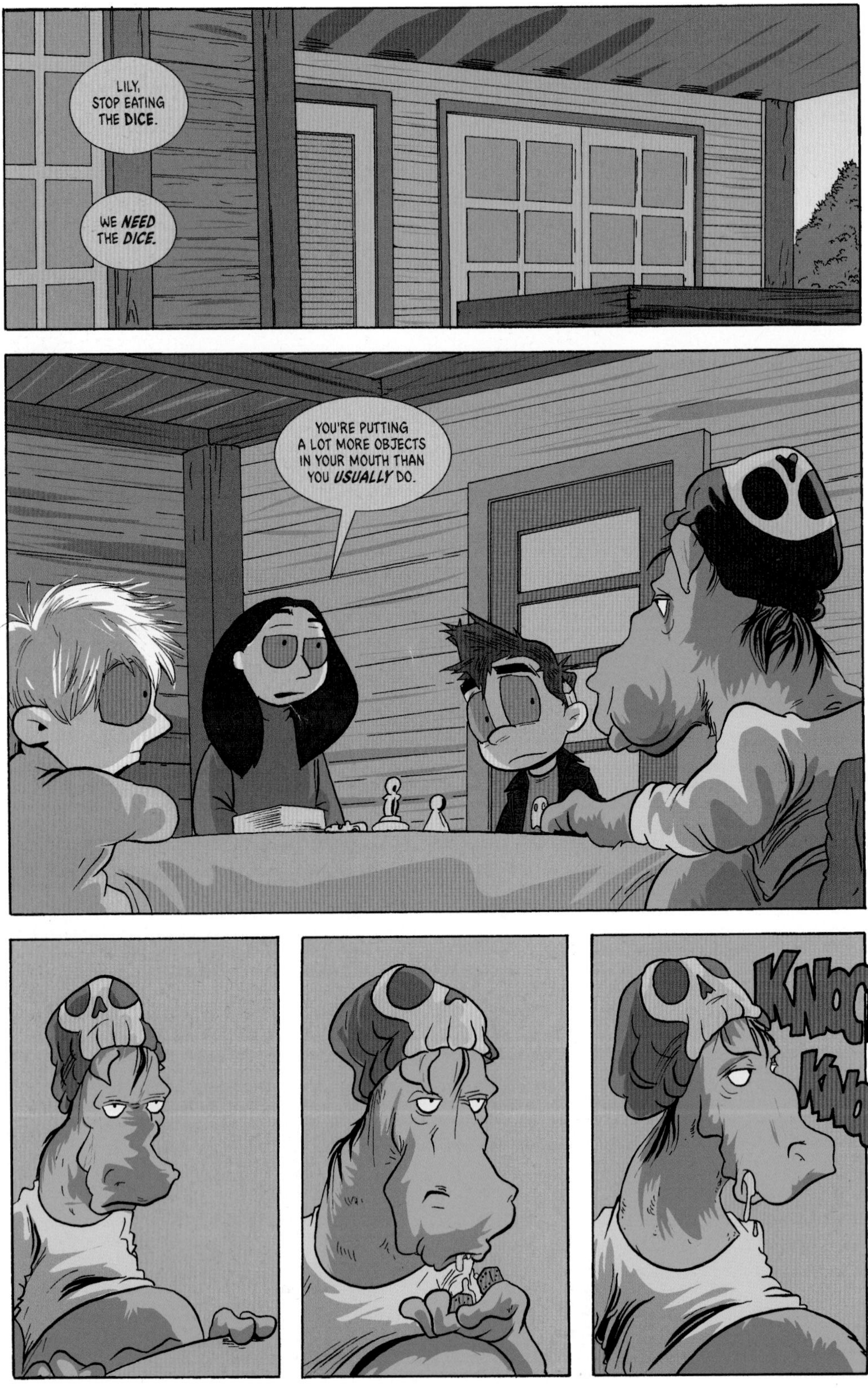
LILY, STOP EATING THE DICE.
WE NEED THE DICE.
YOU'RE PUTTING A LOT MORE OBJECTS IN YOUR MOUTH THAN YOU USUALLY DO.

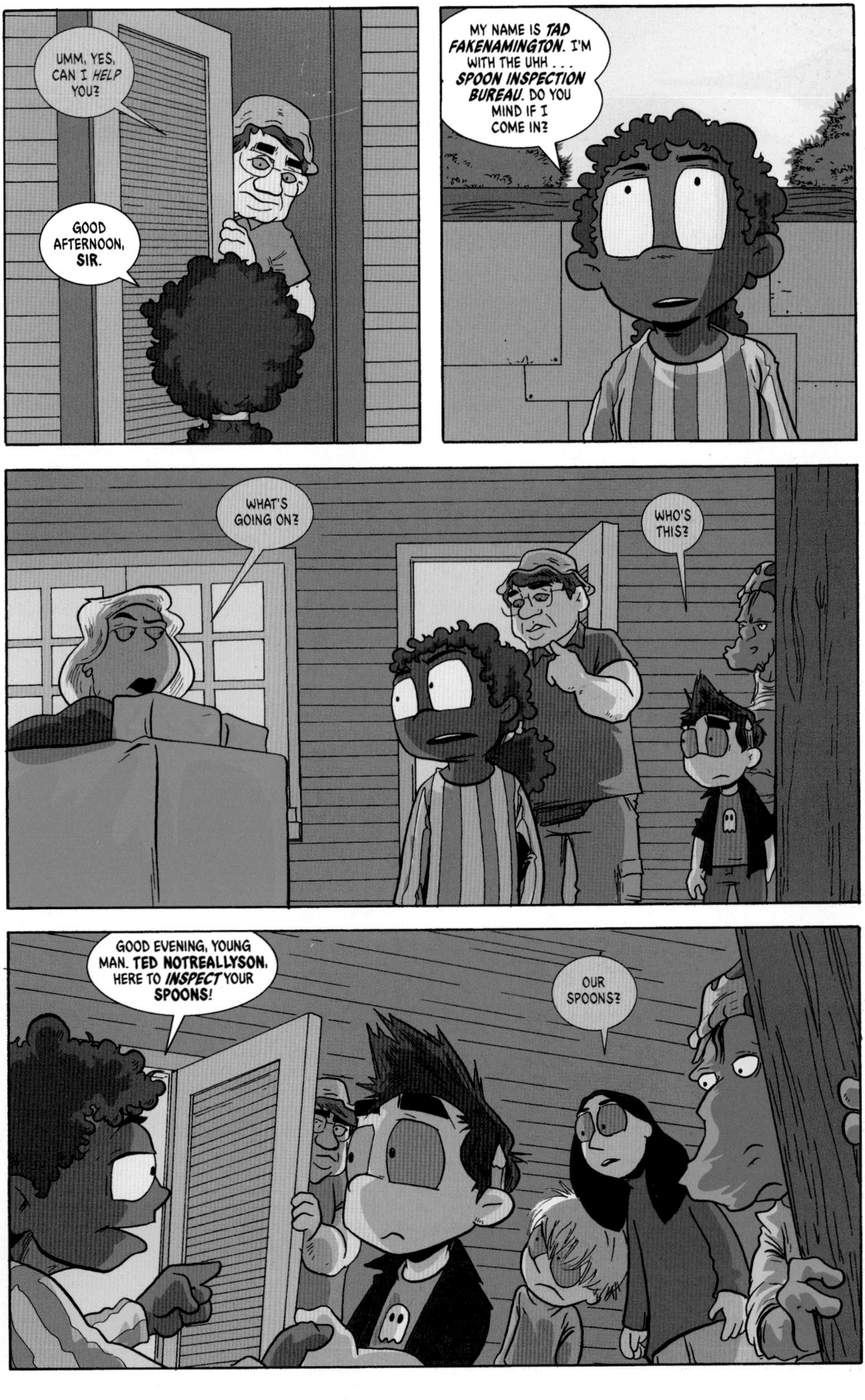
UMM, YES, CAN I *HELP* YOU?
GOOD AFTERNOON, **SIR**.
MY NAME IS ***TAD FAKENAMINGTON***. I'M WITH THE UHH . . . ***SPOON INSPECTION BUREAU***. DO YOU MIND IF I COME IN?
WHAT'S GOING ON?
WHO'S THIS?
GOOD EVENING, YOUNG MAN. **TED NOTREALLYSON**, HERE TO ***INSPECT*** YOUR **SPOONS**!
OUR SPOONS?

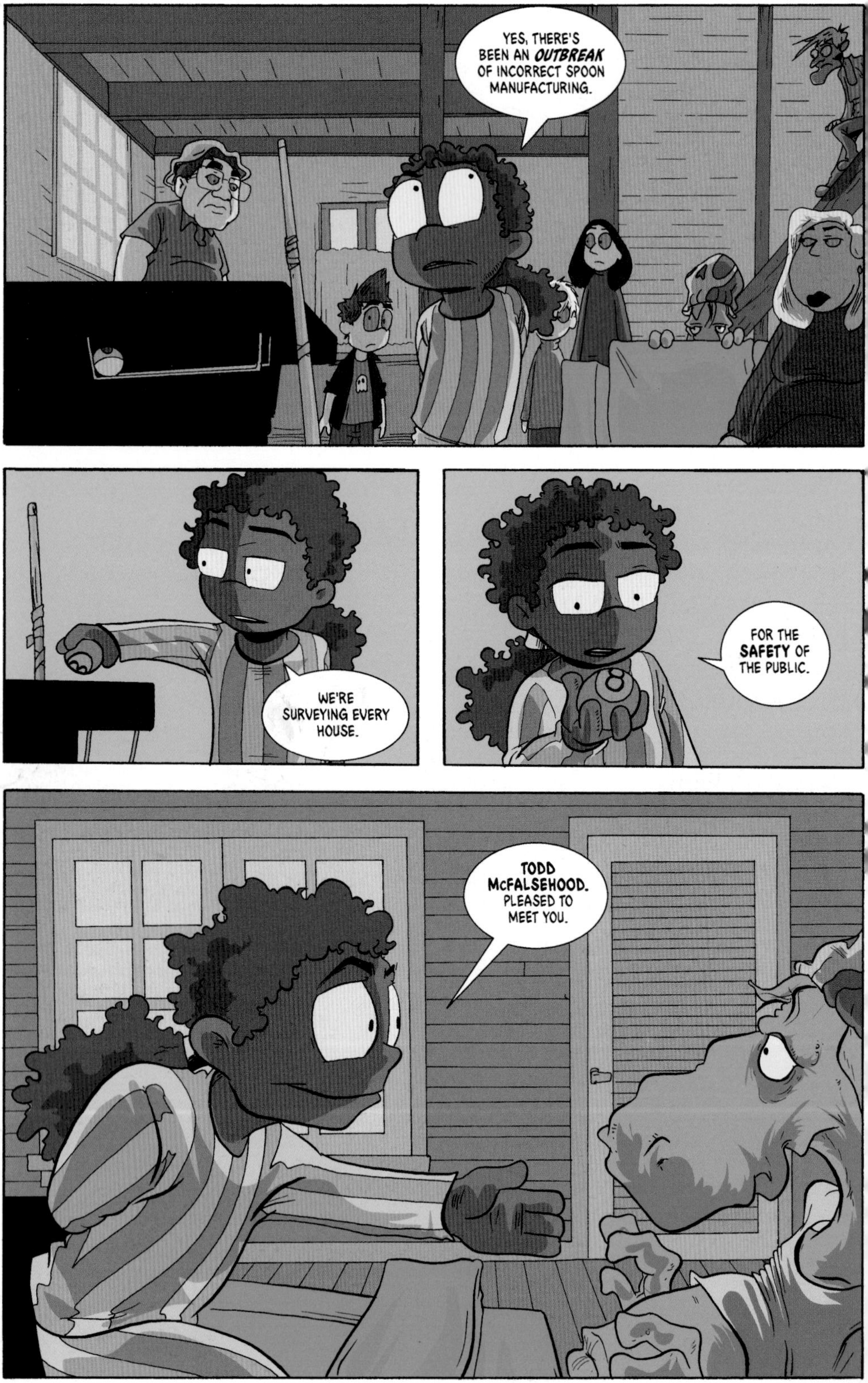
YES, THERE'S BEEN AN *OUTBREAK* OF INCORRECT SPOON MANUFACTURING.
WE'RE SURVEYING EVERY HOUSE.
FOR THE **SAFETY** OF THE PUBLIC.
TODD McFALSEHOOD. PLEASED TO MEET YOU.

HERE! THIS IS OUR BEST AND CLEANEST SPOON.

EXCELLENT. THIS WILL DO NICELY.

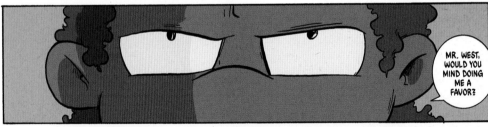

MR. WEST, WOULD YOU MIND DOING ME A FAVOR?

BREATHE SOME HOT AIR ON THIS SPOON AND PRESS IT ON YOUR NOSE.

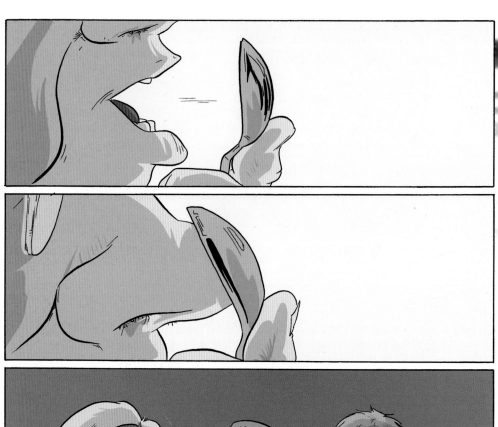

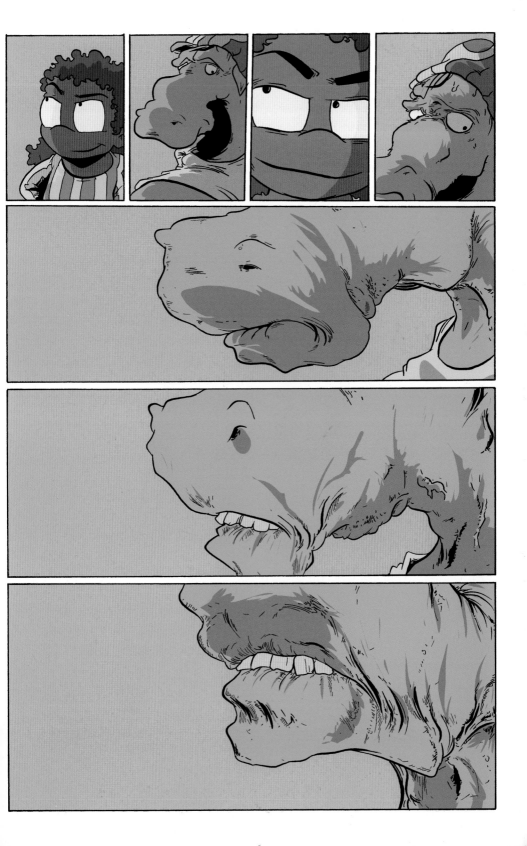

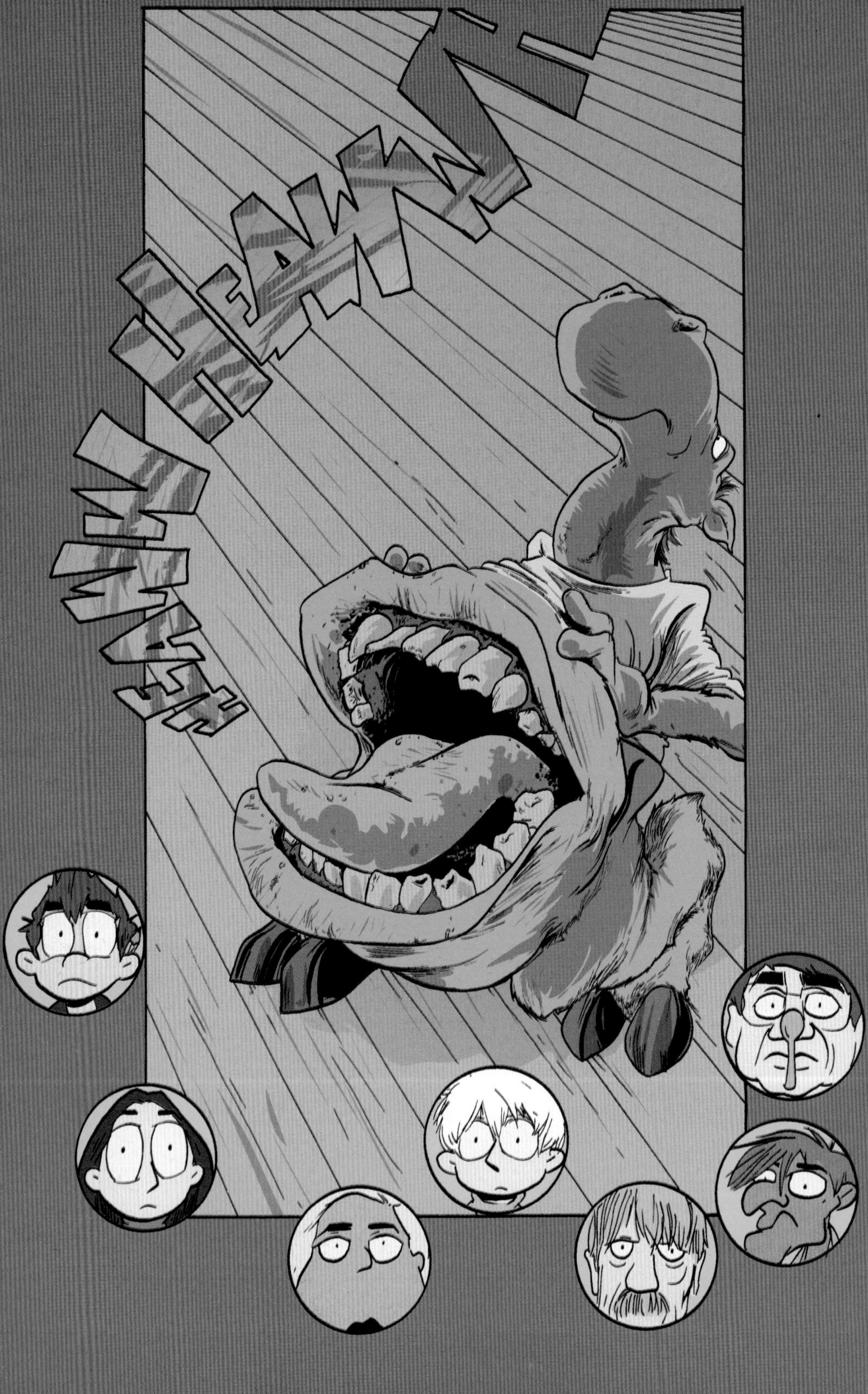
HEAWW HEAWW!

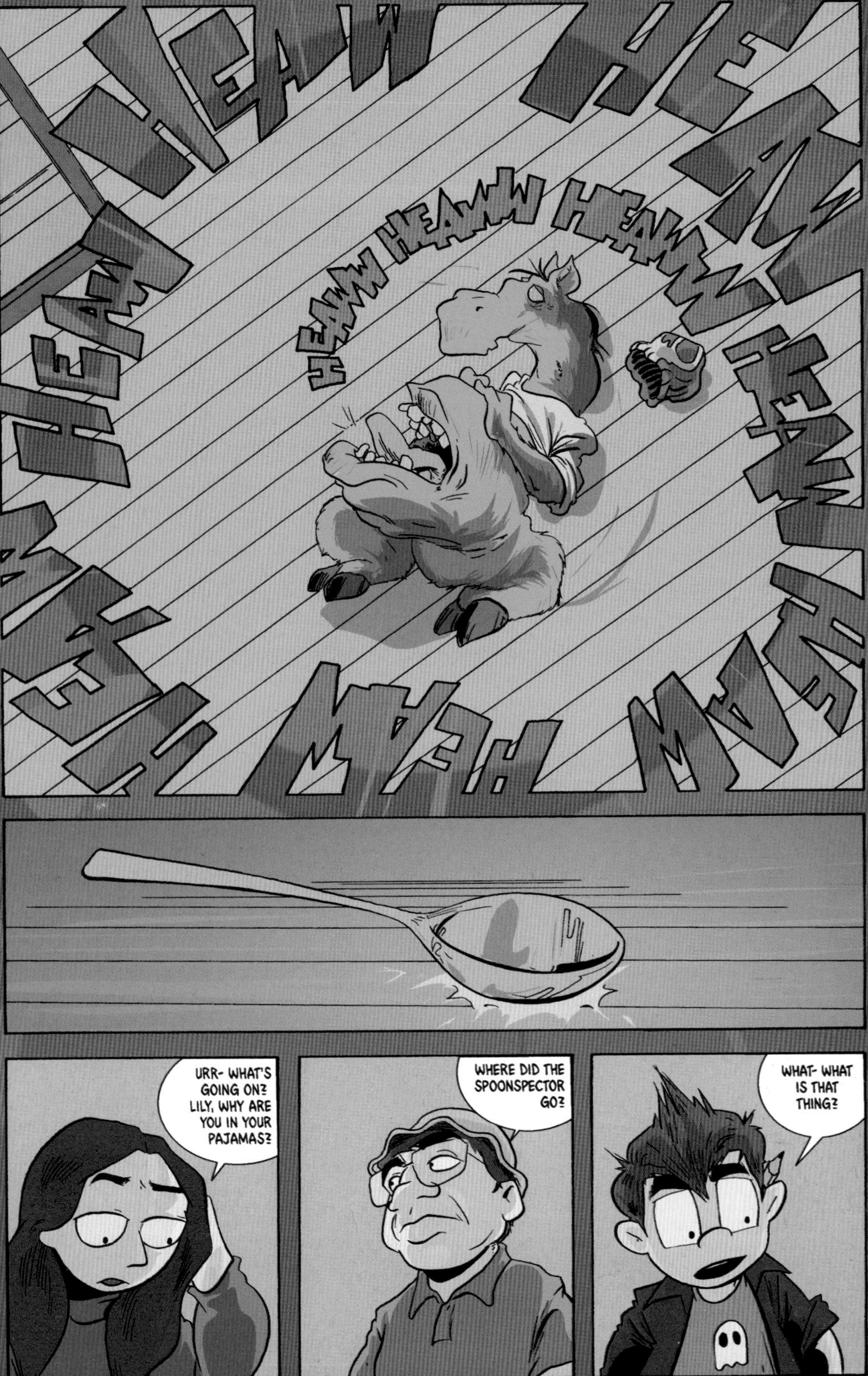
HEAWW HEAWW HEAWW HEAWW
URR- WHAT'S GOING ON? LILY, WHY ARE YOU IN YOUR PAJAMAS?
WHERE DID THE SPOONSPECTOR GO?
WHAT- WHAT IS THAT THING?

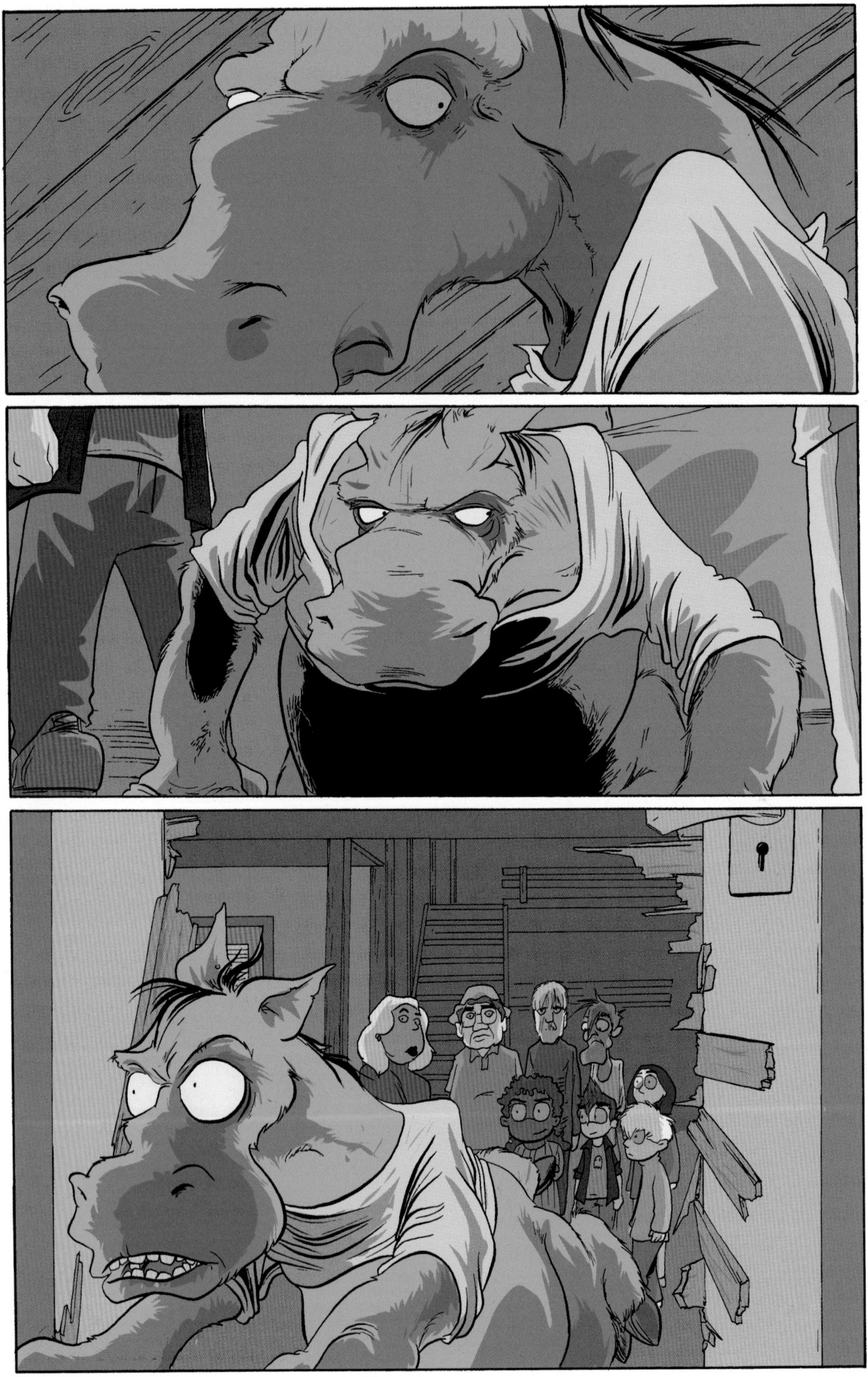

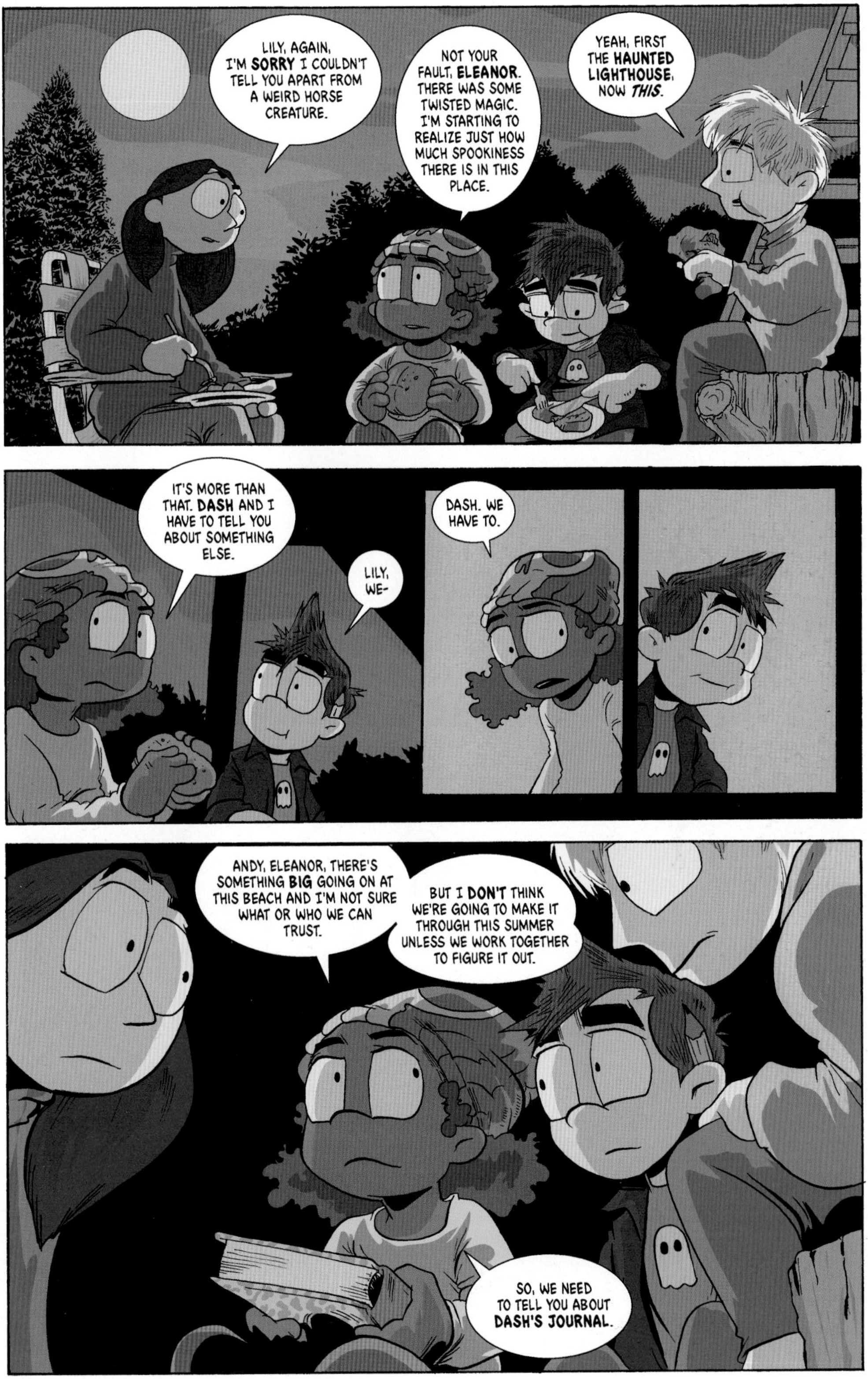
LILY, AGAIN, I'M SORRY I COULDN'T TELL YOU APART FROM A WEIRD HORSE CREATURE.
NOT YOUR FAULT, ELEANOR. THERE WAS SOME TWISTED MAGIC. I'M STARTING TO REALIZE JUST HOW MUCH SPOOKINESS THERE IS IN THIS PLACE.
YEAH, FIRST THE HAUNTED LIGHTHOUSE, NOW THIS.
IT'S MORE THAN THAT. DASH AND I HAVE TO TELL YOU ABOUT SOMETHING ELSE.
LILY, WE-
DASH. WE HAVE TO.
ANDY, ELEANOR, THERE'S SOMETHING BIG GOING ON AT THIS BEACH AND I'M NOT SURE WHAT OR WHO WE CAN TRUST.
BUT I DON'T THINK WE'RE GOING TO MAKE IT THROUGH THIS SUMMER UNLESS WE WORK TOGETHER TO FIGURE IT OUT.
SO, WE NEED TO TELL YOU ABOUT DASH'S JOURNAL.

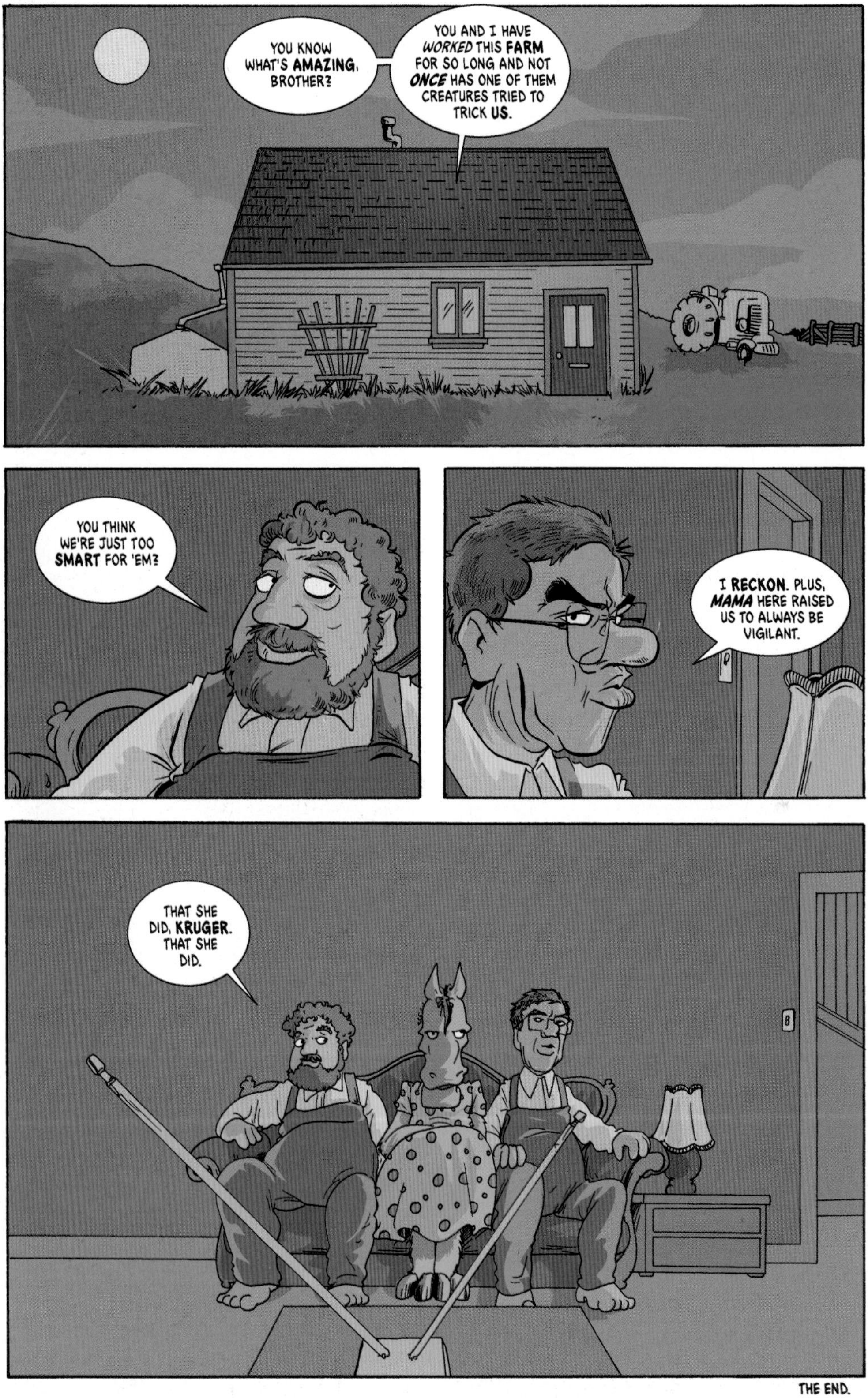
YOU KNOW WHAT'S AMAZING, BROTHER?
YOU AND I HAVE WORKED THIS FARM FOR SO LONG AND NOT ONCE HAS ONE OF THEM CREATURES TRIED TO TRICK US.
YOU THINK WE'RE JUST TOO SMART FOR 'EM?
I RECKON. PLUS, MAMA HERE RAISED US TO ALWAYS BE VIGILANT.
THAT SHE DID, KRUGER. THAT SHE DID.

THE END.

Coming in Summer 2021,

the second book in the **BLACK SAND BEACH** series

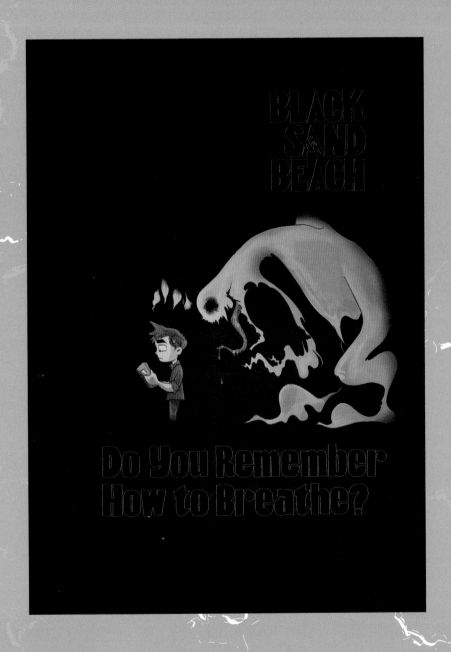

Here's the step by step process of creating a page of comic. I try to do as much as possible with pen and paper because I really hate using a computer. Paper just feels nicer to me. The downside is, it's really hard to change anything if your editor doesn't like it, which means you have to work extra hard to make your editors scared of you. For this, I recommend always wearing a ghost costume to meetings.

Page 47:
They all walk in cautiously, looking around. Inside is a spiral staircase leading up to the viewing deck. There's a big metal pole in the center, rusted but smooth. It goes up through the ceiling and into the light mechanism part. It also goes all the way through the floor, through what was once a perfectly fitted hole, but it now a misshapen gap in the wooden floorboards.

Eleanor:
Well I'd say no one has been in here for a long time. So, if we're th ng that someone was in here t g the light on-

:
n't you say this lighthouse was lly automated.

Eleanor:
Yeah, but I also said it never worked properly.

1: Script

Everyone has a different way of scripting. I switch between excessive descriptions of every panel and nothing but dialogue, with a loose note on what might be going on visually. This page is definitely the latter.

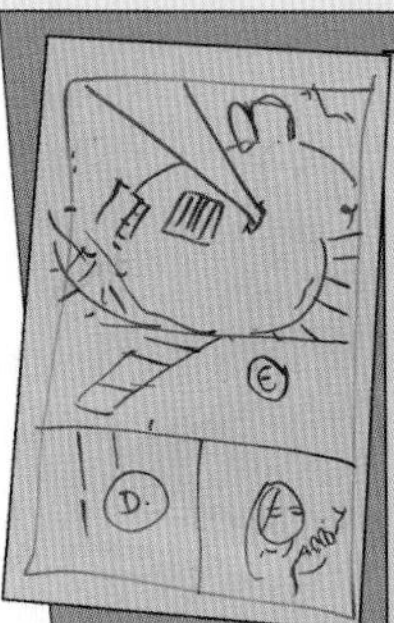

2: Thumbnails

Once the script's written, as messy as it may be, I do thumbnails for every page. This lets me see if the pacing is right or if I'm staying on a scene too long, meaning I have to cram too much in somewhere else.

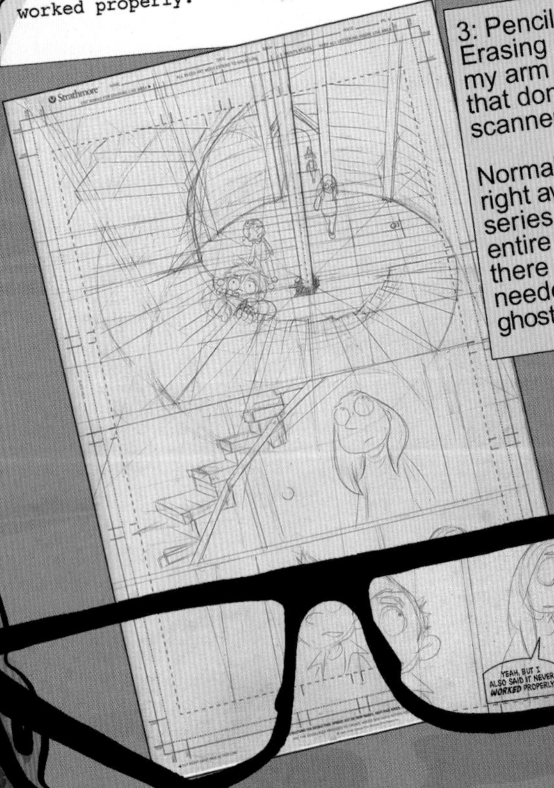

YEAH, BUT I ALSO SAID IT NEVER WORKED PROPERLY.

3: Pencils

Erasing pencils sucks and makes my arm hurt, so I use blue pencils that don't get picked up by scanners. Plus, they look cooler.

Normally I pencil a page then ink it right away, but since this was a new series, I ended up penciling an entire chapter at once, just in case there were any major changes needed. Thanks to my convincing ghost costume, there were not.

4: Lettering

I hate lettering, but I do like how it looks over pencils though, and I do like how it lets me know where I can cut corners on inking and coloring.

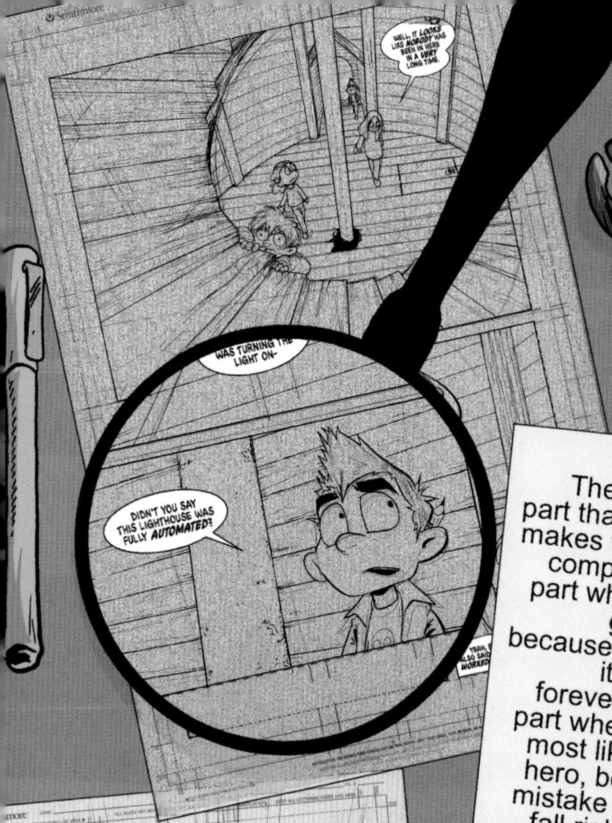
WELL, IT LOOKS LIKE NOBODY HAS BEEN IN HERE IN A VERY LONG TIME.
WAS TURNING THE LIGHT ON-
DIDN'T YOU SAY THIS LIGHTHOUSE WAS FULLY AUTOMATED?

5: Inking
The fun part. The part that immediately makes the page look complete. Also the part where you only get one shot, because if you screw it up it's there forever. This is the part where I feel the most like an action hero, because one mistake and I could fall right out of my exploding helicopter.

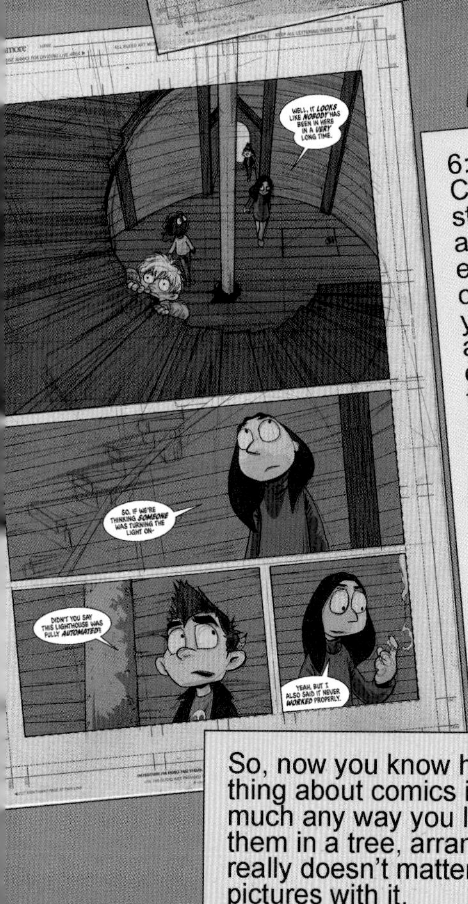
WELL, IT LOOKS LIKE NOBODY HAS BEEN IN HERE IN A VERY LONG TIME.
SO, IF WE'RE THINKING SOMEONE WAS TURNING THE LIGHT ON-
DIDN'T YOU SAY THIS LIGHTHOUSE WAS FULLY AUTOMATED?
YEAH, BUT I ALSO SAID IT NEVER WORKED PROPERLY.

6: Colors.
Coloring is a strange process. I only started coloring about a year ago and I realized that it can be the easiest or hardest part of making a comic. The actual technical skills you need to learn are very simple, and anyone can be an acceptable colorist, because it really is like a faster version of coloring in. Knowing where the shadows and highlights go, knowing when to use an effect, that's the part that comes from really knowing how to put an image together. This is a pretty cartoony looking book, so the coloring is mostly very simple, but I think any more rendering on these characters would detract from the line work and design.

So, now you know how my comics get made, but the best thing about comics is that you can make them pretty much any way you like. Paint them, scribble them, carve them in a tree, arrange gum you find to make pictures, it really doesn't matter. Just write something and put pictures with it.

ACKNOWLEDGMENTS

First off I want to thank Ray. This book took almost three and a half months to write, draw, and color, and he put up with me throughout like a champ. Late nights on the phone from my office, telling him about the stories and all the little details I was seeding for the rest of the series, waking up early to make me coffee so I could get started again the next day, he did it all.

Lucy Campagnolo and Theo Macdonald, thank you for reading each chapter as it was done to make sure it was scary enough.

I need to thank Jacqueline for helping me maintain my energy levels during some of the most intense drawing sessions of my life.

Paul Wolff offered so much inspiration for these stories with his vast knowledge of electrical circuits and all the science that seems like magic to me. He also tolerated me turning our office into a dorm room, with clothes and blankets strewn about for weeks at a time.

To my friend and roommate, Alex Burke. Thank you for calling me every few days when I didn't come home to make sure I was still alive. Thank you for offering to bring me coffee and for trying to remind me there was an outside world.

I cannot overstate how supportive Bethany Buck has been as an editor or how lucky I am that she and I crossed paths. From the moment I met her, I knew we were going to be friends, and I'm so grateful to have her back in my world.

Vicki Marsdon is the kind of agent everyone should be trying to get. She knows exactly when to let me run wild with a thousand new proposals and when to reign me in because I'm about to land on something wonderful.

Finally, I want to thank Nigel, my best friend, my soulmate, the plastic skeleton I never knew I needed. His permanent smile and dapper outfits remind me what I'm working for.

RICHARD FAIRGRAY is a writer, artist, and colorist, best known for his work in comic books such as *Blastosaurus* and *Ghost Ghost*, and picture books such as *Gorillas in our Midst, My Grandpa Is a Dinosaur,* and *If I Had an Elephant*. As a child he firmly believed he would grow up and eat all the candy he wanted and stay up as late as he liked. By drawing pictures when he wasn't meant to and reading all the things people told him not to, he has made his dream come true.

Richard now splits his time between Los Angeles and Surrey, British Columbia, where he is able to work furiously, surrounded by plastic skeletons, dogs, friends, loved ones and (possibly) the most comprehensive collection of Courtney Love bootlegs on the planet.

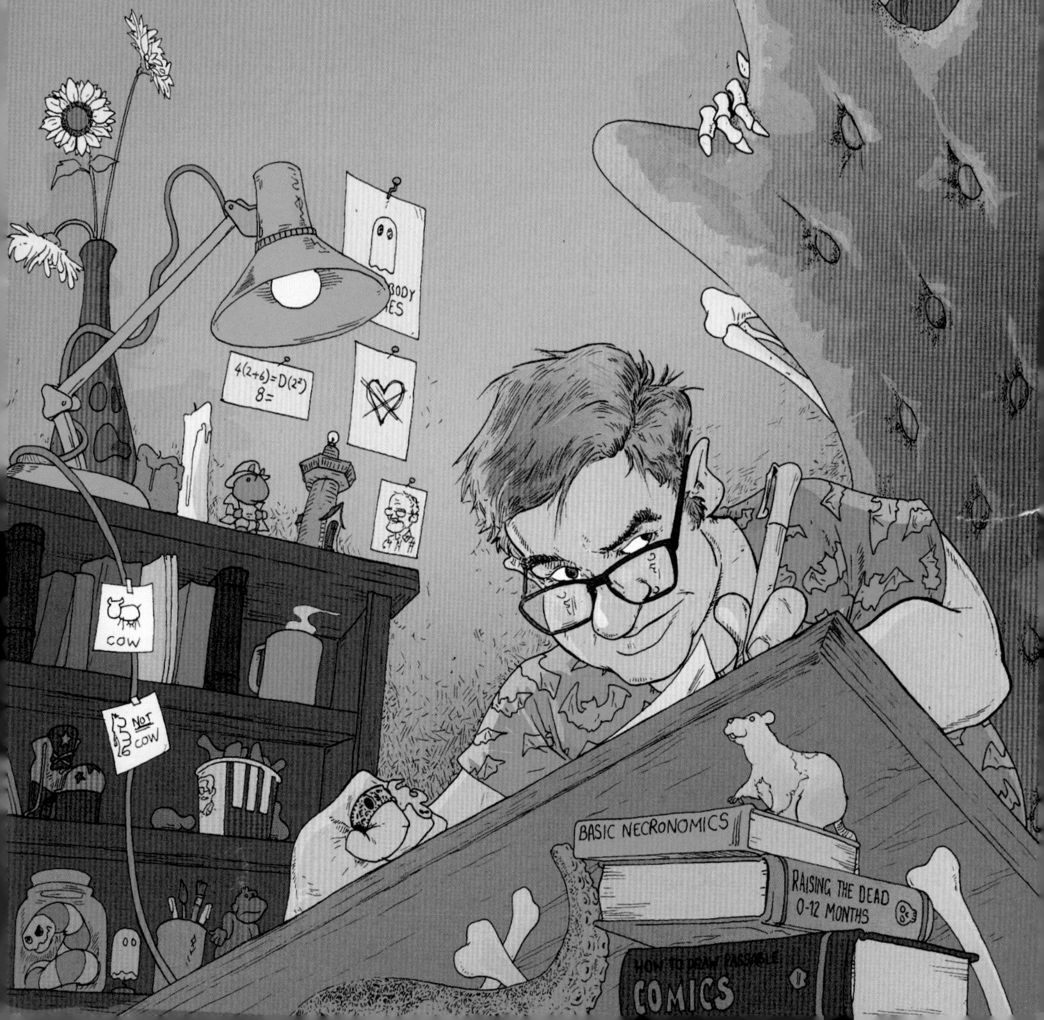

4(2+6)=D(2²)
8=
COW
NOT COW
BASIC NECRONOMICS
RAISING THE DEAD 0-12 MONTHS
HOW TO DRAW PASSABLE
COMICS

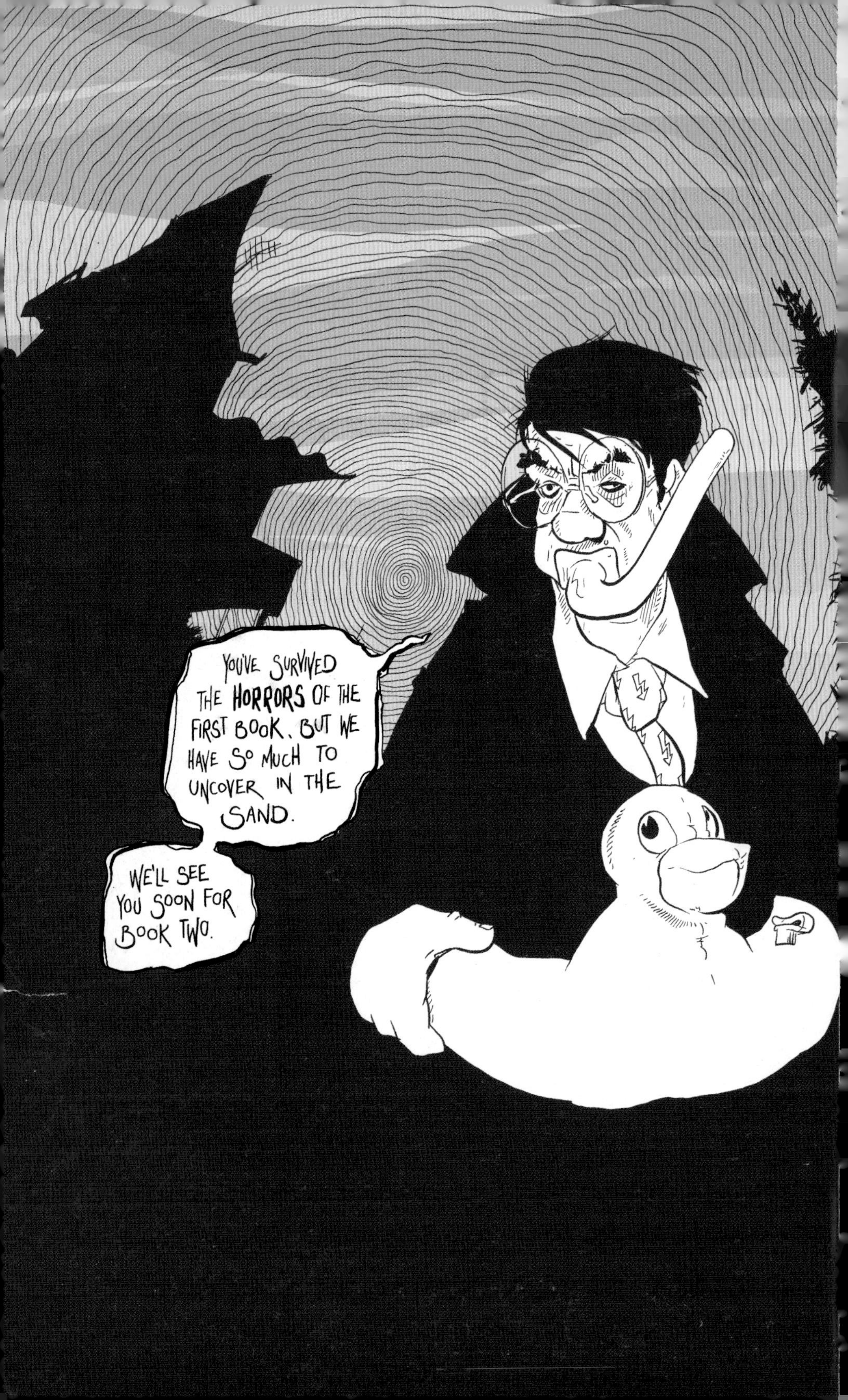
YOU'VE SURVIVED THE **HORRORS** OF THE FIRST BOOK. BUT WE HAVE SO MUCH TO UNCOVER IN THE SAND.
WE'LL SEE YOU SOON FOR BOOK TWO.